MOMOGUMI
PLUS
SENKI

Volume 1

Created by Eri SAKONDO

HAMBURG // LONDON // LOS ANGELES // TOKYO

Momogumi Plus Senki Volume 1
Created by Eri SAKONDO

Translation - Aimi Tokutake
English Adaptation - Rachel Brown
Copy Editor - Shannon Watters
Retouch and Lettering - Star Print Brokers
Production Artist - Rui Kyo
Graphic Designer - Al-Insan Lashley

Editor - Bryce P. Coleman
Print Production Manager - Lucas Rivera
Managing Editor - Vy Nguyen
Senior Designer - Louis Csontos
Director of Sales and Manufacturing - Allyson De Simone
Associate Publisher - Marco F. Pavia
President and C.O.O. - John Parker
C.E.O. and Chief Creative Officer - Stu Levy

A  Manga

TOKYOPOP and  are trademarks or registered trademarks of TOKYOPOP Inc.

TOKYOPOP Inc.
5900 Wilshire Blvd. Suite 2000
Los Angeles, CA 90036

E-mail: info@TOKYOPOP.com
Come visit us online at www.TOKYOPOP.com

MOMOGUMI PLUS SENKI Volume 1 © Eri SAKONDO 2006
First published in Japan in 2006 by KADOKAWA SHOTEN
PUBLISHING CO., LTD., Tokyo. English translation rights
arranged with KADOKAWA SHOTEN PUBLISHING
CO., LTD., Tokyo through TUTTLE–MORI AGENCY, INC., Tokyo.
English text copyright © 2009 TOKYOPOP Inc.

ISBN: 978-1-4278-1562-0

First TOKYOPOP printing: August 2009
10 9 8 7 6 5 4 3 2 1
Printed in the USA

MOMOGUMI PLUS SENKI

Eri SAKONDO

Volume 1

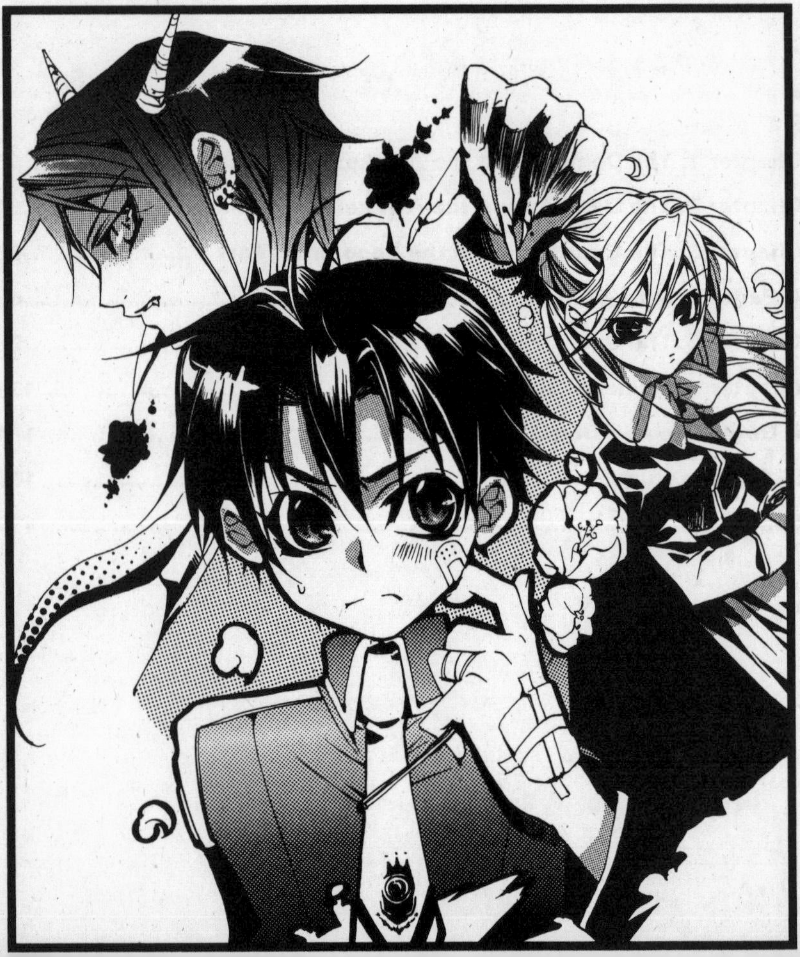

MOMOGUMI PLUS SENKI

CONTENTS

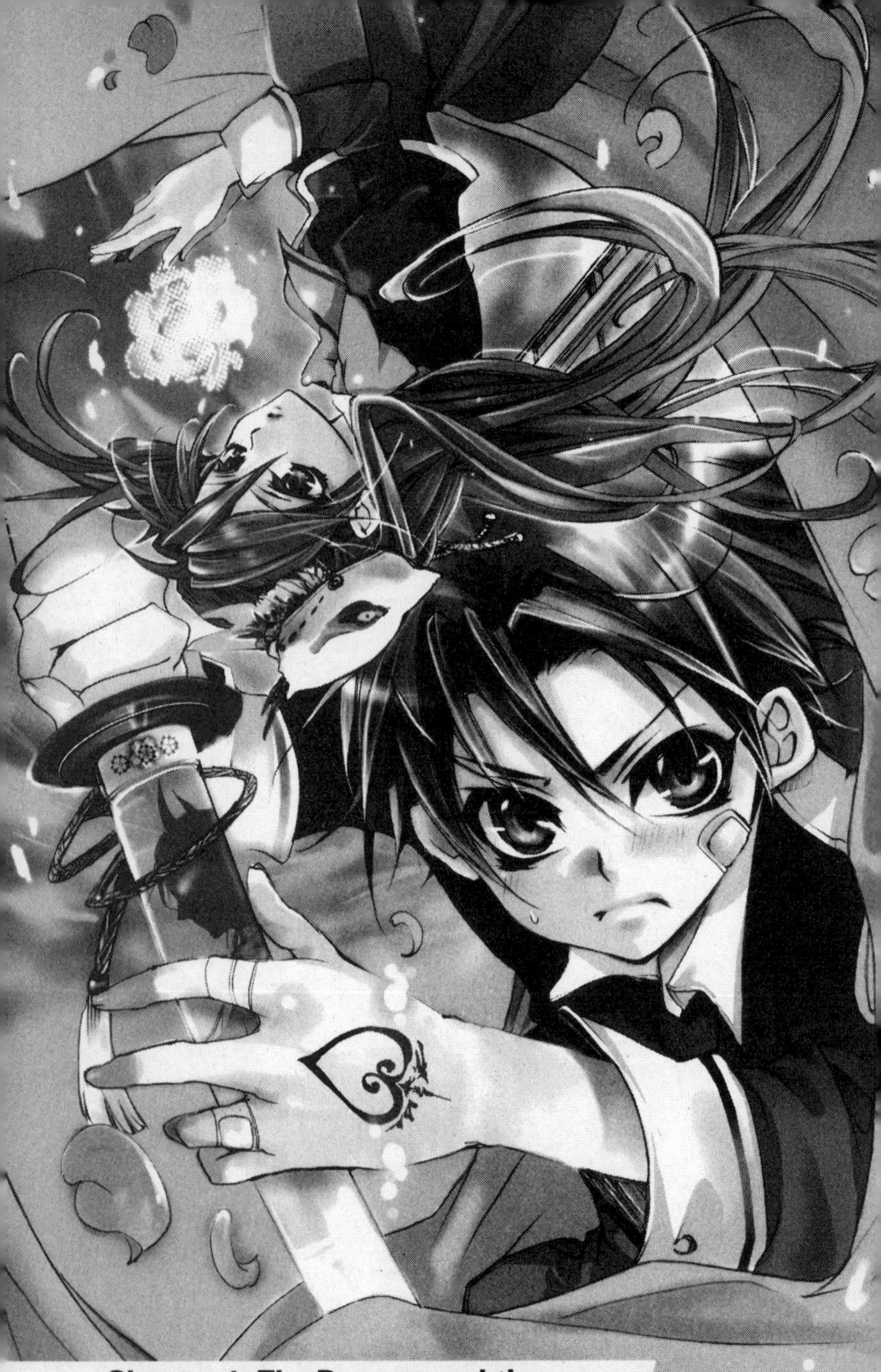

Chapter 1: The Demons and the Awakening of the Blood, Part 1

桃組プラス戦記

もも くみ せん き

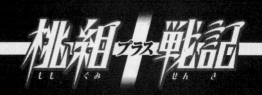

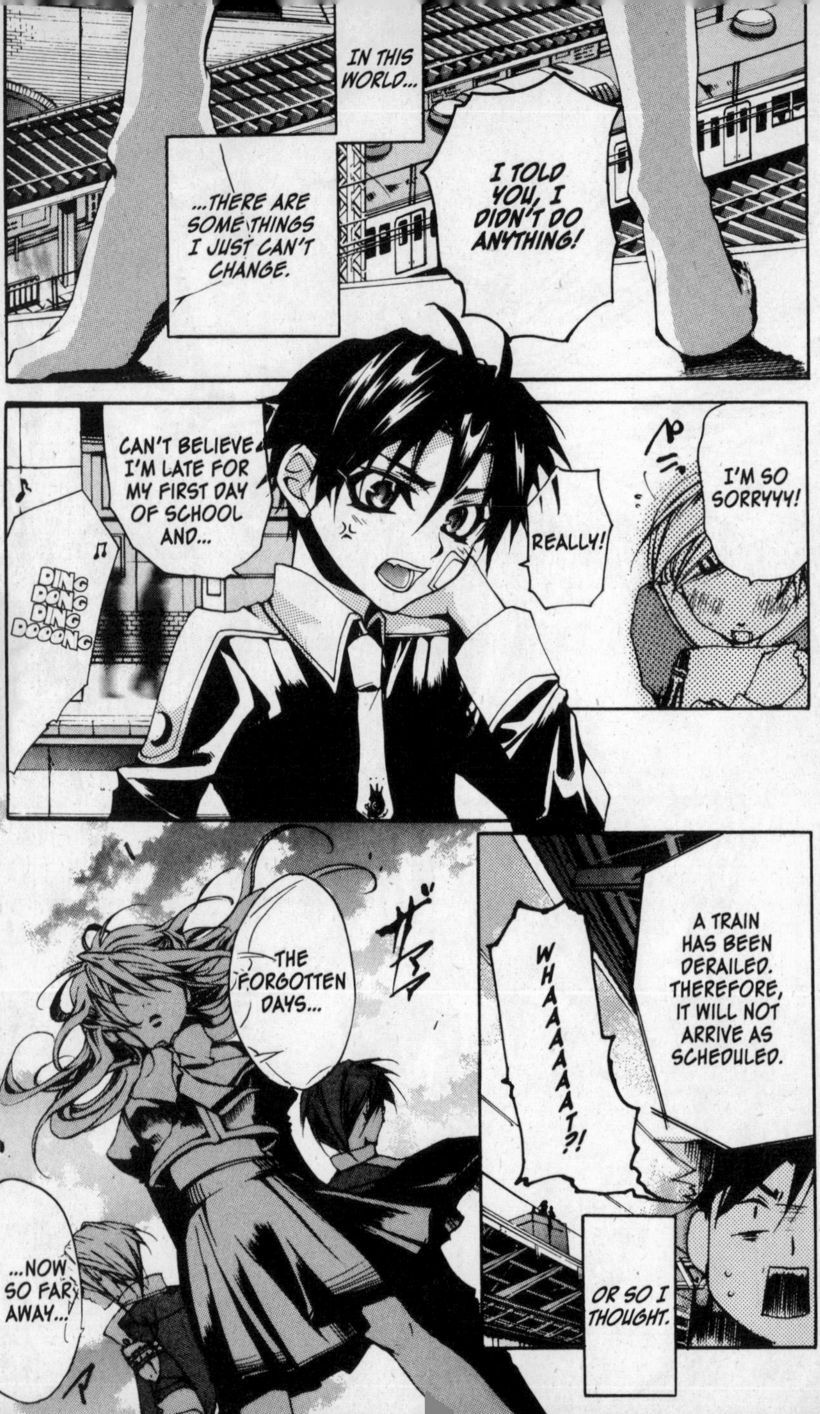
IN THIS WORLD...
I TOLD YOU, I DIDN'T DO ANYTHING!
...THERE ARE SOME THINGS I JUST CAN'T CHANGE.
I'M SO SORRYYY!
REALLY!
CAN'T BELIEVE I'M LATE FOR MY FIRST DAY OF SCHOOL AND...
DING DONG DING DOOONG
A TRAIN HAS BEEN DERAILED. THEREFORE, IT WILL NOT ARRIVE AS SCHEDULED.
WHAAAAAAT?!
OR SO I THOUGHT.
THE FORGOTTEN DAYS...
...NOW SO FAR AWAY...

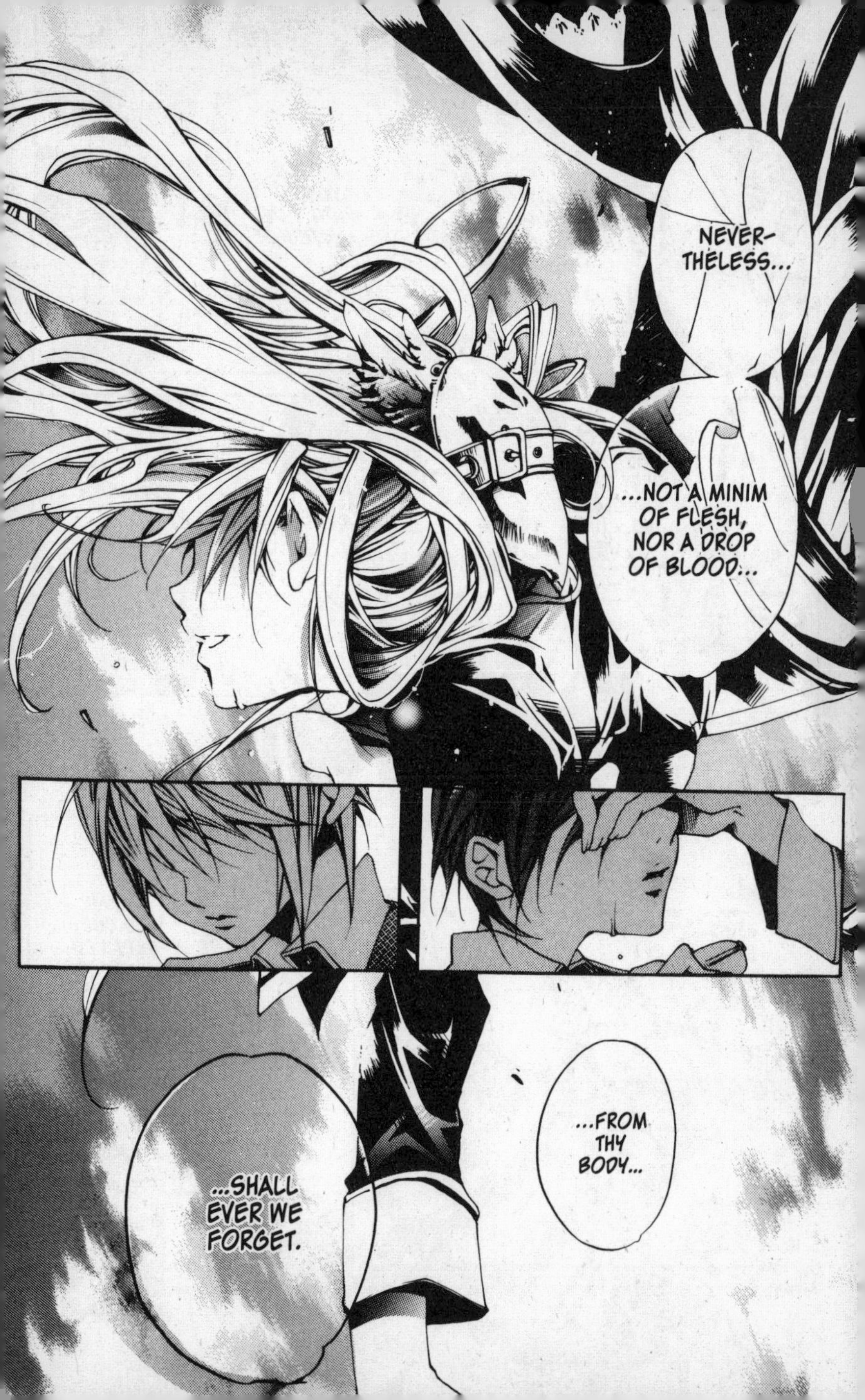
NEVER-THELESS...
...NOT A MINIM OF FLESH, NOR A DROP OF BLOOD...
...FROM THY BODY...
...SHALL EVER WE FORGET.

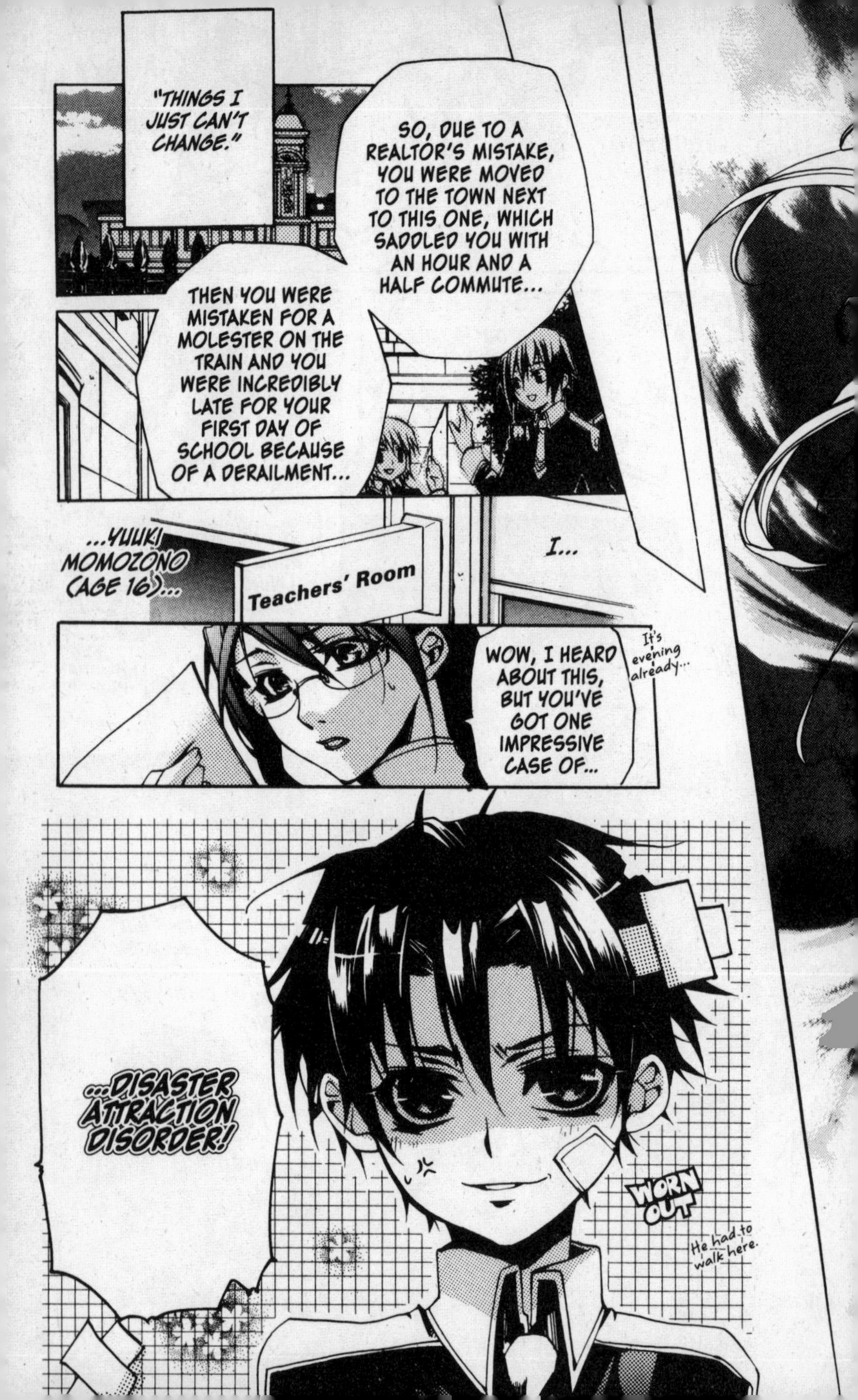
"THINGS I JUST CAN'T CHANGE."
SO, DUE TO A REALTOR'S MISTAKE, YOU WERE MOVED TO THE TOWN NEXT TO THIS ONE, WHICH SADDLED YOU WITH AN HOUR AND A HALF COMMUTE...
THEN YOU WERE MISTAKEN FOR A MOLESTER ON THE TRAIN AND YOU WERE INCREDIBLY LATE FOR YOUR FIRST DAY OF SCHOOL BECAUSE OF A DERAILMENT...
I...
Teachers' Room
...YUUKI MOMOZONO (AGE 16)...
It's evening already...
WOW, I HEARD ABOUT THIS, BUT YOU'VE GOT ONE IMPRESSIVE CASE OF...
...DISASTER ATTRACTION DISORDER!
WORN OUT
He had to walk here.

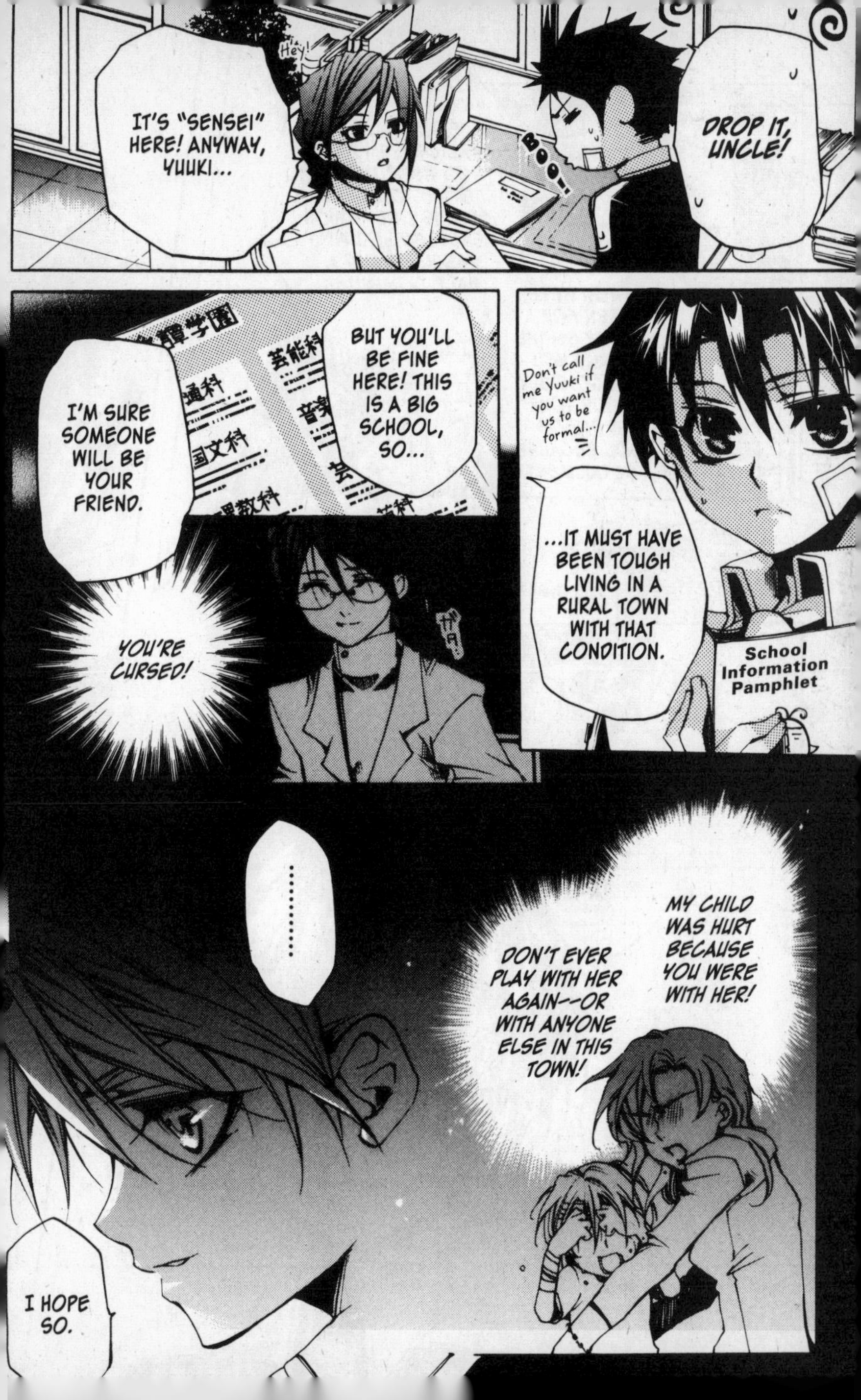
DROP IT, UNCLE!
Hey!
IT'S "SENSEI" HERE! ANYWAY, YUUKI...
Don't call me Yuuki if you want us to be formal...
...IT MUST HAVE BEEN TOUGH LIVING IN A RURAL TOWN WITH THAT CONDITION.
School Information Pamphlet
BUT YOU'LL BE FINE HERE! THIS IS A BIG SCHOOL, SO...
I'M SURE SOMEONE WILL BE YOUR FRIEND.
YOU'RE CURSED!
MY CHILD WAS HURT BECAUSE YOU WERE WITH HER!
DON'T EVER PLAY WITH HER AGAIN--OR WITH ANYONE ELSE IN THIS TOWN!
......
I HOPE SO.

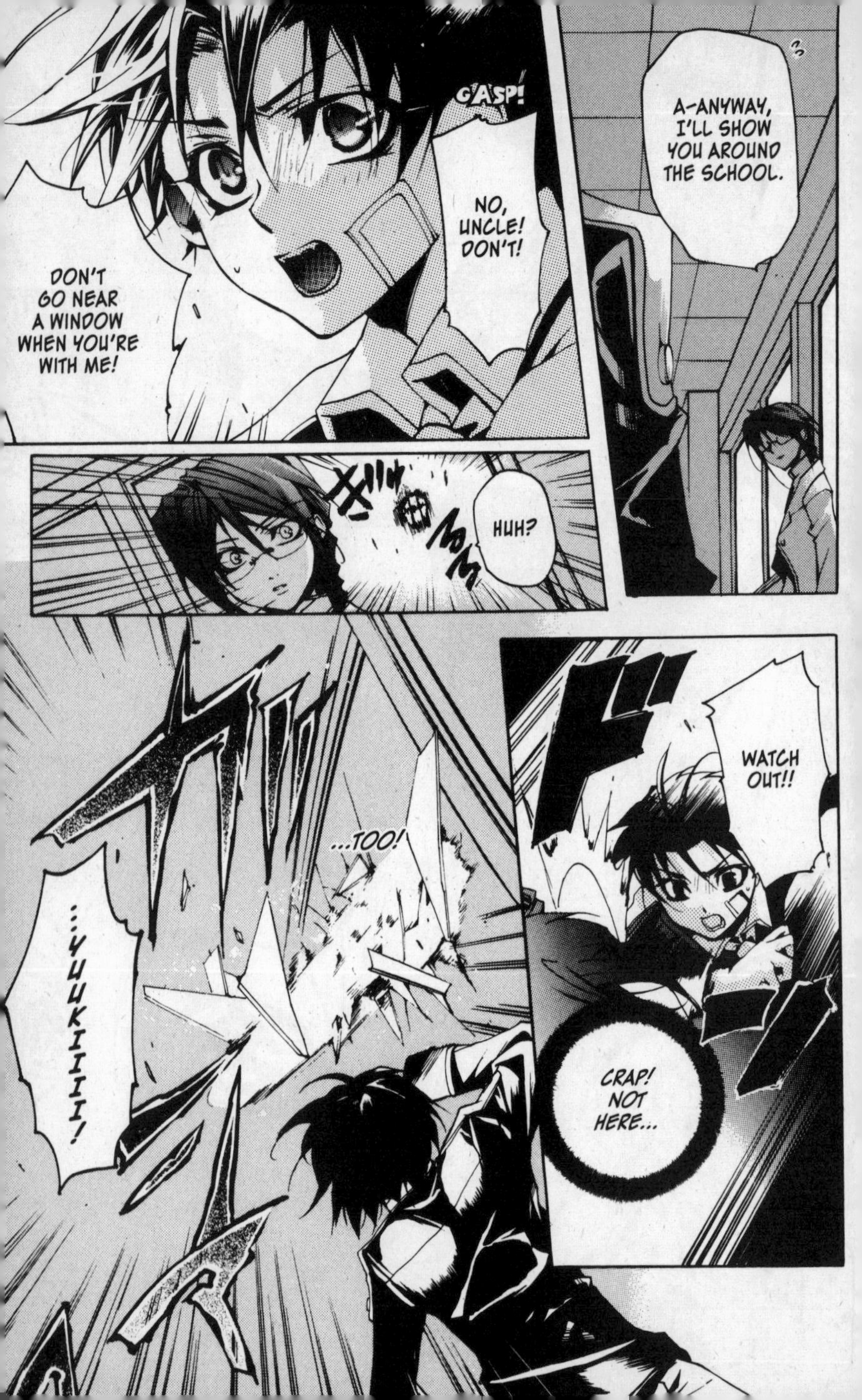
A-ANYWAY, I'LL SHOW YOU AROUND THE SCHOOL.
GASP!
NO, UNCLE! DON'T!
DON'T GO NEAR A WINDOW WHEN YOU'RE WITH ME!
HUH?
WATCH OUT!!
CRAP! NOT HERE...
...TOO!
...YUUKIIIIII!

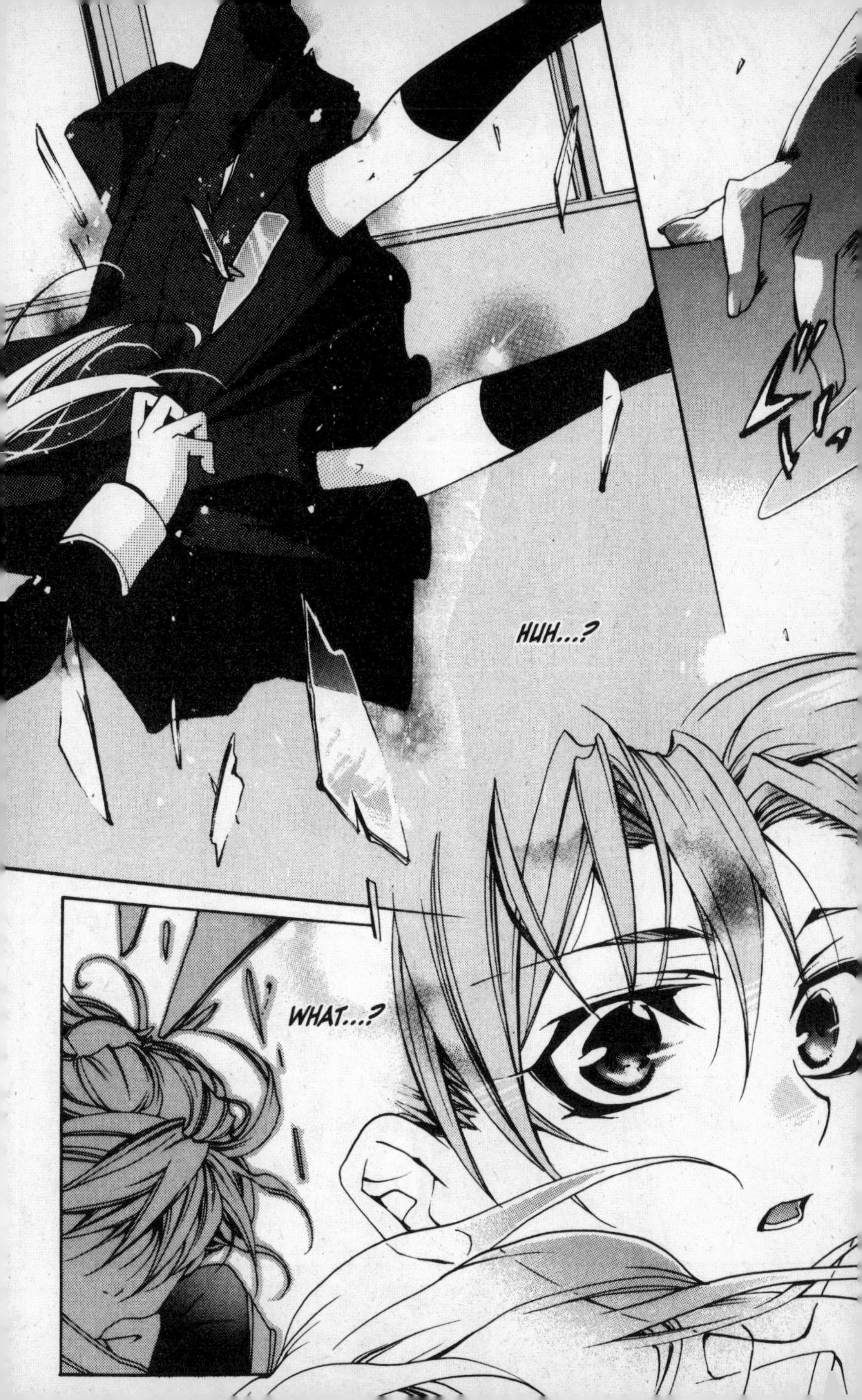
HUH...?
WHAT...?

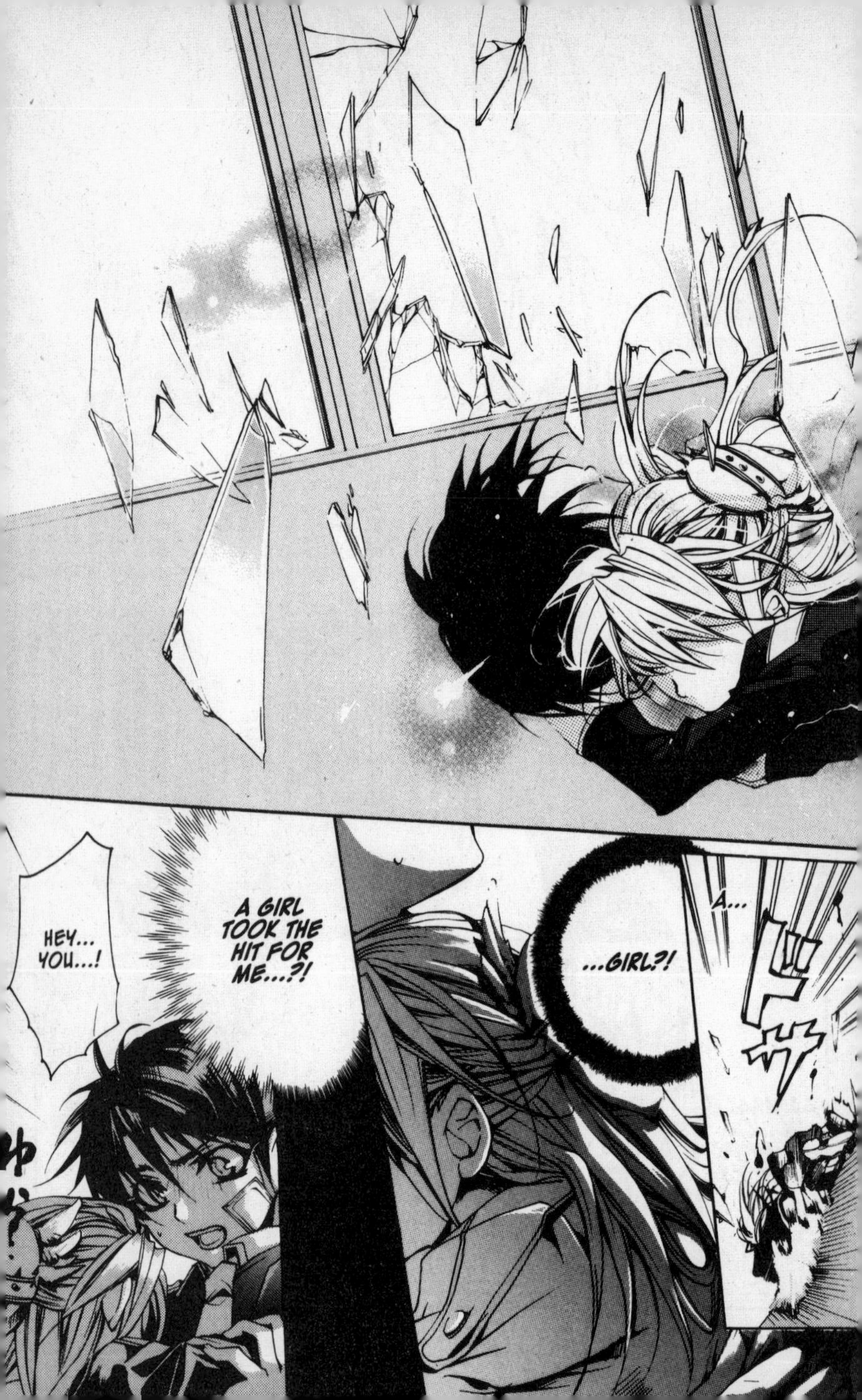
A...
...GIRL?!
A GIRL TOOK THE HIT FOR ME...?!
HEY... YOU...!

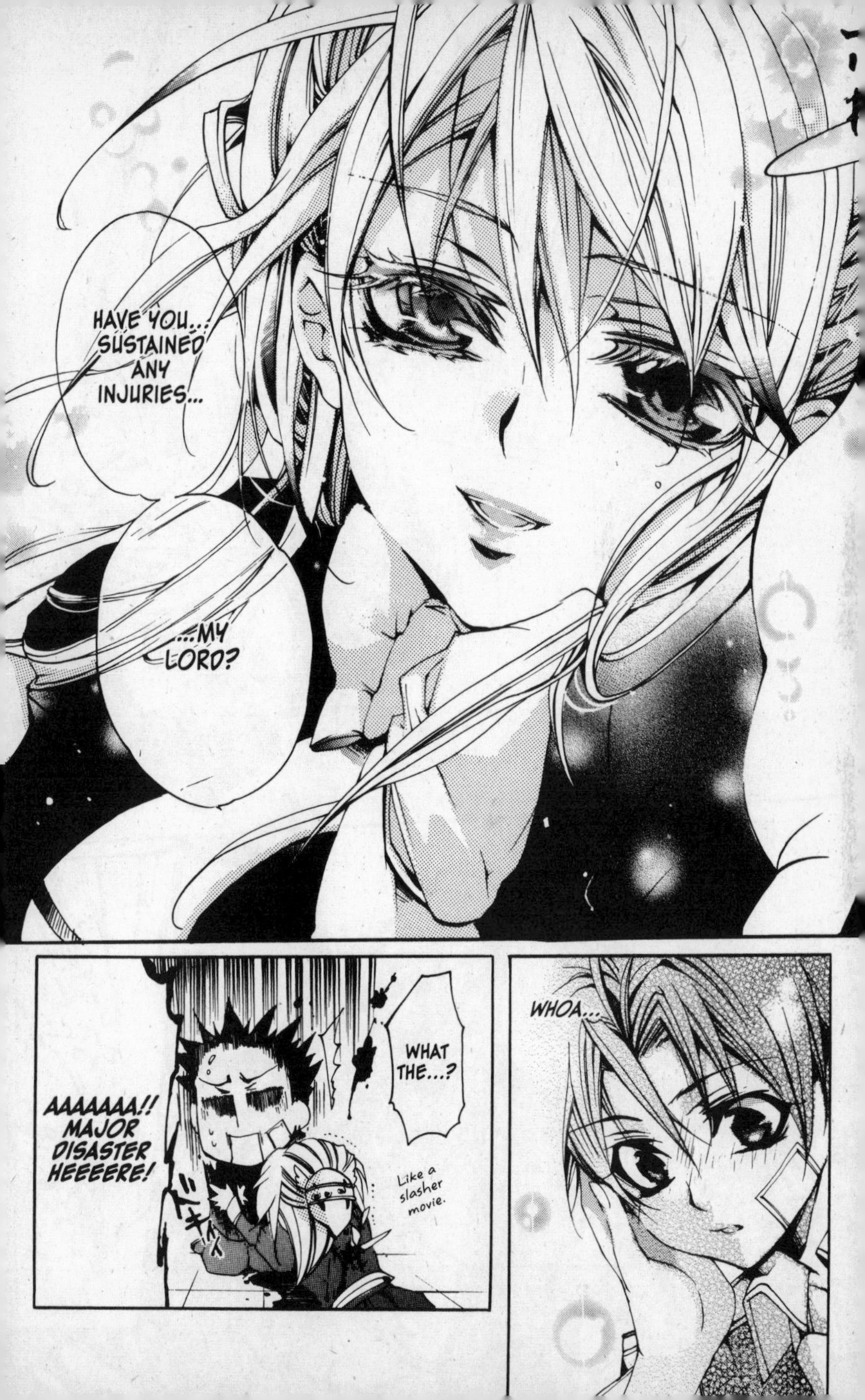
HAVE YOU... SUSTAINED ANY INJURIES...
...MY LORD?
WHOA...
WHAT THE...?
AAAAAAA!! MAJOR DISASTER HEEEERE!
Like a slasher movie.

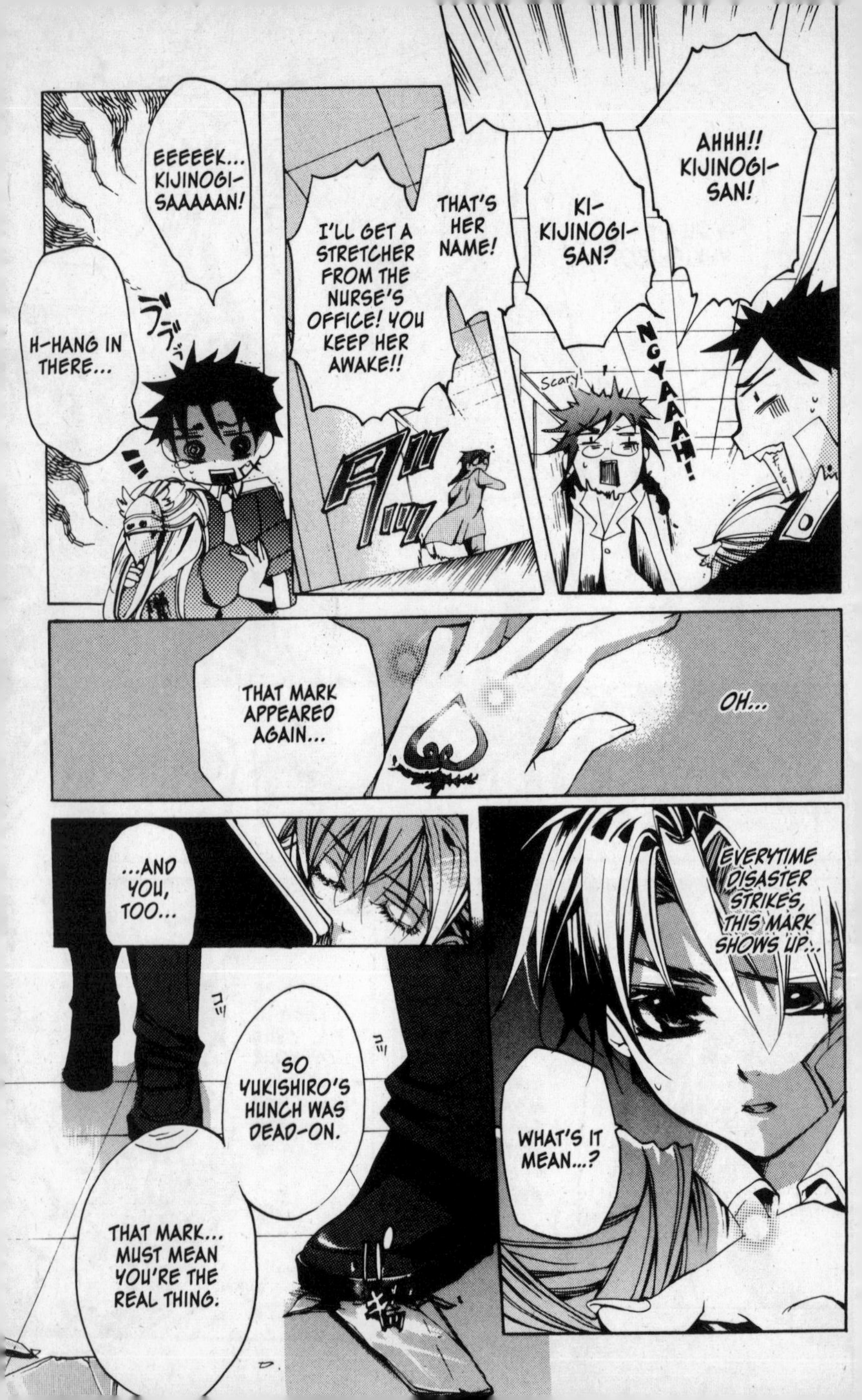
AHHH!! KIJINOGI-SAN!
KI-KIJINOGI-SAN?
NGYAAAAH!
Scary!
THAT'S HER NAME!
I'LL GET A STRETCHER FROM THE NURSE'S OFFICE! YOU KEEP HER AWAKE!!
EEEEEK... KIJINOGI-SAAAAAN!
H-HANG IN THERE...
OH...
THAT MARK APPEARED AGAIN...
EVERYTIME DISASTER STRIKES, THIS MARK SHOWS UP...
WHAT'S IT MEAN...?
...AND YOU, TOO...
SO YUKISHIRO'S HUNCH WAS DEAD-ON.
THAT MARK... MUST MEAN YOU'RE THE REAL THING.

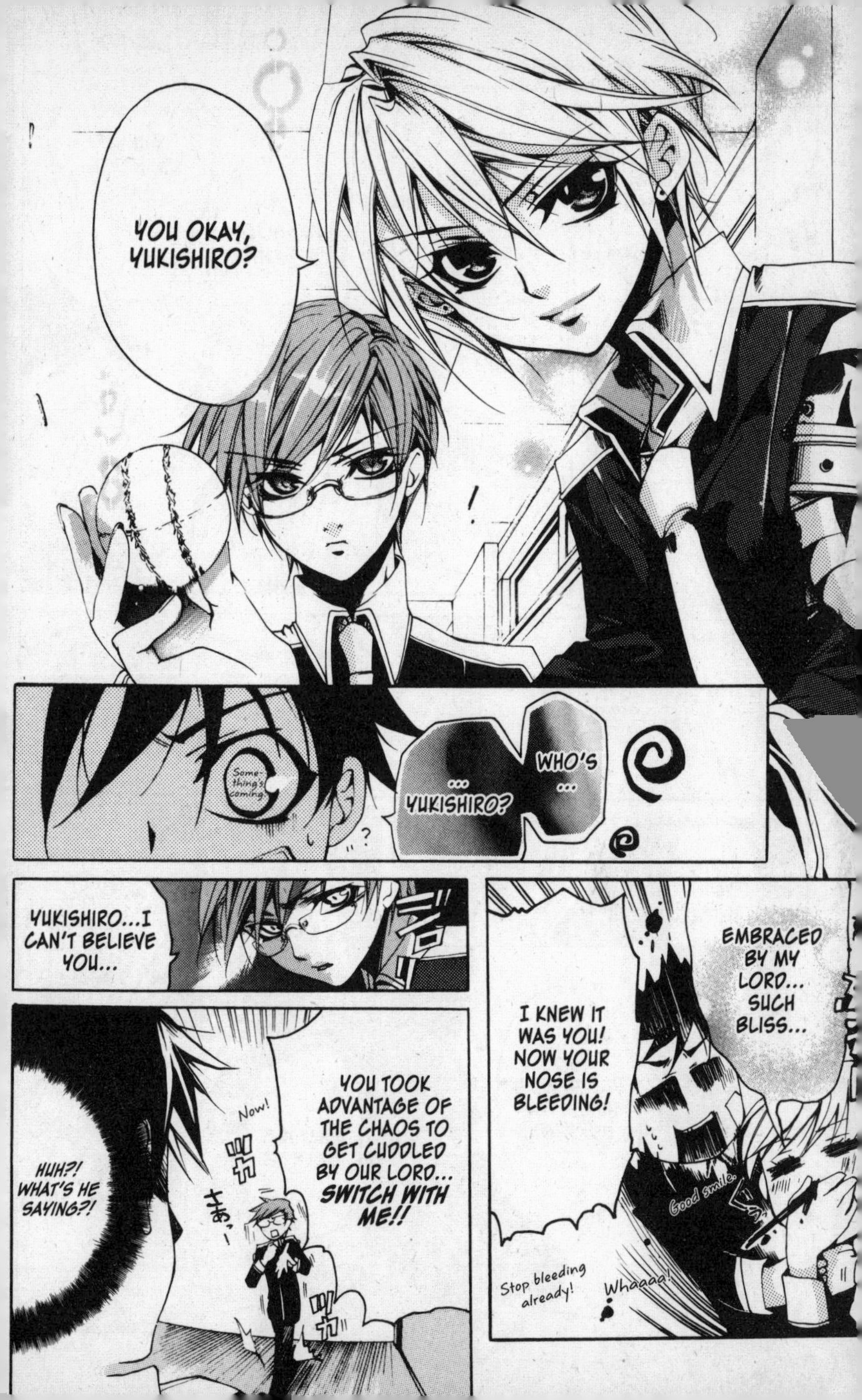
YOU OKAY, YUKISHIRO?
WHO'S ...
... YUKISHIRO?
Something's coming.
EMBRACED BY MY LORD... SUCH BLISS...
I KNEW IT WAS YOU! NOW YOUR NOSE IS BLEEDING!
Good smile.
Whaaaa!
Stop bleeding already!
YUKISHIRO...I CAN'T BELIEVE YOU...
YOU TOOK ADVANTAGE OF THE CHAOS TO GET CUDDLED BY OUR LORD... SWITCH WITH ME!!
Now!
HUH?! WHAT'S HE SAYING?!

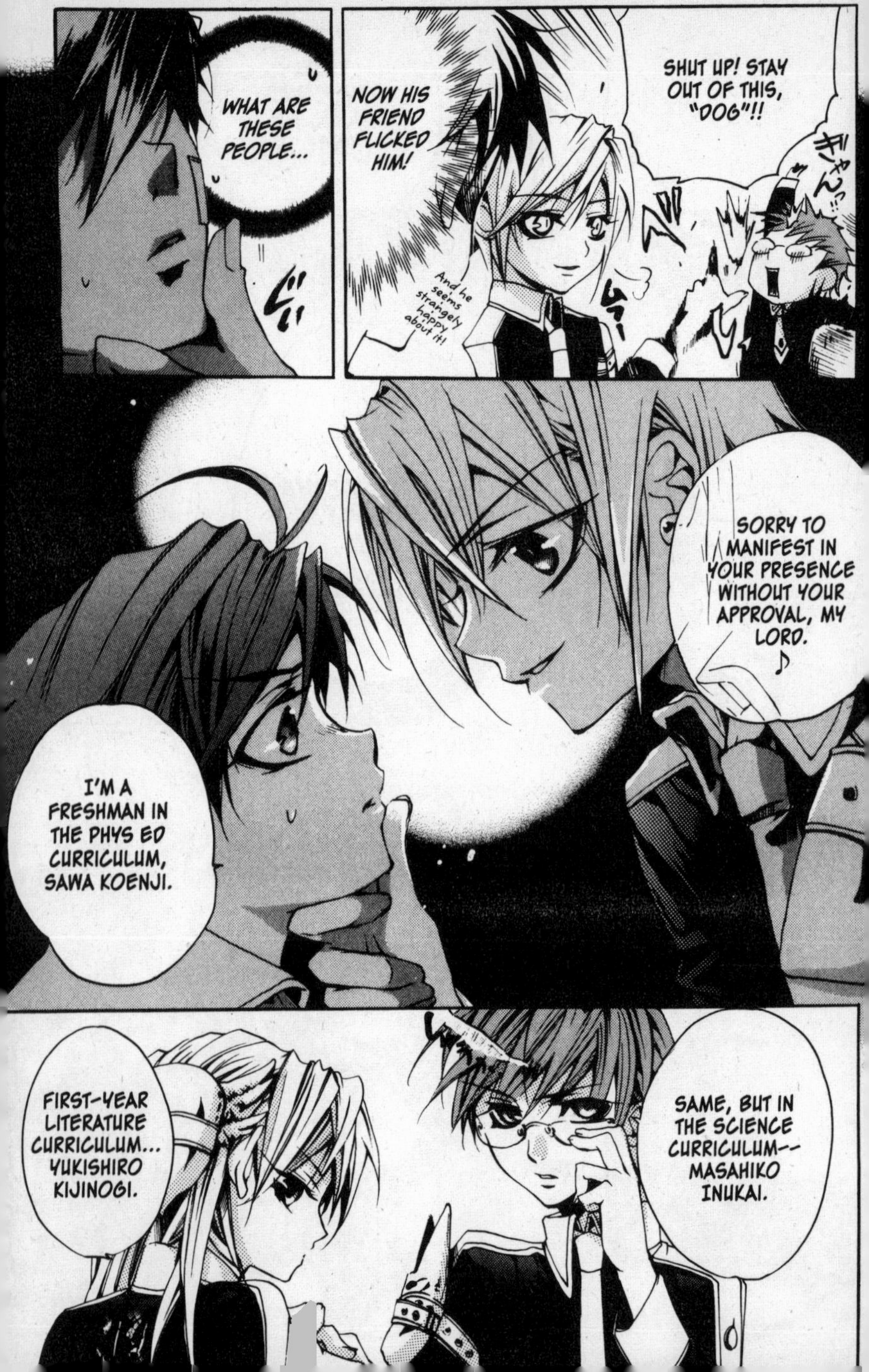

SHUT UP! STAY OUT OF THIS, "DOG"!!
ぎゃん!!
NOW HIS FRIEND FLICKED HIM!
And he seems strangely happy about it!
WHAT ARE THESE PEOPLE...
SORRY TO MANIFEST IN YOUR PRESENCE WITHOUT YOUR APPROVAL, MY LORD. ♪
I'M A FRESHMAN IN THE PHYS ED CURRICULUM, SAWA KOENJI.
FIRST-YEAR LITERATURE CURRICULUM... YUKISHIRO KIJINOGI.
SAME, BUT IN THE SCIENCE CURRICULUM-- MASAHIKO INUKAI.

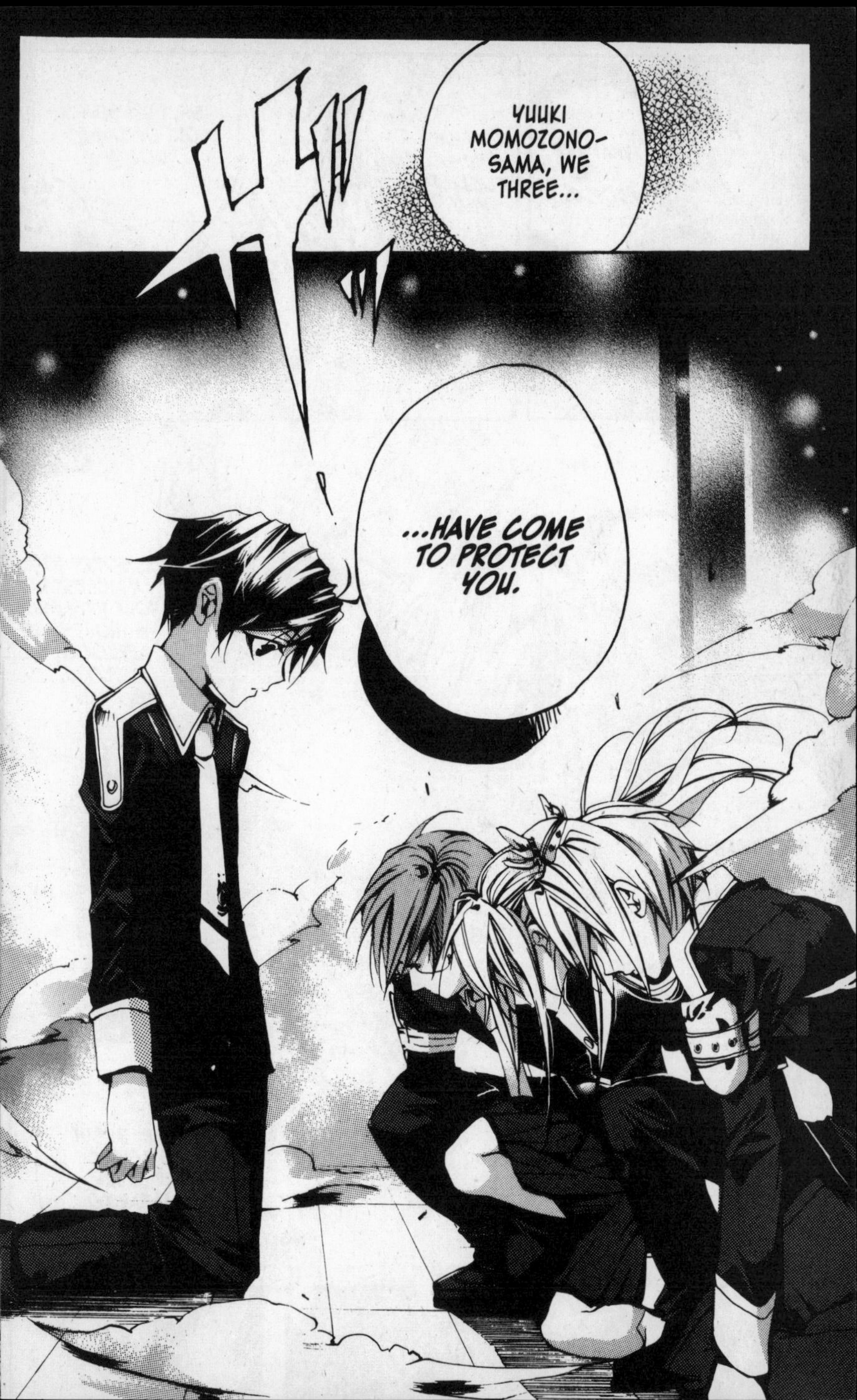
YUUKI MOMOZONO-SAMA, WE THREE...
...HAVE COME TO PROTECT YOU.

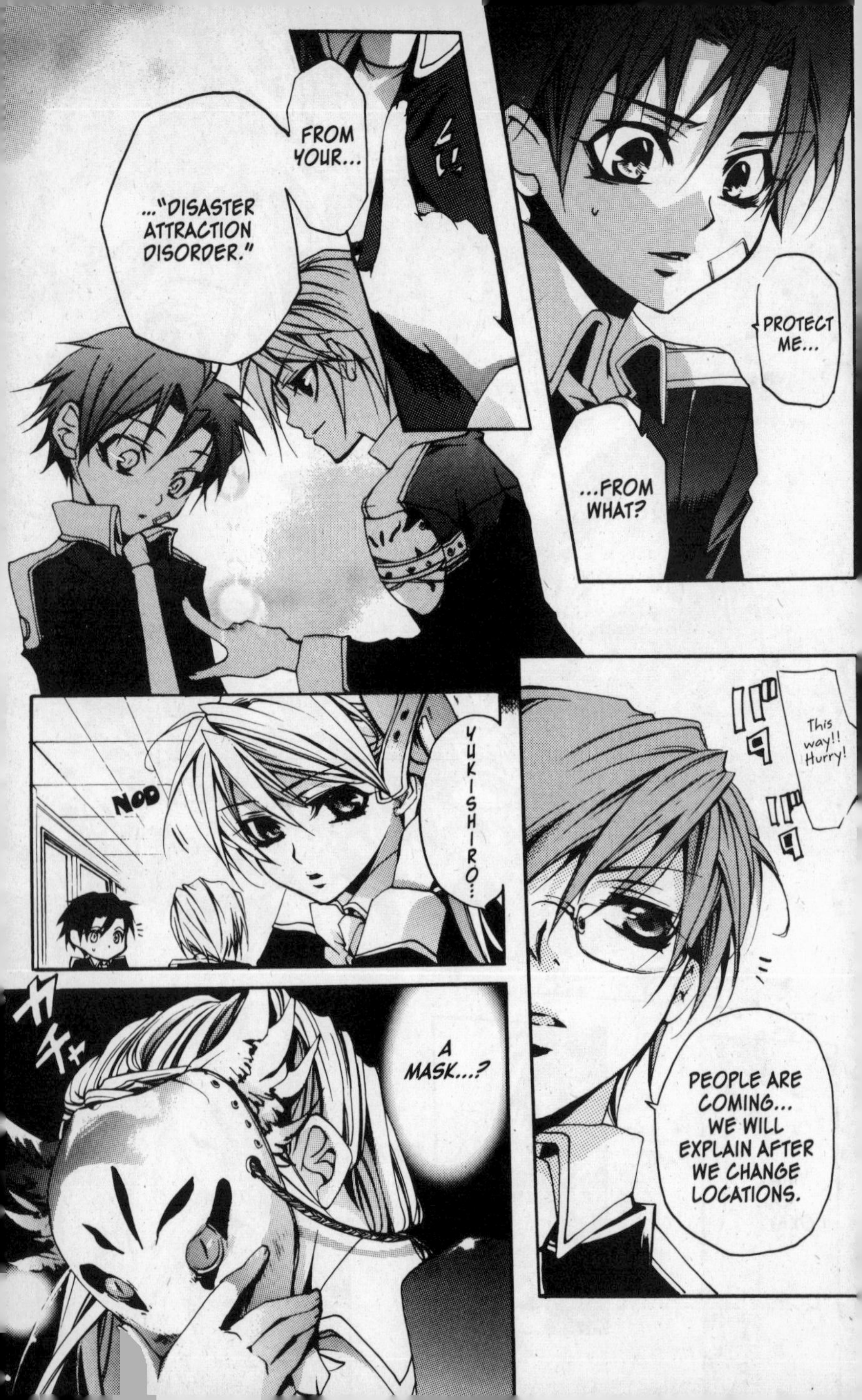
PROTECT ME...
...FROM WHAT?
FROM YOUR...
..."DISASTER ATTRACTION DISORDER."
This way!! Hurry!
PEOPLE ARE COMING... WE WILL EXPLAIN AFTER WE CHANGE LOCATIONS.
YUKISHIRO...
NOD
A MASK...?

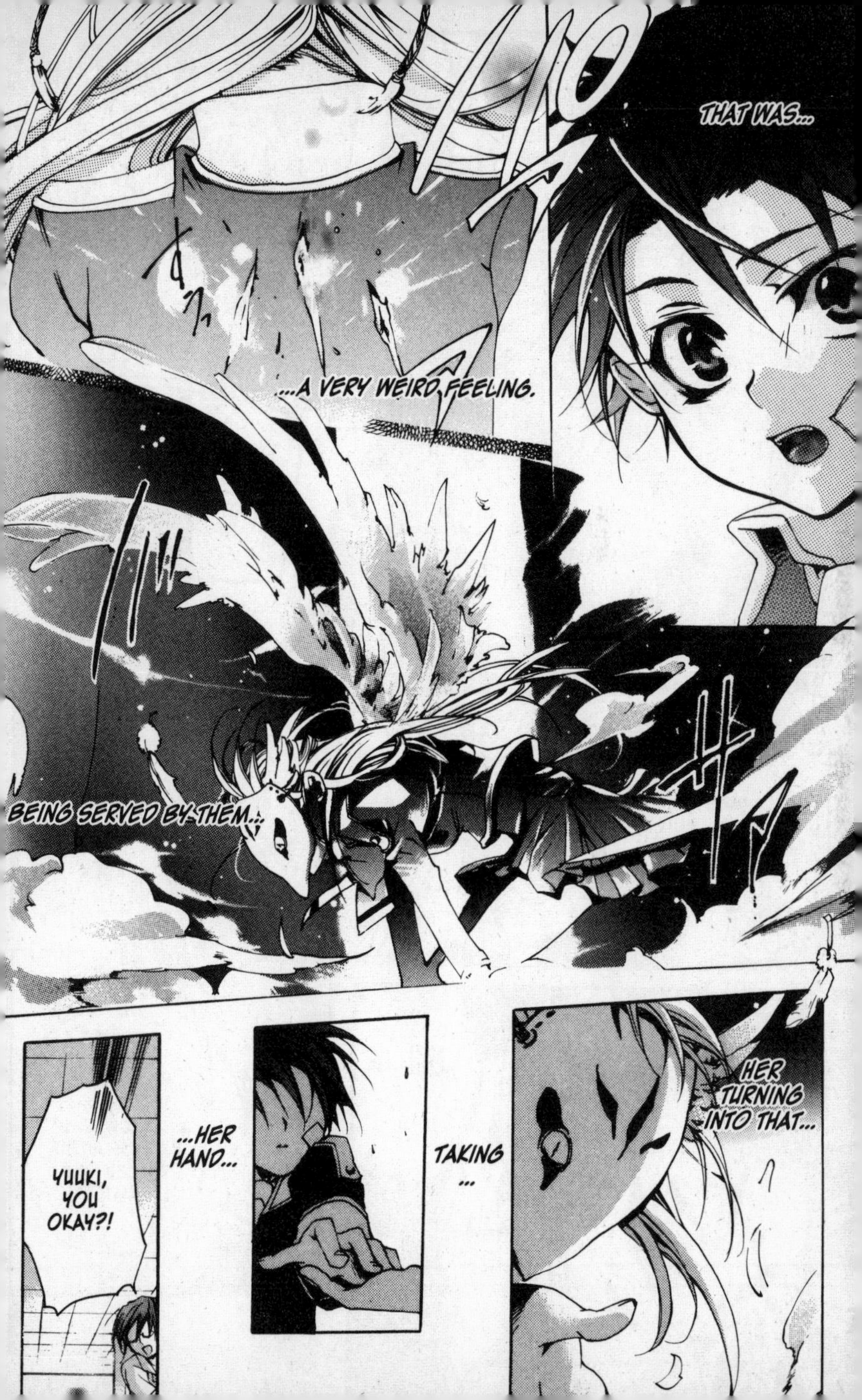
THAT WAS...
...A VERY WEIRD FEELING.
BEING SERVED BY THEM...
HER TURNING INTO THAT...
TAKING ...
...HER HAND...
YUUKI, YOU OKAY?!

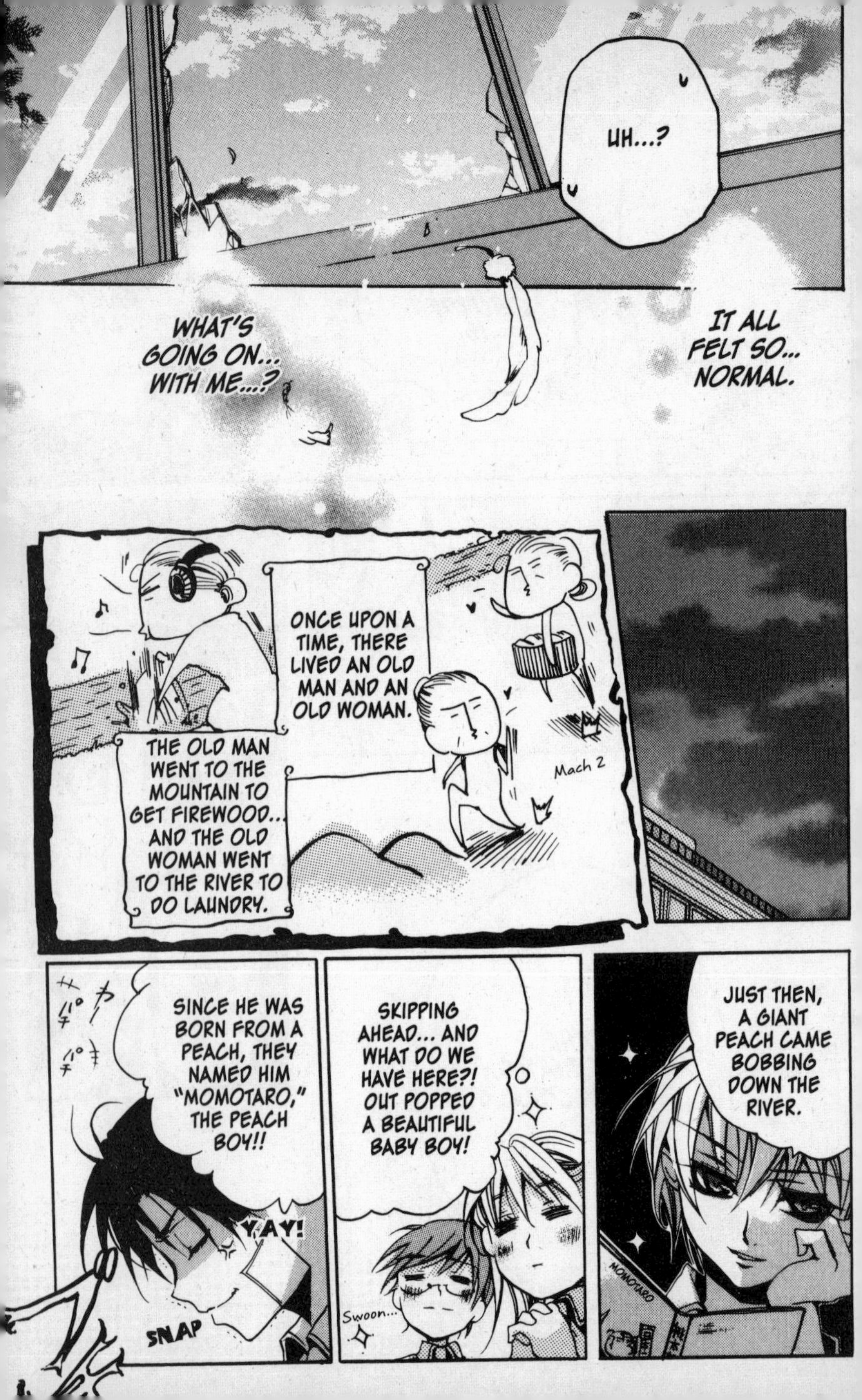
UH...?
IT ALL FELT SO... NORMAL.
WHAT'S GOING ON... WITH ME...?
ONCE UPON A TIME, THERE LIVED AN OLD MAN AND AN OLD WOMAN.
Mach 2
THE OLD MAN WENT TO THE MOUNTAIN TO GET FIREWOOD... AND THE OLD WOMAN WENT TO THE RIVER TO DO LAUNDRY.
JUST THEN, A GIANT PEACH CAME BOBBING DOWN THE RIVER.
MOMOTARO
SKIPPING AHEAD... AND WHAT DO WE HAVE HERE?! OUT POPPED A BEAUTIFUL BABY BOY!
Swoon...
SINCE HE WAS BORN FROM A PEACH, THEY NAMED HIM "MOMOTARO," THE PEACH BOY!!
YAY!
SNAP

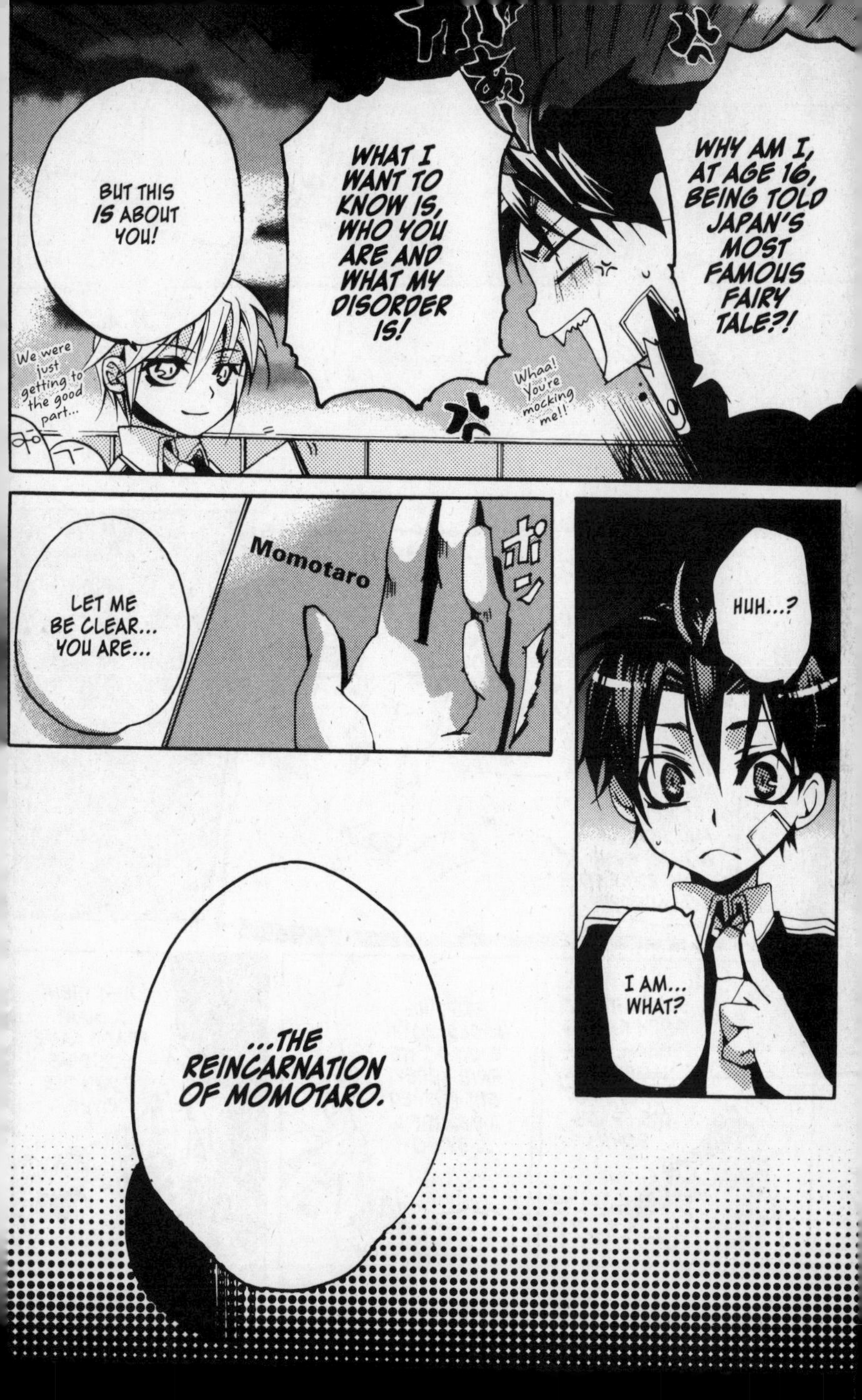
WHY AM I, AT AGE 16, BEING TOLD JAPAN'S MOST FAMOUS FAIRY TALE?!
Whaa! You're mocking me!!
WHAT I WANT TO KNOW IS, WHO YOU ARE AND WHAT MY DISORDER IS!
BUT THIS IS ABOUT YOU!
We were just getting to the good part...
HUH...?
I AM... WHAT?
Momotaro
LET ME BE CLEAR... YOU ARE...
...THE REINCARNATION OF MOMOTARO.

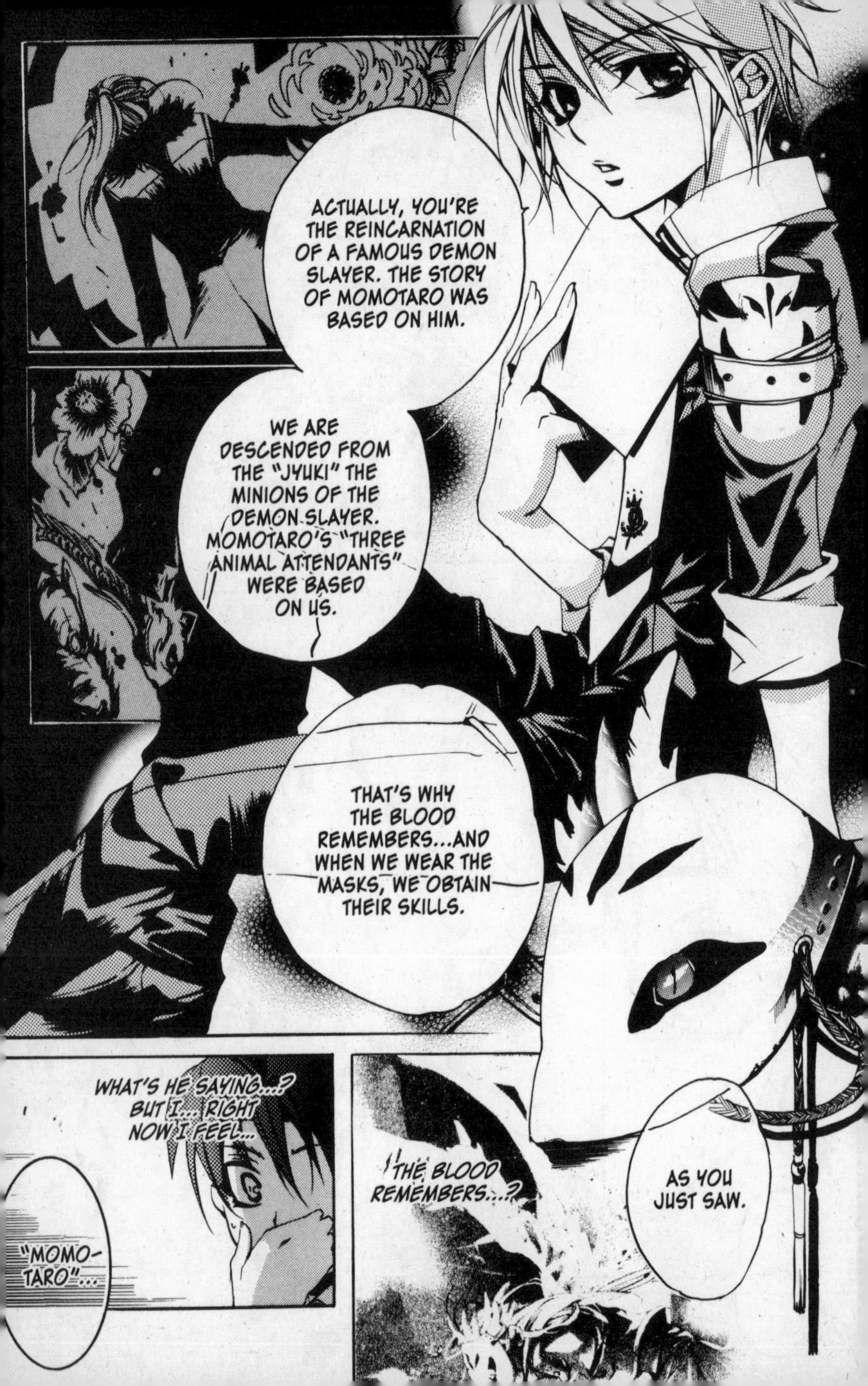
ACTUALLY, YOU'RE THE REINCARNATION OF A FAMOUS DEMON SLAYER. THE STORY OF MOMOTARO WAS BASED ON HIM.
WE ARE DESCENDED FROM THE "JYUKI" THE MINIONS OF THE DEMON SLAYER. MOMOTARO'S "THREE ANIMAL ATTENDANTS" WERE BASED ON US.
THAT'S WHY THE BLOOD REMEMBERS...AND WHEN WE WEAR THE MASKS, WE OBTAIN THEIR SKILLS.
AS YOU JUST SAW.
THE BLOOD REMEMBERS...?
WHAT'S HE SAYING...? BUT I... RIGHT NOW I FEEL...
"MOMO-TARO"...

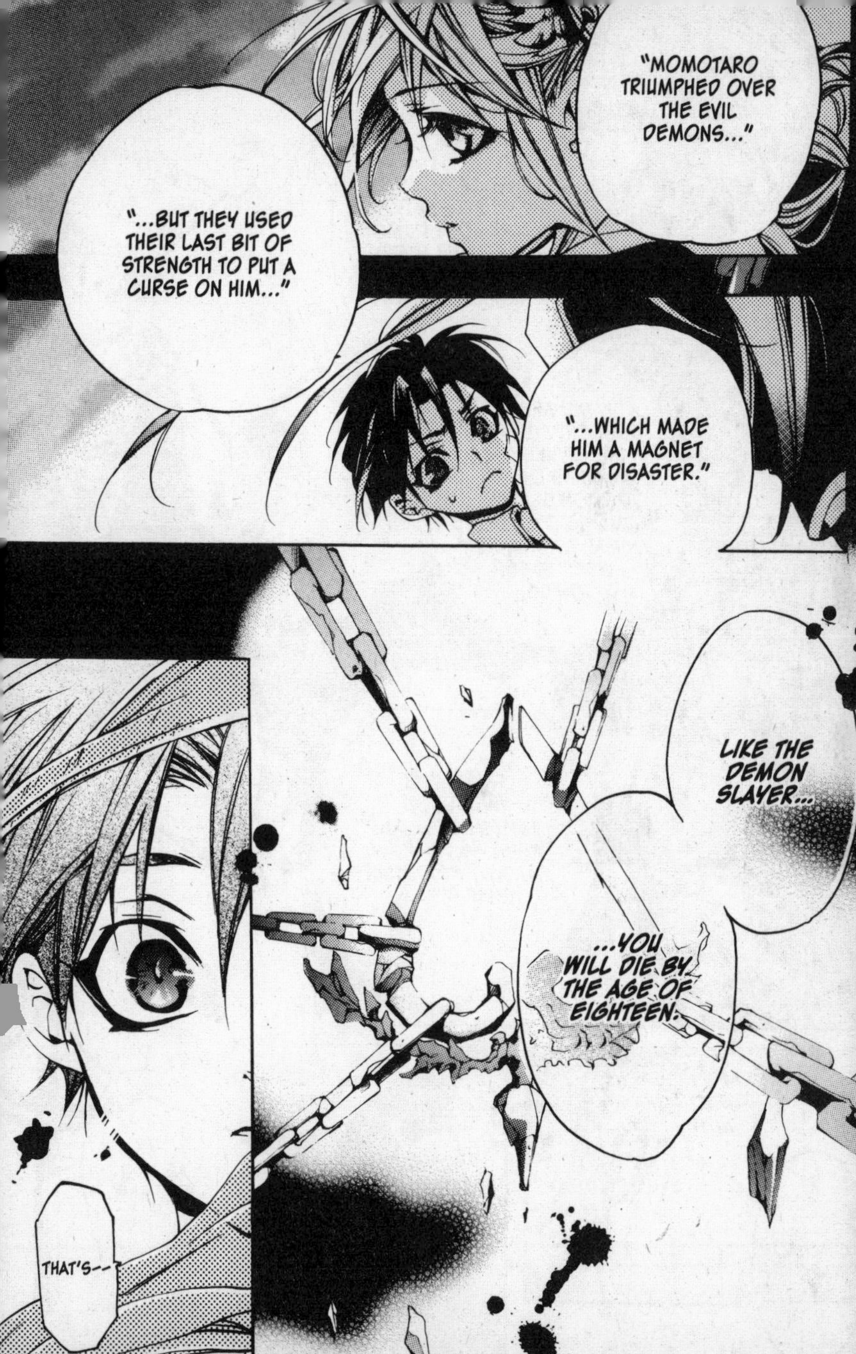
"MOMOTARO TRIUMPHED OVER THE EVIL DEMONS..."
"...BUT THEY USED THEIR LAST BIT OF STRENGTH TO PUT A CURSE ON HIM..."
"...WHICH MADE HIM A MAGNET FOR DISASTER."
LIKE THE DEMON SLAYER...
...YOU WILL DIE BY THE AGE OF EIGHTEEN.
THAT'S--

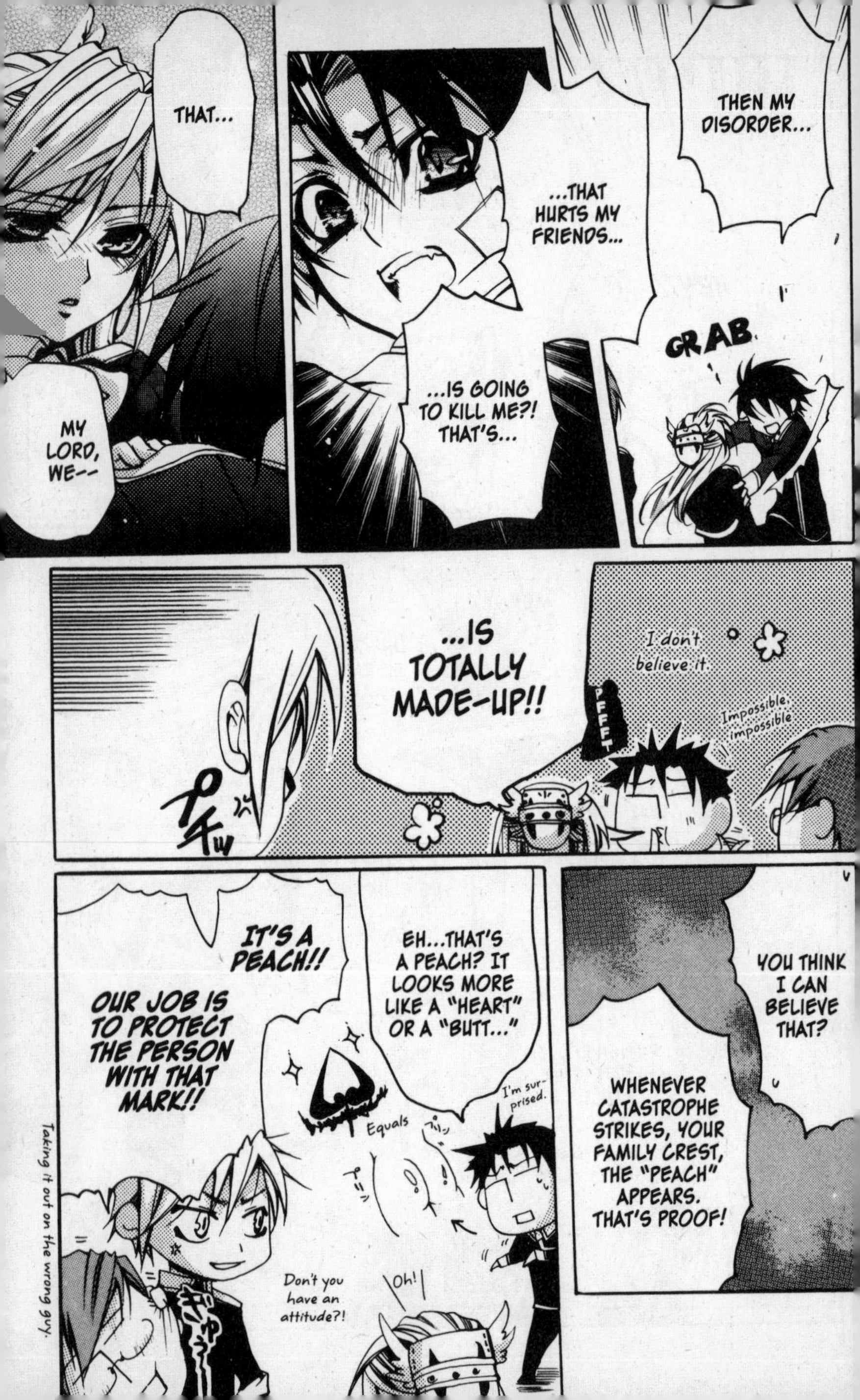
THEN MY DISORDER...
GRAB
...THAT HURTS MY FRIENDS...
...IS GOING TO KILL ME?! THAT'S...
THAT...
MY LORD, WE--
I don't believe it.
Impossible, impossible
PFFFT
...IS TOTALLY MADE-UP!!
YOU THINK I CAN BELIEVE THAT?
WHENEVER CATASTROPHE STRIKES, YOUR FAMILY CREST, THE "PEACH" APPEARS. THAT'S PROOF!
EH...THAT'S A PEACH? IT LOOKS MORE LIKE A "HEART" OR A "BUTT..."
I'm surprised.
IT'S A PEACH!!
OUR JOB IS TO PROTECT THE PERSON WITH THAT MARK!!
Equals
Oh!
Don't you have an attitude?!
Taking it out on the wrong guy.

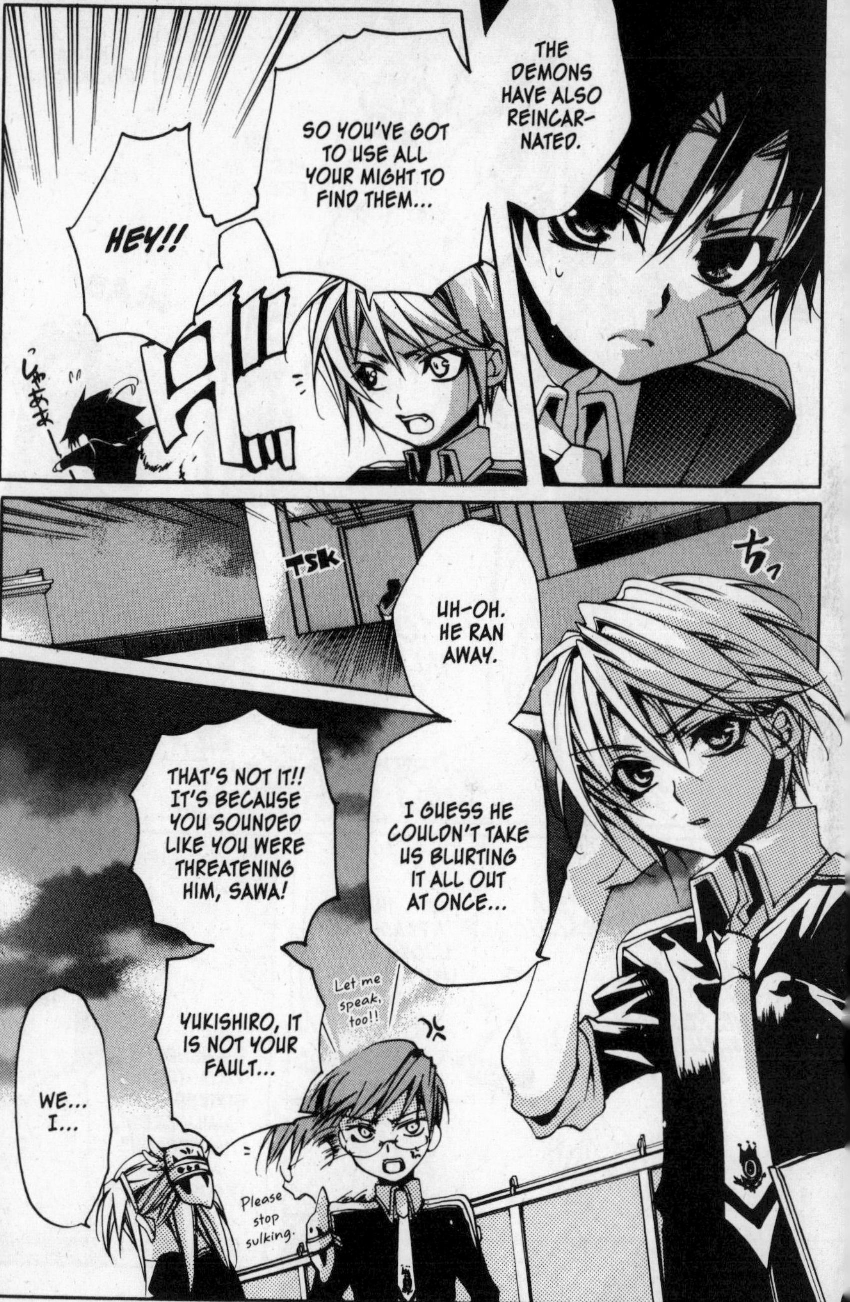
THE DEMONS HAVE ALSO REINCARNATED.
SO YOU'VE GOT TO USE ALL YOUR MIGHT TO FIND THEM...
HEY!!
ちっ
UH-OH. HE RAN AWAY.
TSK
I GUESS HE COULDN'T TAKE US BLURTING IT ALL OUT AT ONCE...
THAT'S NOT IT!! IT'S BECAUSE YOU SOUNDED LIKE YOU WERE THREATENING HIM, SAWA!
Let me speak, too!!
YUKISHIRO, IT IS NOT YOUR FAULT...
WE... I...
Please stop sulking.

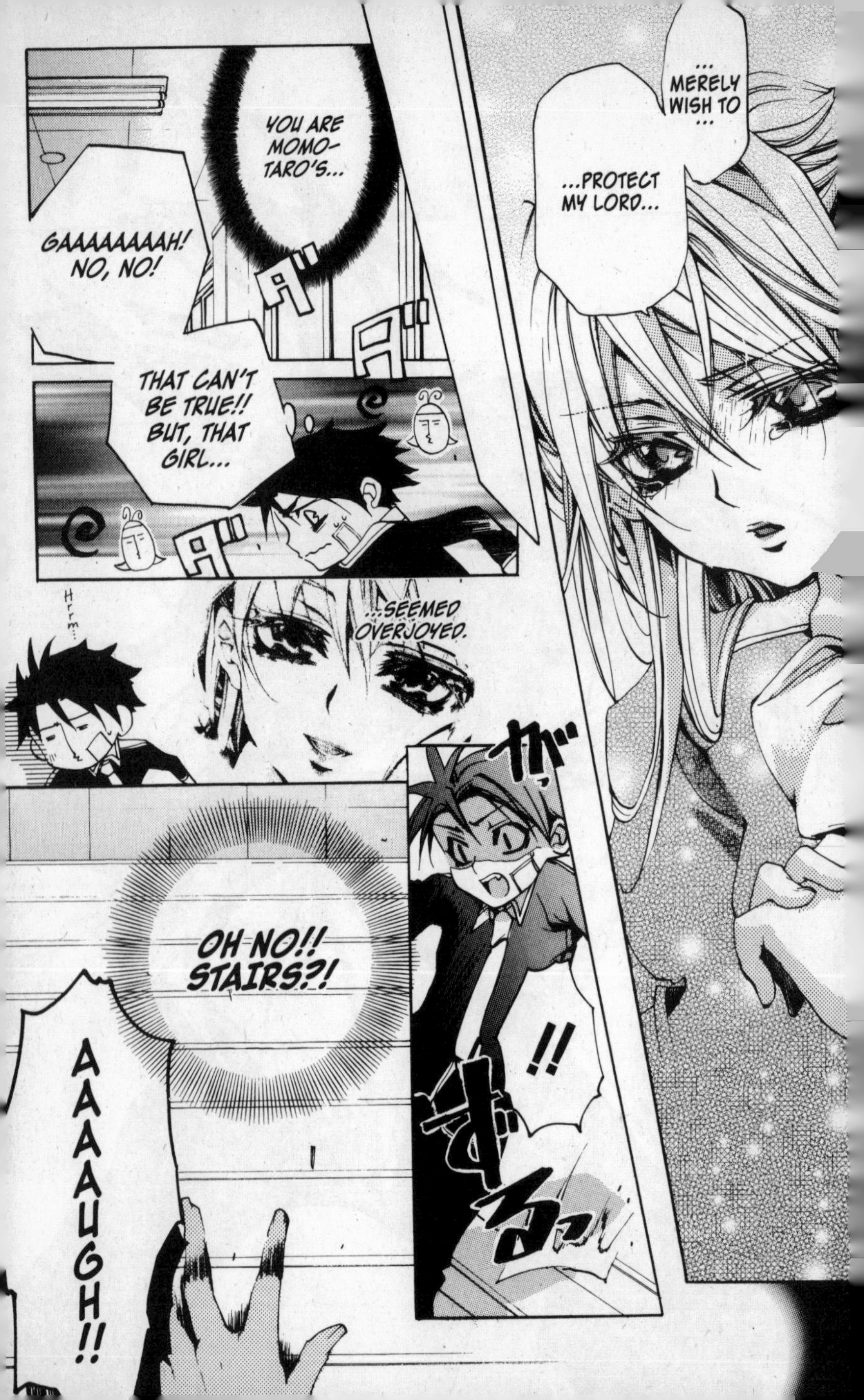
... MERELY WISH TO ...
...PROTECT MY LORD...
YOU ARE MOMO-TARO'S...
GAAAAAAAAH! NO, NO!
THAT CAN'T BE TRUE!! BUT, THAT GIRL...
Hrrm...
...SEEMED OVERJOYED.
!!
OH NO!! STAIRS?!
AAAAUGH!!

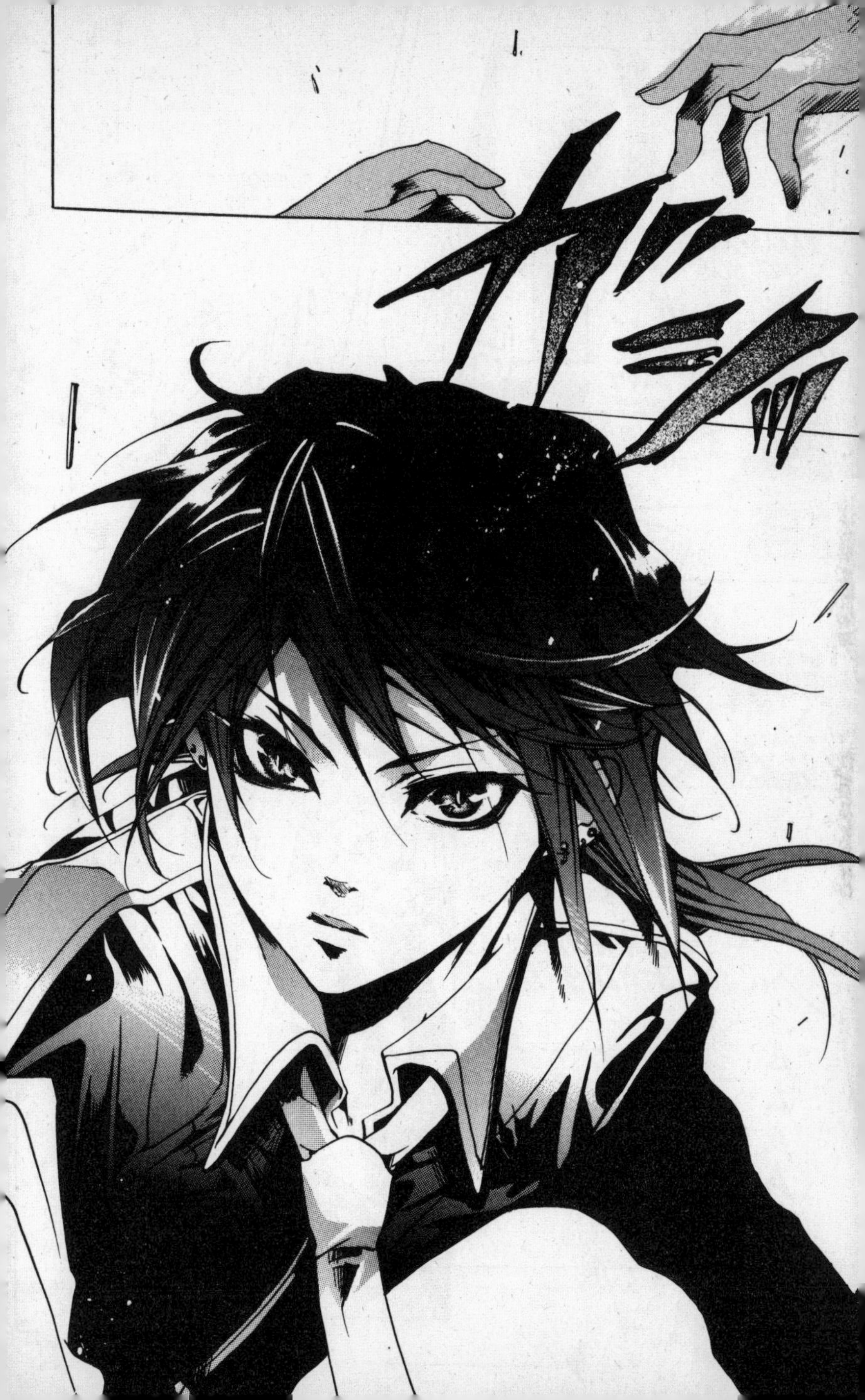

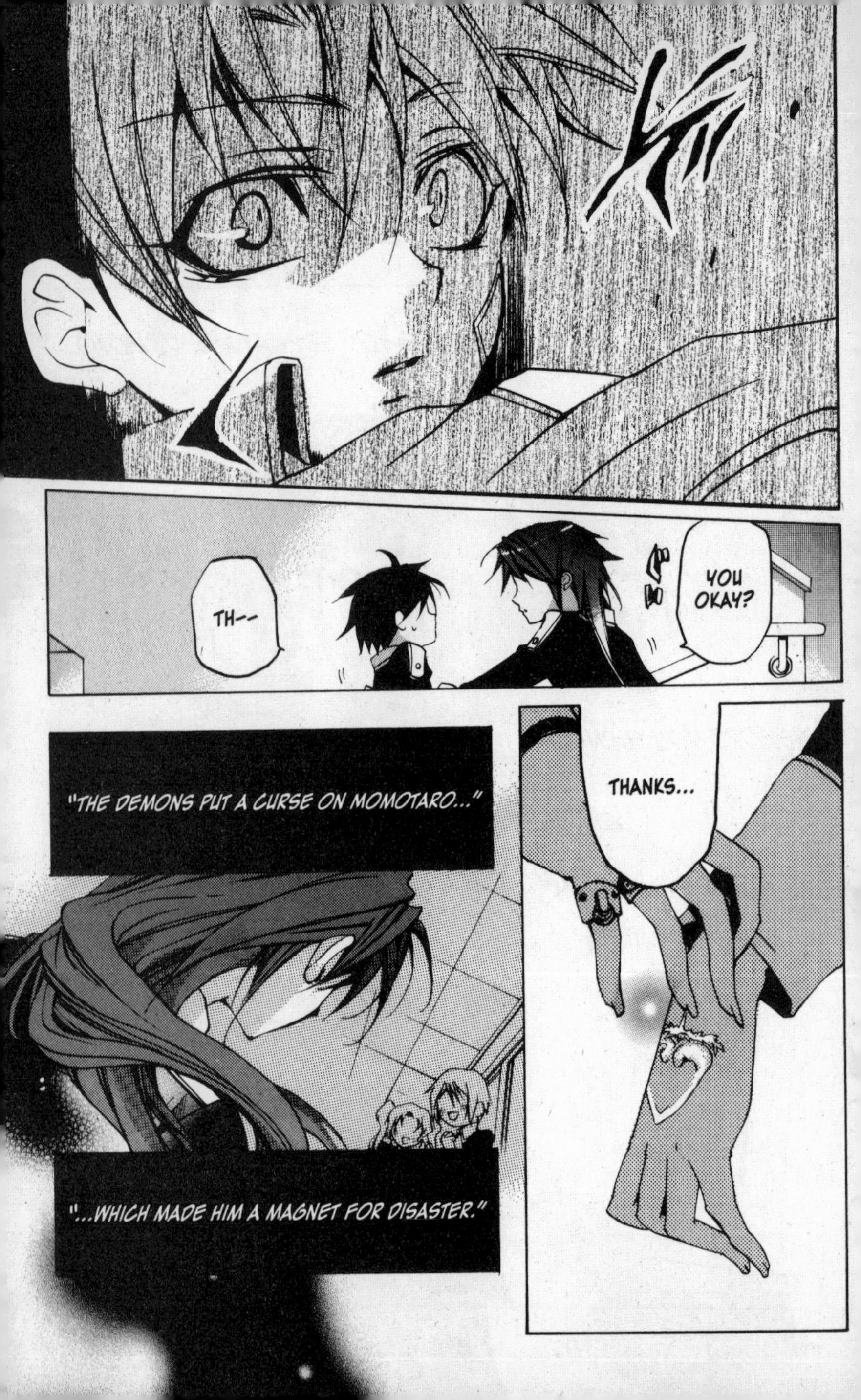
YOU OKAY?
TH--
THANKS...
"THE DEMONS PUT A CURSE ON MOMOTARO..."
"...WHICH MADE HIM A MAGNET FOR DISASTER."

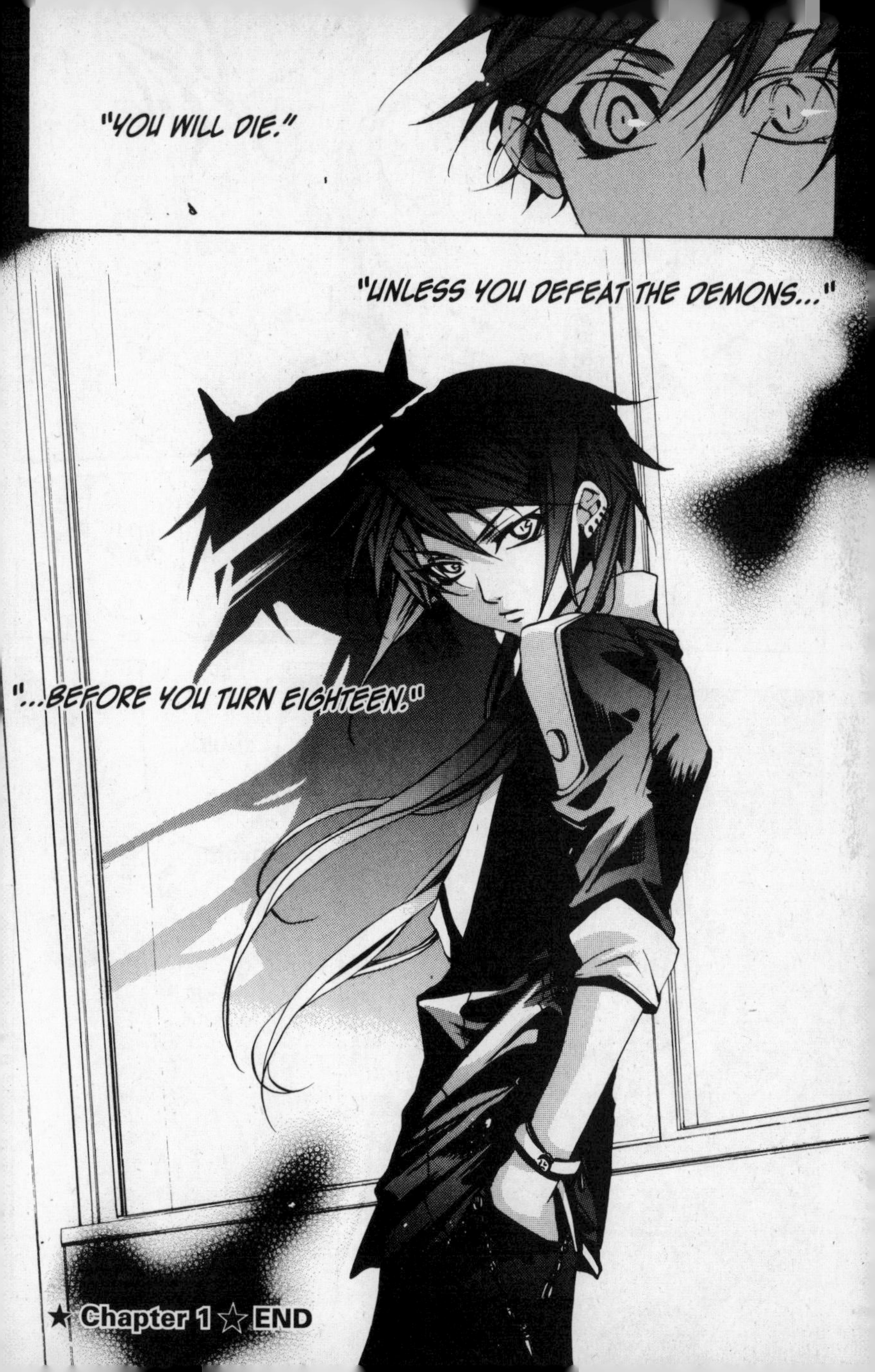
"YOU WILL DIE."
"UNLESS YOU DEFEAT THE DEMONS..."
"...BEFORE YOU TURN EIGHTEEN."
★ Chapter 1 ☆ END

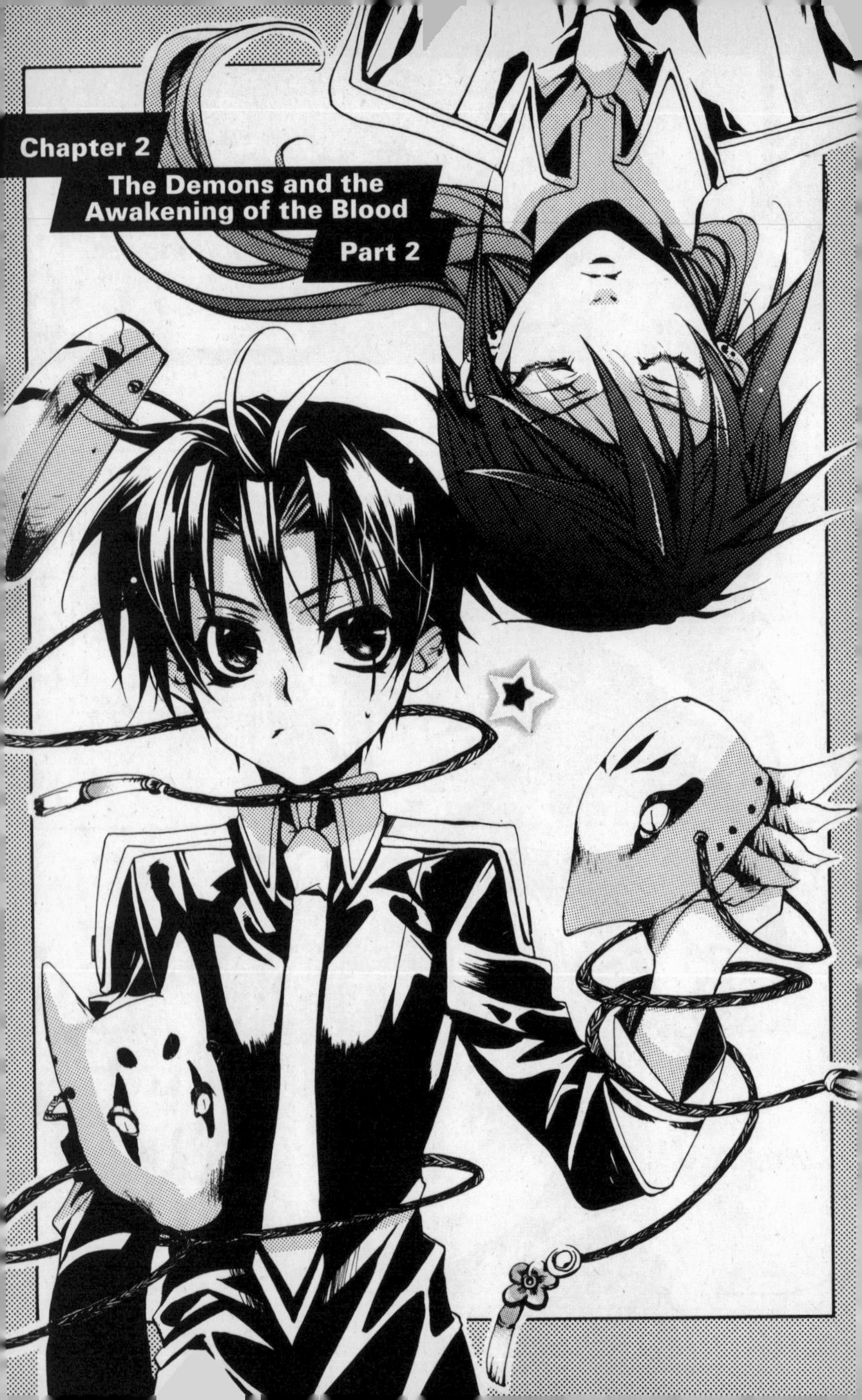

Chapter 2
The Demons and the Awakening of the Blood
Part 2

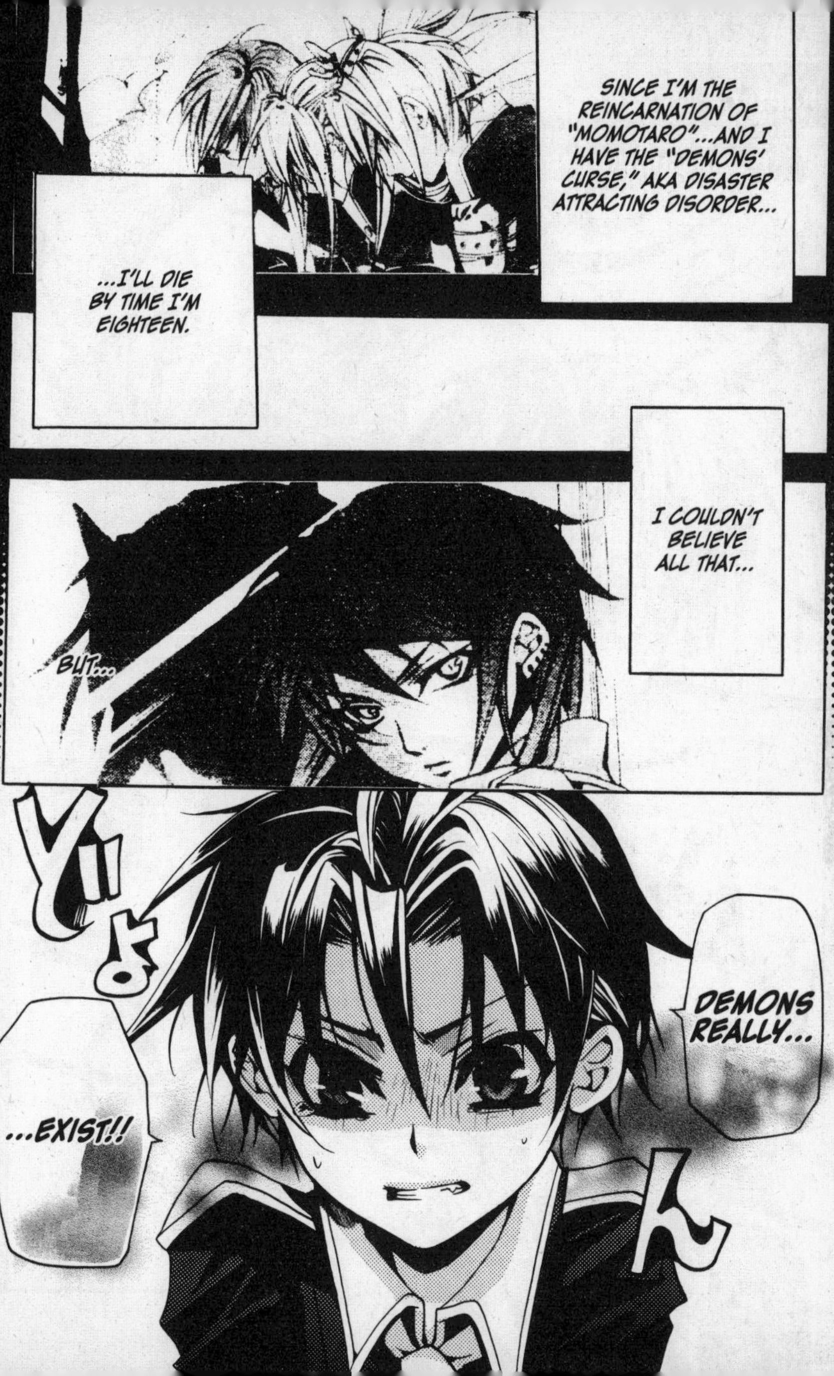
SINCE I'M THE REINCARNATION OF "MOMOTARO"...AND I HAVE THE "DEMONS' CURSE," AKA DISASTER ATTRACTING DISORDER...
...I'LL DIE BY TIME I'M EIGHTEEN.
I COULDN'T BELIEVE ALL THAT...
BUT...
DEMONS REALLY...
...EXIST!!

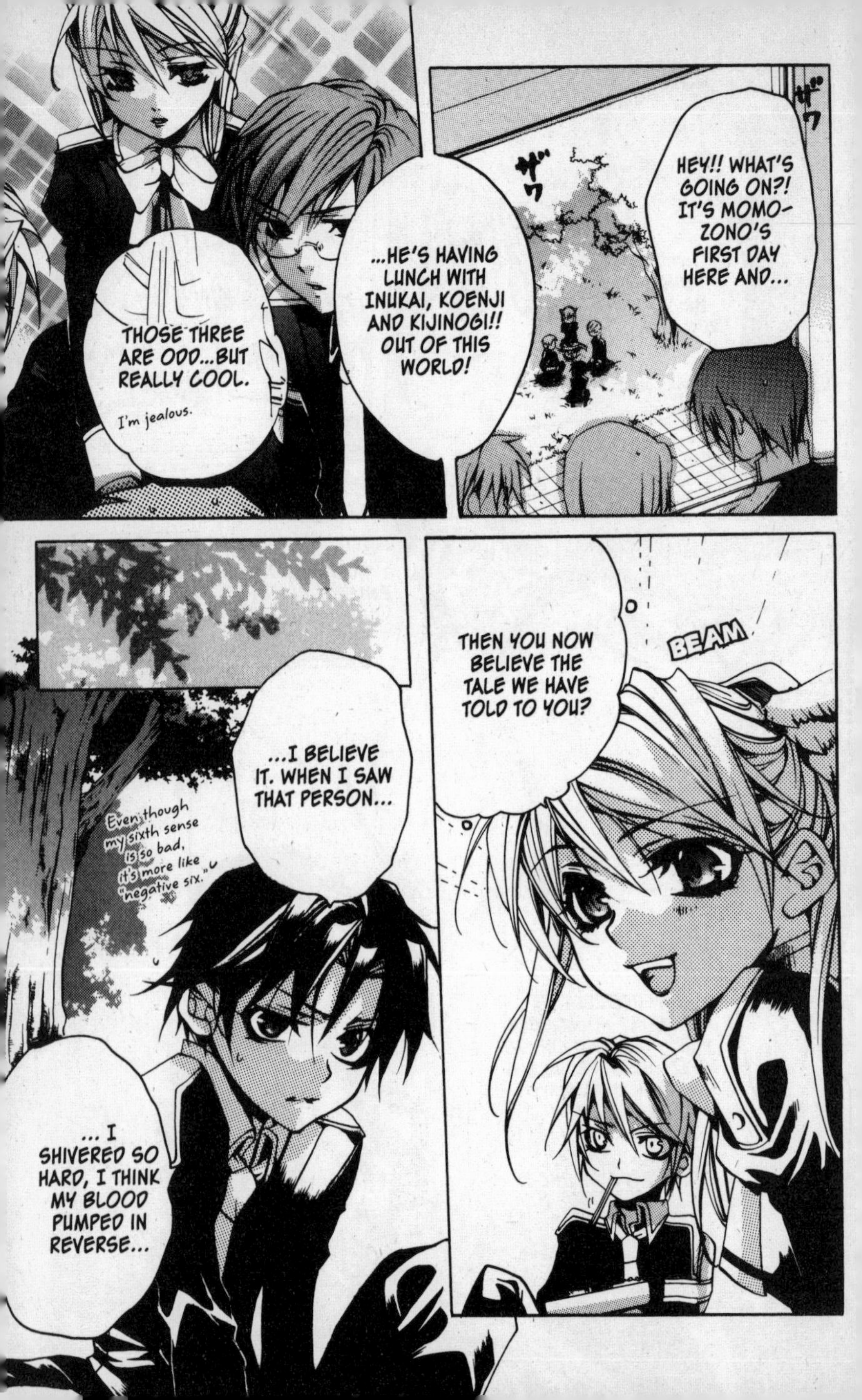
ザワ
ザワ
HEY!! WHAT'S GOING ON?! IT'S MOMO-ZONO'S FIRST DAY HERE AND...
...HE'S HAVING LUNCH WITH INUKAI, KOENJI AND KIJINOGI!! OUT OF THIS WORLD!
THOSE THREE ARE ODD...BUT REALLY COOL.
I'm jealous.
THEN YOU NOW BELIEVE THE TALE WE HAVE TOLD TO YOU?
BEAM
...I BELIEVE IT. WHEN I SAW THAT PERSON...
Even though my sixth sense is so bad, it's more like "negative six."
... I SHIVERED SO HARD, I THINK MY BLOOD PUMPED IN REVERSE...

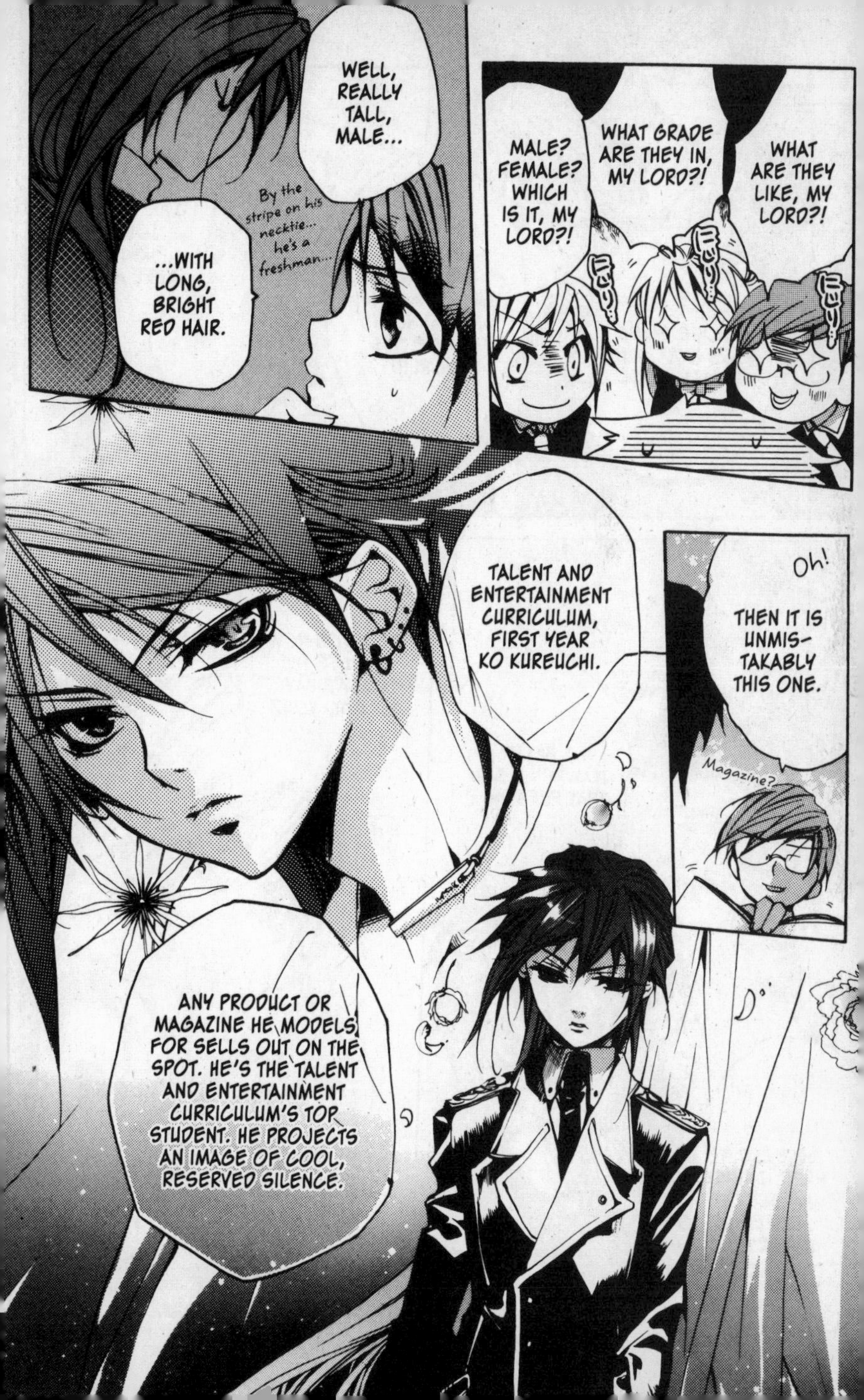
WHAT ARE THEY LIKE, MY LORD?!
WHAT GRADE ARE THEY IN, MY LORD?!
MALE? FEMALE? WHICH IS IT, MY LORD?!
WELL, REALLY TALL, MALE...
By the stripe on his necktie... he's a freshman...
...WITH LONG, BRIGHT RED HAIR.
Oh!
THEN IT IS UNMIS-TAKABLY THIS ONE.
Magazine?
TALENT AND ENTERTAINMENT CURRICULUM, FIRST YEAR KO KUREUCHI.
ANY PRODUCT OR MAGAZINE HE MODELS FOR SELLS OUT ON THE SPOT. HE'S THE TALENT AND ENTERTAINMENT CURRICULUM'S TOP STUDENT. HE PROJECTS AN IMAGE OF COOL, RESERVED SILENCE.

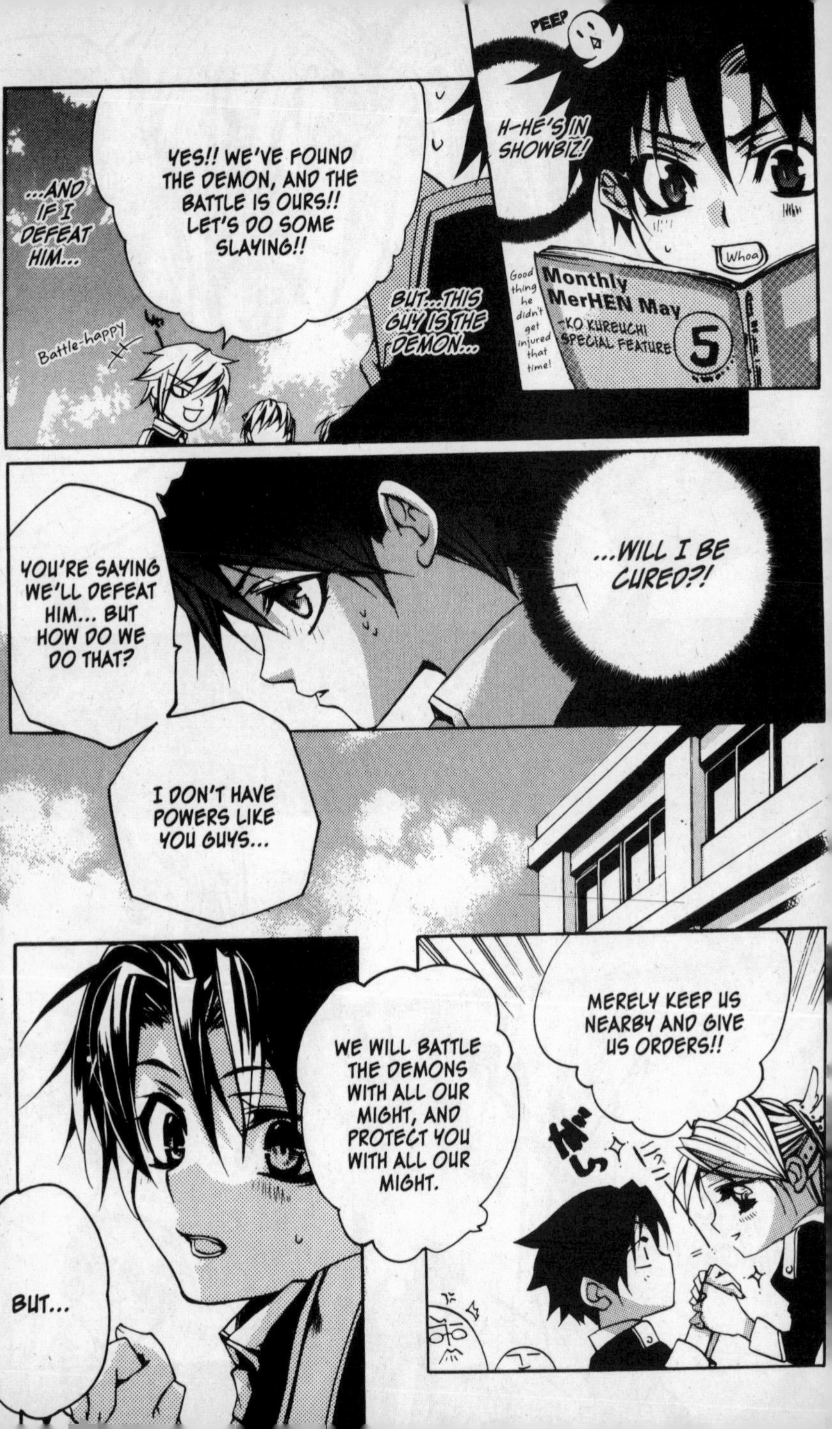
PEEP
H-HE'S IN SHOWBIZ!
Whoa
Monthly MerHEN May
-KO KUREUCHI SPECIAL FEATURE
5
Good thing he didn't get injured that time!
BUT...THIS GUY IS THE DEMON...
YES!! WE'VE FOUND THE DEMON, AND THE BATTLE IS OURS!! LET'S DO SOME SLAYING!!
...AND IF I DEFEAT HIM...
Battle-happy
...WILL I BE CURED?!
YOU'RE SAYING WE'LL DEFEAT HIM... BUT HOW DO WE DO THAT?
I DON'T HAVE POWERS LIKE YOU GUYS...
WE WILL BATTLE THE DEMONS WITH ALL OUR MIGHT, AND PROTECT YOU WITH ALL OUR MIGHT.
MERELY KEEP US NEARBY AND GIVE US ORDERS!!
BUT...

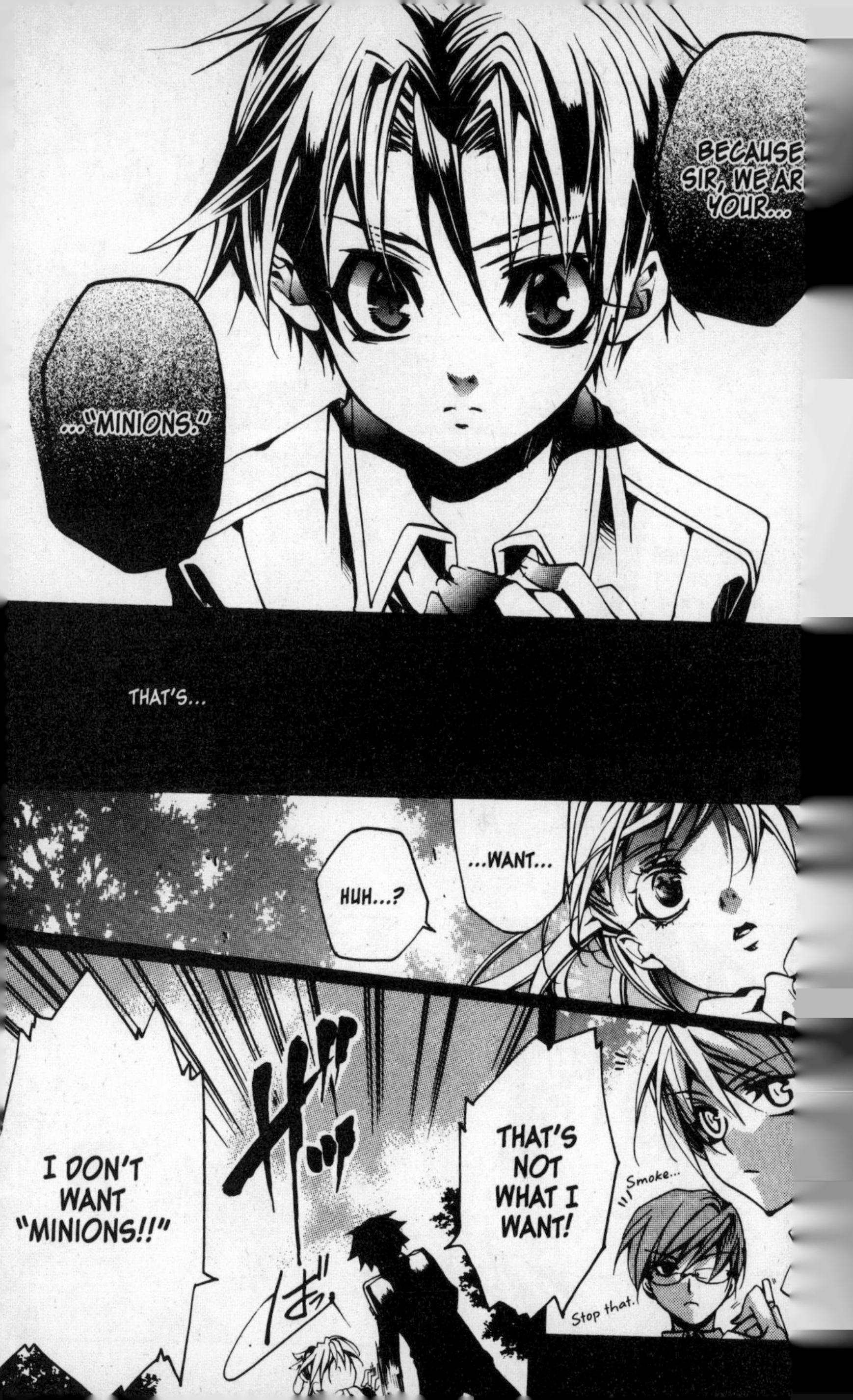
BECAUSE SIR, WE AR YOUR...
..."MINIONS."
THAT'S...
...WANT...
HUH...?
THAT'S NOT WHAT I WANT!
Smoke...
I DON'T WANT "MINIONS!!"
Stop that.

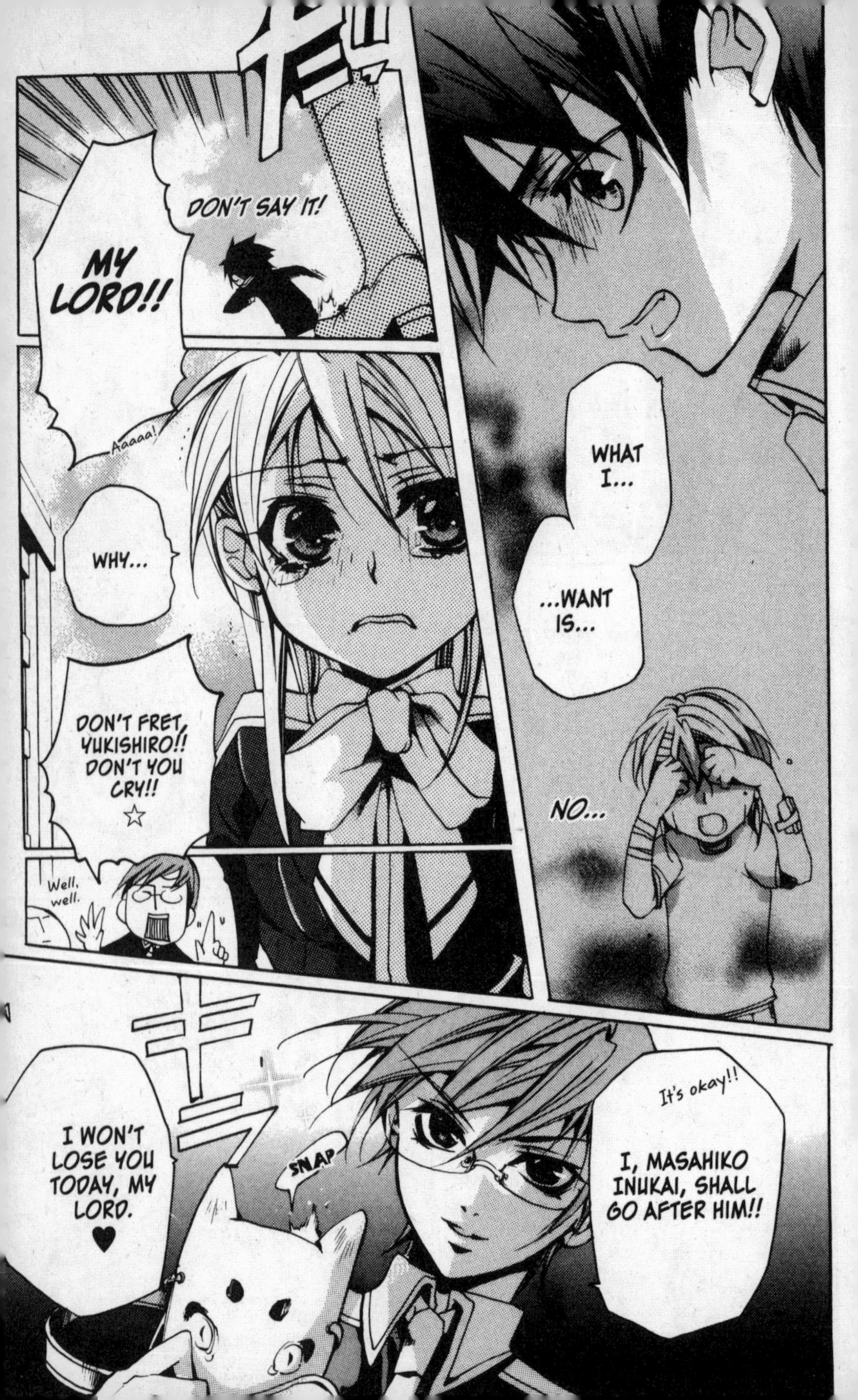
WHAT I...
...WANT IS...
NO...
DON'T SAY IT!
MY LORD!!
Aaaaa!
WHY...
DON'T FRET, YUKISHIRO!! DON'T YOU CRY!! ☆
Well, well.
It's okay!!
I, MASAHIKO INUKAI, SHALL GO AFTER HIM!!
SNAP
I WON'T LOSE YOU TODAY, MY LORD. ♥

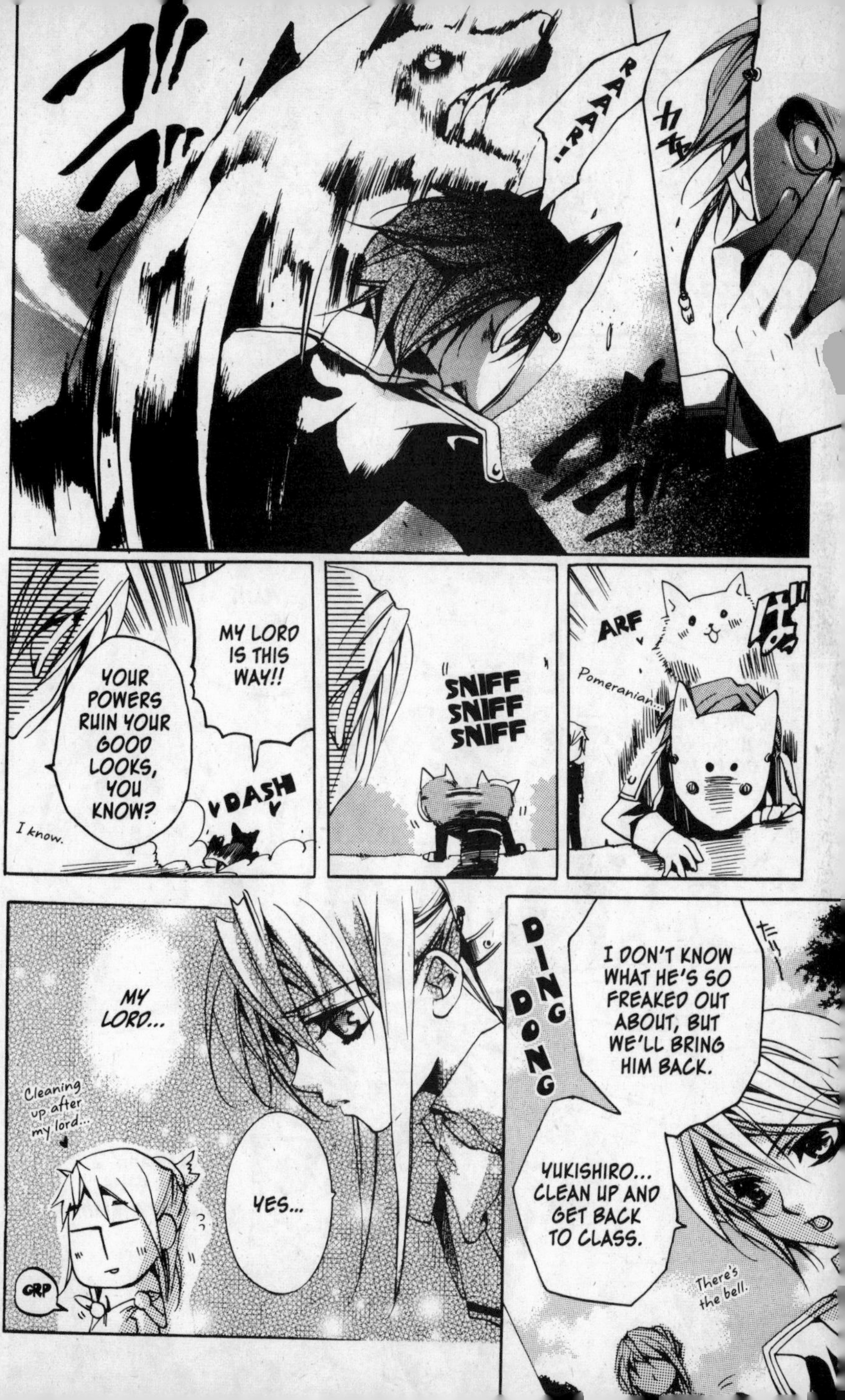
RAAAR!!
ARF
Pomeranian...
SNIFF SNIFF SNIFF
MY LORD IS THIS WAY!!
DASH
YOUR POWERS RUIN YOUR GOOD LOOKS, YOU KNOW?
I know.
DING DONG
I DON'T KNOW WHAT HE'S SO FREAKED OUT ABOUT, BUT WE'LL BRING HIM BACK.
YUKISHIRO... CLEAN UP AND GET BACK TO CLASS.
There's the bell.
MY LORD...
YES...
Cleaning up after my lord...
GRP

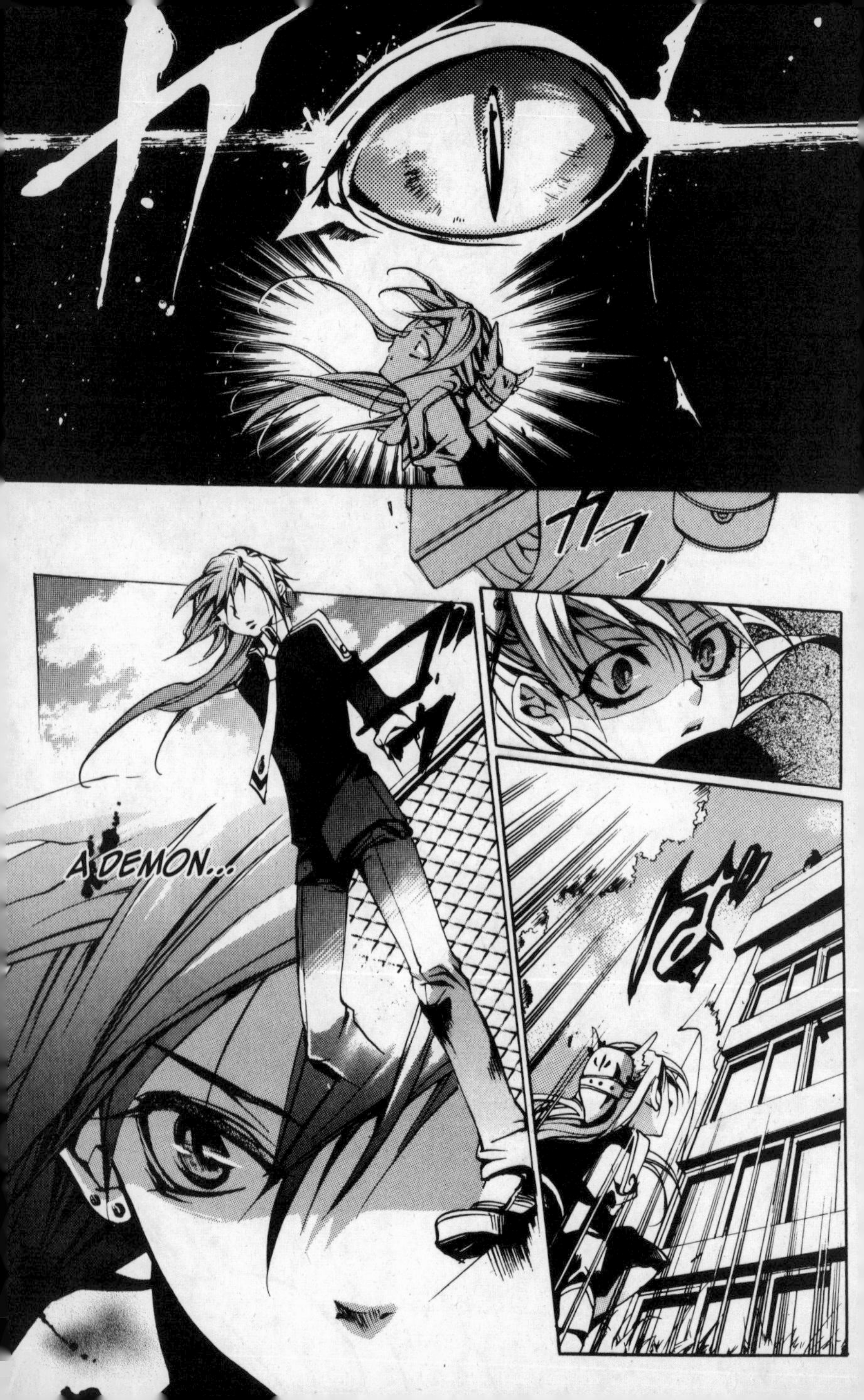
A DEMON...

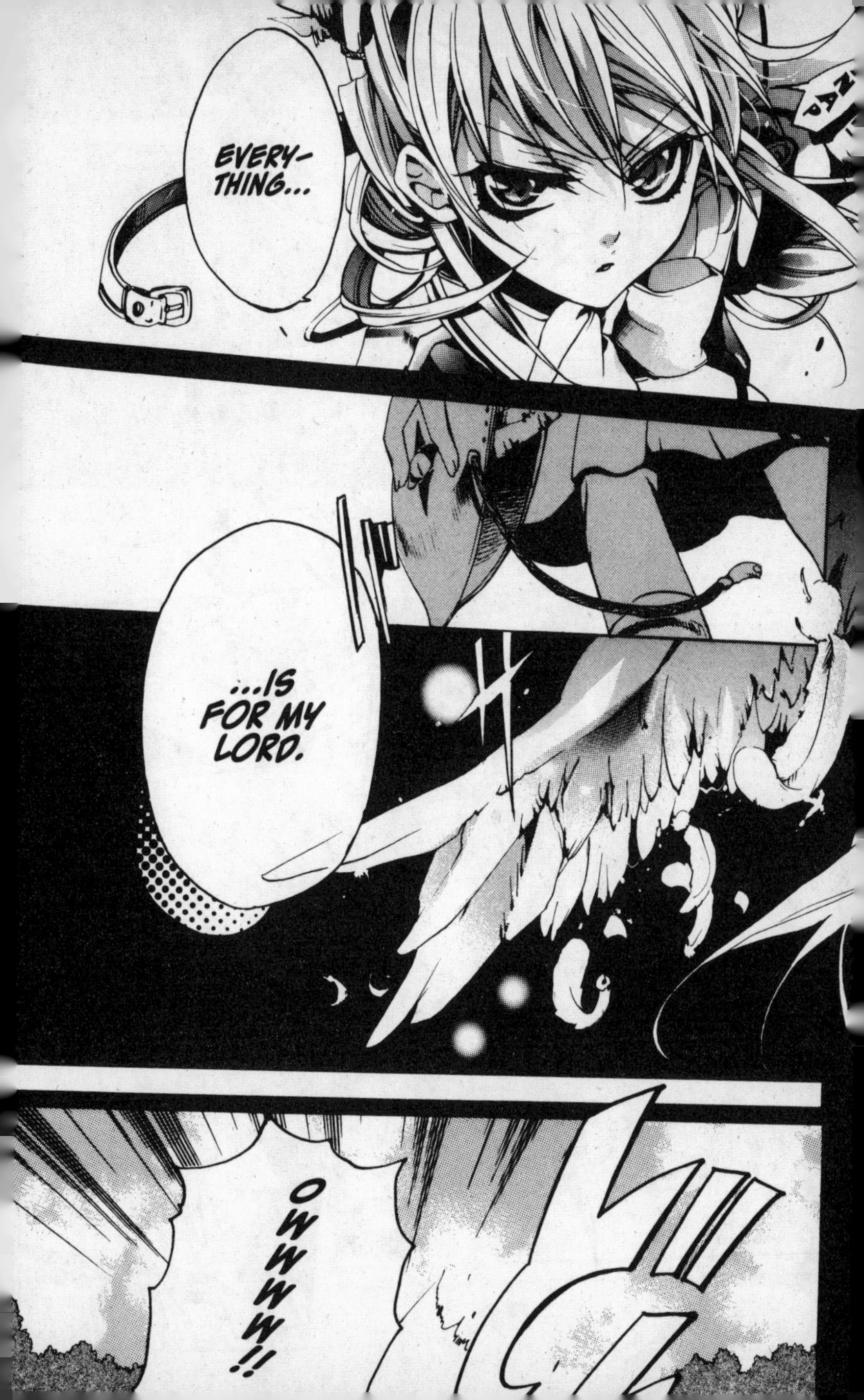
EVERY-THING...
...IS FOR MY LORD.
OWWWWW!!

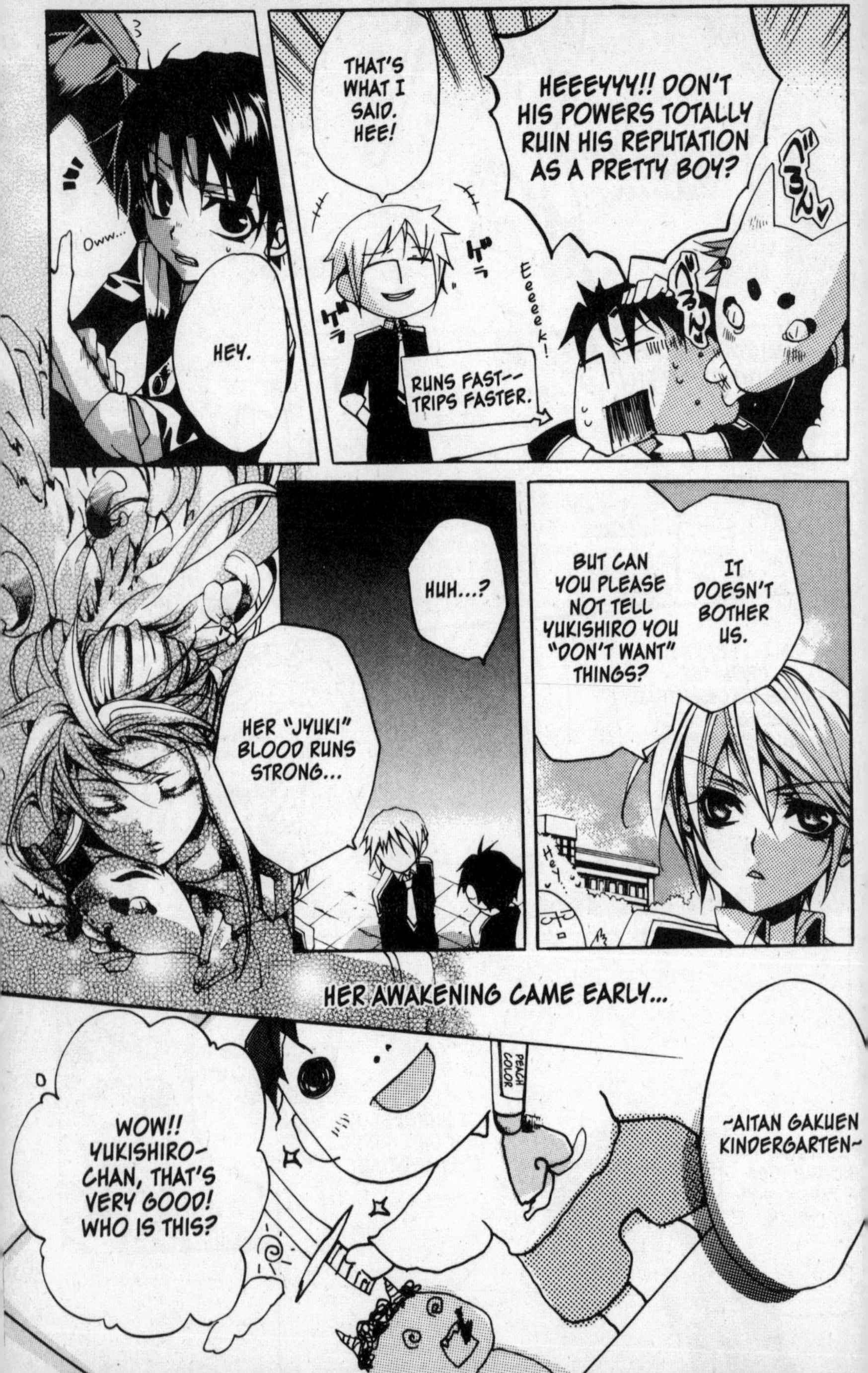
HEEEYYY!! DON'T HIS POWERS TOTALLY RUIN HIS REPUTATION AS A PRETTY BOY?
Eeeeek!
THAT'S WHAT I SAID. HEE!
RUNS FAST--TRIPS FASTER.
Oww...
HEY.
IT DOESN'T BOTHER US.
BUT CAN YOU PLEASE NOT TELL YUKISHIRO YOU "DON'T WANT" THINGS?
Hey...
HUH...?
HER "JYUKI" BLOOD RUNS STRONG...
HER AWAKENING CAME EARLY...
~AITAN GAKUEN KINDERGARTEN~
PEACH COLOR
WOW!! YUKISHIRO-CHAN, THAT'S VERY GOOD! WHO IS THIS?

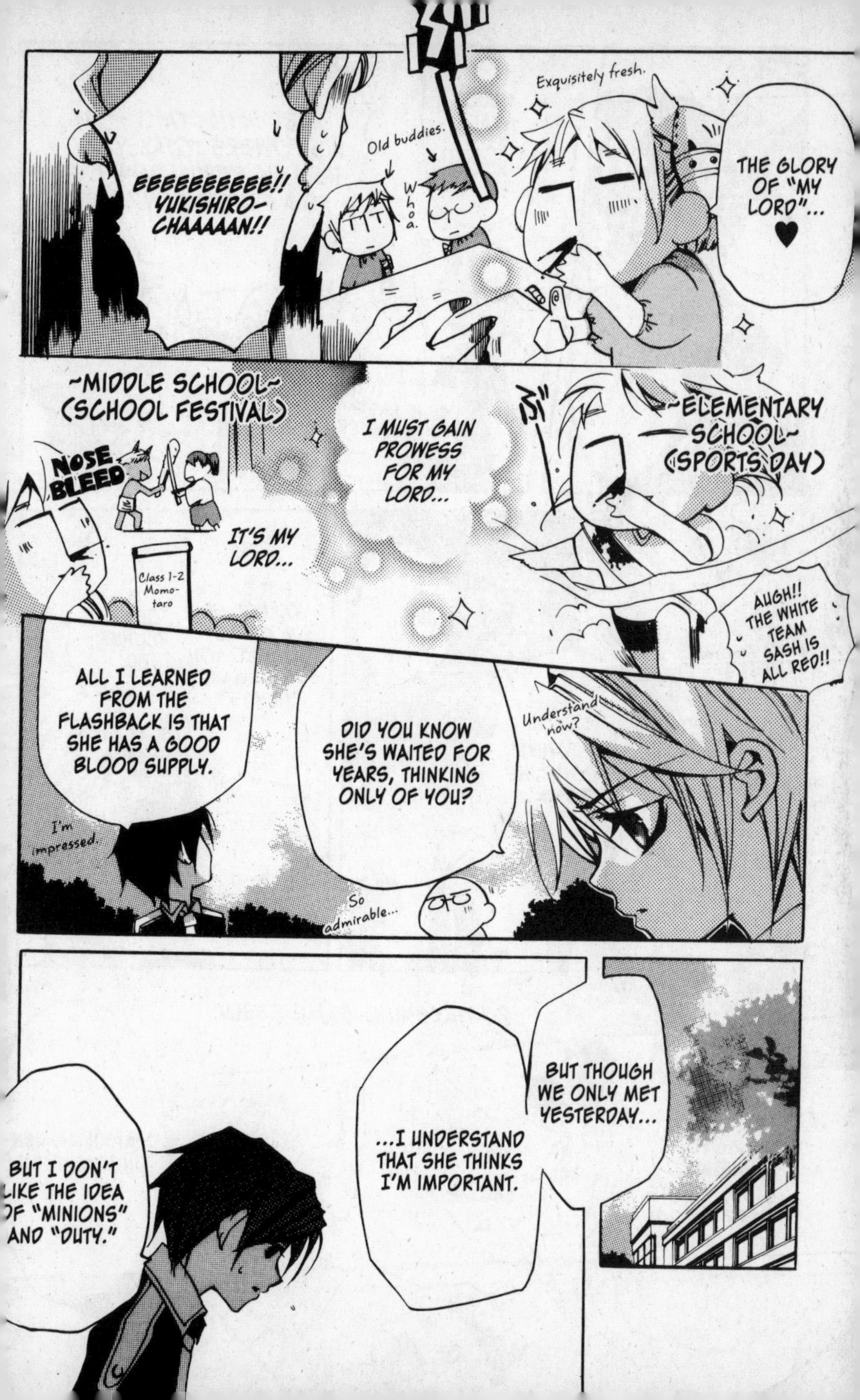
Exquisitely fresh.
THE GLORY OF "MY LORD"... ♥
Old buddies.
Whoa.
EEEEEEEEEE!! YUKISHIRO-CHAAAAAN!!
ぶ
~ELEMENTARY SCHOOL~ (SPORTS DAY)
AUGH!! THE WHITE TEAM SASH IS ALL RED!!
I MUST GAIN PROWESS FOR MY LORD...
~MIDDLE SCHOOL~ (SCHOOL FESTIVAL)
IT'S MY LORD...
NOSE BLEED
Class 1-2 Momo-taro
Understand now?
DID YOU KNOW SHE'S WAITED FOR YEARS, THINKING ONLY OF YOU?
So admirable...
ALL I LEARNED FROM THE FLASHBACK IS THAT SHE HAS A GOOD BLOOD SUPPLY.
I'm impressed.
BUT THOUGH WE ONLY MET YESTERDAY...
...I UNDERSTAND THAT SHE THINKS I'M IMPORTANT.
BUT I DON'T LIKE THE IDEA OF "MINIONS" AND "DUTY."

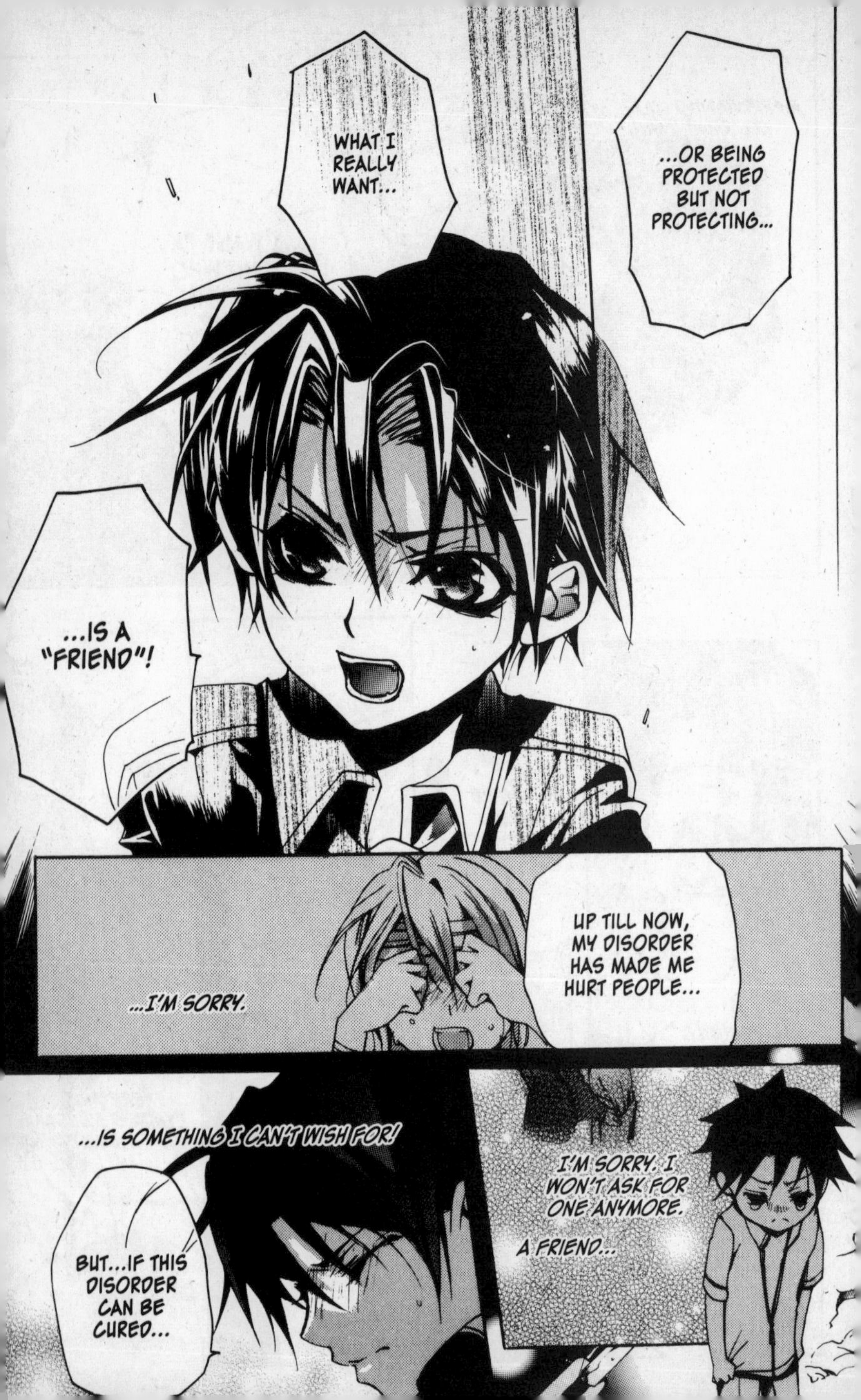
...OR BEING PROTECTED BUT NOT PROTECTING...
WHAT I REALLY WANT...
...IS A "FRIEND"!
UP TILL NOW, MY DISORDER HAS MADE ME HURT PEOPLE...
...I'M SORRY.
I'M SORRY. I WON'T ASK FOR ONE ANYMORE.
A FRIEND...
...IS SOMETHING I CAN'T WISH FOR!
BUT...IF THIS DISORDER CAN BE CURED...

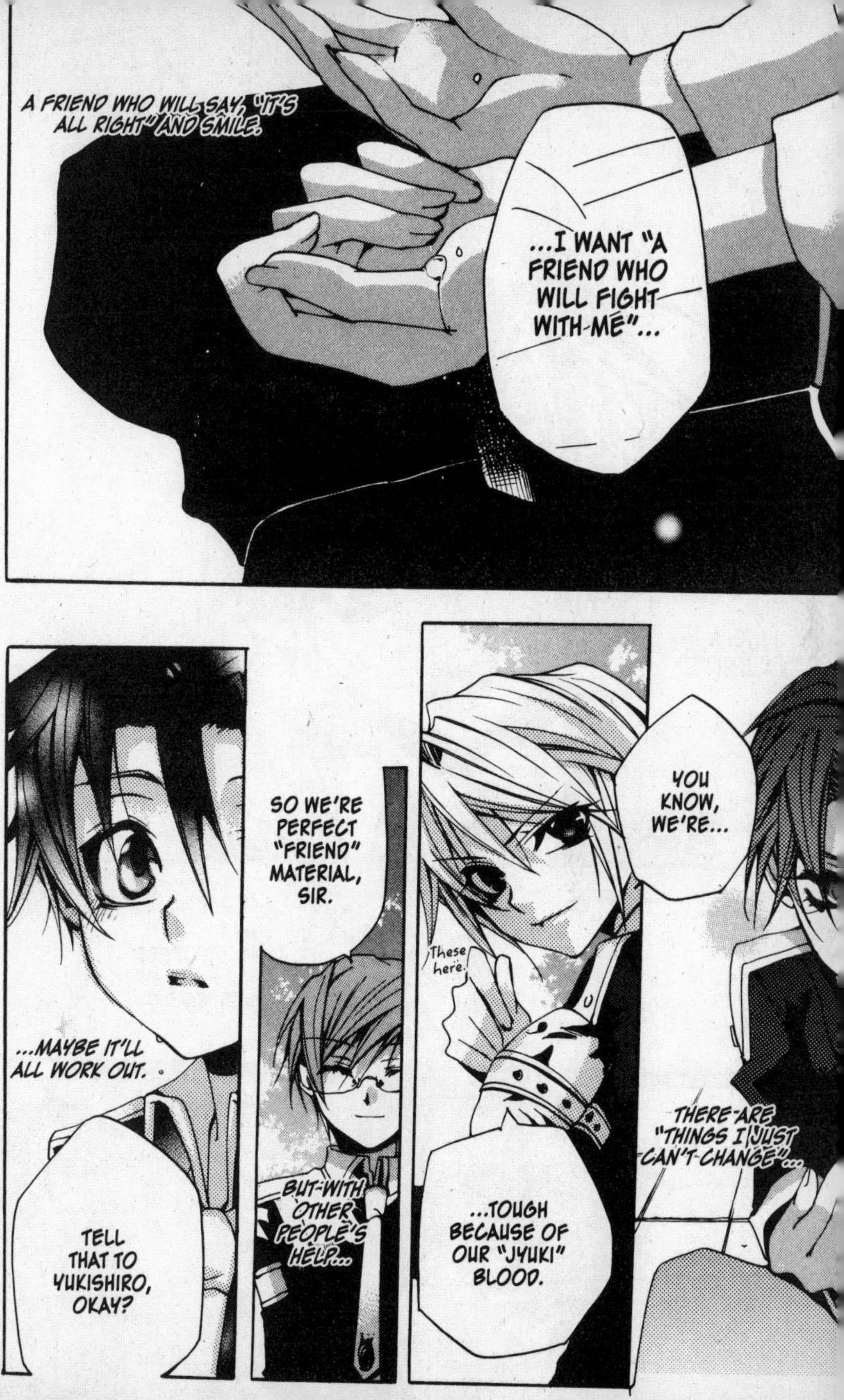
...I WANT "A FRIEND WHO WILL FIGHT WITH ME"...
A FRIEND WHO WILL SAY, "IT'S ALL RIGHT" AND SMILE.
YOU KNOW, WE'RE...
THERE ARE "THINGS I JUST CAN'T CHANGE"...
These here.
...TOUGH BECAUSE OF OUR "JYUKI" BLOOD.
SO WE'RE PERFECT "FRIEND" MATERIAL, SIR.
BUT WITH OTHER PEOPLE'S HELP...
...MAYBE IT'LL ALL WORK OUT.
TELL THAT TO YUKISHIRO, OKAY?

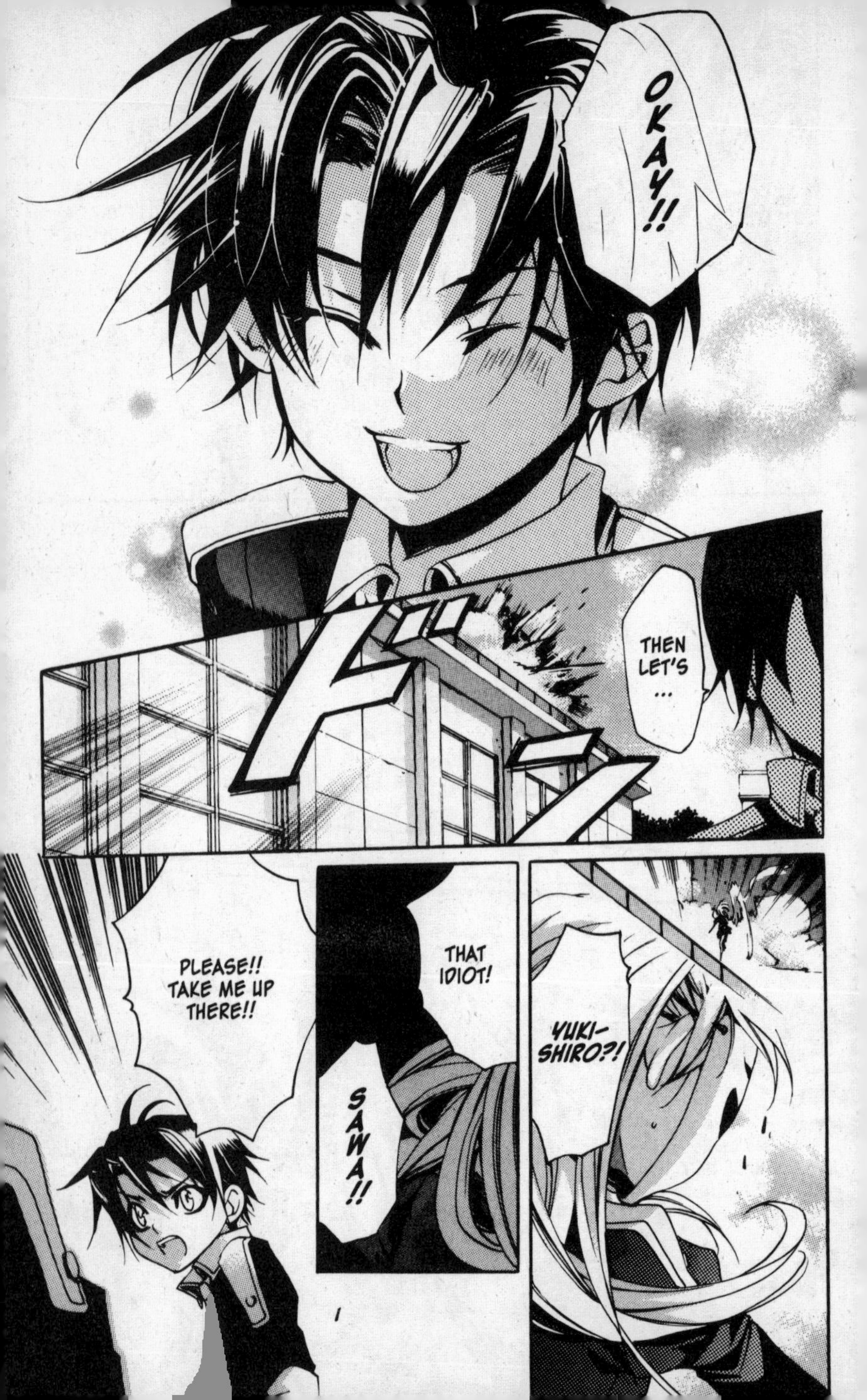
OKAY!!
THEN LET'S ...
YUKI-SHIRO?!
THAT IDIOT!
SAWA!!
PLEASE!! TAKE ME UP THERE!!

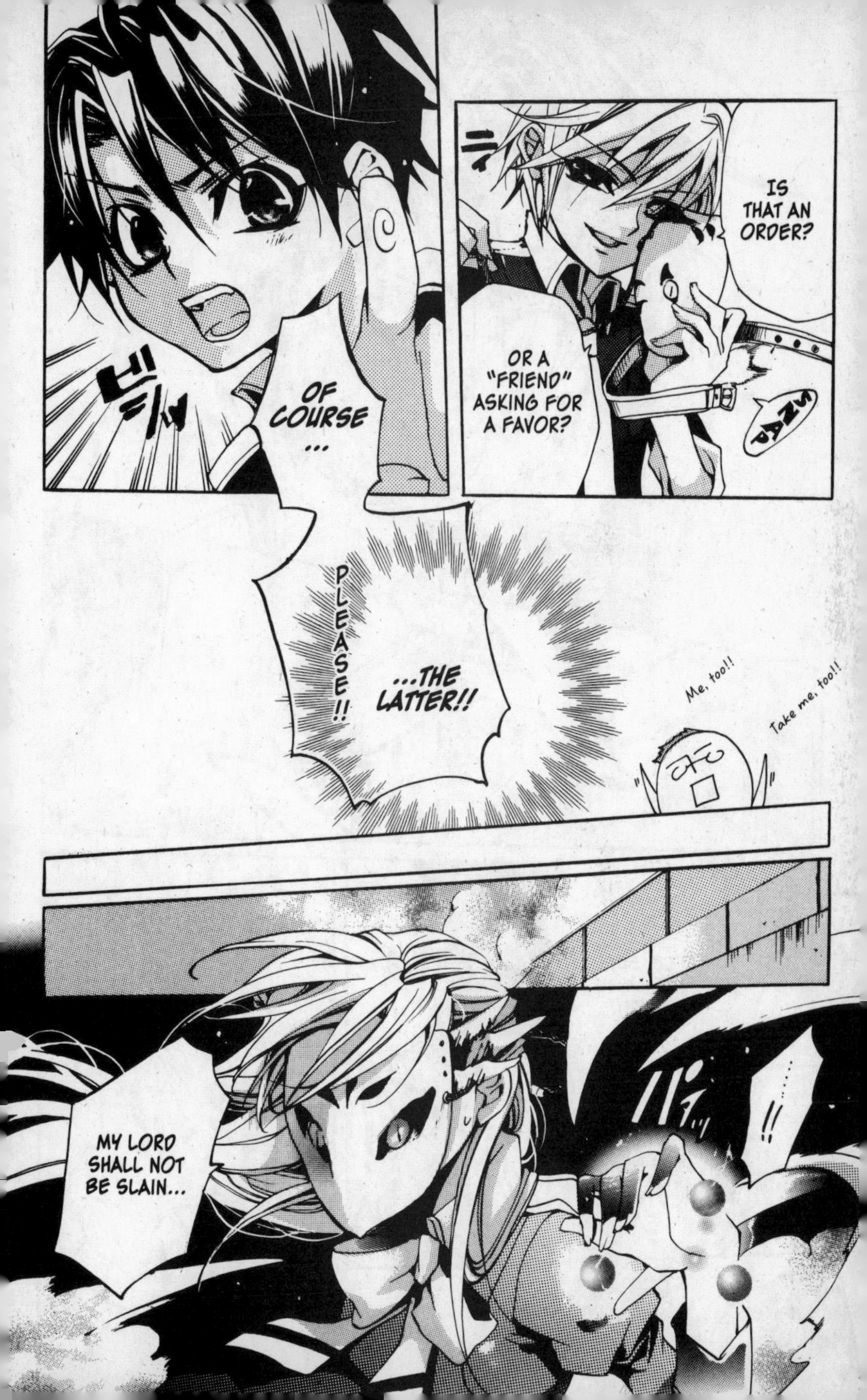
IS THAT AN ORDER?
OR A "FRIEND" ASKING FOR A FAVOR?
PANS
OF COURSE ...
...THE LATTER!!
PLEASE!!
Me, too!!
Take me, too!!
!! ......
MY LORD SHALL NOT BE SLAIN...

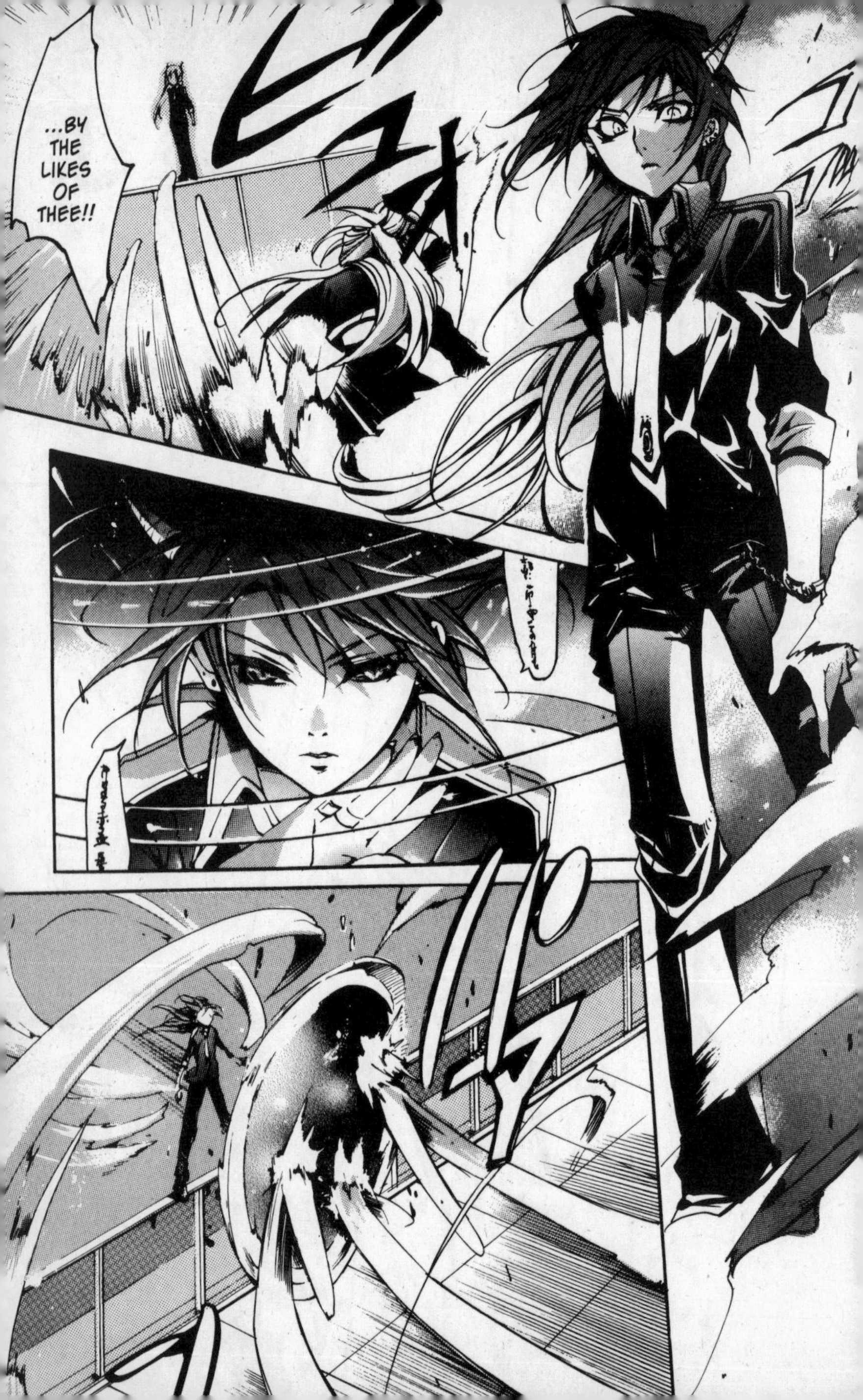
...BY THE LIKES OF THEE!!

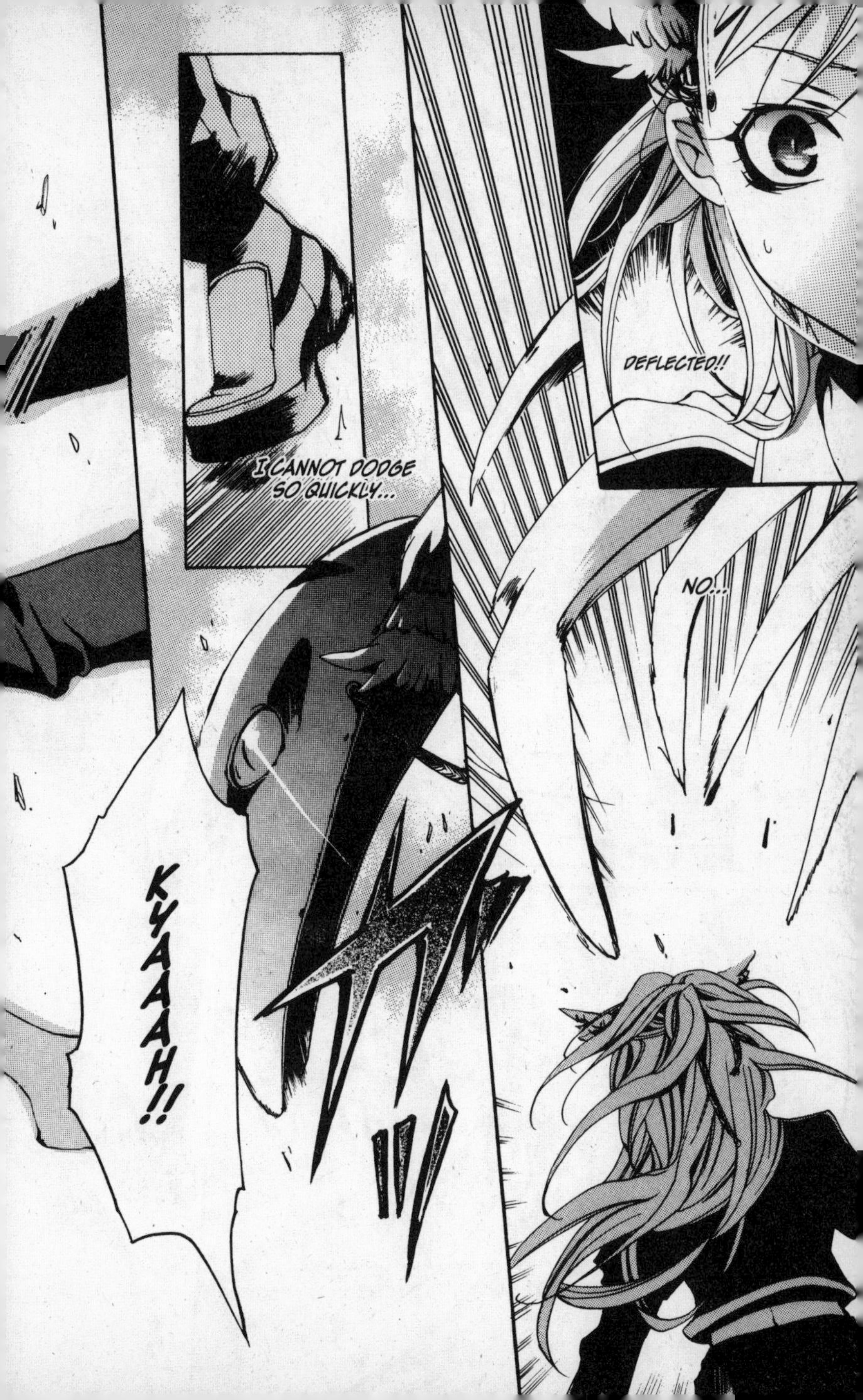
DEFLECTED!!
I CANNOT DODGE SO QUICKLY...
NO...
KYAAAAH!!

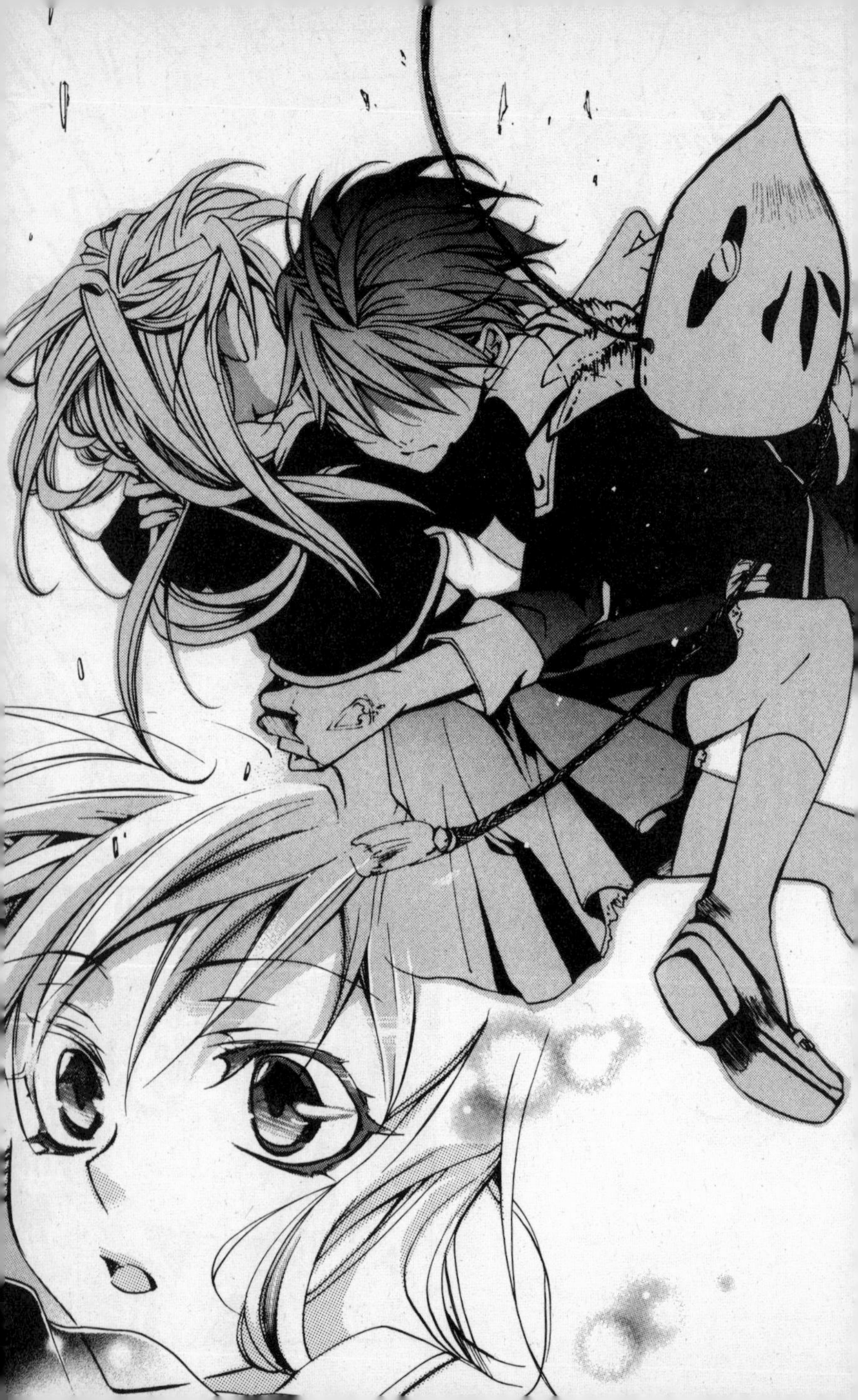

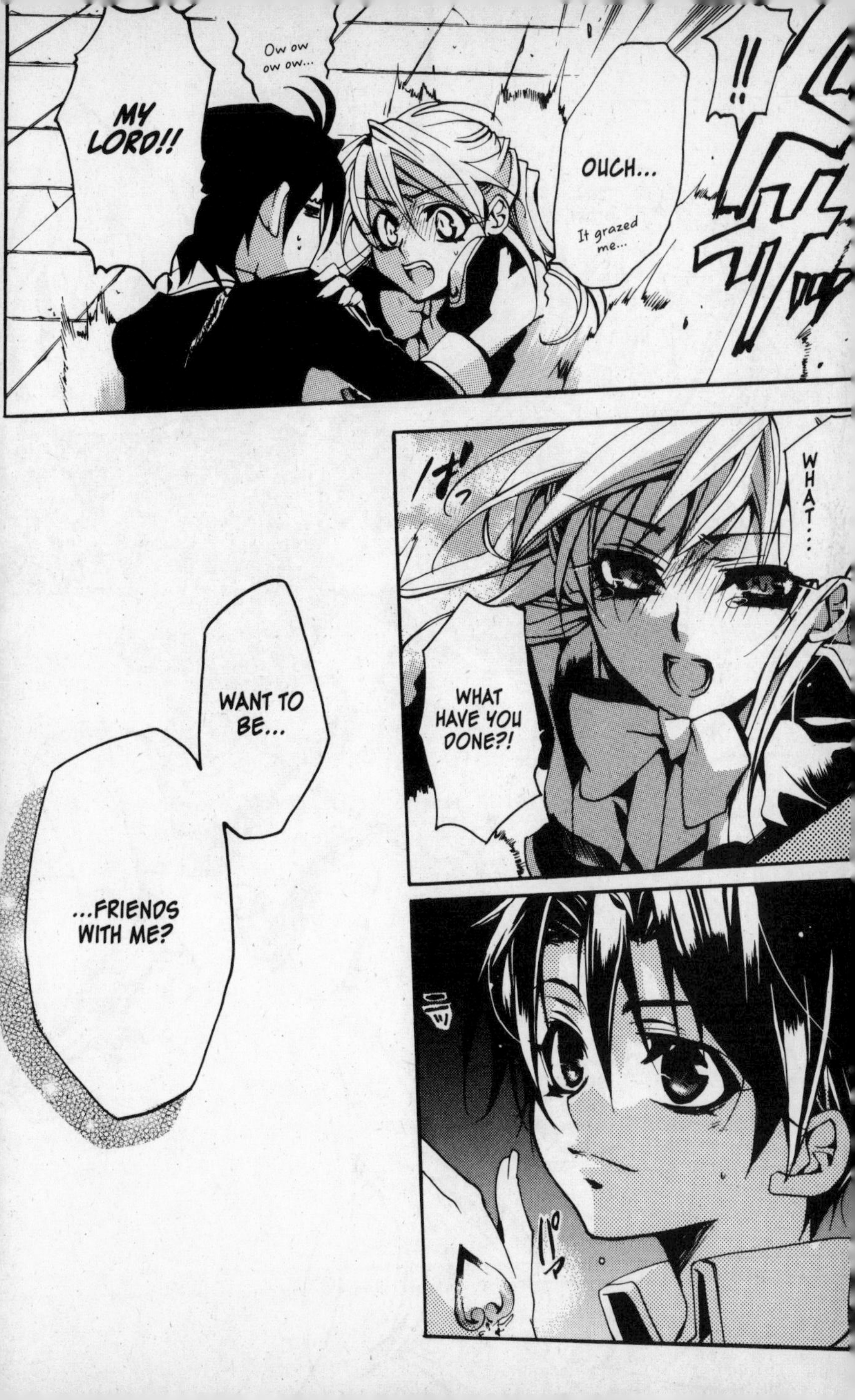
OUCH...
It grazed me...
Ow ow ow ow...
MY LORD!!
WHAT...
WHAT HAVE YOU DONE?!
WANT TO BE...
...FRIENDS WITH ME?

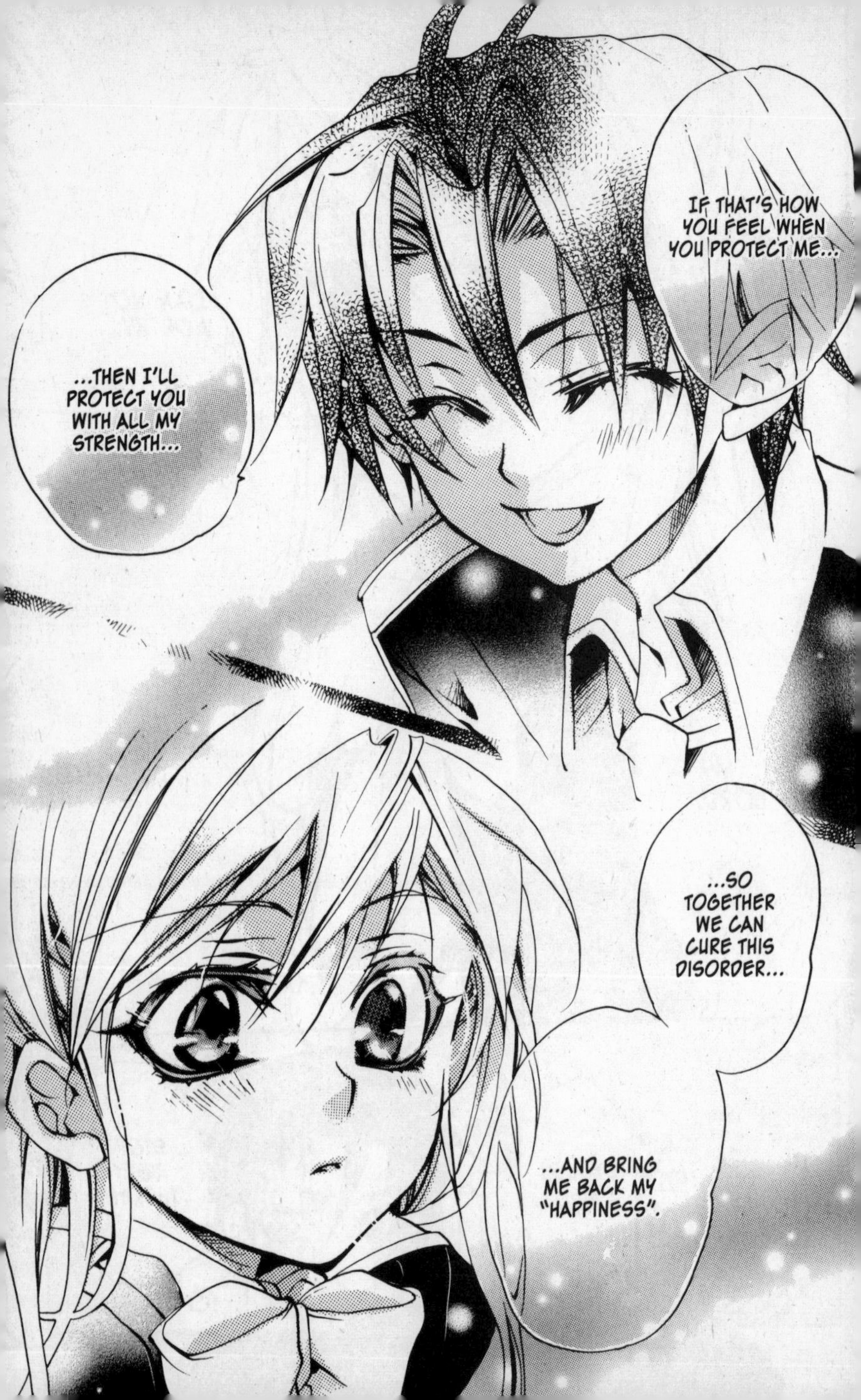
IF THAT'S HOW YOU FEEL WHEN YOU PROTECT ME...
...THEN I'LL PROTECT YOU WITH ALL MY STRENGTH...
...SO TOGETHER WE CAN CURE THIS DISORDER...
...AND BRING ME BACK MY "HAPPINESS".

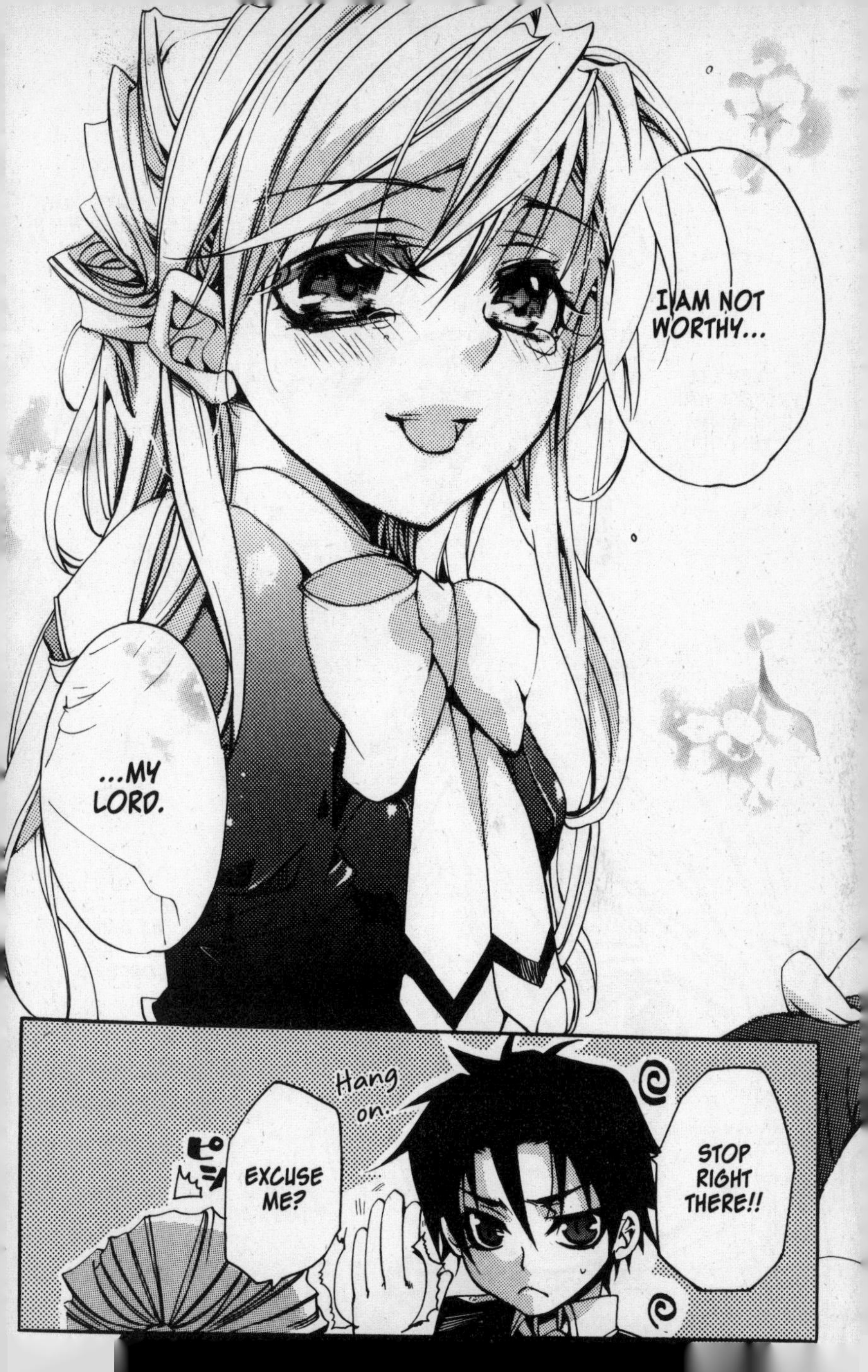
I AM NOT WORTHY...
...MY LORD.
STOP RIGHT THERE!!
Hang on..
EXCUSE ME?

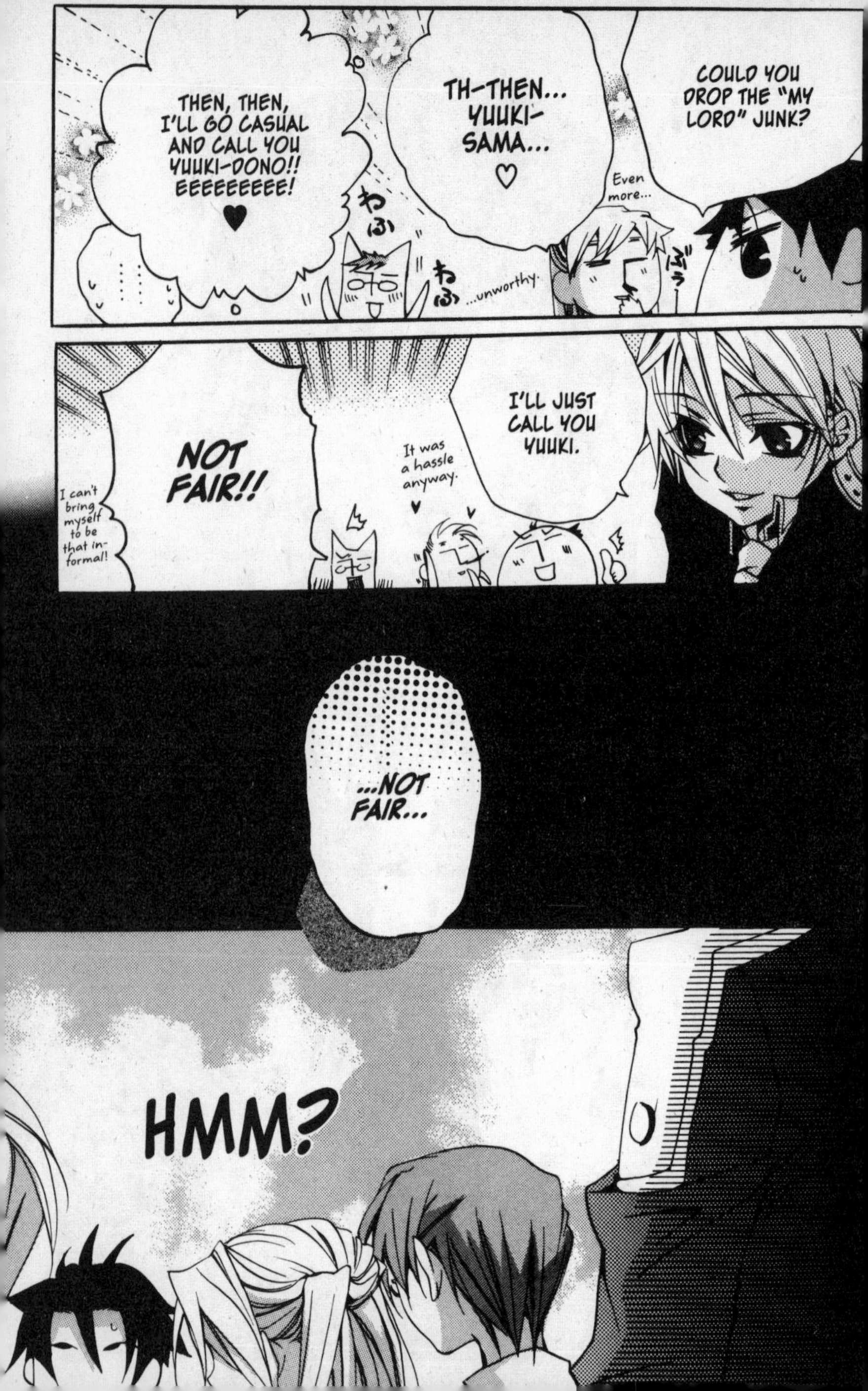
COULD YOU DROP THE "MY LORD" JUNK?
Even more... ...unworthy.
TH-THEN... YUUKI-SAMA... ♡
わふ わふ
THEN, THEN, I'LL GO CASUAL AND CALL YOU YUUKI-DONO!! EEEEEEEEE! ♥
......
I'LL JUST CALL YOU YUUKI.
It was a hassle anyway.
NOT FAIR!!
I can't bring myself to be that informal!
...NOT FAIR...
HMM?

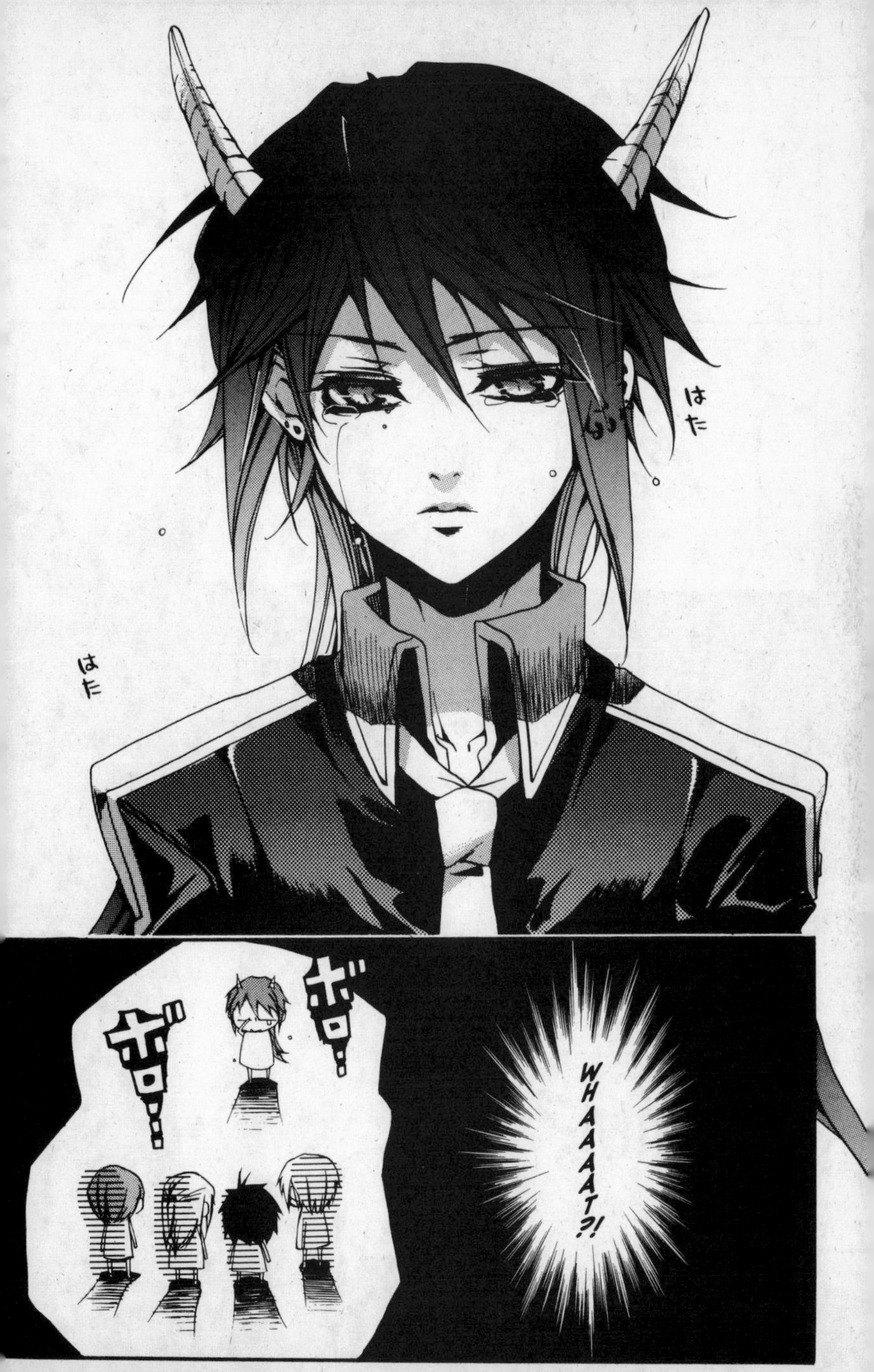
はた
はた
WHAAAAT?!
ボロ…
ボロ…

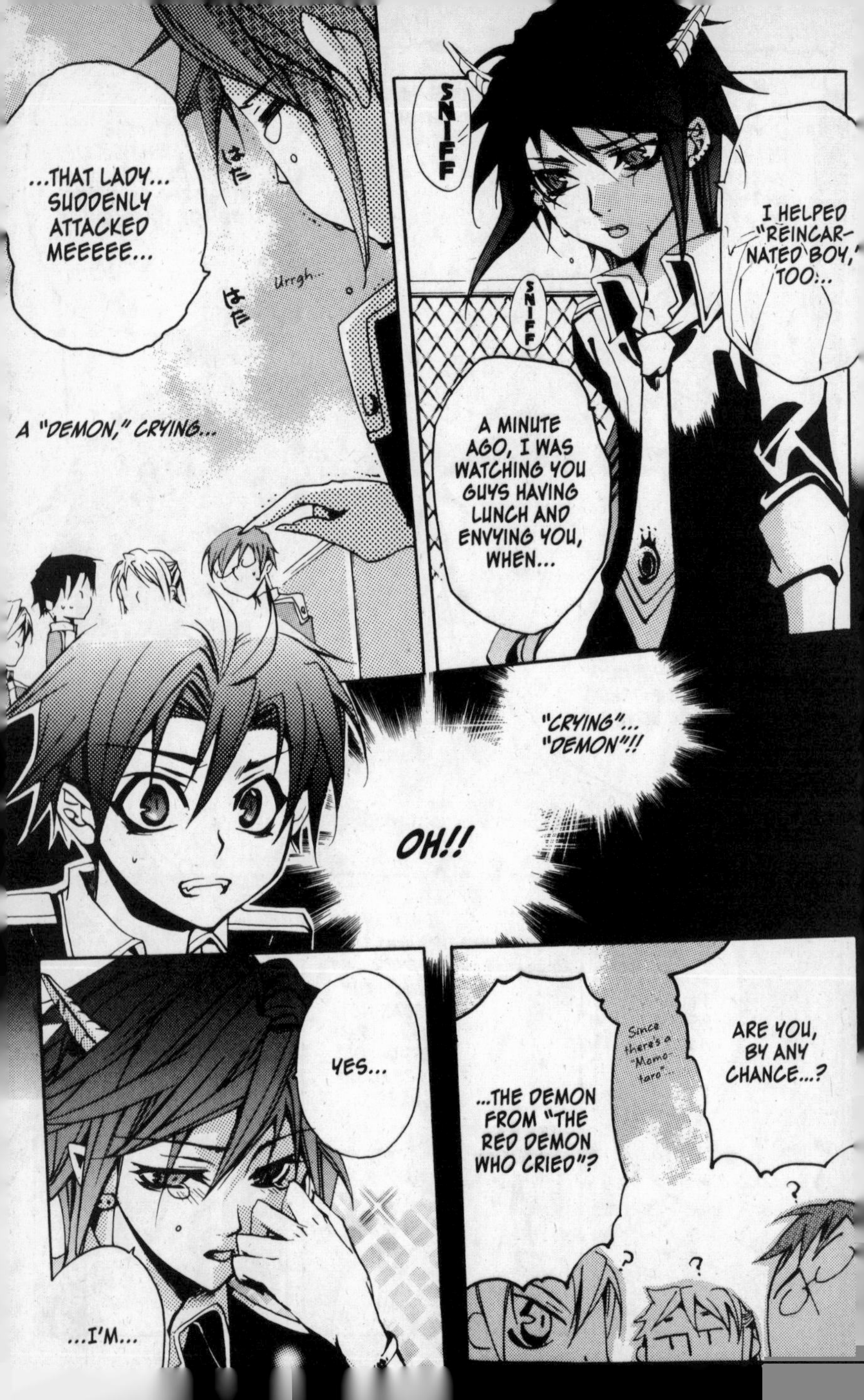
SNIFF
I HELPED "REINCARNATED BOY," TOO...
SNIFF
A MINUTE AGO, I WAS WATCHING YOU GUYS HAVING LUNCH AND ENVYING YOU, WHEN...
...THAT LADY... SUDDENLY ATTACKED MEEEEE...
はた
はた
Urrgh...
A "DEMON," CRYING...
"CRYING"... "DEMON"!!
OH!!
ARE YOU, BY ANY CHANCE...?
Since there's a "Momotaro"...
...THE DEMON FROM "THE RED DEMON WHO CRIED"?
?
?
?
YES...
...I'M...

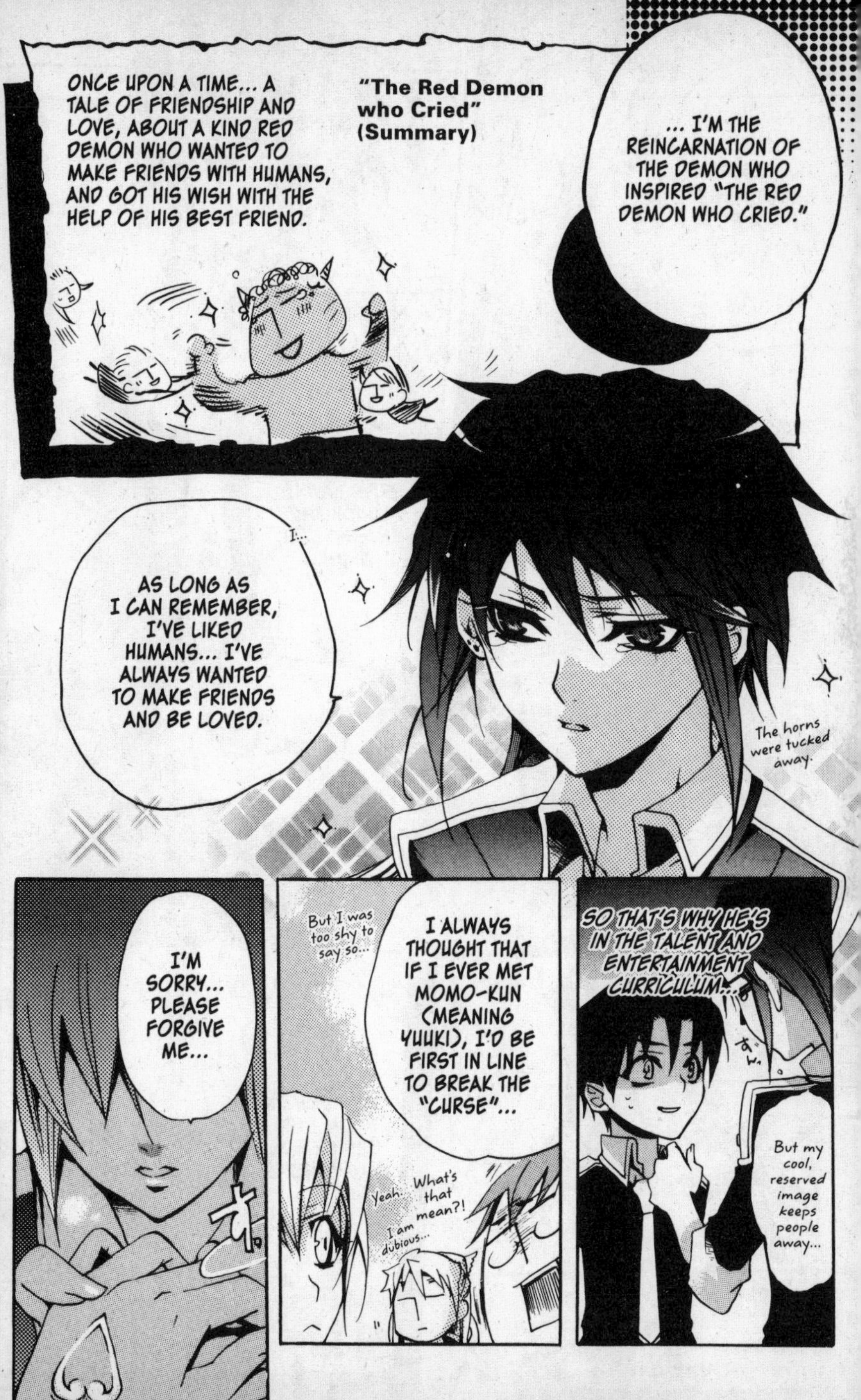
... I'M THE REINCARNATION OF THE DEMON WHO INSPIRED "THE RED DEMON WHO CRIED."
"The Red Demon who Cried" (Summary)
ONCE UPON A TIME... A TALE OF FRIENDSHIP AND LOVE, ABOUT A KIND RED DEMON WHO WANTED TO MAKE FRIENDS WITH HUMANS, AND GOT HIS WISH WITH THE HELP OF HIS BEST FRIEND.
I...
AS LONG AS I CAN REMEMBER, I'VE LIKED HUMANS... I'VE ALWAYS WANTED TO MAKE FRIENDS AND BE LOVED.
The horns were tucked away.
SO THAT'S WHY HE'S IN THE TALENT AND ENTERTAINMENT CURRICULUM...
But my cool, reserved image keeps people away...
I ALWAYS THOUGHT THAT IF I EVER MET MOMO-KUN (MEANING YUUKI), I'D BE FIRST IN LINE TO BREAK THE "CURSE"...
But I was too shy to say so...
What's that mean?!
Yeah.
I am dubious...
I'M SORRY... PLEASE FORGIVE ME...

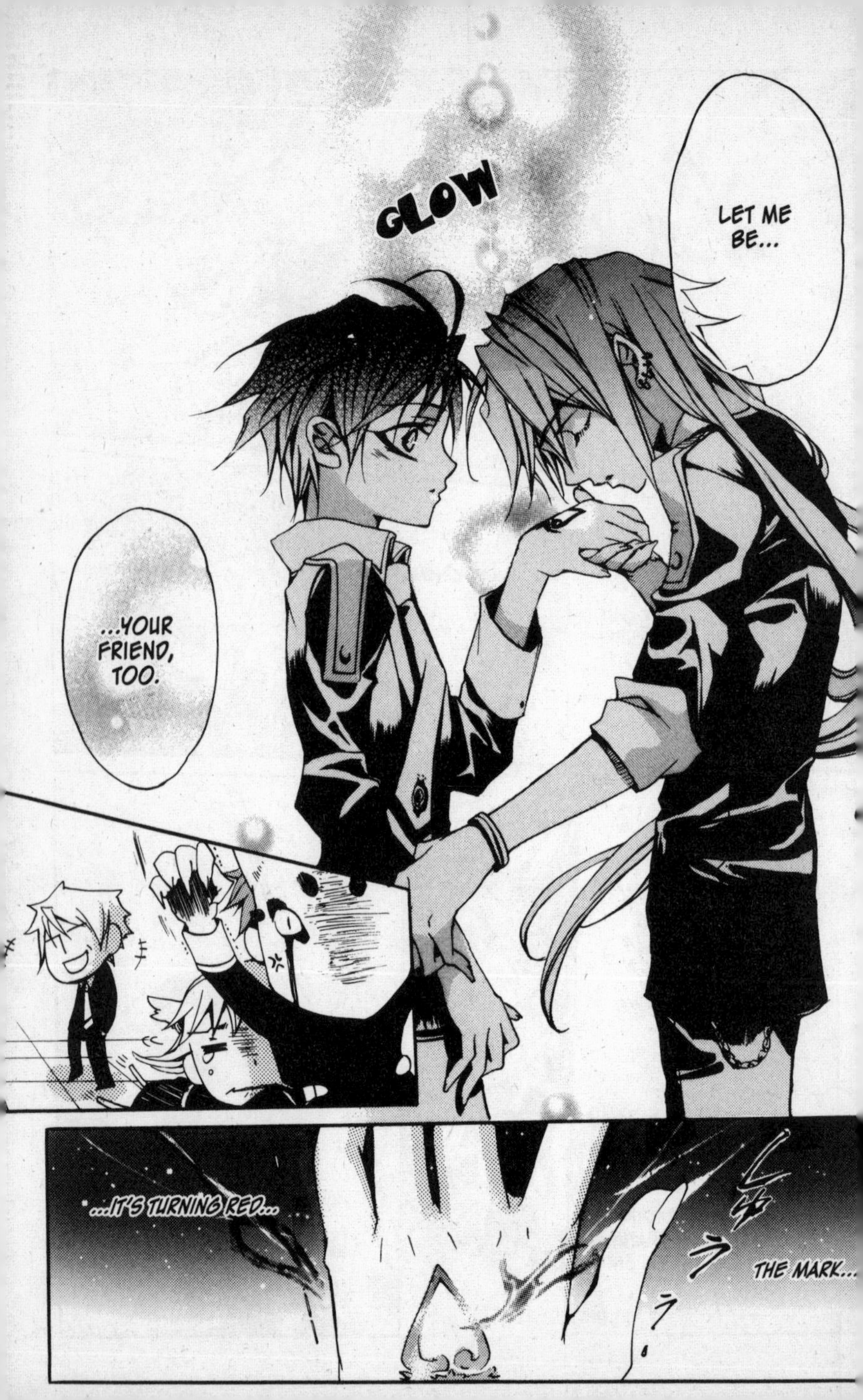
LET ME BE...
GLOW
...YOUR FRIEND, TOO.
THE MARK...
...IT'S TURNING RED...

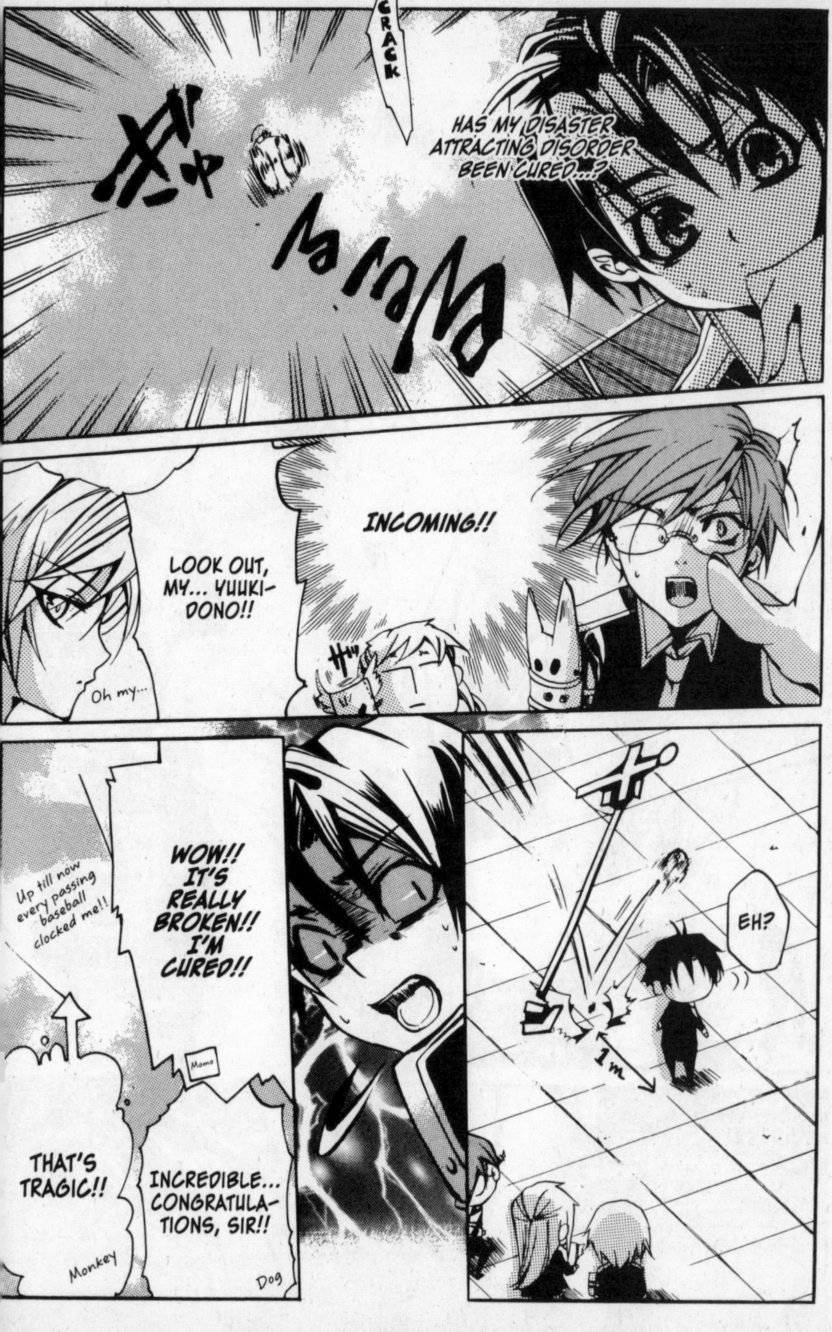

GRACK
HAS MY DISASTER ATTRACTING DISORDER BEEN CURED...?
INCOMING!!
LOOK OUT, MY... YUUKI-DONO!!
Oh my...
EH?
1 m
WOW!! IT'S REALLY BROKEN!! I'M CURED!!
Momo
Up till now every passing baseball clocked me!!
INCREDIBLE... CONGRATULA-TIONS, SIR!!
Dog
THAT'S TRAGIC!!
Monkey

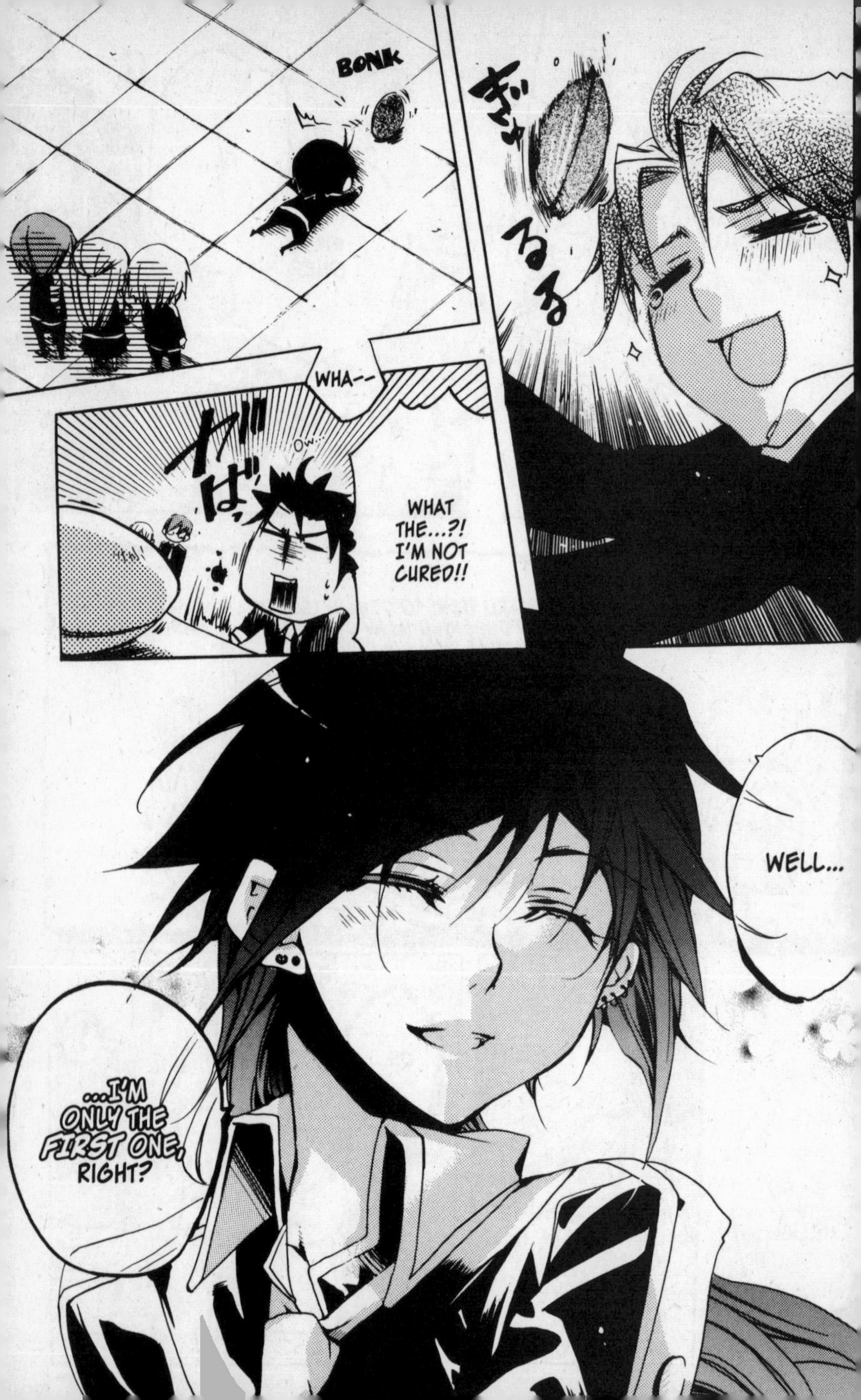
ぎゅるる
BONK
WHA--
Ow...
WHAT THE...?! I'M NOT CURED!!
WELL...
...I'M ONLY THE FIRST ONE, RIGHT?

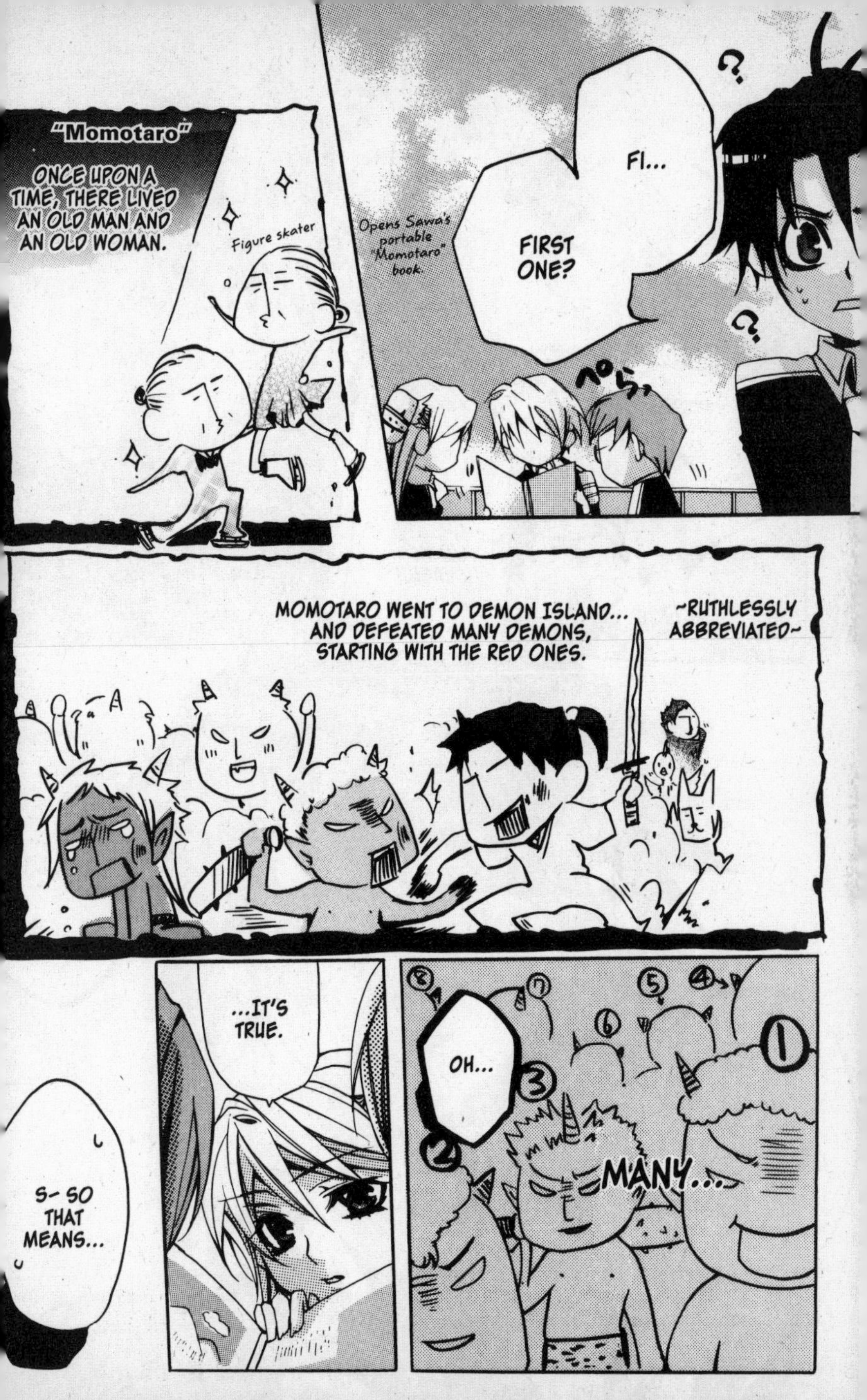
FI...
FIRST ONE?
Opens Sawa's portable "Momotaro" book.
"Momotaro"
ONCE UPON A TIME, THERE LIVED AN OLD MAN AND AN OLD WOMAN.
Figure skater
~RUTHLESSLY ABBREVIATED~
MOMOTARO WENT TO DEMON ISLAND... AND DEFEATED MANY DEMONS, STARTING WITH THE RED ONES.
OH...
MANY...
...IT'S TRUE.
S- SO THAT MEANS...

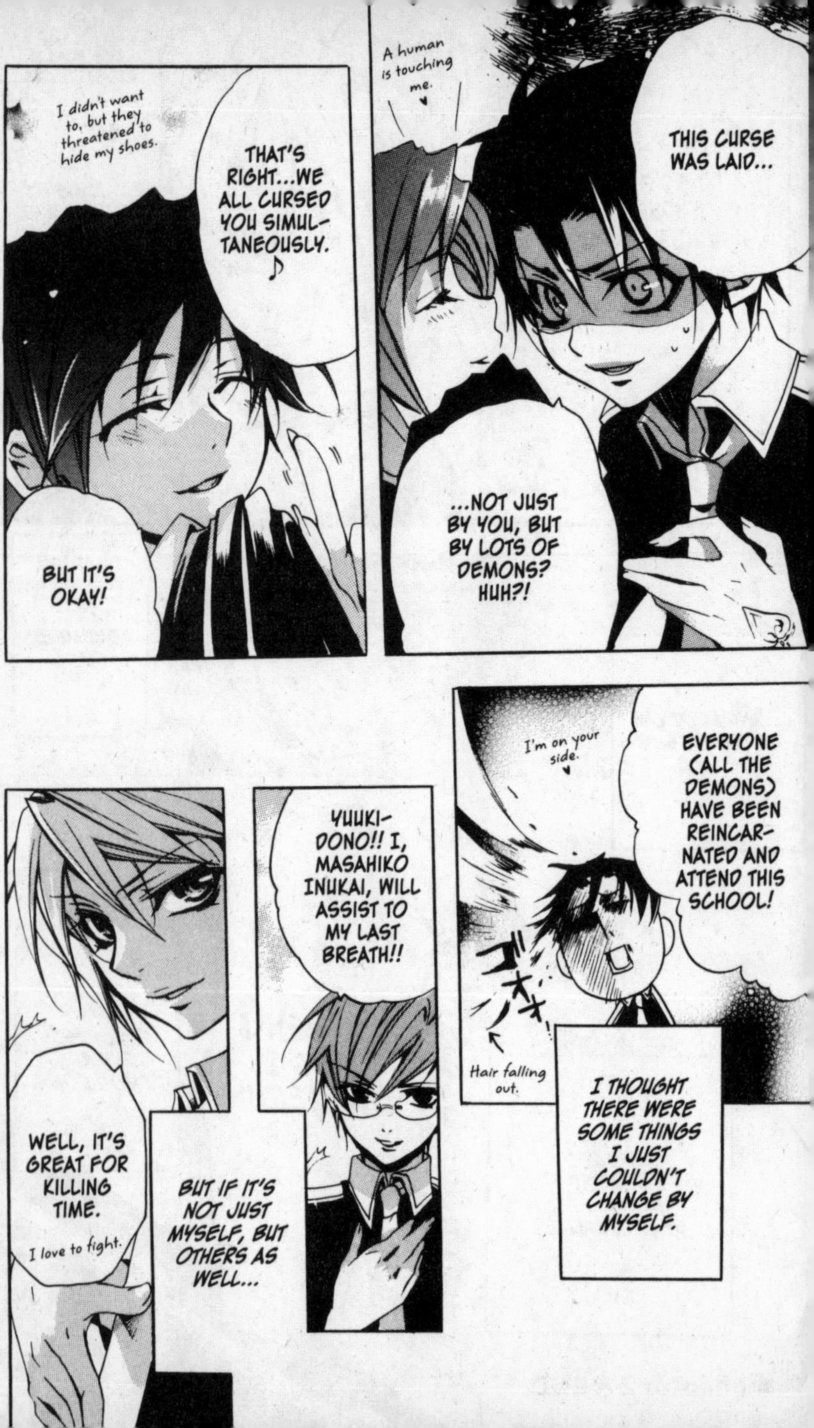
A human is touching me.
THIS CURSE WAS LAID...
...NOT JUST BY YOU, BUT BY LOTS OF DEMONS? HUH?!
I didn't want to, but they threatened to hide my shoes.
THAT'S RIGHT...WE ALL CURSED YOU SIMULTANEOUSLY. ♪
BUT IT'S OKAY!
EVERYONE (ALL THE DEMONS) HAVE BEEN REINCARNATED AND ATTEND THIS SCHOOL!
I'm on your side.
Hair falling out.
I THOUGHT THERE WERE SOME THINGS I JUST COULDN'T CHANGE BY MYSELF.
YUUKI-DONO!! I, MASAHIKO INUKAI, WILL ASSIST TO MY LAST BREATH!!
BUT IF IT'S NOT JUST MYSELF, BUT OTHERS AS WELL...
WELL, IT'S GREAT FOR KILLING TIME.
I love to fight.

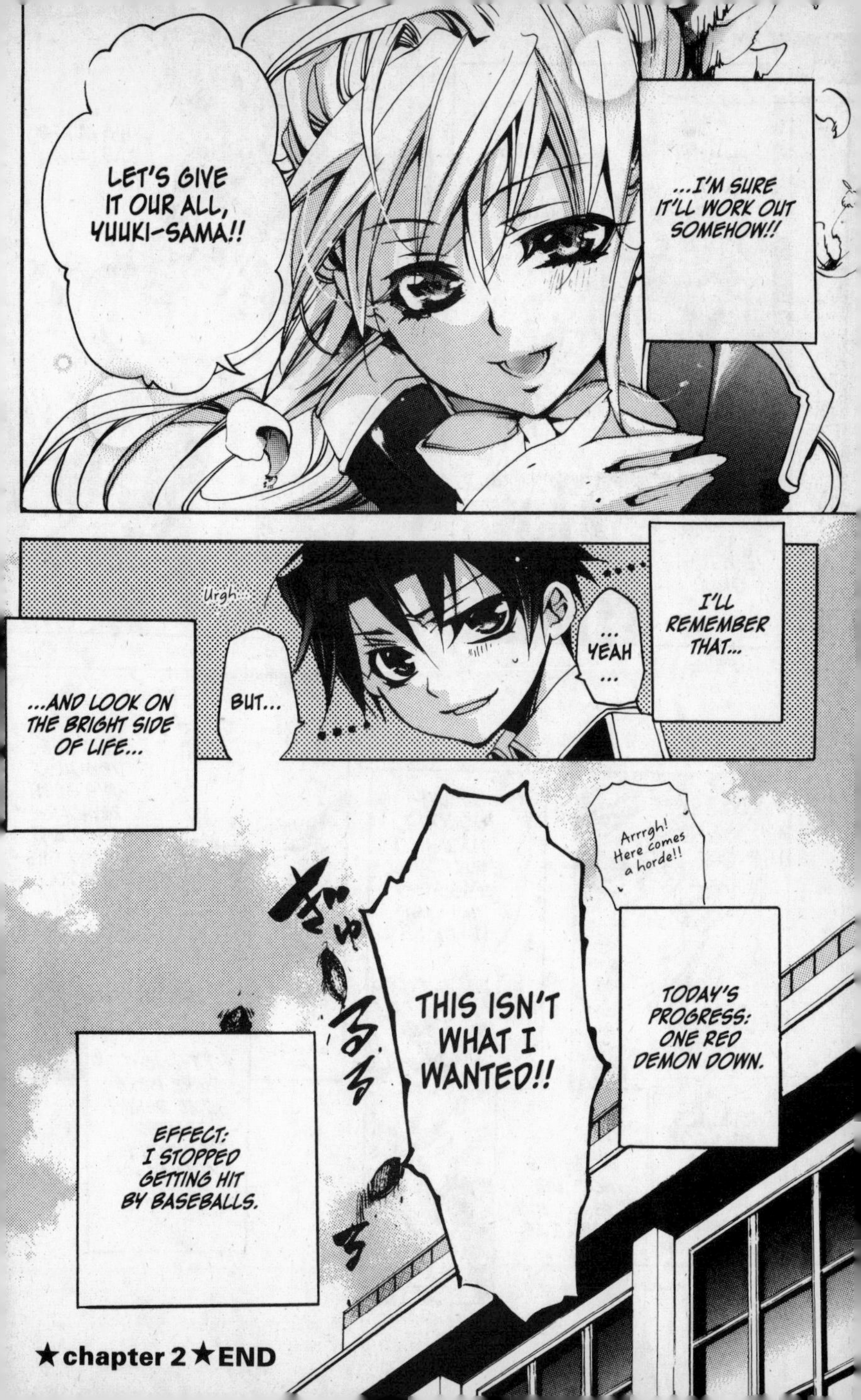
...I'M SURE IT'LL WORK OUT SOMEHOW!!
LET'S GIVE IT OUR ALL, YUUKI-SAMA!!
I'LL REMEMBER THAT...
... YEAH ...
Urgh...
BUT...
...AND LOOK ON THE BRIGHT SIDE OF LIFE...
Arrrgh! Here comes a horde!!
TODAY'S PROGRESS: ONE RED DEMON DOWN.
THIS ISN'T WHAT I WANTED!!
EFFECT: I STOPPED GETTING HIT BY BASEBALLS.
★chapter 2★END

Chapter 3

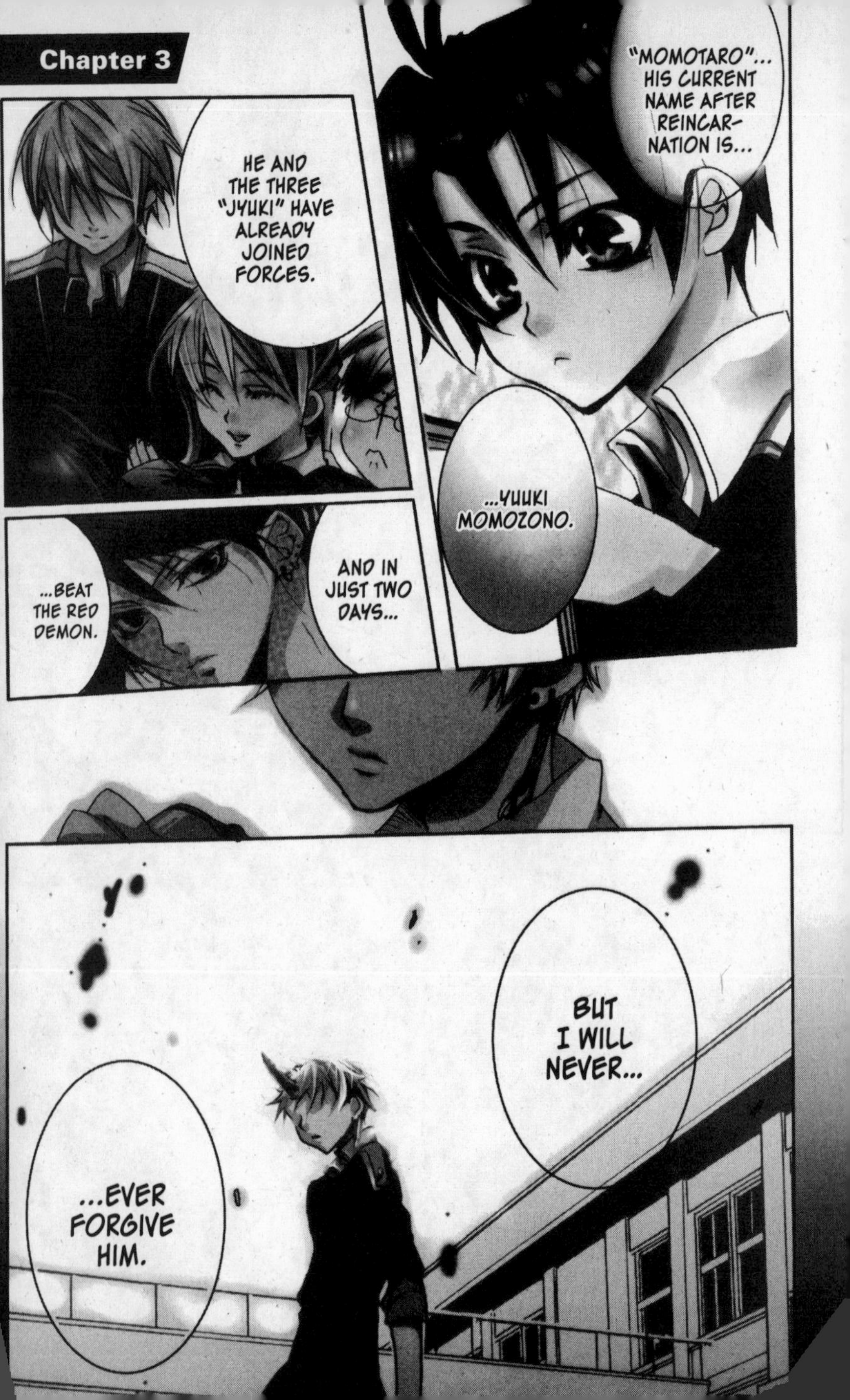
"MOMOTARO"... HIS CURRENT NAME AFTER REINCAR-NATION IS...
...YUUKI MOMOZONO.
HE AND THE THREE "JYUKI" HAVE ALREADY JOINED FORCES.
AND IN JUST TWO DAYS...
...BEAT THE RED DEMON.
BUT I WILL NEVER...
...EVER FORGIVE HIM.

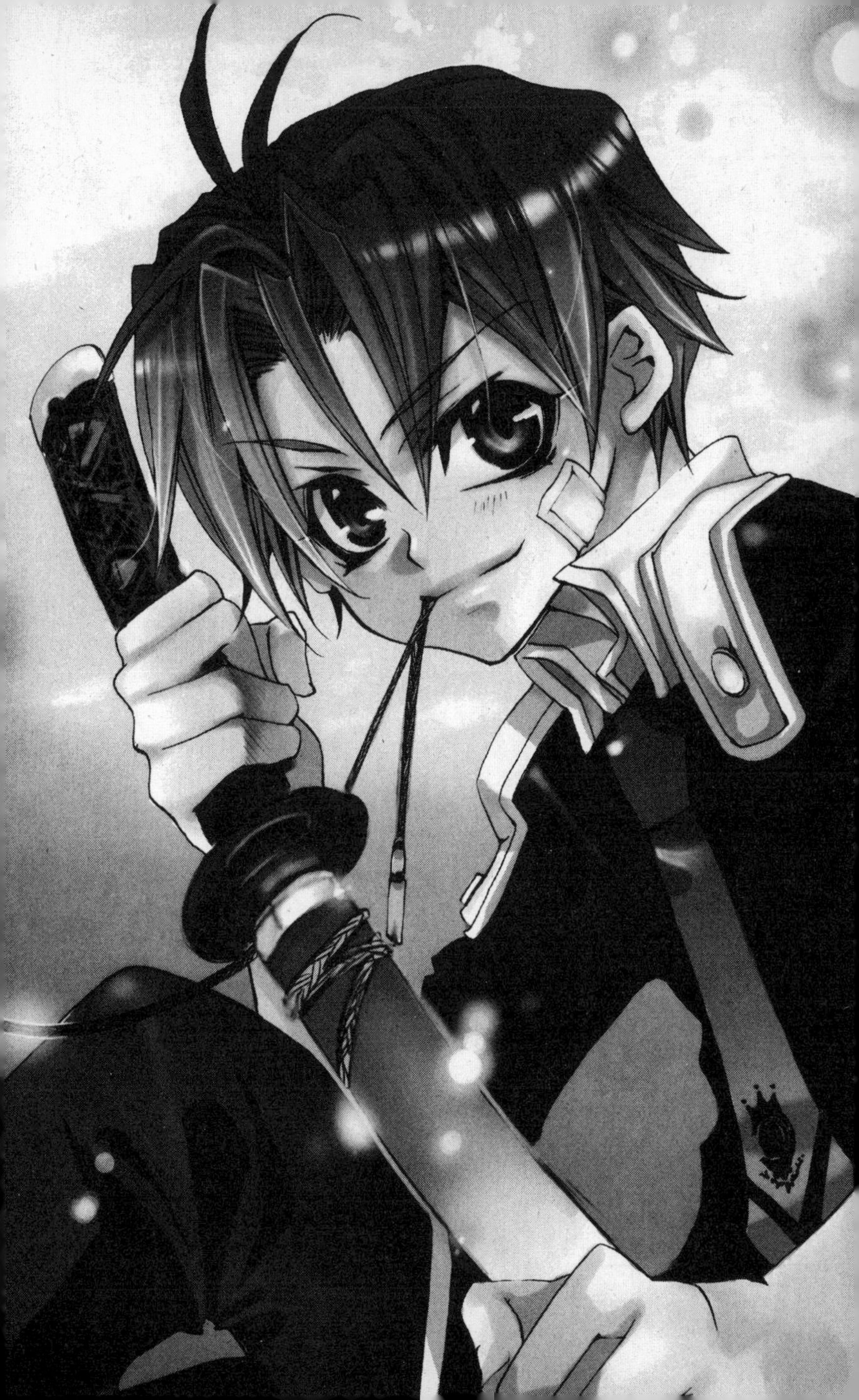

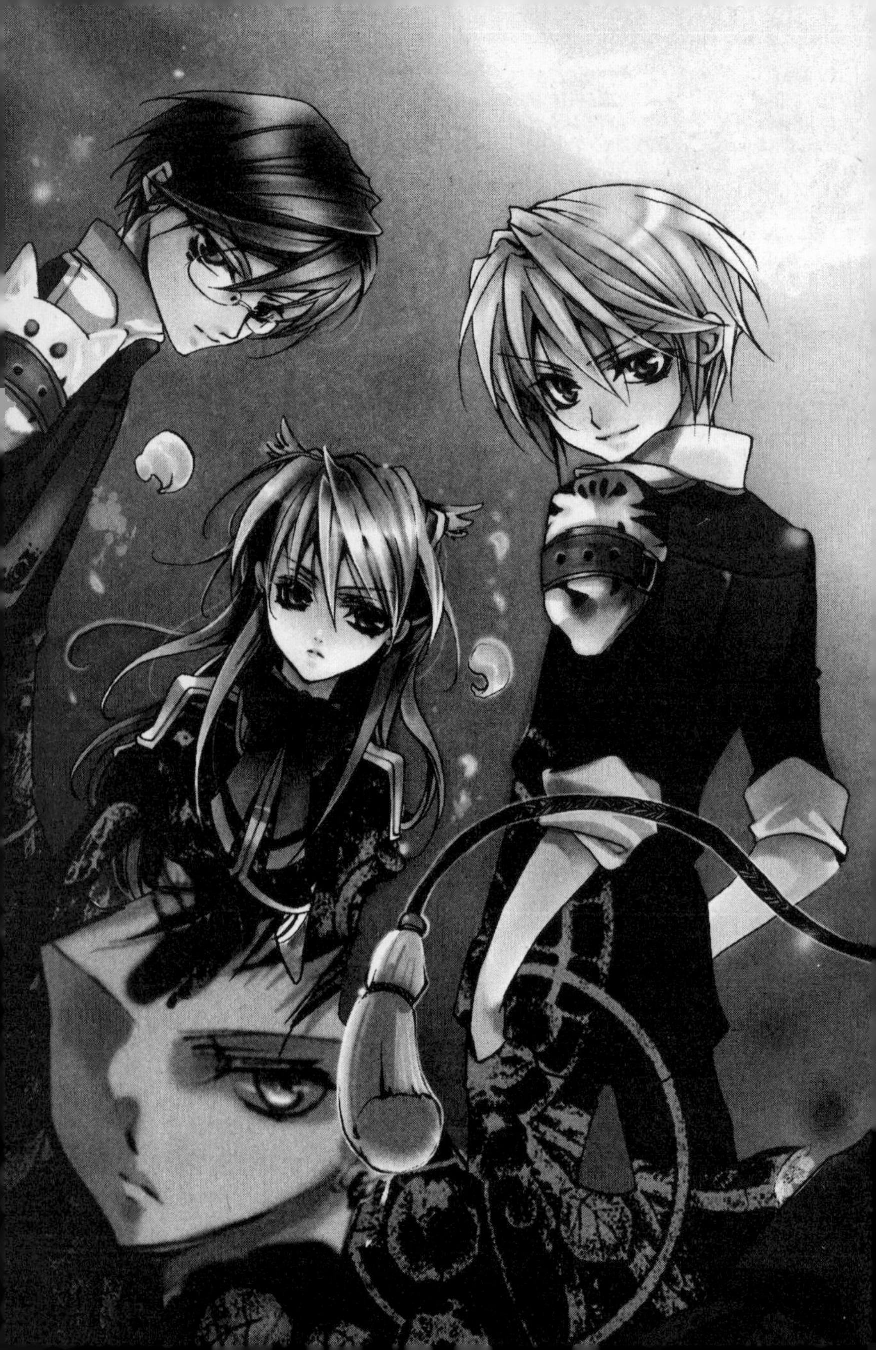

A Page for the Dog

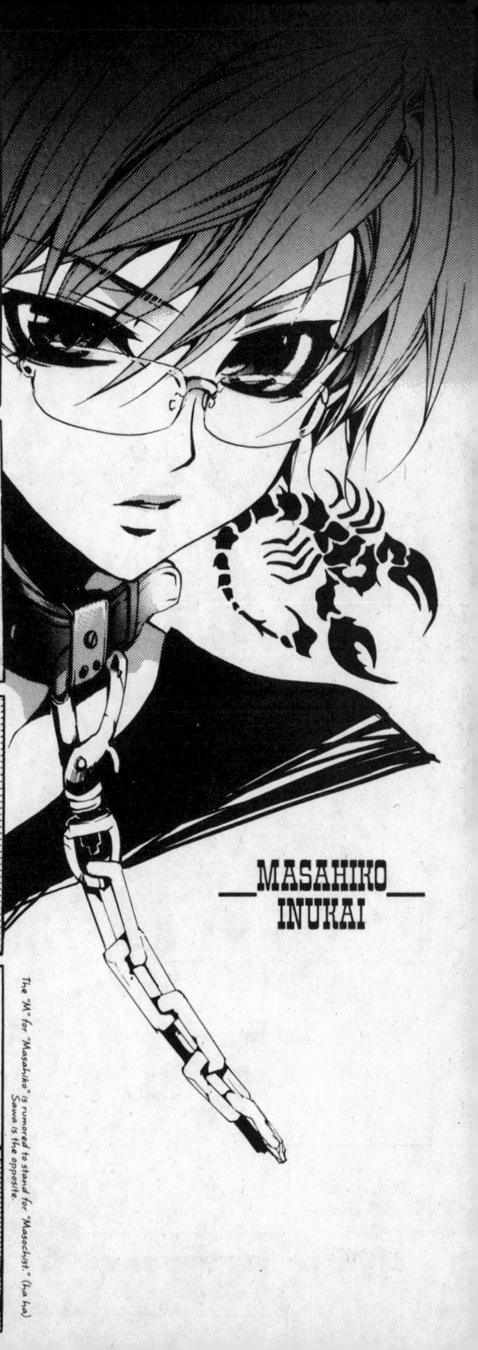
MASAHIKO INUKAI
The "M" for "Masahiko" is rumored to stand for "Masochist." (ha ha) Sawa is the opposite.

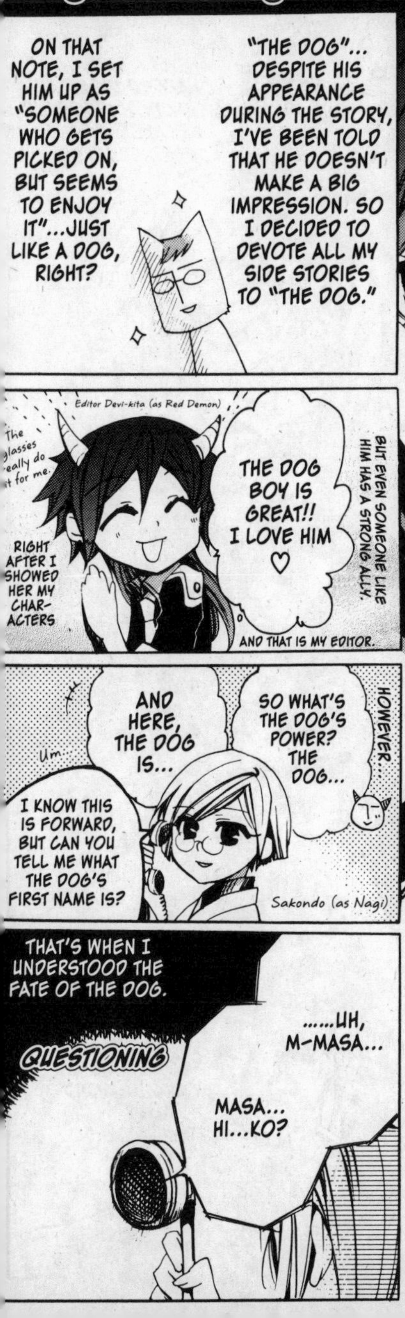
"THE DOG"... DESPITE HIS APPEARANCE DURING THE STORY, I'VE BEEN TOLD THAT HE DOESN'T MAKE A BIG IMPRESSION. SO I DECIDED TO DEVOTE ALL MY SIDE STORIES TO "THE DOG."
ON THAT NOTE, I SET HIM UP AS "SOMEONE WHO GETS PICKED ON, BUT SEEMS TO ENJOY IT"...JUST LIKE A DOG, RIGHT?
BUT EVEN SOMEONE LIKE HIM HAS A STRONG ALLY.
AND THAT IS MY EDITOR.
THE DOG BOY IS GREAT!! I LOVE HIM ♡
Editor Devi-kita (as Red Demon)
The glasses really do it for me.
RIGHT AFTER I SHOWED HER MY CHARACTERS
HOWEVER
SO WHAT'S THE DOG'S POWER? THE DOG...
AND HERE, THE DOG IS...
Um
I KNOW THIS IS FORWARD, BUT CAN YOU TELL ME WHAT THE DOG'S FIRST NAME IS?
Sakondo (as Nagi)
THAT'S WHEN I UNDERSTOOD THE FATE OF THE DOG.
......UH, M-MASA...
QUESTIONING
MASA... HI...KO?

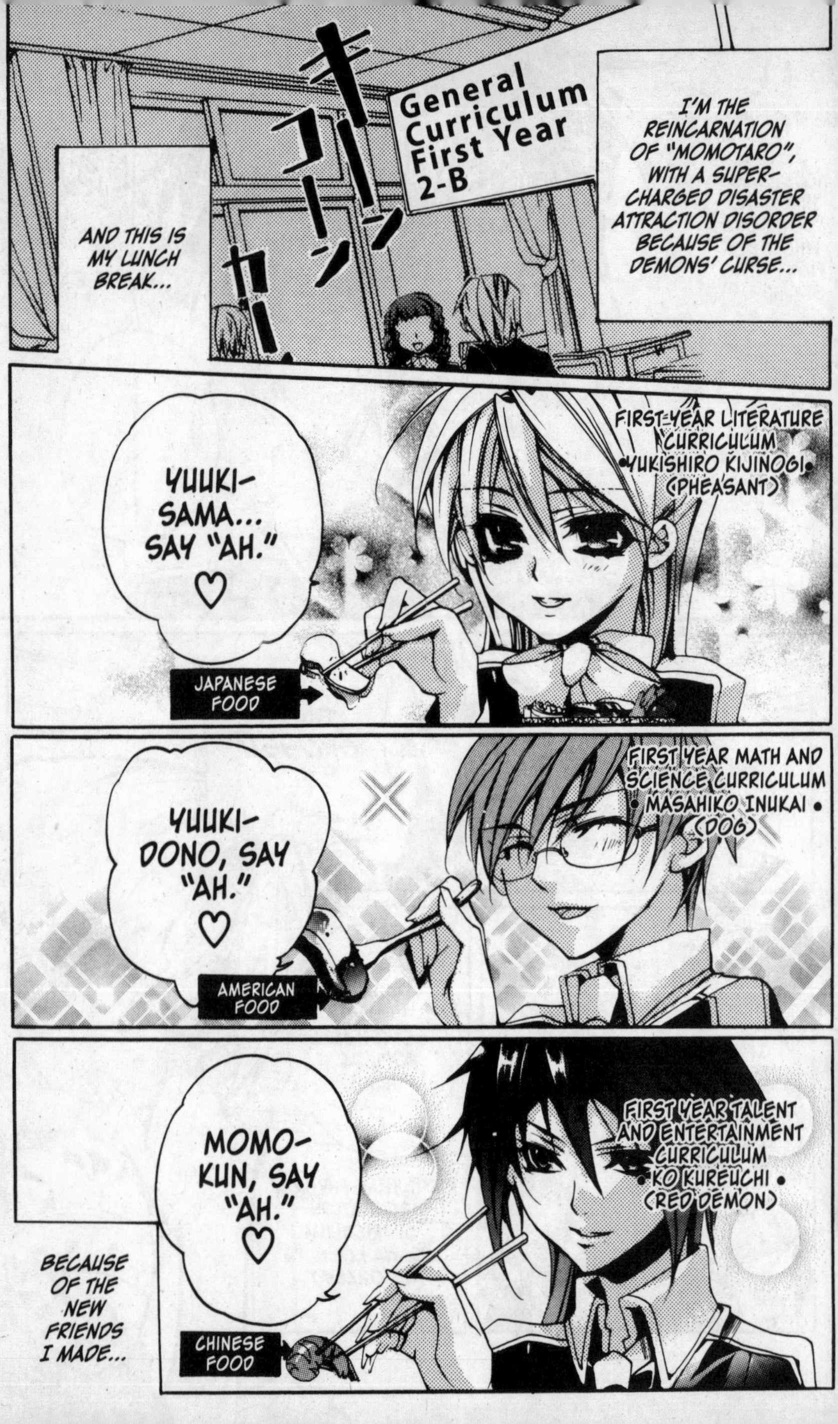
I'M THE REINCARNATION OF "MOMOTARO", WITH A SUPER-CHARGED DISASTER ATTRACTION DISORDER BECAUSE OF THE DEMONS' CURSE...
General Curriculum First Year 2-B
AND THIS IS MY LUNCH BREAK...
FIRST-YEAR LITERATURE CURRICULUM •YUKISHIRO KIJINOGI• (PHEASANT)
YUUKI-SAMA... SAY "AH." ♡
JAPANESE FOOD
FIRST YEAR MATH AND SCIENCE CURRICULUM • MASAHIKO INUKAI • (DOG)
YUUKI-DONO, SAY "AH." ♡
AMERICAN FOOD
FIRST YEAR TALENT AND ENTERTAINMENT CURRICULUM • KO KUREUCHI • (RED DEMON)
MOMO-KUN, SAY "AH." ♡
CHINESE FOOD
BECAUSE OF THE NEW FRIENDS I MADE...

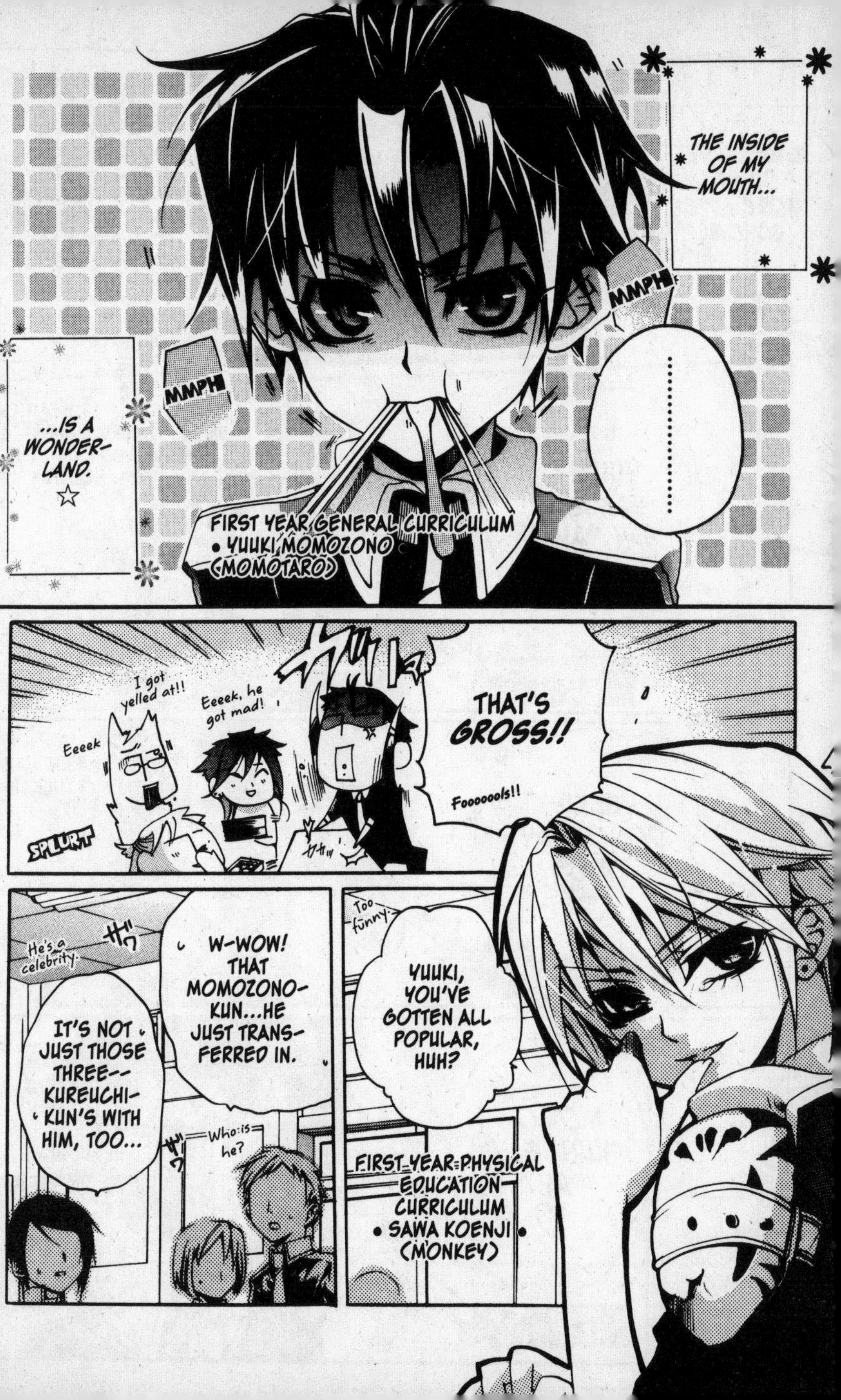
THE INSIDE OF MY MOUTH...
MMPH!
......
MMPH!
...IS A WONDERLAND. ☆
FIRST YEAR GENERAL CURRICULUM • YUUKI MOMOZONO (MOMOTARO)
THAT'S GROSS!!
Foooooools!!
Eeeek, he got mad!
I got yelled at!!
Eeeek
SPLURT
Too funny.
YUUKI, YOU'VE GOTTEN ALL POPULAR, HUH?
FIRST YEAR PHYSICAL EDUCATION CURRICULUM • SAWA KOENJI (MONKEY)
He's a celebrity.
W-WOW! THAT MOMOZONO-KUN...HE JUST TRANSFERRED IN.
IT'S NOT JUST THOSE THREE--KUREUCHI-KUN'S WITH HIM, TOO...
Who is he?

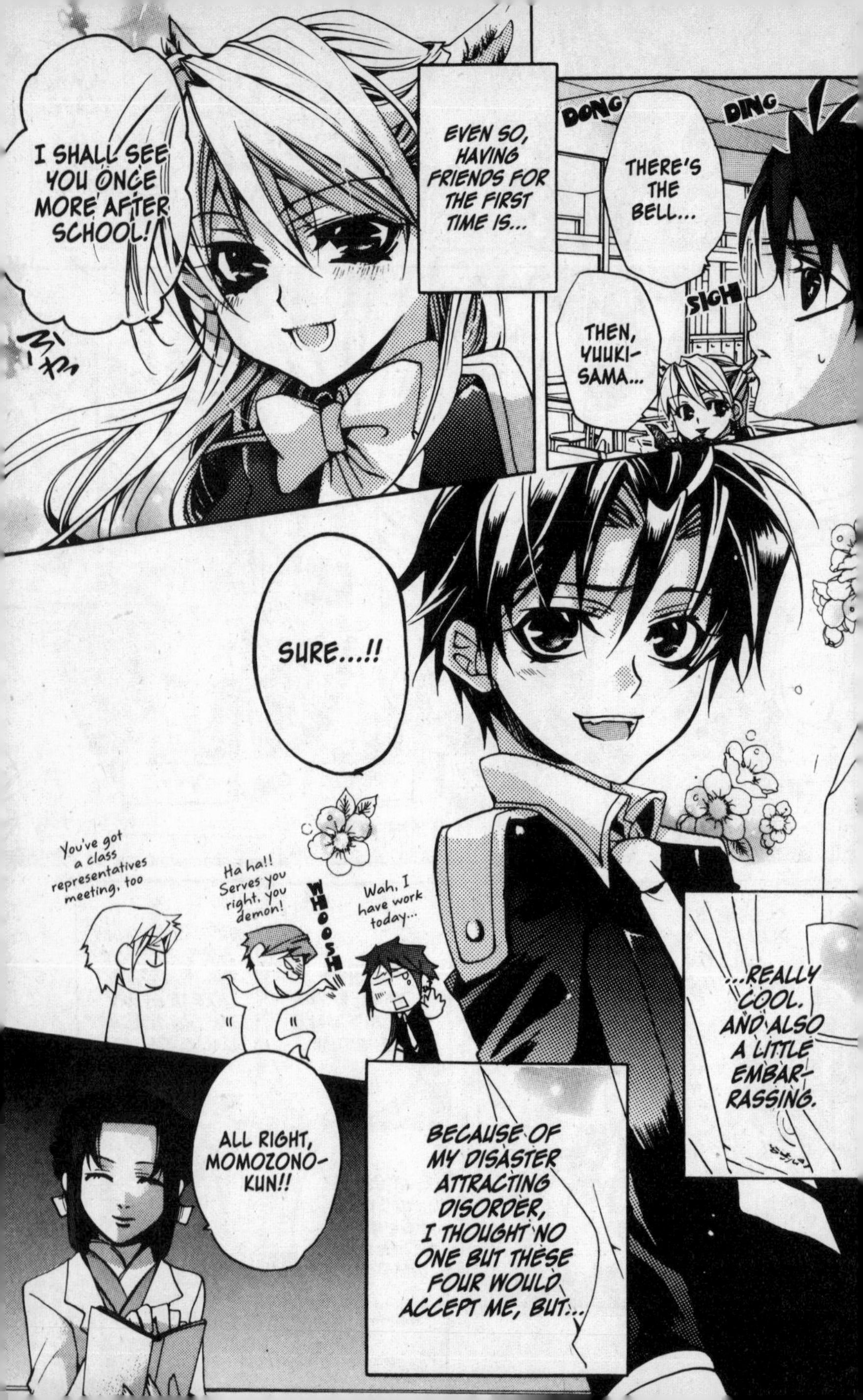
DONG
DING
THERE'S THE BELL...
SIGH
THEN, YUUKI-SAMA...
EVEN SO, HAVING FRIENDS FOR THE FIRST TIME IS...
I SHALL SEE YOU ONCE MORE AFTER SCHOOL!
SURE...!!
...REALLY COOL. AND ALSO A LITTLE EMBAR-RASSING.
Wah, I have work today...
WHOOSH
Ha ha!! Serves you right, you demon!
You've got a class representatives meeting, too
BECAUSE OF MY DISASTER ATTRACTING DISORDER, I THOUGHT NO ONE BUT THESE FOUR WOULD ACCEPT ME, BUT...
ALL RIGHT, MOMOZONO-KUN!!

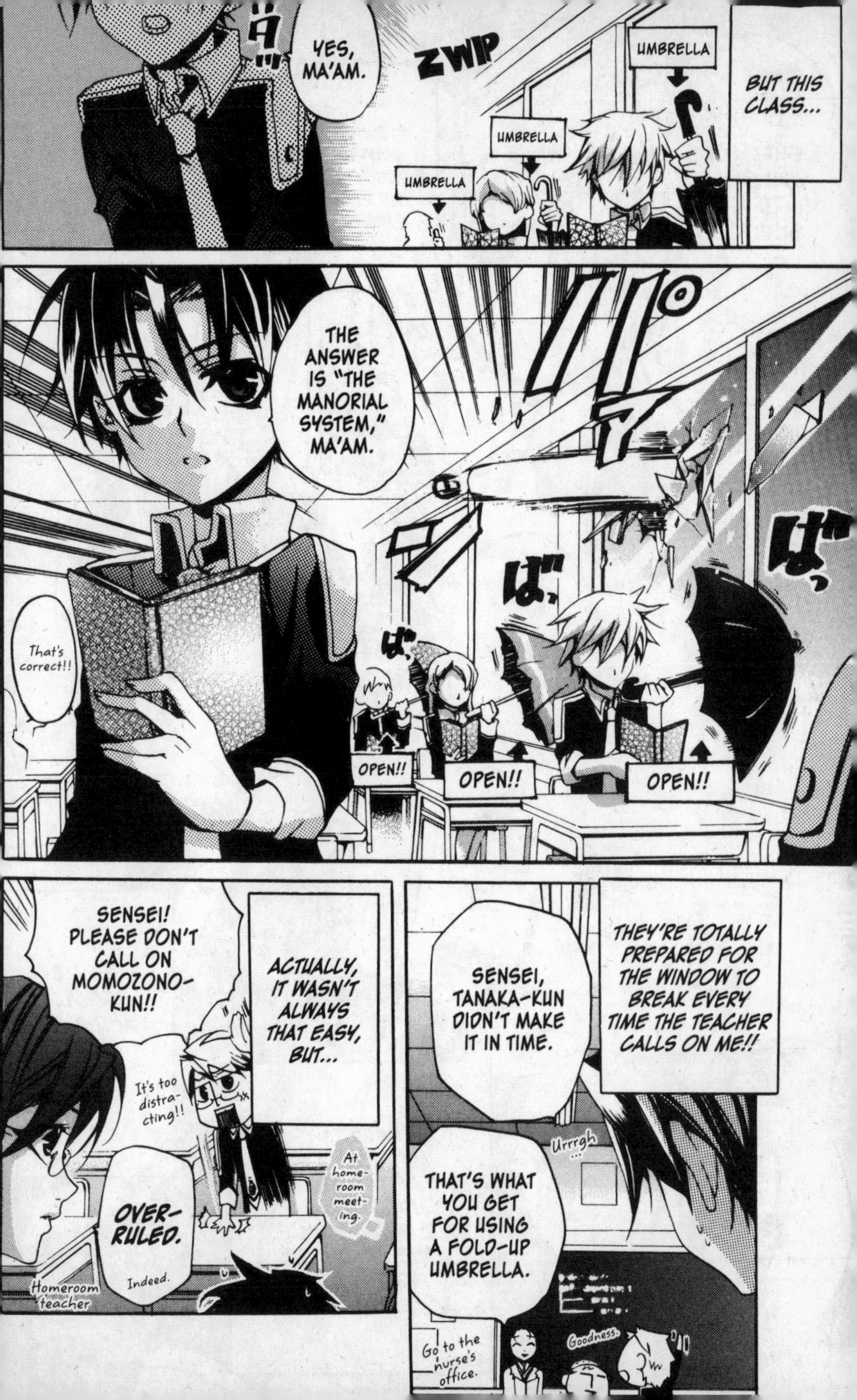

BUT THIS CLASS...
UMBRELLA
UMBRELLA
UMBRELLA
ZWIP
YES, MA'AM.
THE ANSWER IS "THE MANORIAL SYSTEM," MA'AM.
OPEN!!
OPEN!!
OPEN!!
That's correct!!
THEY'RE TOTALLY PREPARED FOR THE WINDOW TO BREAK EVERY TIME THE TEACHER CALLS ON ME!!
SENSEI, TANAKA-KUN DIDN'T MAKE IT IN TIME.
Urrrgh...
THAT'S WHAT YOU GET FOR USING A FOLD-UP UMBRELLA.
Goodness.
Go to the nurse's office.
ACTUALLY, IT WASN'T ALWAYS THAT EASY, BUT...
SENSEI! PLEASE DON'T CALL ON MOMOZONO-KUN!!
It's too distracting!!
At homeroom meeting.
OVER-RULED.
Indeed.
Homeroom teacher

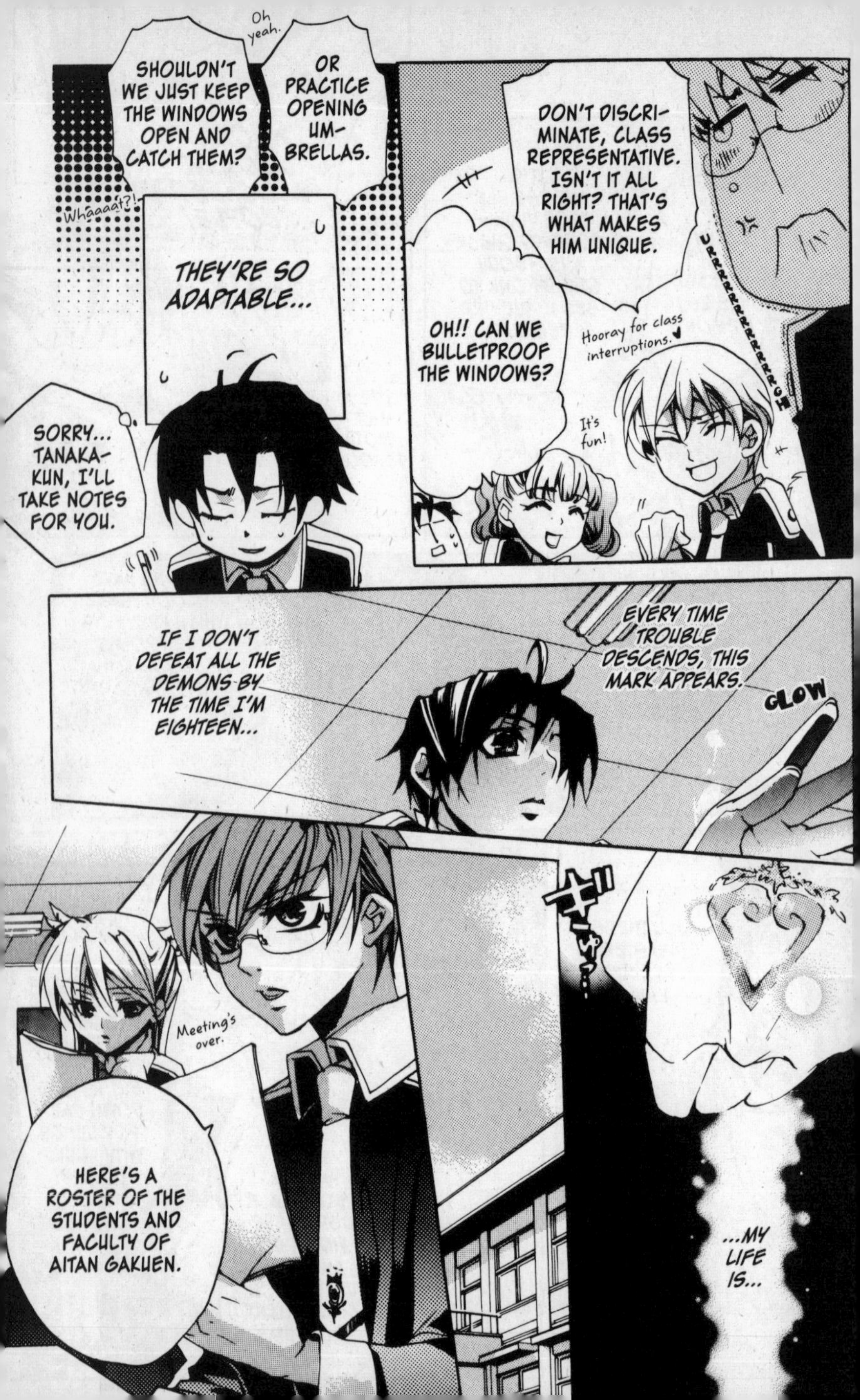
DON'T DISCRIMINATE, CLASS REPRESENTATIVE. ISN'T IT ALL RIGHT? THAT'S WHAT MAKES HIM UNIQUE.
URRRRRRRRRRRRGH
OH!! CAN WE BULLETPROOF THE WINDOWS?
Hooray for class interruptions.♥
It's fun!
Oh yeah.
OR PRACTICE OPENING UM-BRELLAS.
SHOULDN'T WE JUST KEEP THE WINDOWS OPEN AND CATCH THEM?
Whaaaat?!
THEY'RE SO ADAPTABLE...
SORRY... TANAKA-KUN, I'LL TAKE NOTES FOR YOU.
EVERY TIME TROUBLE DESCENDS, THIS MARK APPEARS.
GLOW
IF I DON'T DEFEAT ALL THE DEMONS BY THE TIME I'M EIGHTEEN...
...MY LIFE IS...
Meeting's over.
HERE'S A ROSTER OF THE STUDENTS AND FACULTY OF AITAN GAKUEN.

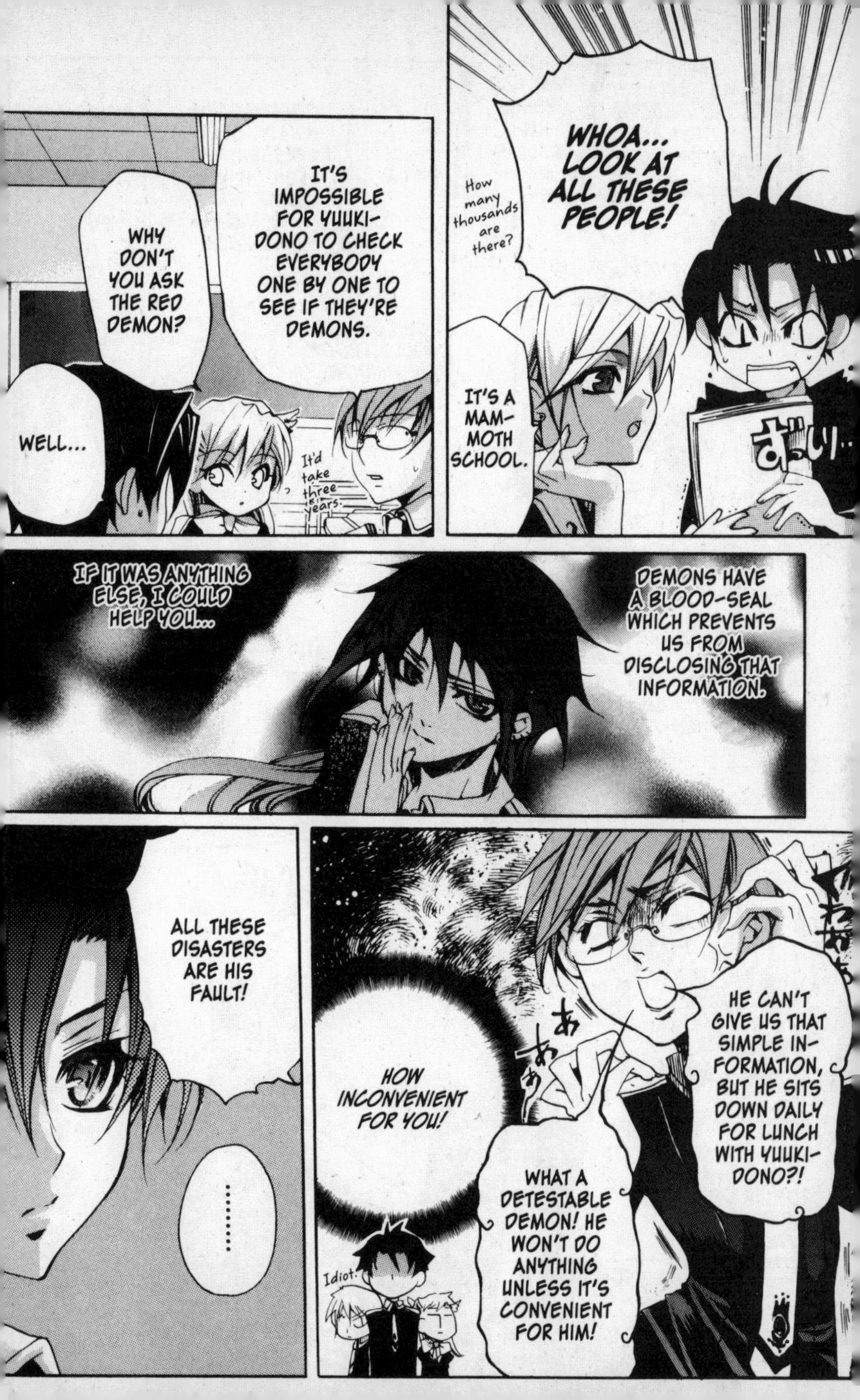
WHOA... LOOK AT ALL THESE PEOPLE!
How many thousands are there?
IT'S A MAM-MOTH SCHOOL.
IT'S IMPOSSIBLE FOR YUUKI-DONO TO CHECK EVERYBODY ONE BY ONE TO SEE IF THEY'RE DEMONS.
It'd take three years.
WHY DON'T YOU ASK THE RED DEMON?
WELL...
DEMONS HAVE A BLOOD-SEAL WHICH PREVENTS US FROM DISCLOSING THAT INFORMATION.
IF IT WAS ANYTHING ELSE, I COULD HELP YOU...
HE CAN'T GIVE US THAT SIMPLE IN-FORMATION, BUT HE SITS DOWN DAILY FOR LUNCH WITH YUUKI-DONO?!
WHAT A DETESTABLE DEMON! HE WON'T DO ANYTHING UNLESS IT'S CONVENIENT FOR HIM!
HOW INCONVENIENT FOR YOU!
Idiot.
ALL THESE DISASTERS ARE HIS FAULT!
......

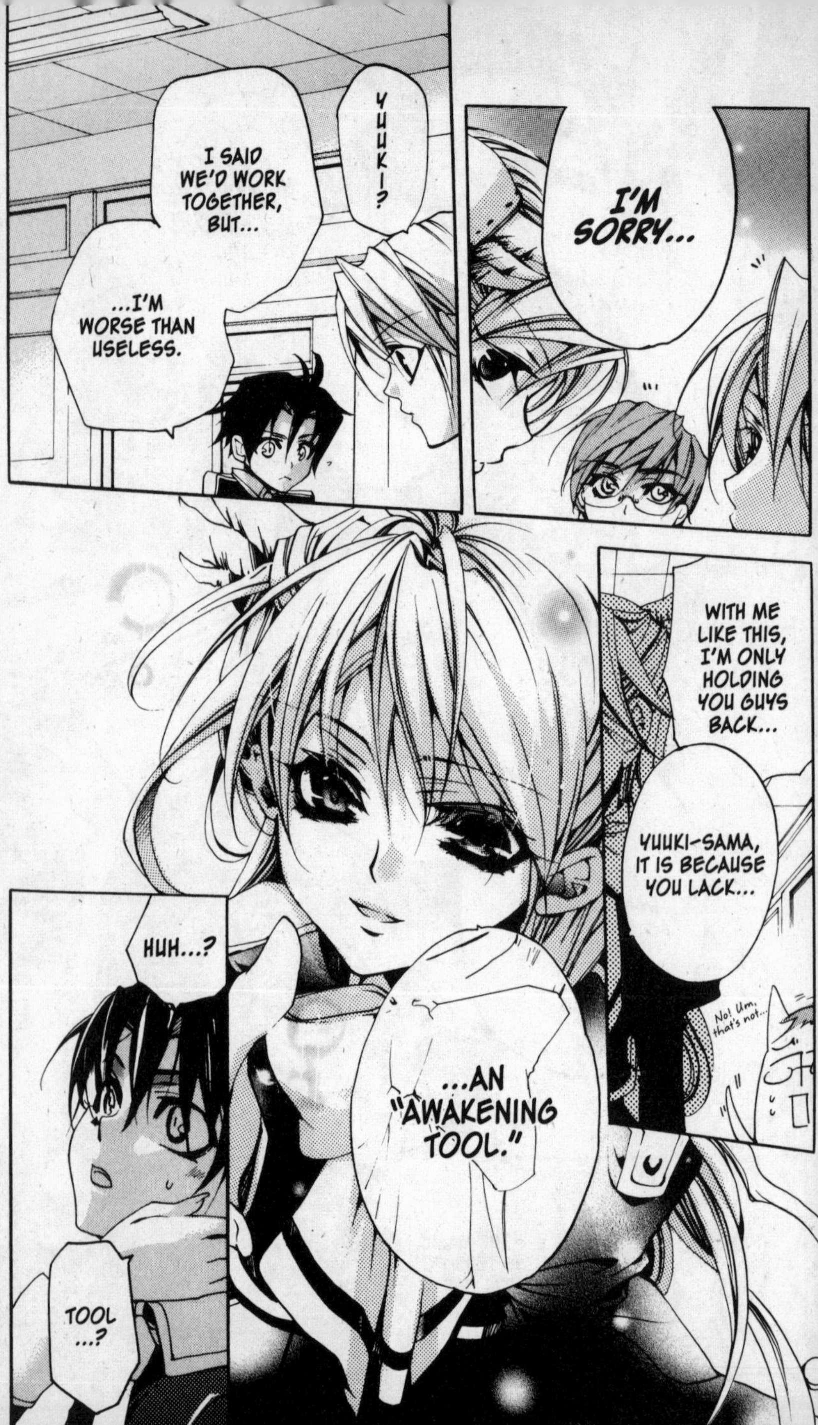
I'M SORRY...
YUUKI-?
I SAID WE'D WORK TOGETHER, BUT...
...I'M WORSE THAN USELESS.
WITH ME LIKE THIS, I'M ONLY HOLDING YOU GUYS BACK...
YUUKI-SAMA, IT IS BECAUSE YOU LACK...
No! Um, that's not...
...AN "AWAKENING TOOL."
HUH...?
TOOL...?

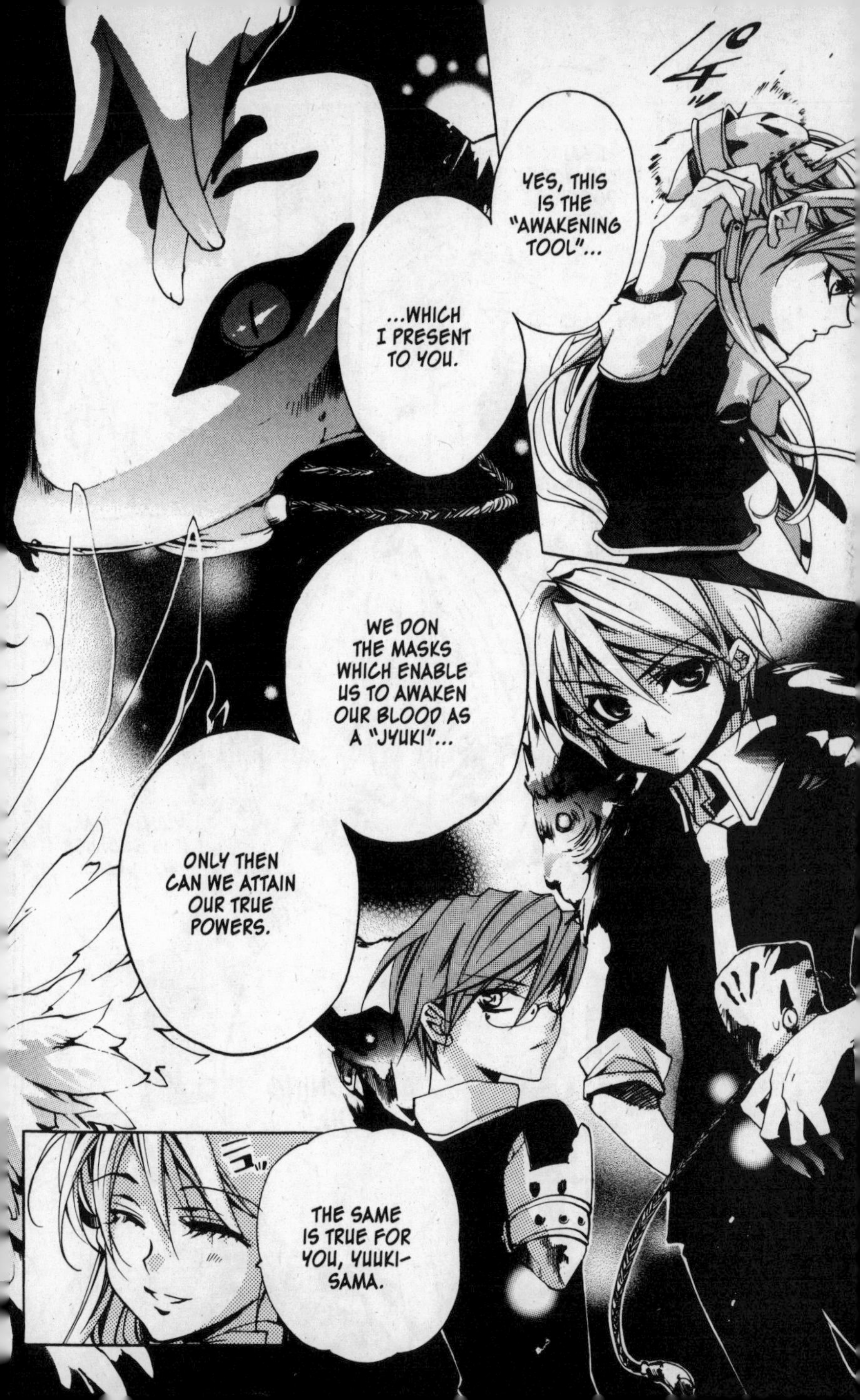
YES, THIS IS THE "AWAKENING TOOL"...
...WHICH I PRESENT TO YOU.
WE DON THE MASKS WHICH ENABLE US TO AWAKEN OUR BLOOD AS A "JYUKI"...
ONLY THEN CAN WE ATTAIN OUR TRUE POWERS.
THE SAME IS TRUE FOR YOU, YUUKI-SAMA.

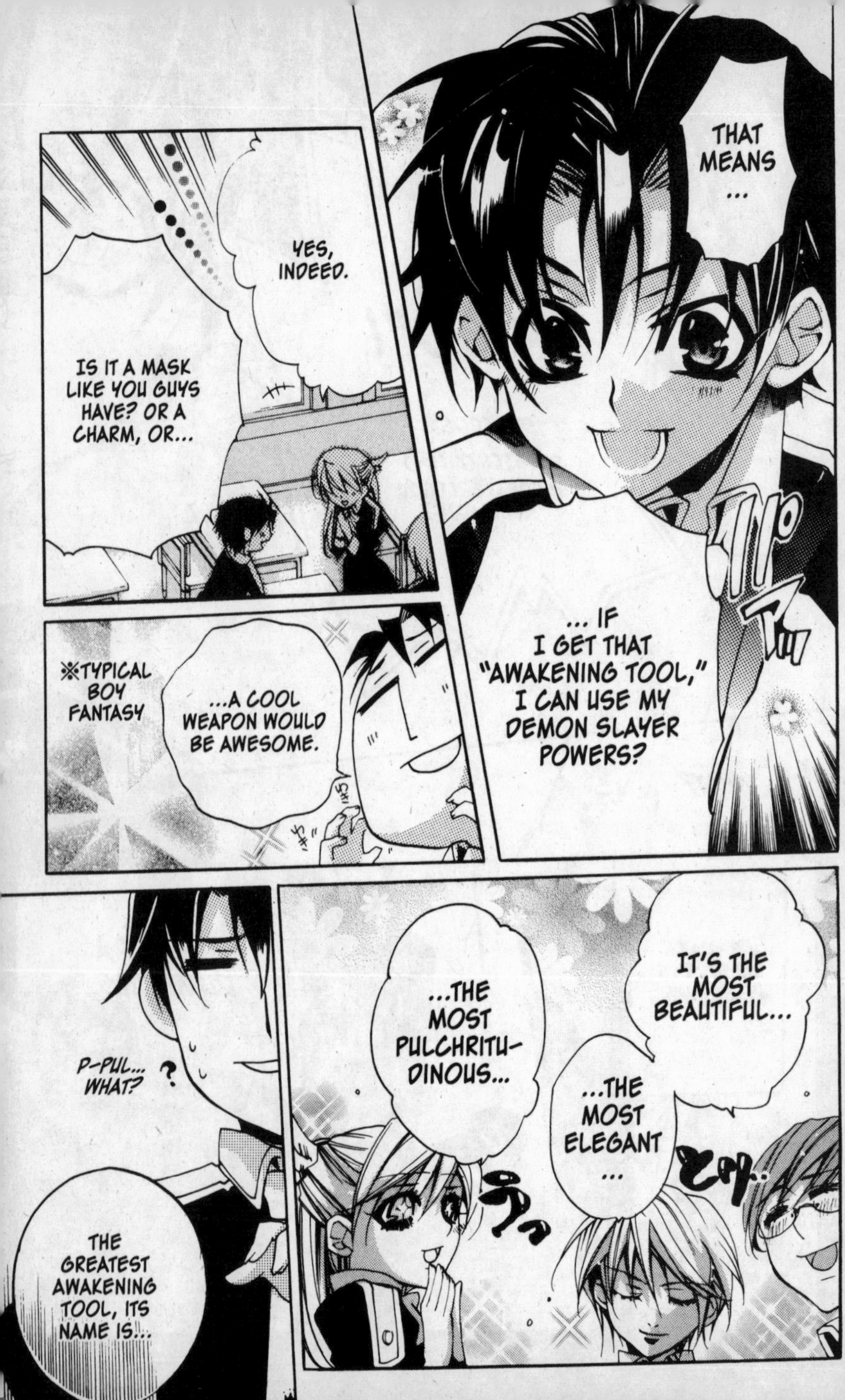

THAT MEANS ...
... IF I GET THAT "AWAKENING TOOL," I CAN USE MY DEMON SLAYER POWERS?
YES, INDEED.
IS IT A MASK LIKE YOU GUYS HAVE? OR A CHARM, OR...
※TYPICAL BOY FANTASY
...A COOL WEAPON WOULD BE AWESOME.
IT'S THE MOST BEAUTIFUL...
...THE MOST PULCHRITU-DINOUS...
...THE MOST ELEGANT ...
P-PUL... WHAT?
THE GREATEST AWAKENING TOOL, ITS NAME IS...

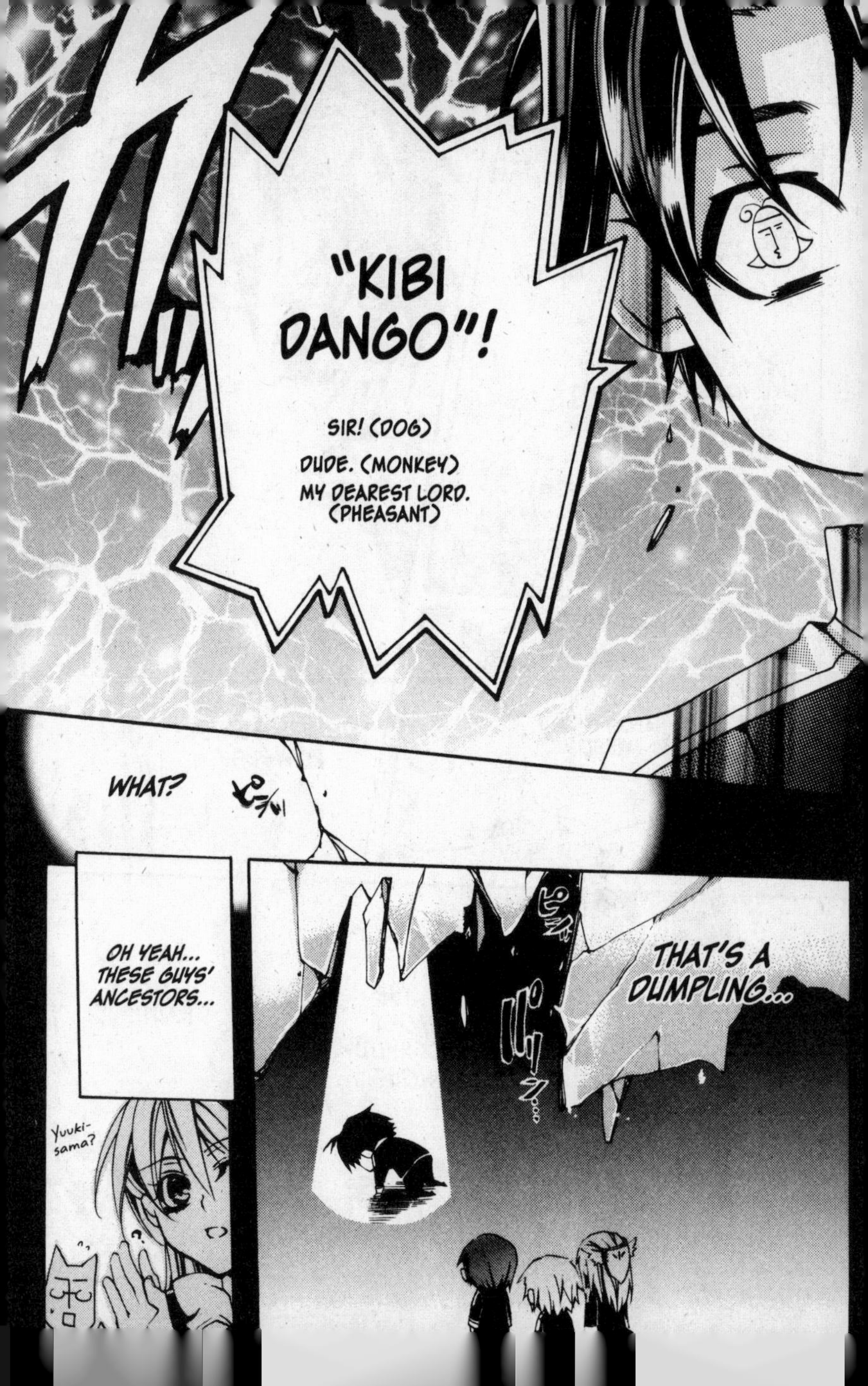
"KIBI DANGO"!
SIR! (DOG)
DUDE. (MONKEY)
MY DEAREST LORD. (PHEASANT)
WHAT?
THAT'S A DUMPLING...
OH YEAH... THESE GUYS' ANCESTORS...
Yuuki-sama?

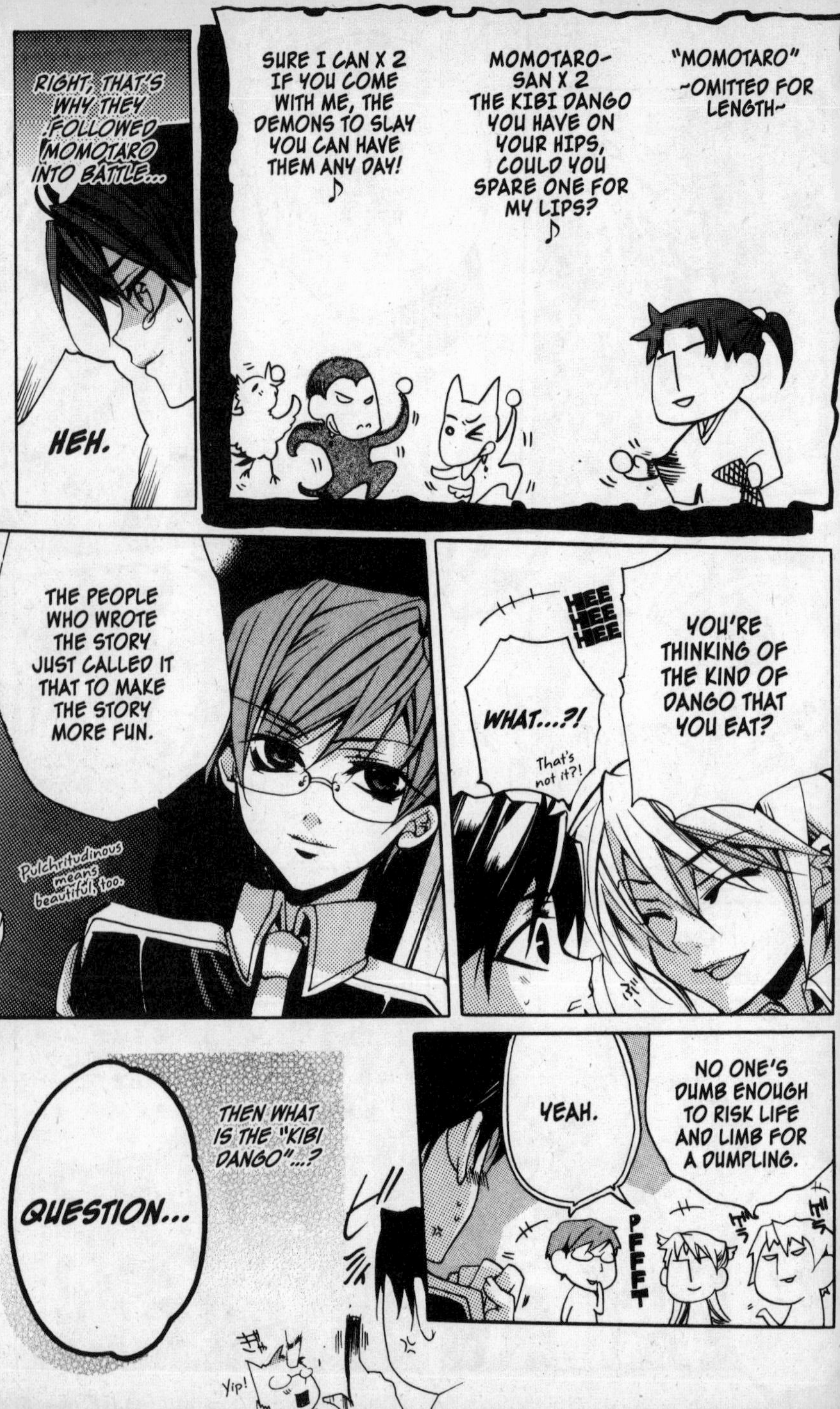
"MOMOTARO"
~OMITTED FOR LENGTH~
MOMOTARO-SAN X 2 THE KIBI DANGO YOU HAVE ON YOUR HIPS, COULD YOU SPARE ONE FOR MY LIPS? ♪
SURE I CAN X 2 IF YOU COME WITH ME, THE DEMONS TO SLAY YOU CAN HAVE THEM ANY DAY! ♪
RIGHT, THAT'S WHY THEY FOLLOWED MOMOTARO INTO BATTLE...
HEH.
YOU'RE THINKING OF THE KIND OF DANGO THAT YOU EAT?
HEE HEE HEE
WHAT...?!
That's not it?!
THE PEOPLE WHO WROTE THE STORY JUST CALLED IT THAT TO MAKE THE STORY MORE FUN.
Pulchritudinous means beautiful, too.
NO ONE'S DUMB ENOUGH TO RISK LIFE AND LIMB FOR A DUMPLING.
YEAH.
PFFFT
THEN WHAT IS THE "KIBI DANGO"...?
QUESTION...
Yip!

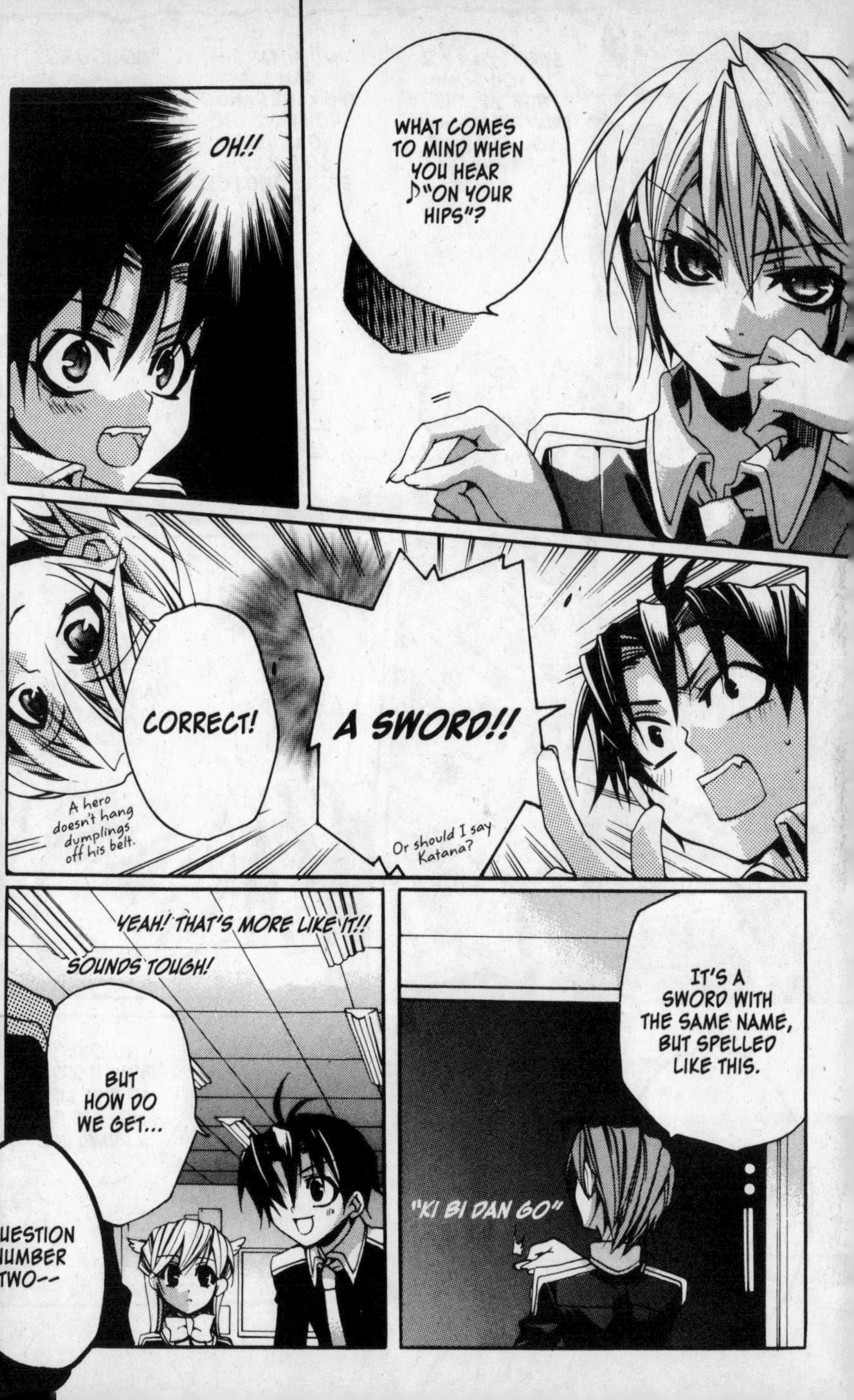
WHAT COMES TO MIND WHEN YOU HEAR ♪"ON YOUR HIPS"?
OH!!
A SWORD!!
Or should I say Katana?
CORRECT!
A hero doesn't hang dumplings off his belt.
IT'S A SWORD WITH THE SAME NAME, BUT SPELLED LIKE THIS.
"KI BI DAN GO"
YEAH! THAT'S MORE LIKE IT!!
SOUNDS TOUGH!
BUT HOW DO WE GET...
UESTION NUMBER TWO--

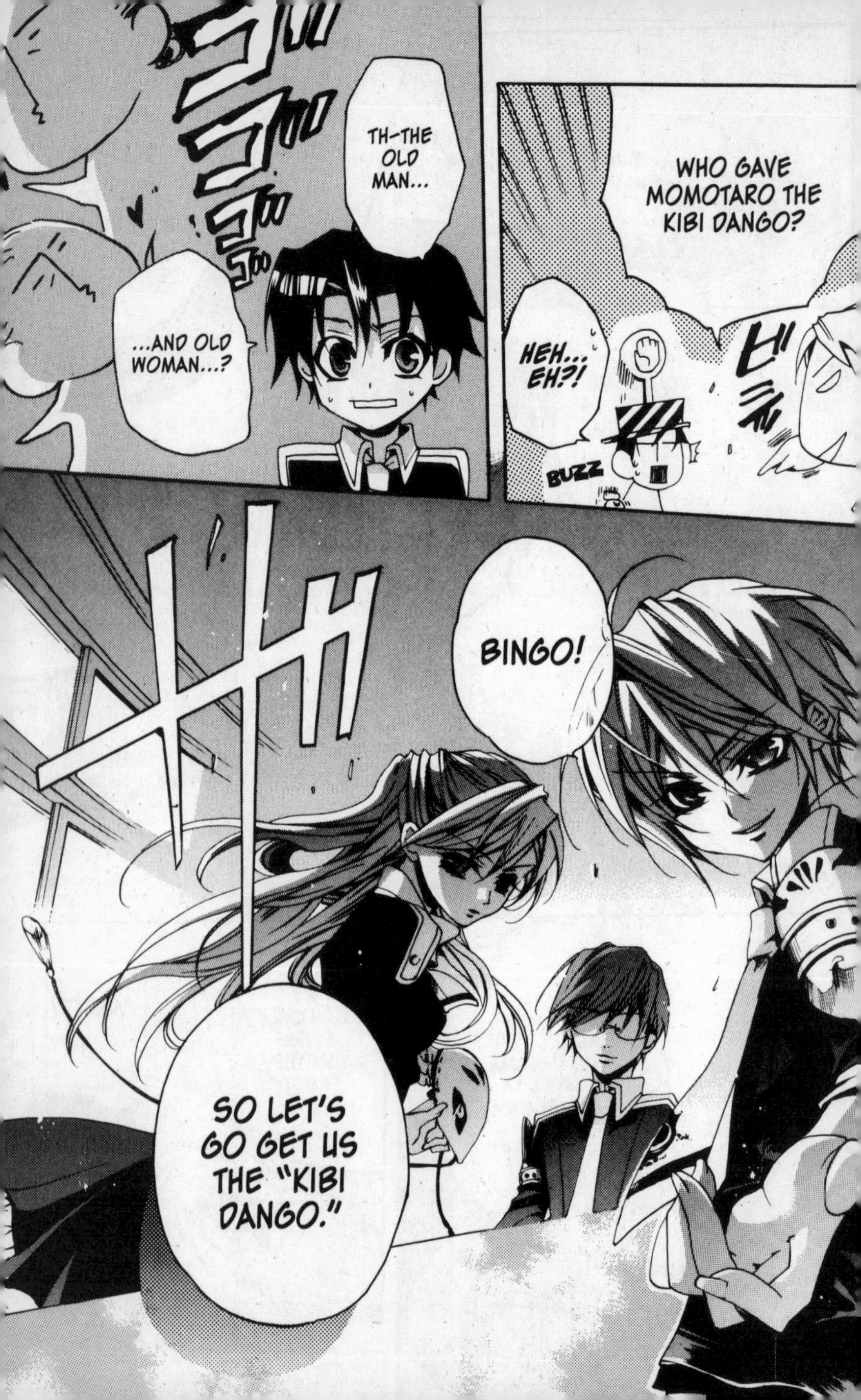
WHO GAVE MOMOTARO THE KIBI DANGO?
HEH... EH?!
BUZZ
TH-THE OLD MAN...
...AND OLD WOMAN...?
BINGO!
SO LET'S GO GET US THE "KIBI DANGO."

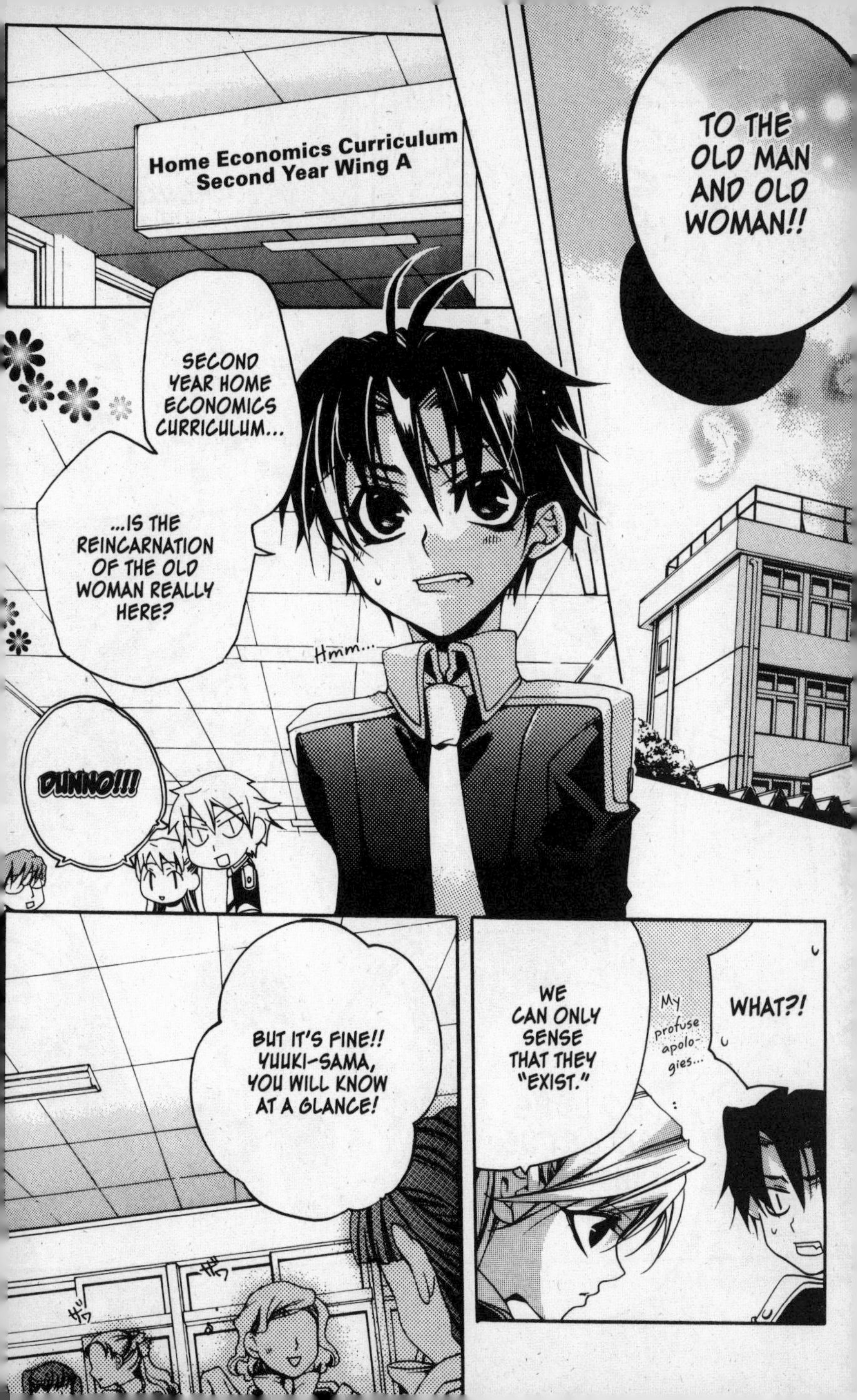
TO THE OLD MAN AND OLD WOMAN!!
Home Economics Curriculum Second Year Wing A
SECOND YEAR HOME ECONOMICS CURRICULUM...
...IS THE REINCARNATION OF THE OLD WOMAN REALLY HERE?
Hmm...
DUNNO!!!
WHAT?!
My profuse apologies...
WE CAN ONLY SENSE THAT THEY "EXIST."
BUT IT'S FINE!! YUUKI-SAMA, YOU WILL KNOW AT A GLANCE!

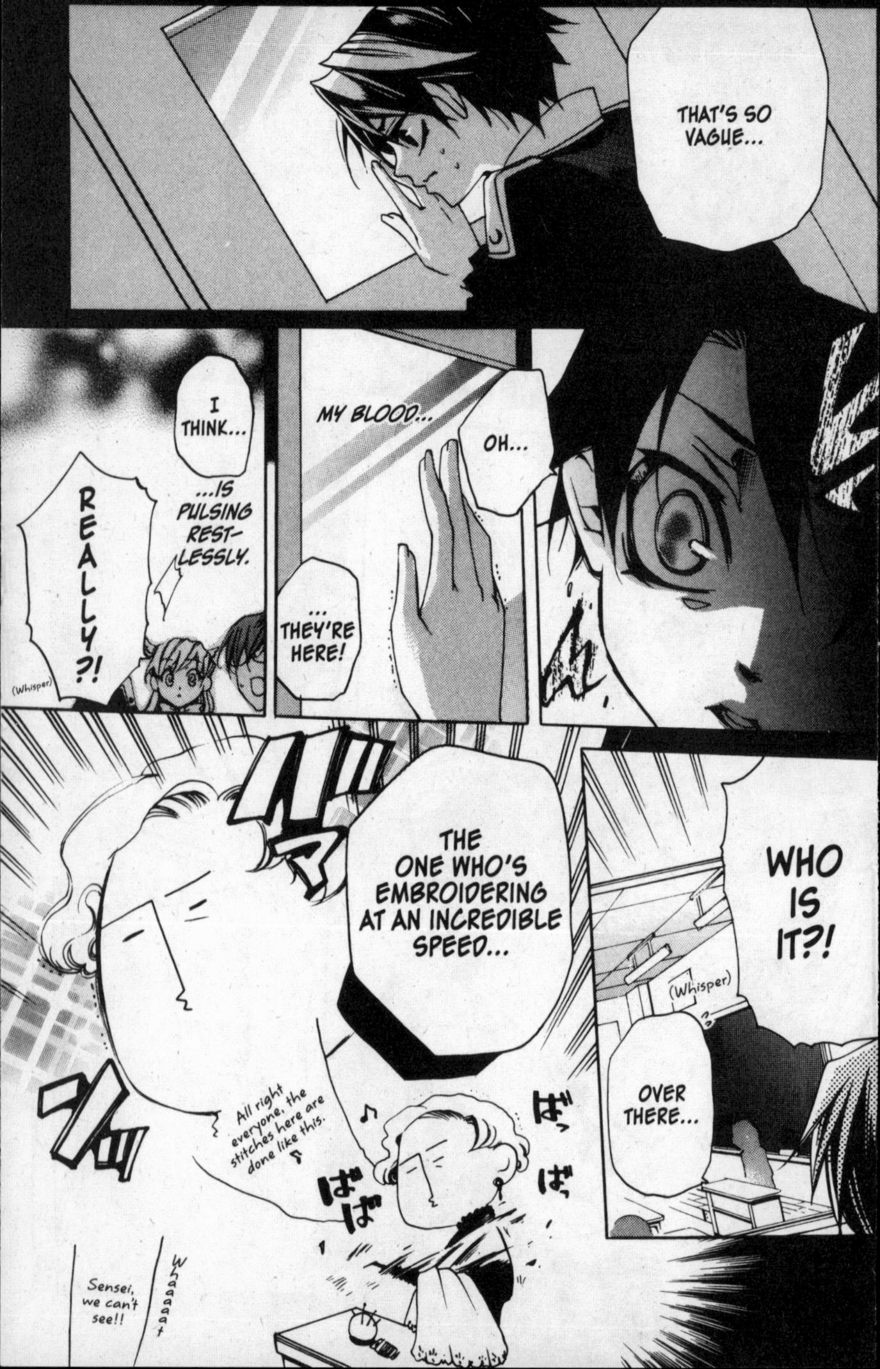
THAT'S SO VAGUE...
OH...
MY BLOOD...
...THEY'RE HERE!
I THINK...
...IS PULSING RESTLESSLY.
REALLY?!
(Whisper)
WHO IS IT?!
(Whisper)
OVER THERE...
THE ONE WHO'S EMBROIDERING AT AN INCREDIBLE SPEED...
ばっ
ば
ばば
All right everyone, the stitches here are done like this.
Whaaaaaat
Sensei, we can't see!!

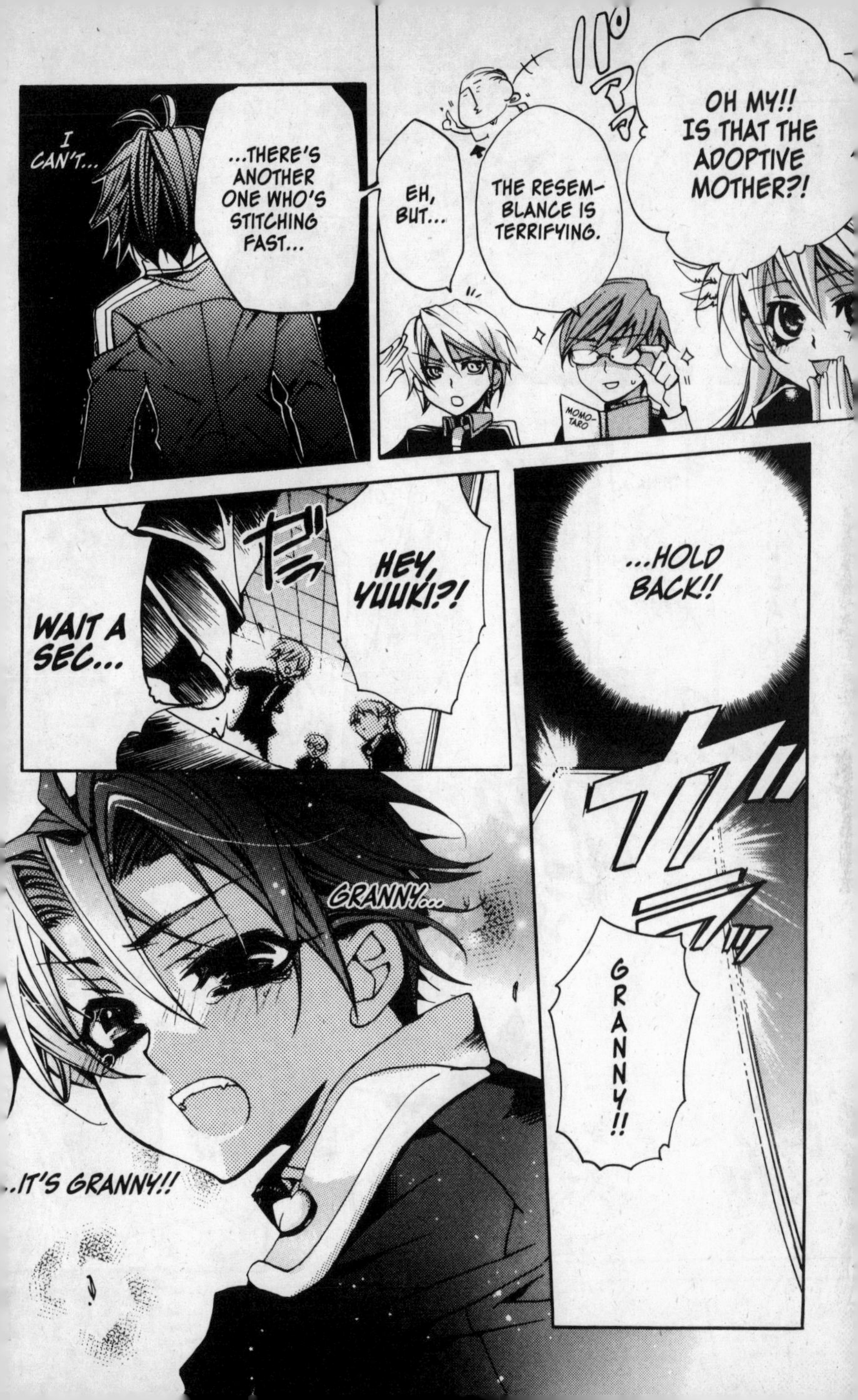

OH MY!! IS THAT THE ADOPTIVE MOTHER?!
THE RESEM-BLANCE IS TERRIFYING.
MOMO-TARO
EH, BUT...
...THERE'S ANOTHER ONE WHO'S STITCHING FAST...
I CAN'T...
...HOLD BACK!!
GRANNY!!
HEY, YUUKI?!
WAIT A SEC...
GRANNY...
..IT'S GRANNY!!

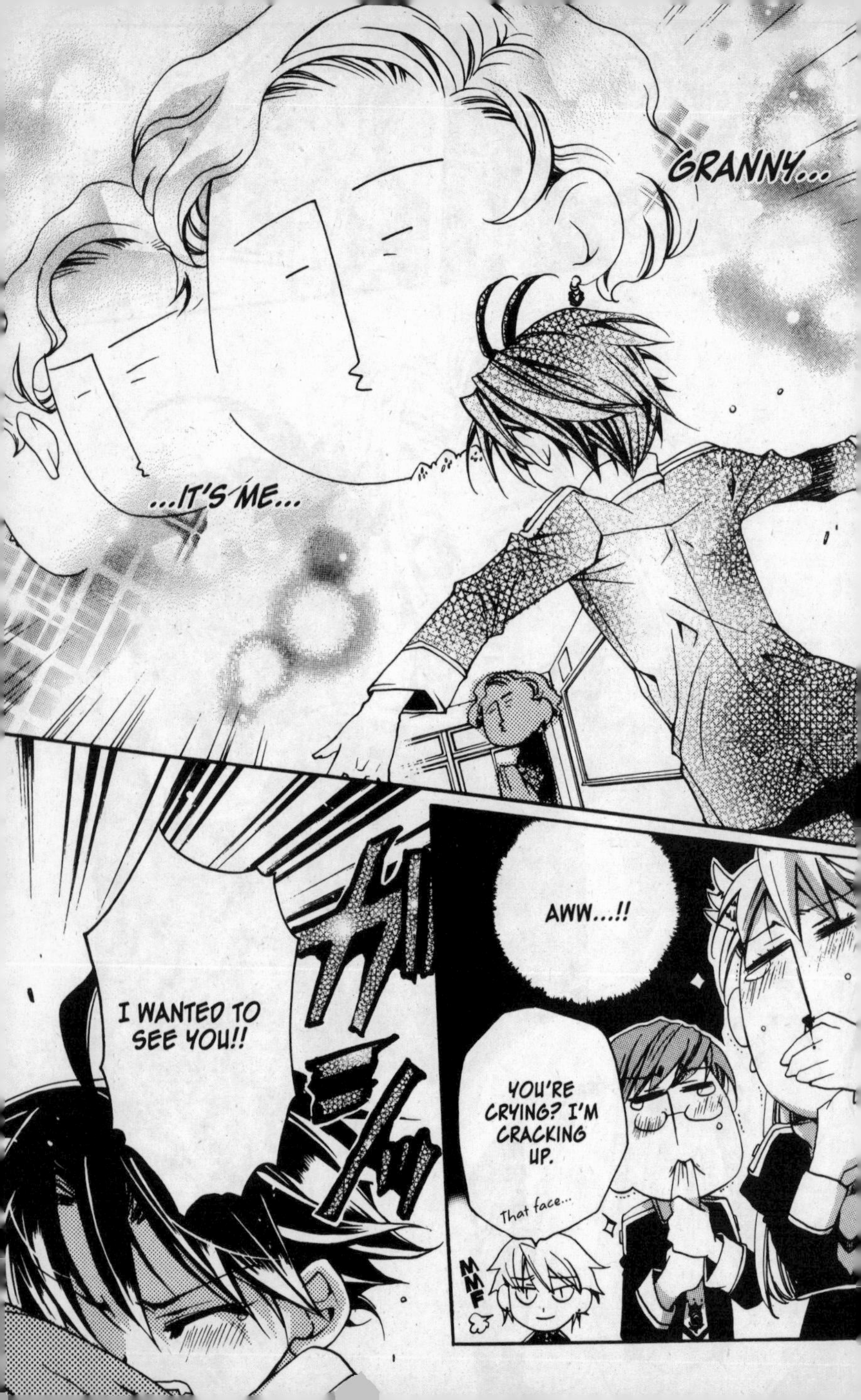
GRANNY...
...IT'S ME...
I WANTED TO SEE YOU!!
AWW...!!
YOU'RE CRYING? I'M CRACKING UP.
That face...
MMF

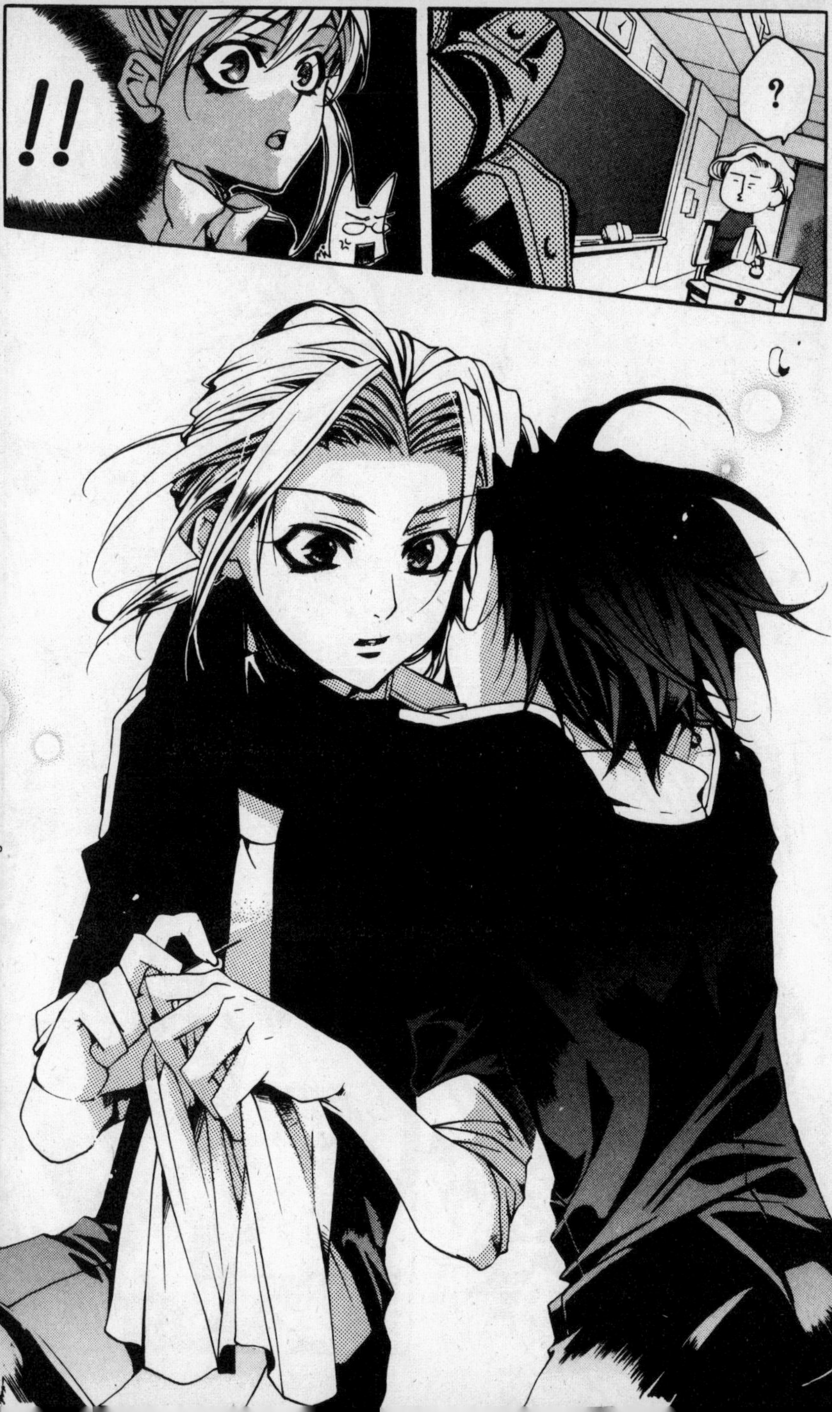
?
!!

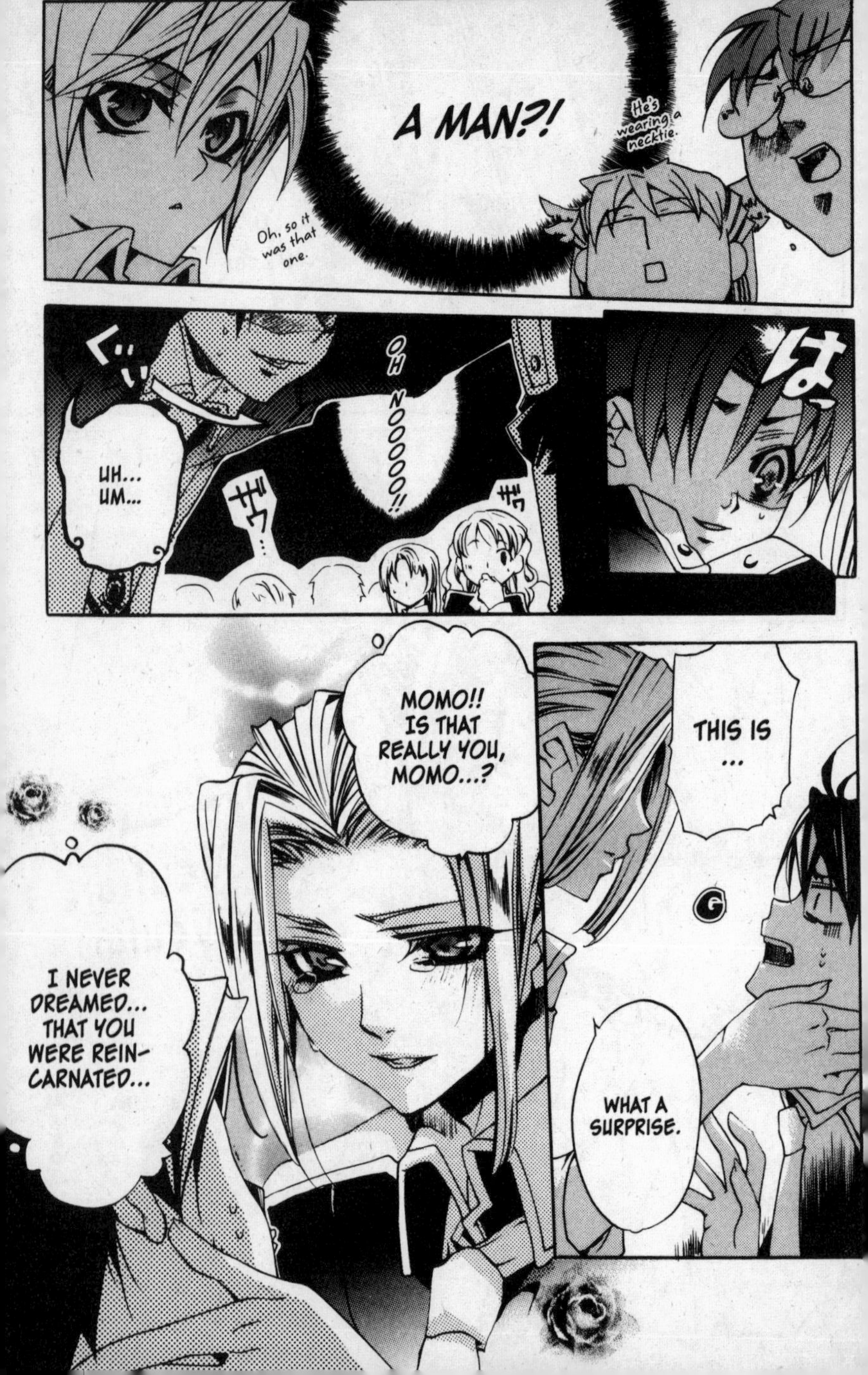
He's wearing a necktie.
A MAN?!
Oh, so it was that one.
は
OH NOOOOOO!!
ザワ
ザワ…
UH... UM...
ぐい
THIS IS ...
WHAT A SURPRISE.
MOMO!! IS THAT REALLY YOU, MOMO...?
I NEVER DREAMED... THAT YOU WERE REIN-CARNATED...

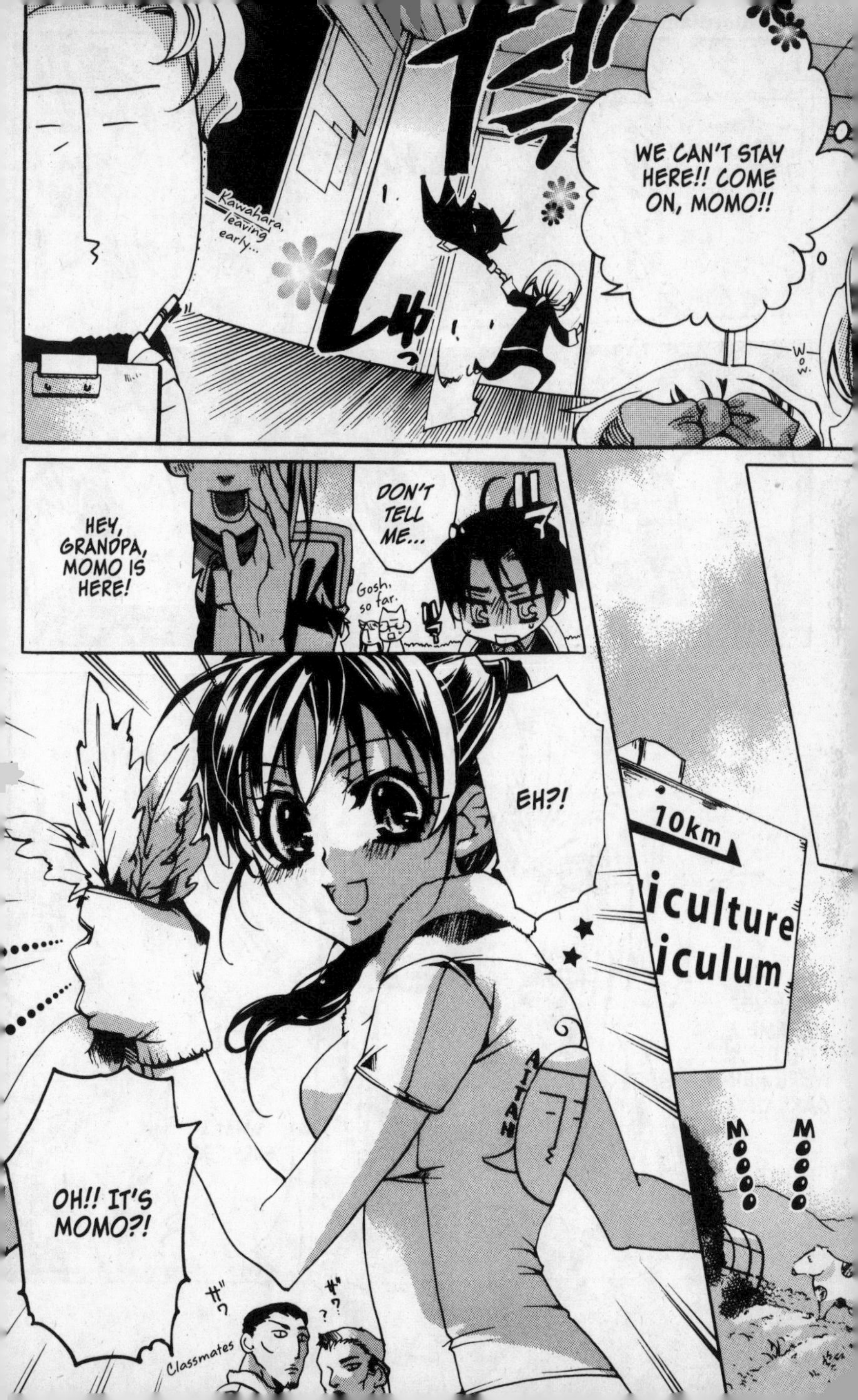
WE CAN'T STAY HERE!! COME ON, MOMO!!
Wow.
Kawahara, leaving early...
DON'T TELL ME...
Gosh, so far.
HEY, GRANDPA, MOMO IS HERE!
MOOOO
MOOOO
10km
iculture
iculum
EH?!
OH!! IT'S MOMO?!
Classmates

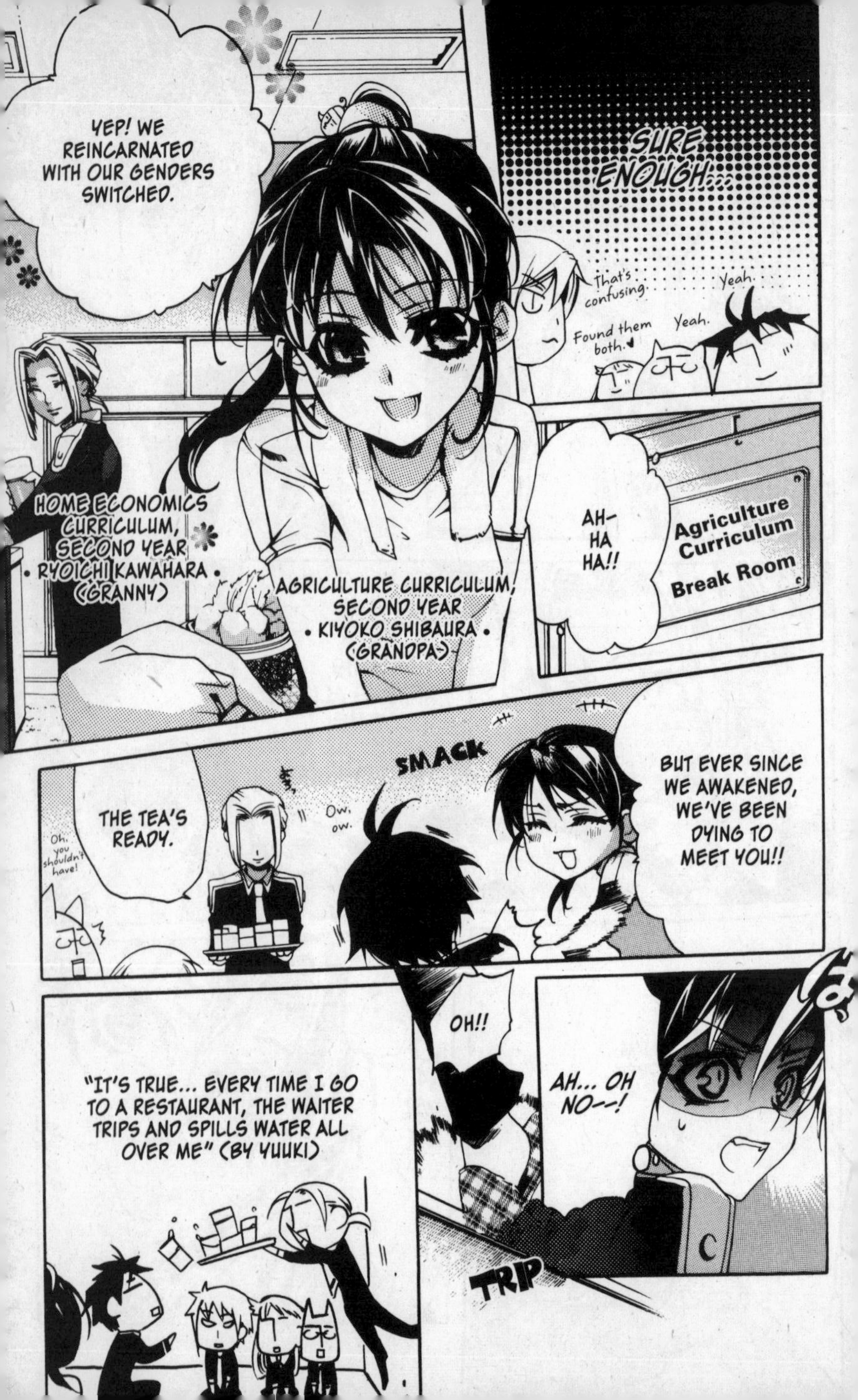
SURE ENOUGH...
Yeah.
That's confusing.
Yeah.
Found them both.♥
Agriculture Curriculum Break Room
AH-HA HA!!
YEP! WE REINCARNATED WITH OUR GENDERS SWITCHED.
AGRICULTURE CURRICULUM, SECOND YEAR • KIYOKO SHIBAURA • (GRANDPA)
HOME ECONOMICS CURRICULUM, SECOND YEAR • RYOICHI KAWAHARA • (GRANNY)
BUT EVER SINCE WE AWAKENED, WE'VE BEEN DYING TO MEET YOU!!
SMACK
Ow, ow.
THE TEA'S READY.
Oh, you shouldn't have!
AH... OH NO--!
OH!!
TRIP
"IT'S TRUE... EVERY TIME I GO TO A RESTAURANT, THE WAITER TRIPS AND SPILLS WATER ALL OVER ME" (BY YUUKI)

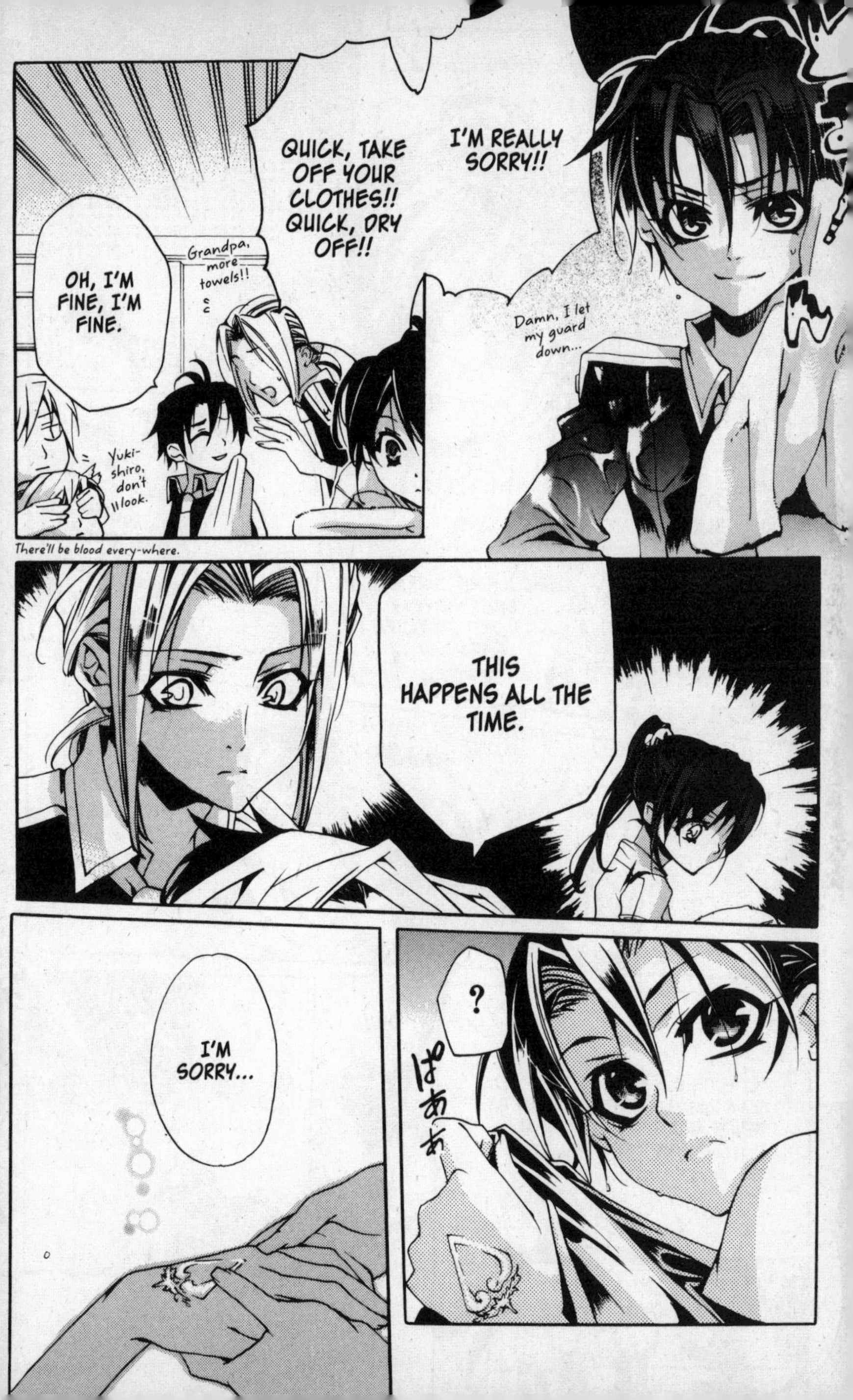
I'M REALLY SORRY!!
Damn, I let my guard down...
QUICK, TAKE OFF YOUR CLOTHES!! QUICK, DRY OFF!!
Grandpa, more towels!!
OH, I'M FINE, I'M FINE.
Yuki-shiro, don't look.
There'll be blood every-where.
THIS HAPPENS ALL THE TIME.
?
ぱああ
I'M SORRY...

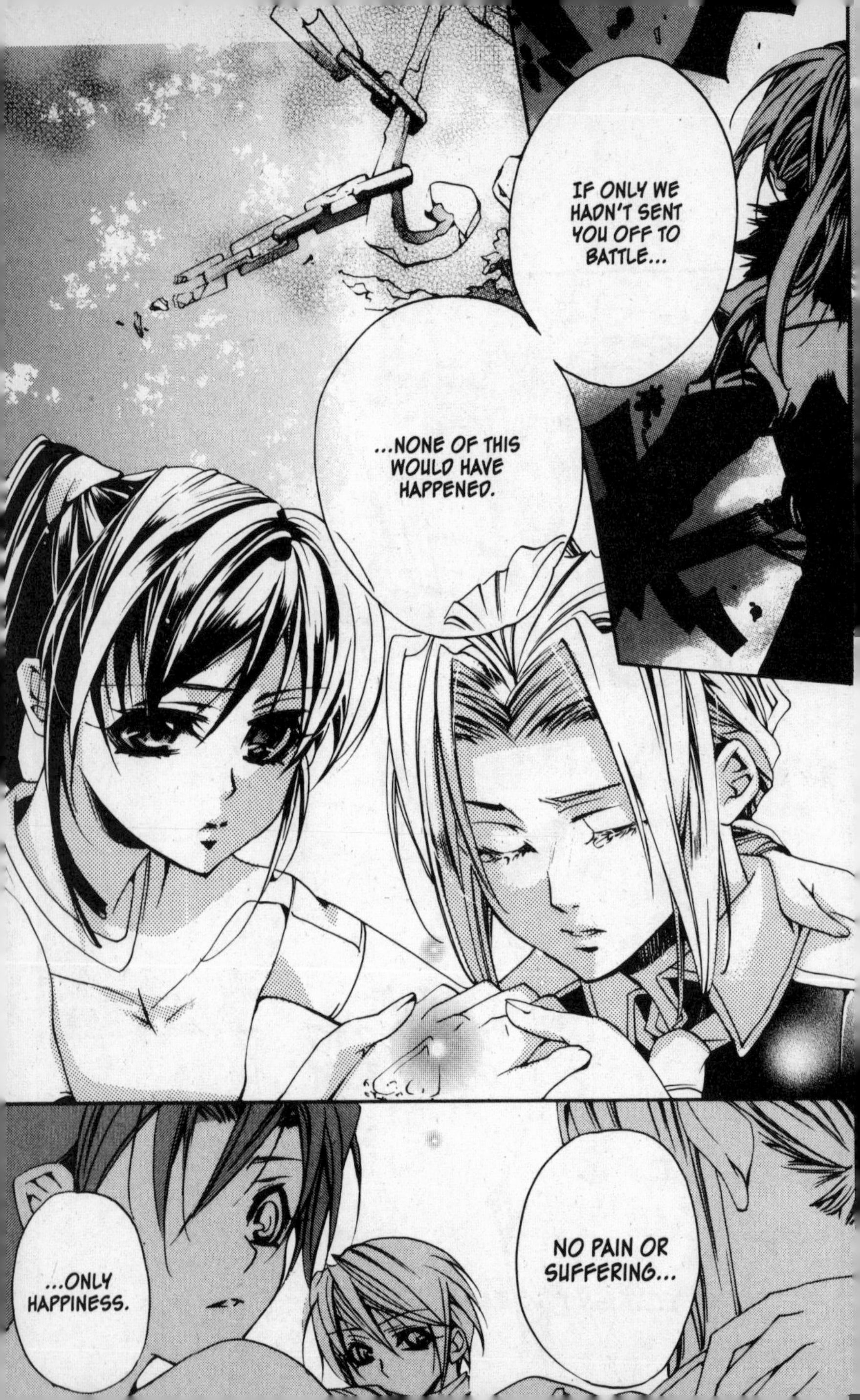
IF ONLY WE HADN'T SENT YOU OFF TO BATTLE...
...NONE OF THIS WOULD HAVE HAPPENED.
NO PAIN OR SUFFERING...
...ONLY HAPPINESS.

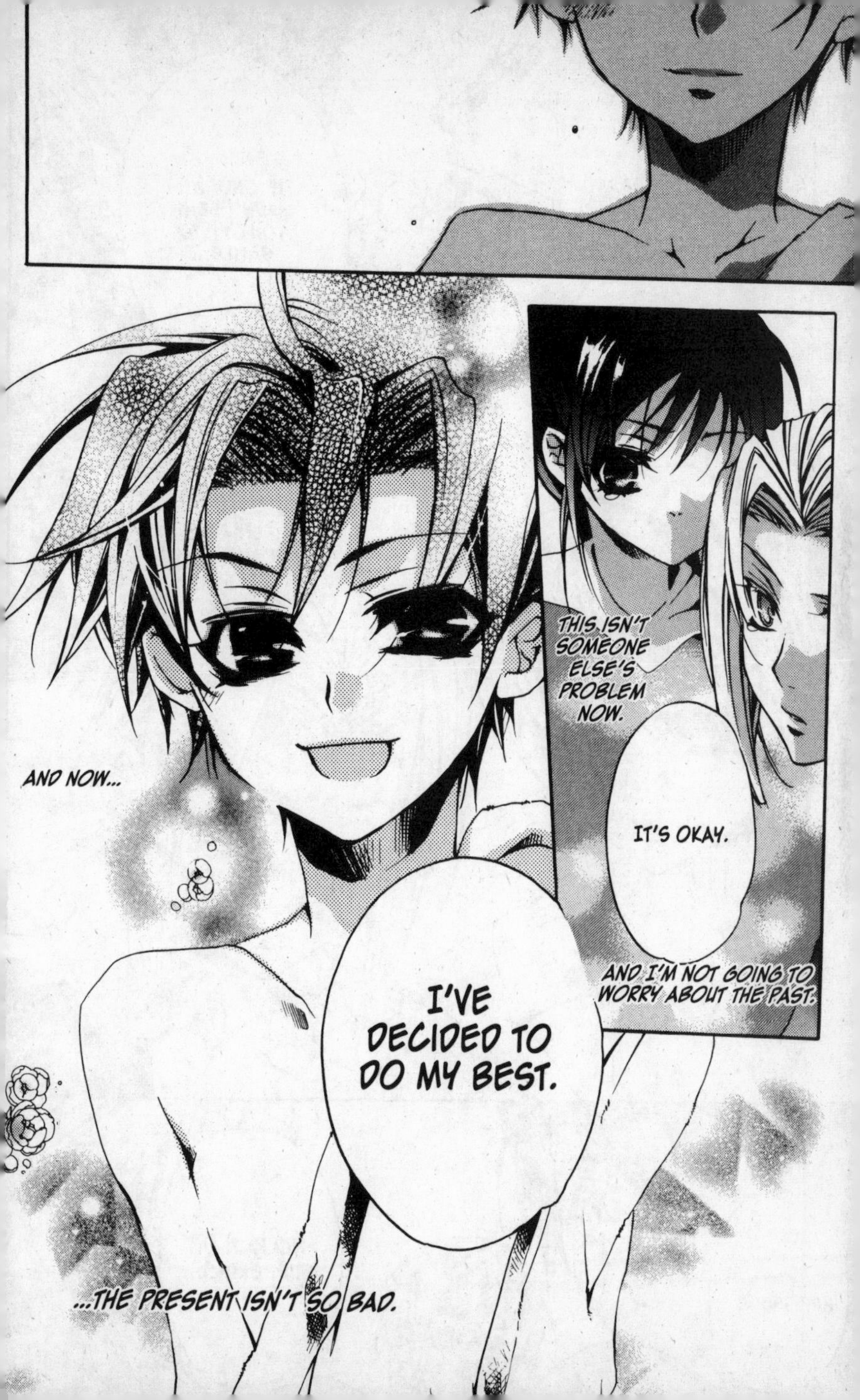
THIS ISN'T SOMEONE ELSE'S PROBLEM NOW.
IT'S OKAY.
AND I'M NOT GOING TO WORRY ABOUT THE PAST.
AND NOW...
I'VE DECIDED TO DO MY BEST.
...THE PRESENT ISN'T SO BAD.

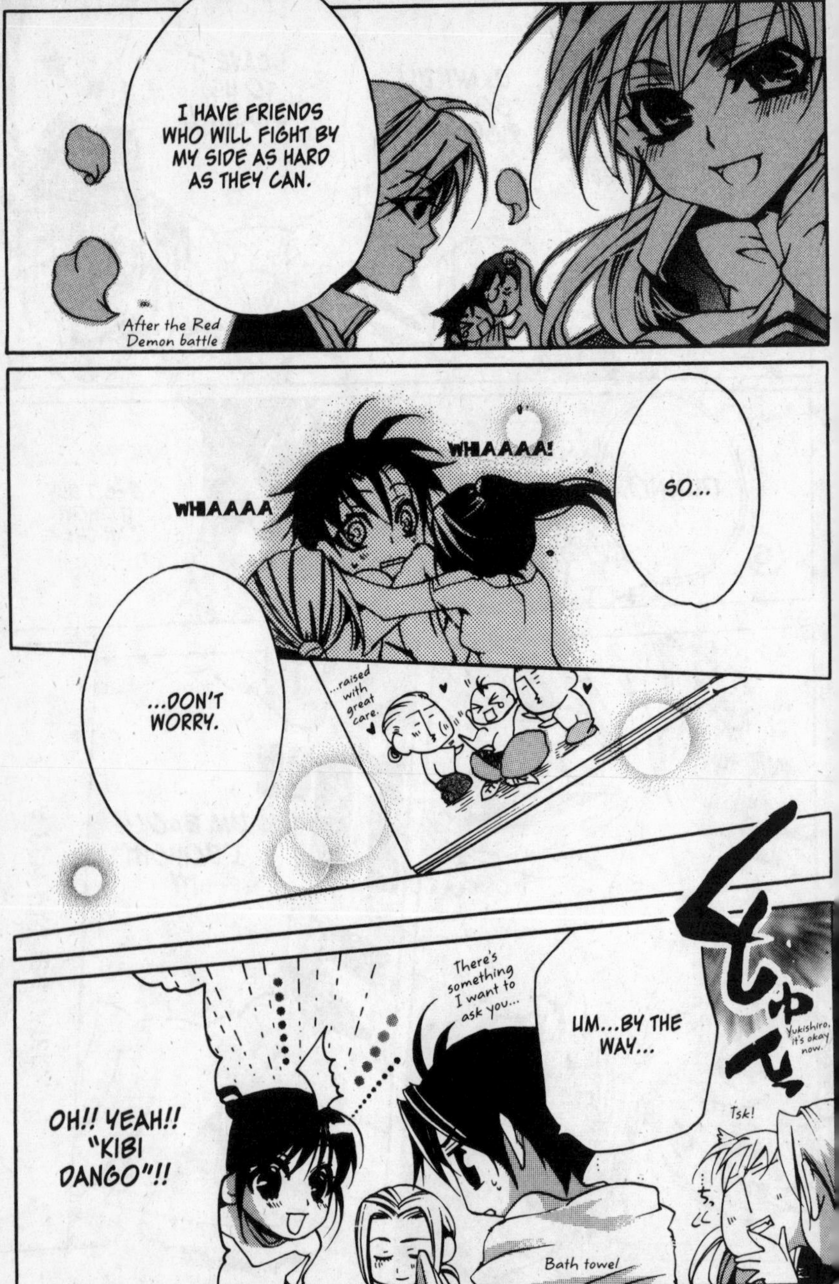
I HAVE FRIENDS WHO WILL FIGHT BY MY SIDE AS HARD AS THEY CAN.
After the Red Demon battle
SO...
WHIAAAA!
WHIAAAA
...raised with great care.
...DON'T WORRY.
Yukishiro, it's okay now.
Tsk!
UM...BY THE WAY...
There's something I want to ask you...
Bath towel
OH!! YEAH!! "KIBI DANGO"!!

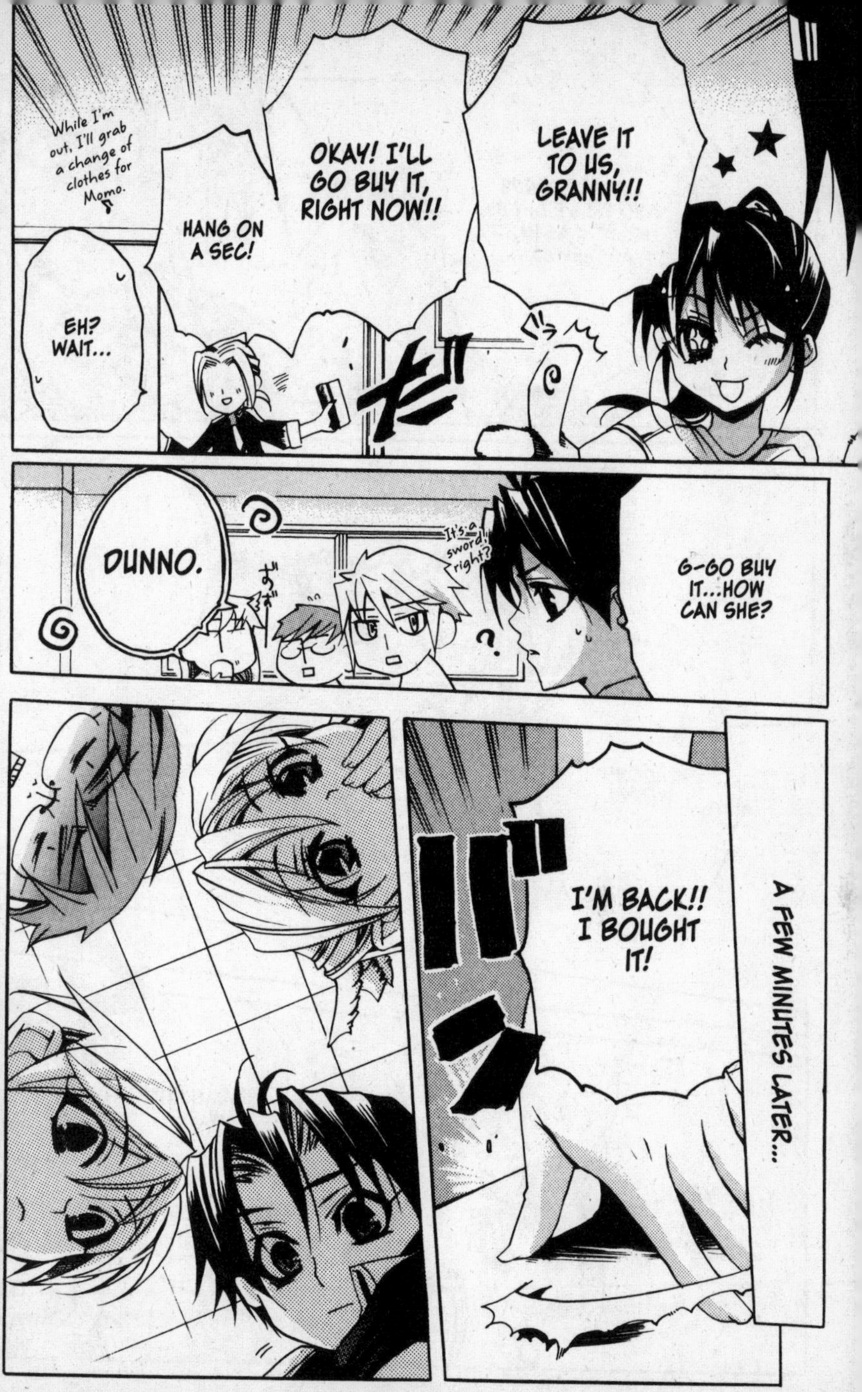
LEAVE IT TO US, GRANNY!!
OKAY! I'LL GO BUY IT, RIGHT NOW!!
HANG ON A SEC!
While I'm out, I'll grab a change of clothes for Momo. ♪
EH? WAIT...
G-GO BUY IT...HOW CAN SHE?
It's a sword, right?
DUNNO.
A FEW MINUTES LATER...
I'M BACK!! I BOUGHT IT!

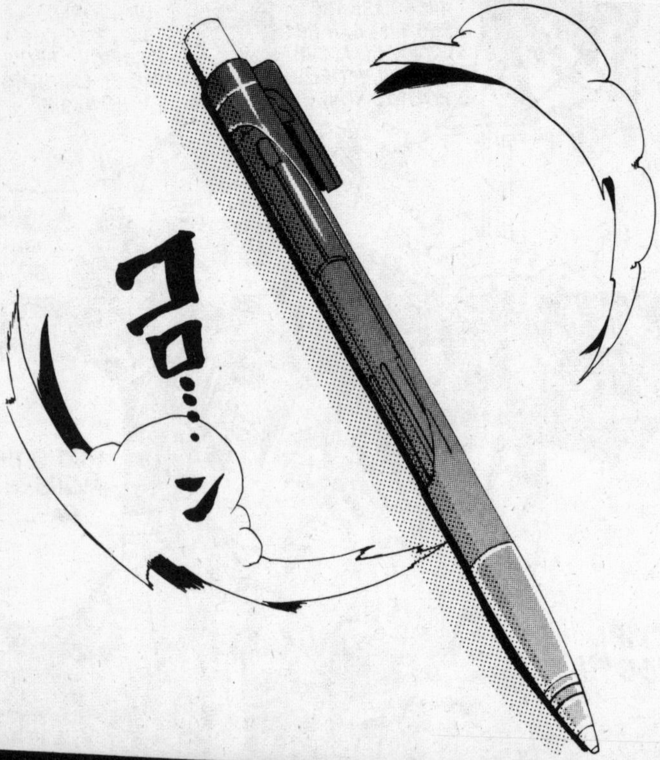
コロ…ン

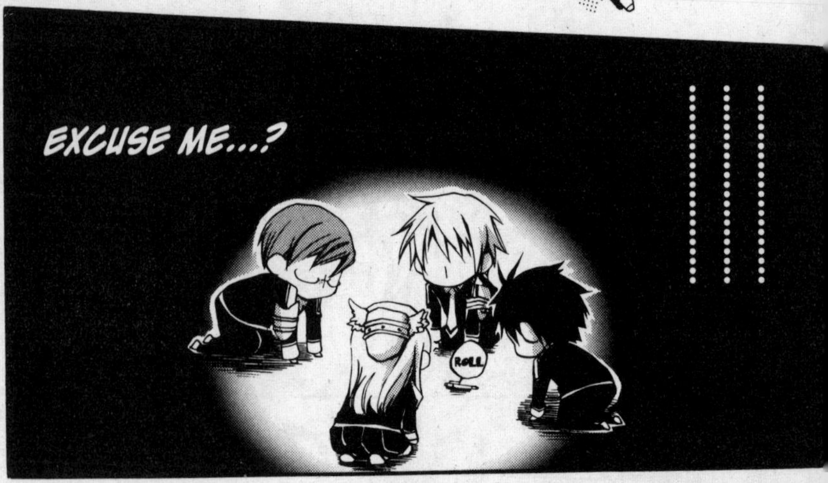
......
EXCUSE ME...?
ROLL

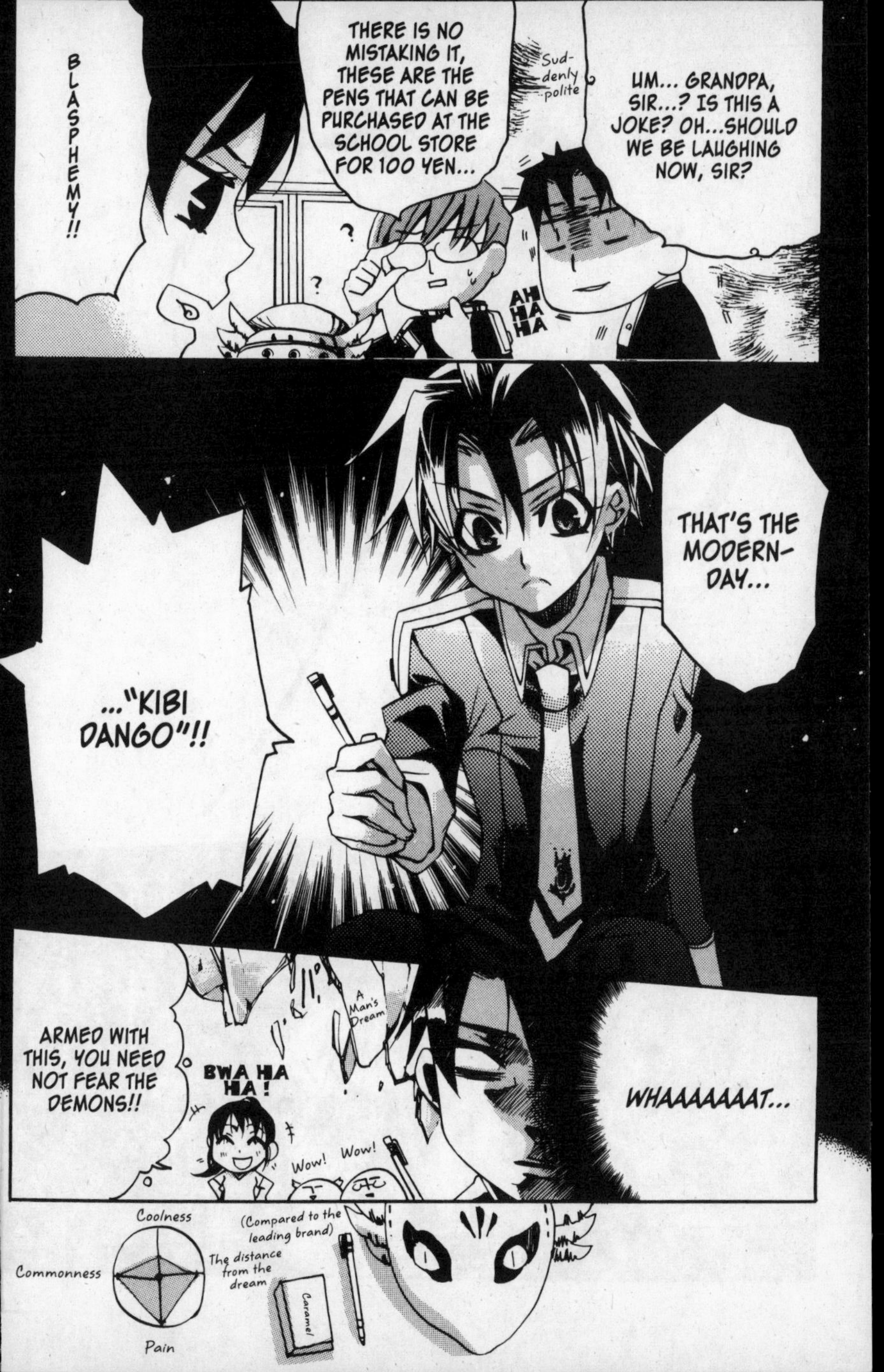
UM... GRANDPA, SIR...? IS THIS A JOKE? OH...SHOULD WE BE LAUGHING NOW, SIR?
Sud-denly polite
THERE IS NO MISTAKING IT, THESE ARE THE PENS THAT CAN BE PURCHASED AT THE SCHOOL STORE FOR 100 YEN...
BLASPHEMY!!
AH HA HA HA
?
?
THAT'S THE MODERN-DAY...
..."KIBI DANGO"!!
WHAAAAAAAT...
A Man's Dream
ARMED WITH THIS, YOU NEED NOT FEAR THE DEMONS!!
BWA HA HA HA!
Wow! Wow!
(Compared to the leading brand)
Coolness
Commonness
The distance from the dream
Pain
Caramel

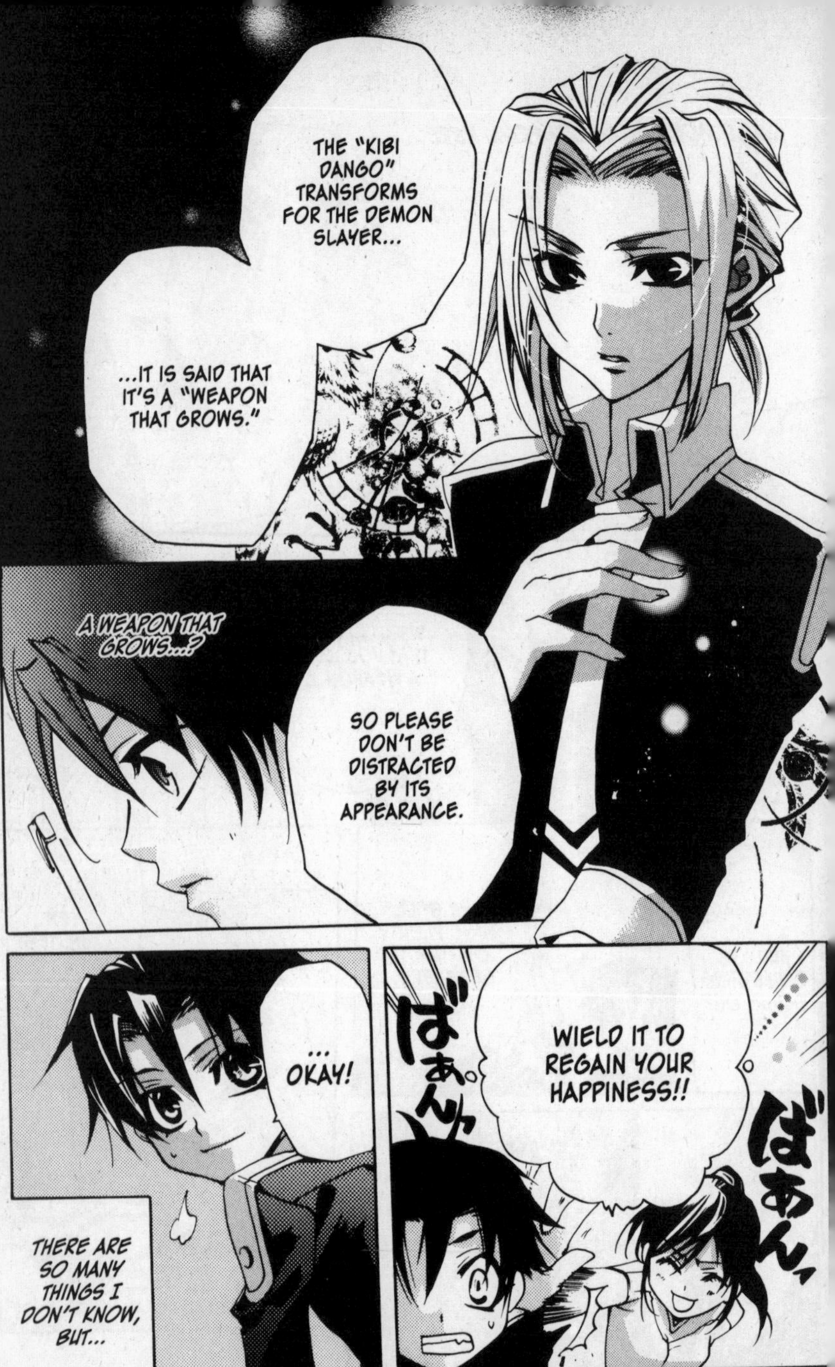
THE "KIBI DANGO" TRANSFORMS FOR THE DEMON SLAYER...
...IT IS SAID THAT IT'S A "WEAPON THAT GROWS."
A WEAPON THAT GROWS...?
SO PLEASE DON'T BE DISTRACTED BY ITS APPEARANCE.
ばぁん
WIELD IT TO REGAIN YOUR HAPPINESS!!
ばぁん
... OKAY!
THERE ARE SO MANY THINGS I DON'T KNOW, BUT...

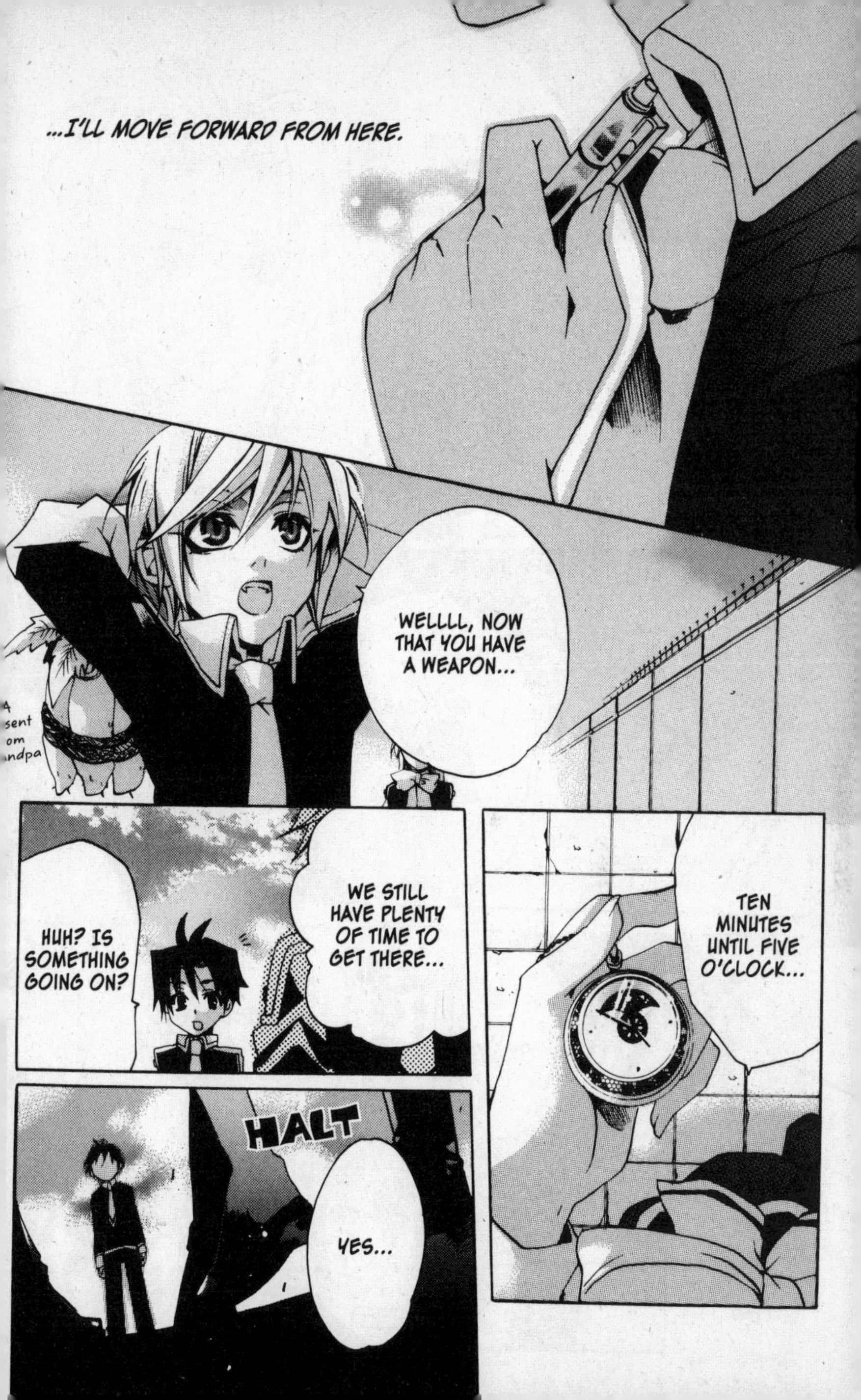
...I'LL MOVE FORWARD FROM HERE.
WELLLL, NOW THAT YOU HAVE A WEAPON...
TEN MINUTES UNTIL FIVE O'CLOCK...
WE STILL HAVE PLENTY OF TIME TO GET THERE...
HUH? IS SOMETHING GOING ON?
HALT
YES...

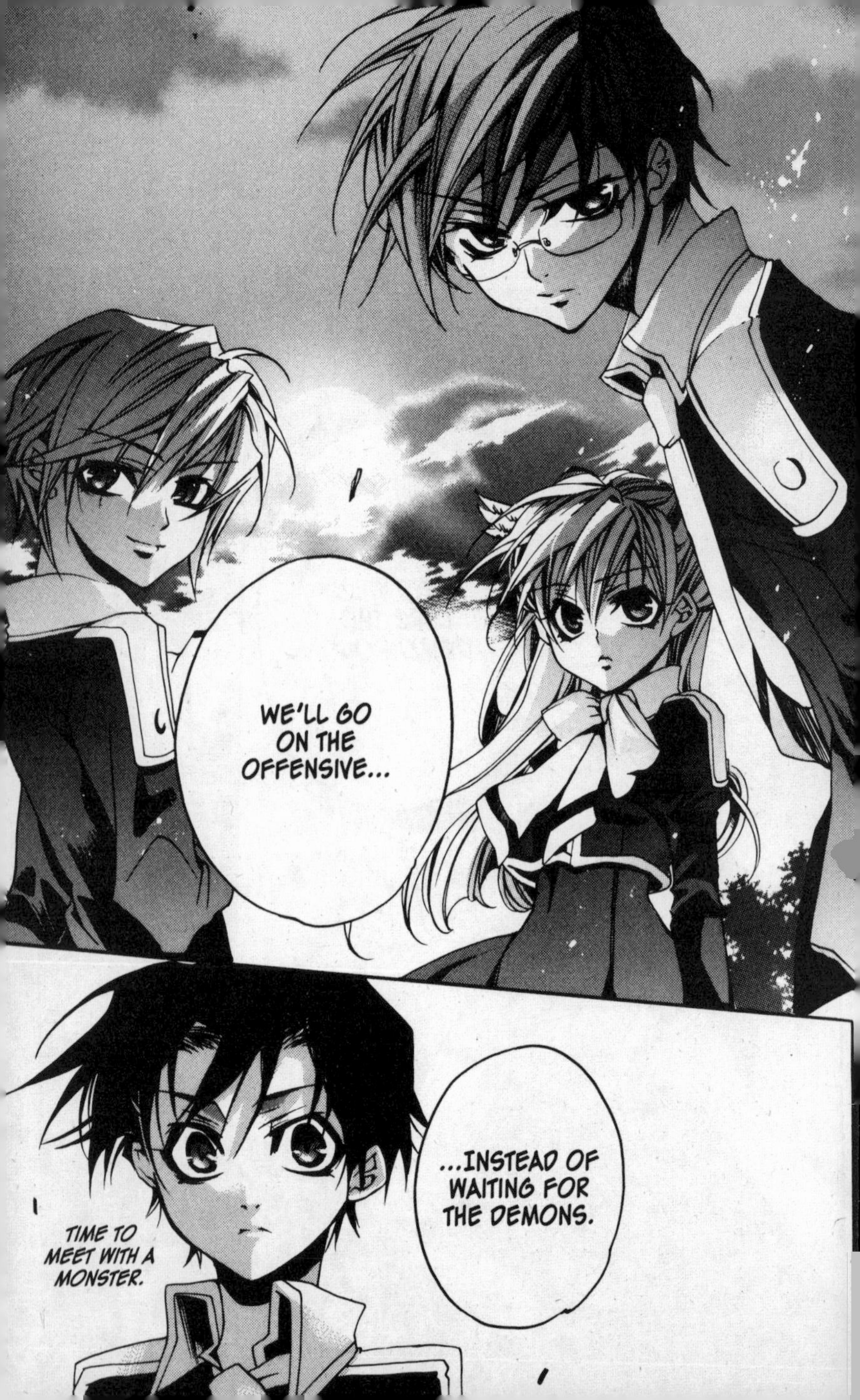
WE'LL GO ON THE OFFENSIVE...
...INSTEAD OF WAITING FOR THE DEMONS.
TIME TO MEET WITH A MONSTER.

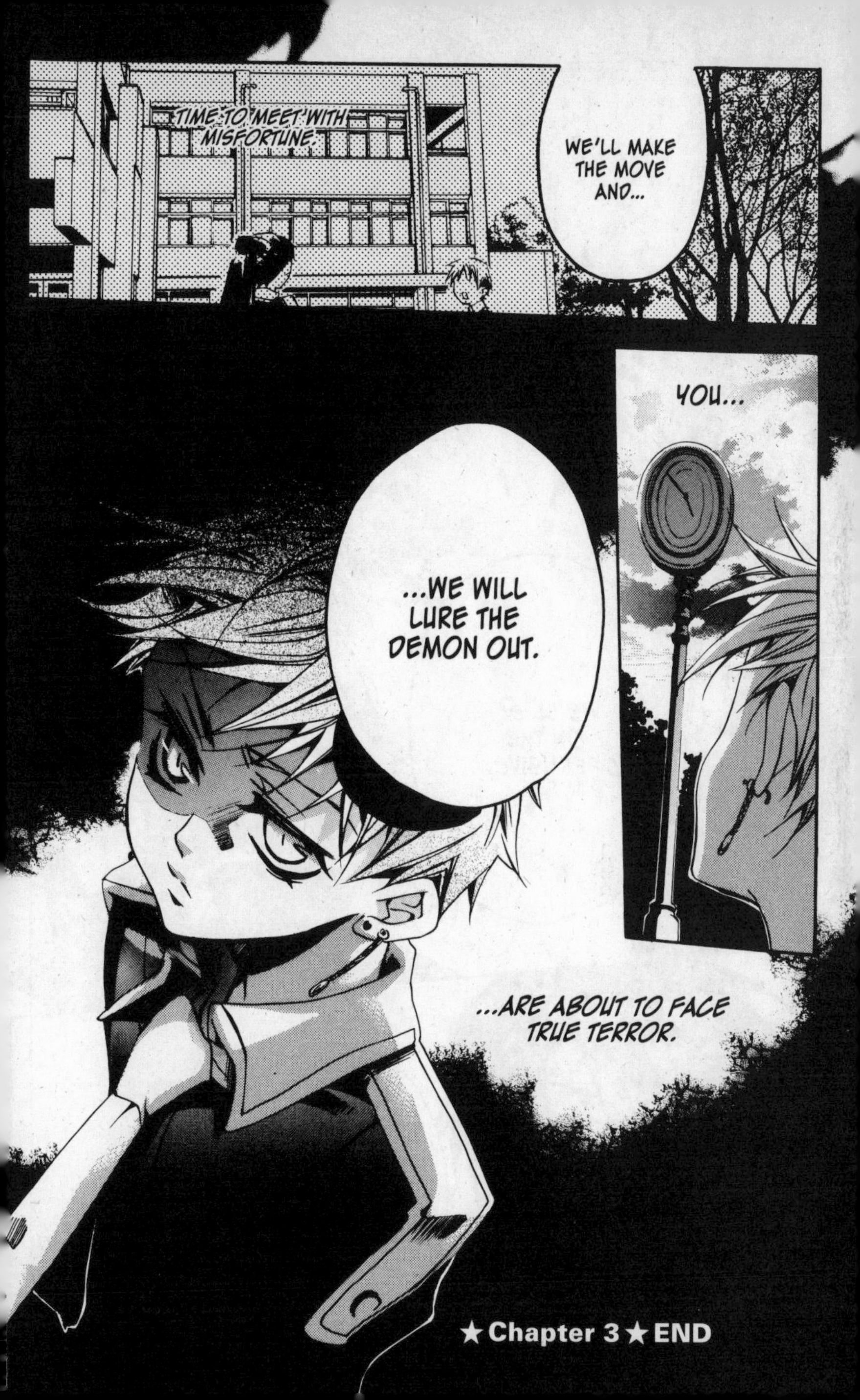
WE'LL MAKE THE MOVE AND...
TIME TO MEET WITH MISFORTUNE.
YOU...
...WE WILL LURE THE DEMON OUT.
...ARE ABOUT TO FACE TRUE TERROR.
★Chapter 3★END

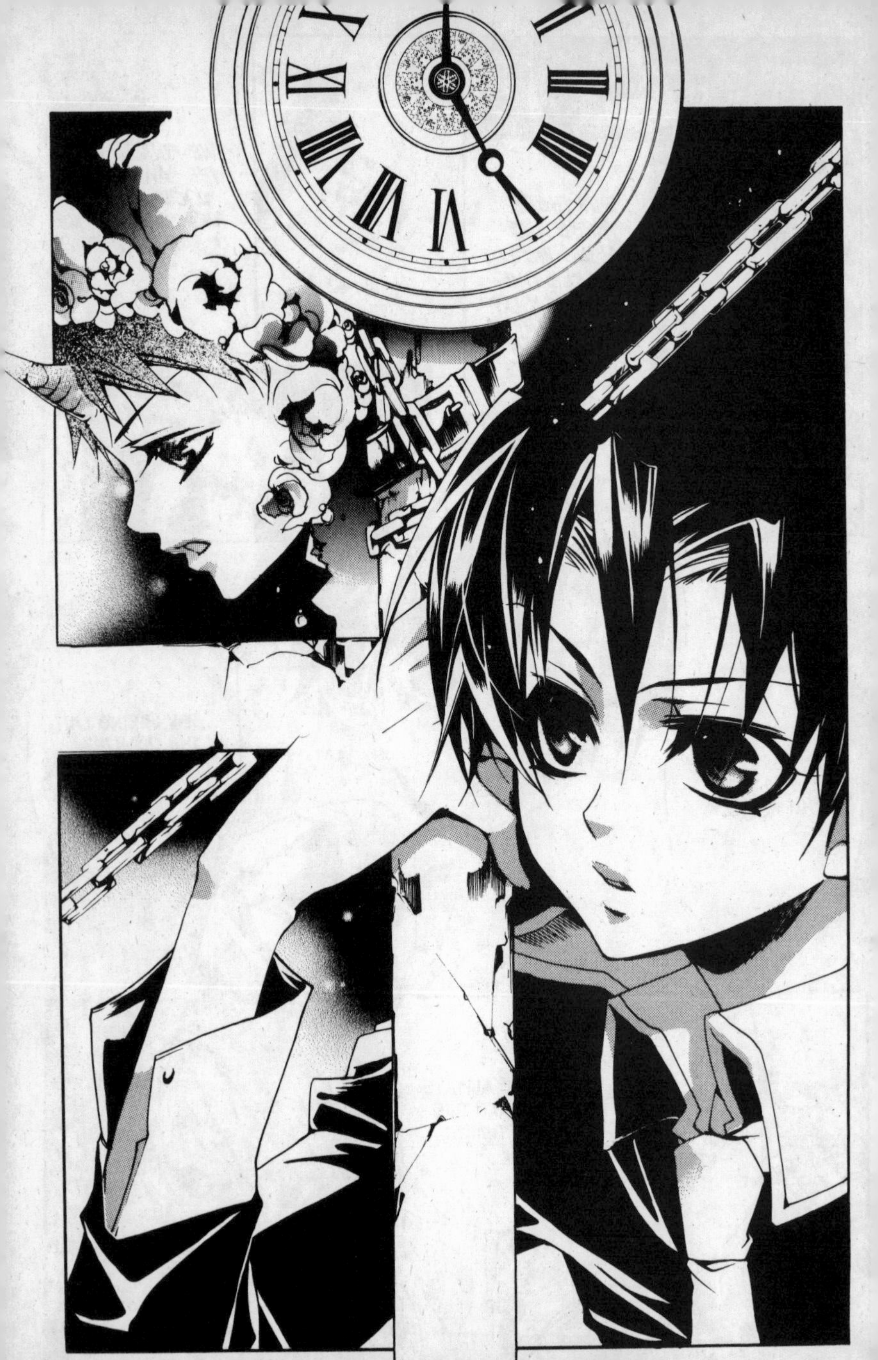

Chapter 4: The Guardians and

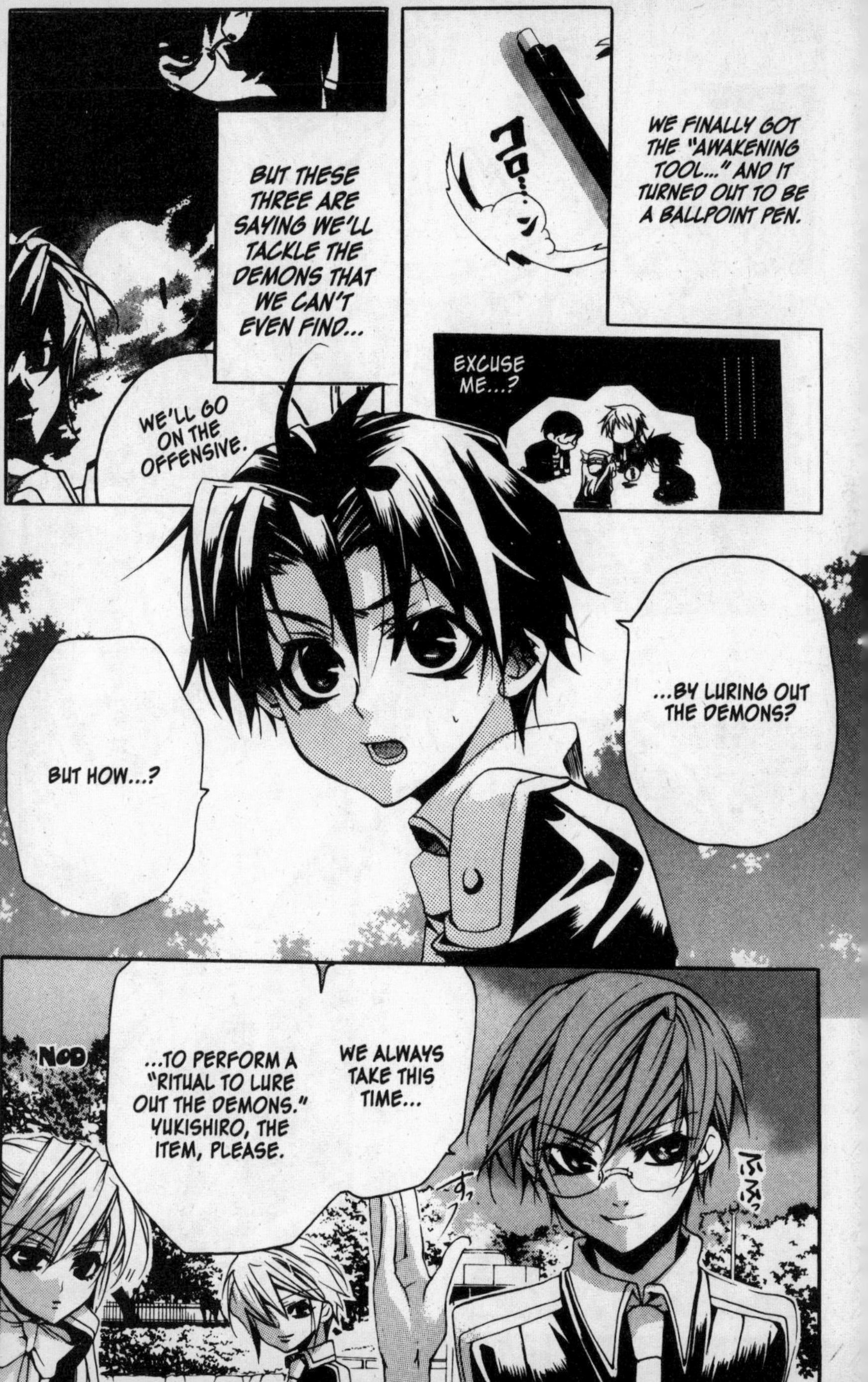
WE FINALLY GOT THE "AWAKENING TOOL..." AND IT TURNED OUT TO BE A BALLPOINT PEN.
EXCUSE ME...?
BUT THESE THREE ARE SAYING WE'LL TACKLE THE DEMONS THAT WE CAN'T EVEN FIND...
WE'LL GO ON THE OFFENSIVE.
...BY LURING OUT THE DEMONS?
BUT HOW...?
WE ALWAYS TAKE THIS TIME...
...TO PERFORM A "RITUAL TO LURE OUT THE DEMONS." YUKISHIRO, THE ITEM, PLEASE.
NOD
ふふっ

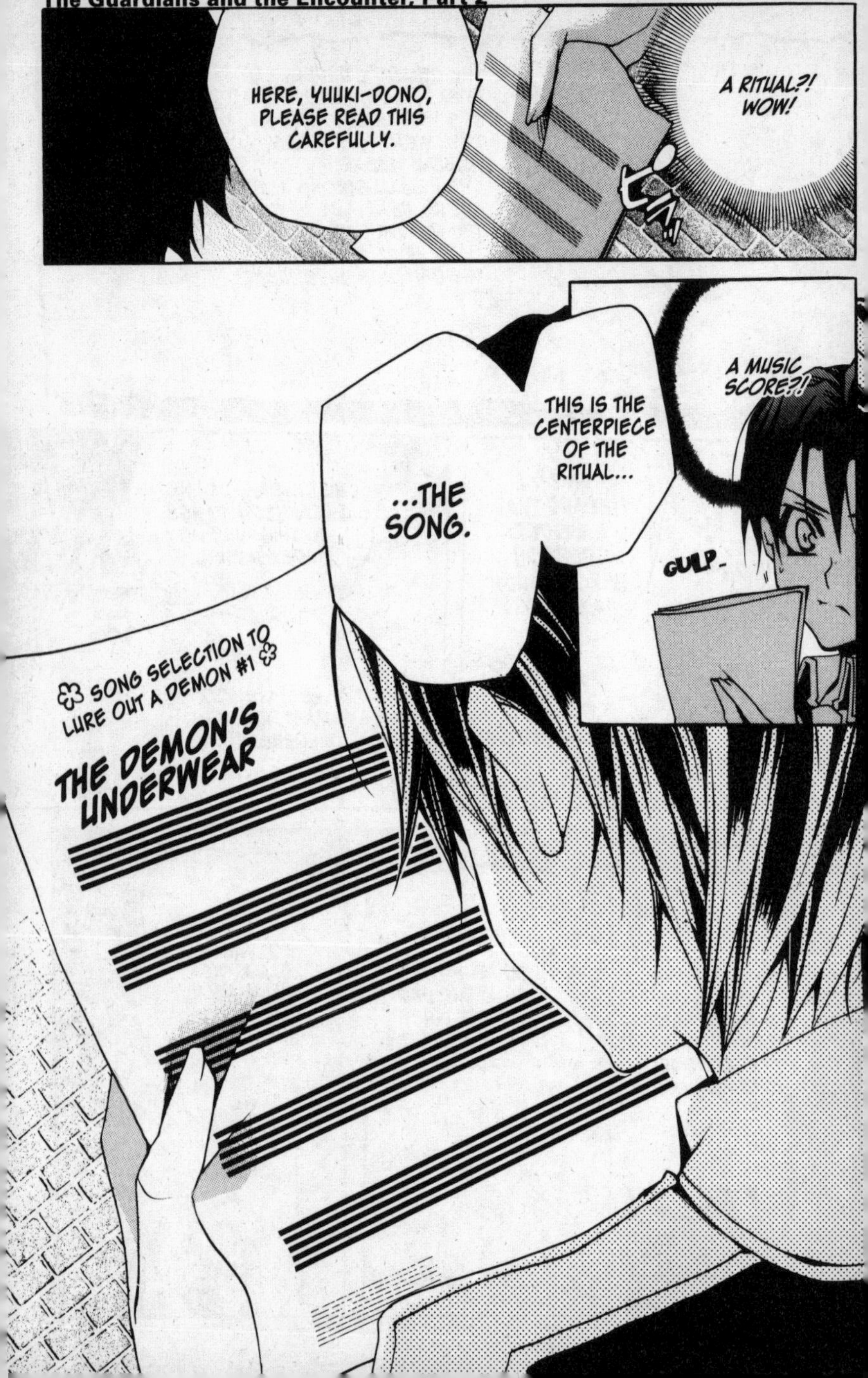
A RITUAL?! WOW!
HERE, YUUKI-DONO, PLEASE READ THIS CAREFULLY.
A MUSIC SCORE?!
GULP
THIS IS THE CENTERPIECE OF THE RITUAL...
...THE SONG.
SONG SELECTION TO LURE OUT A DEMON #1
THE DEMON'S UNDERWEAR

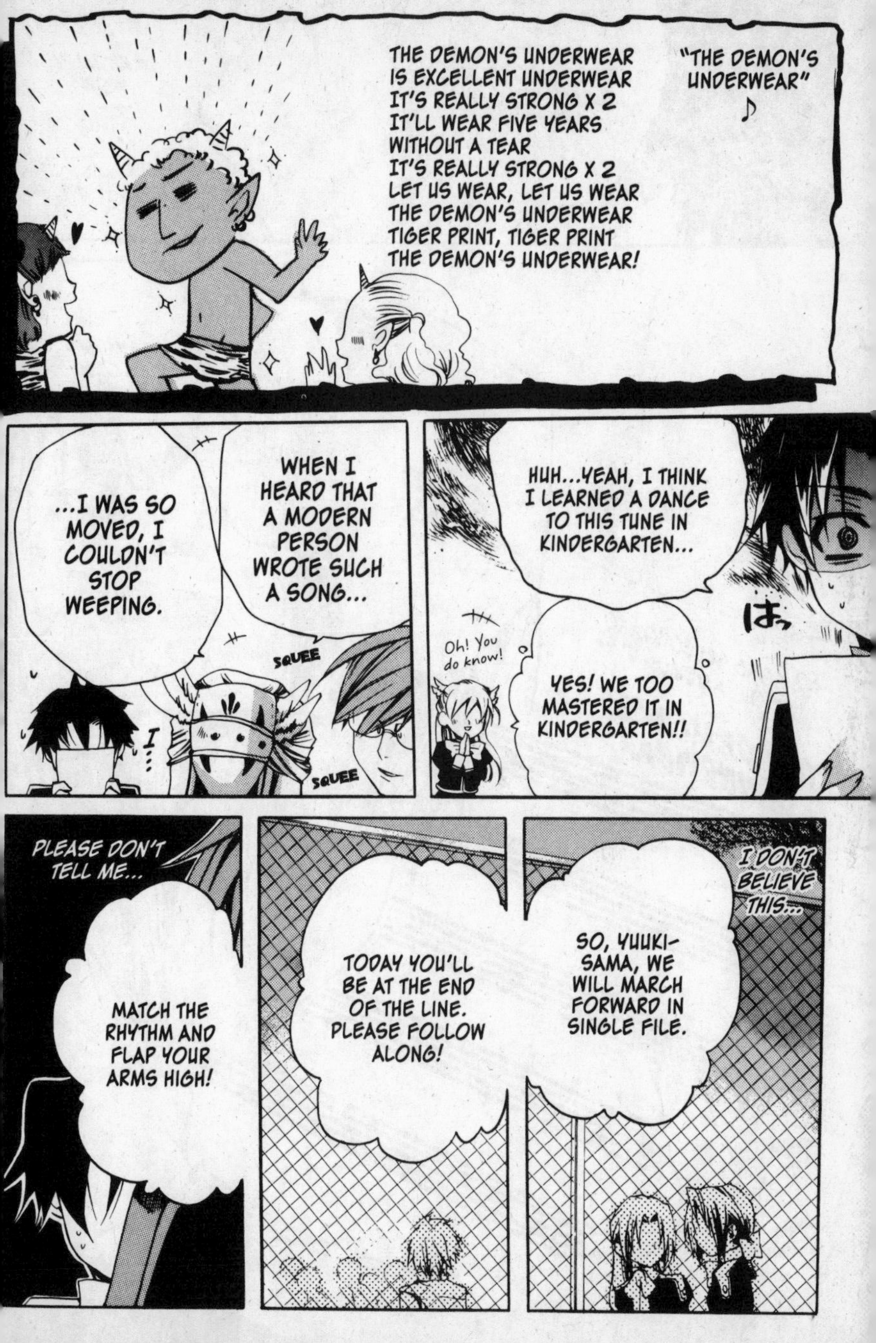
"THE DEMON'S UNDERWEAR" ♪
THE DEMON'S UNDERWEAR
IS EXCELLENT UNDERWEAR
IT'S REALLY STRONG X 2
IT'LL WEAR FIVE YEARS
WITHOUT A TEAR
IT'S REALLY STRONG X 2
LET US WEAR, LET US WEAR
THE DEMON'S UNDERWEAR
TIGER PRINT, TIGER PRINT
THE DEMON'S UNDERWEAR!
HUH...YEAH, I THINK I LEARNED A DANCE TO THIS TUNE IN KINDERGARTEN...
はっ
Oh! You do know!
YES! WE TOO MASTERED IT IN KINDERGARTEN!!
WHEN I HEARD THAT A MODERN PERSON WROTE SUCH A SONG...
...I WAS SO MOVED, I COULDN'T STOP WEEPING.
SQUEE
SQUEE
I...
I DON'T BELIEVE THIS...
SO, YUUKI-SAMA, WE WILL MARCH FORWARD IN SINGLE FILE.
TODAY YOU'LL BE AT THE END OF THE LINE. PLEASE FOLLOW ALONG!
PLEASE DON'T TELL ME...
MATCH THE RHYTHM AND FLAP YOUR ARMS HIGH!

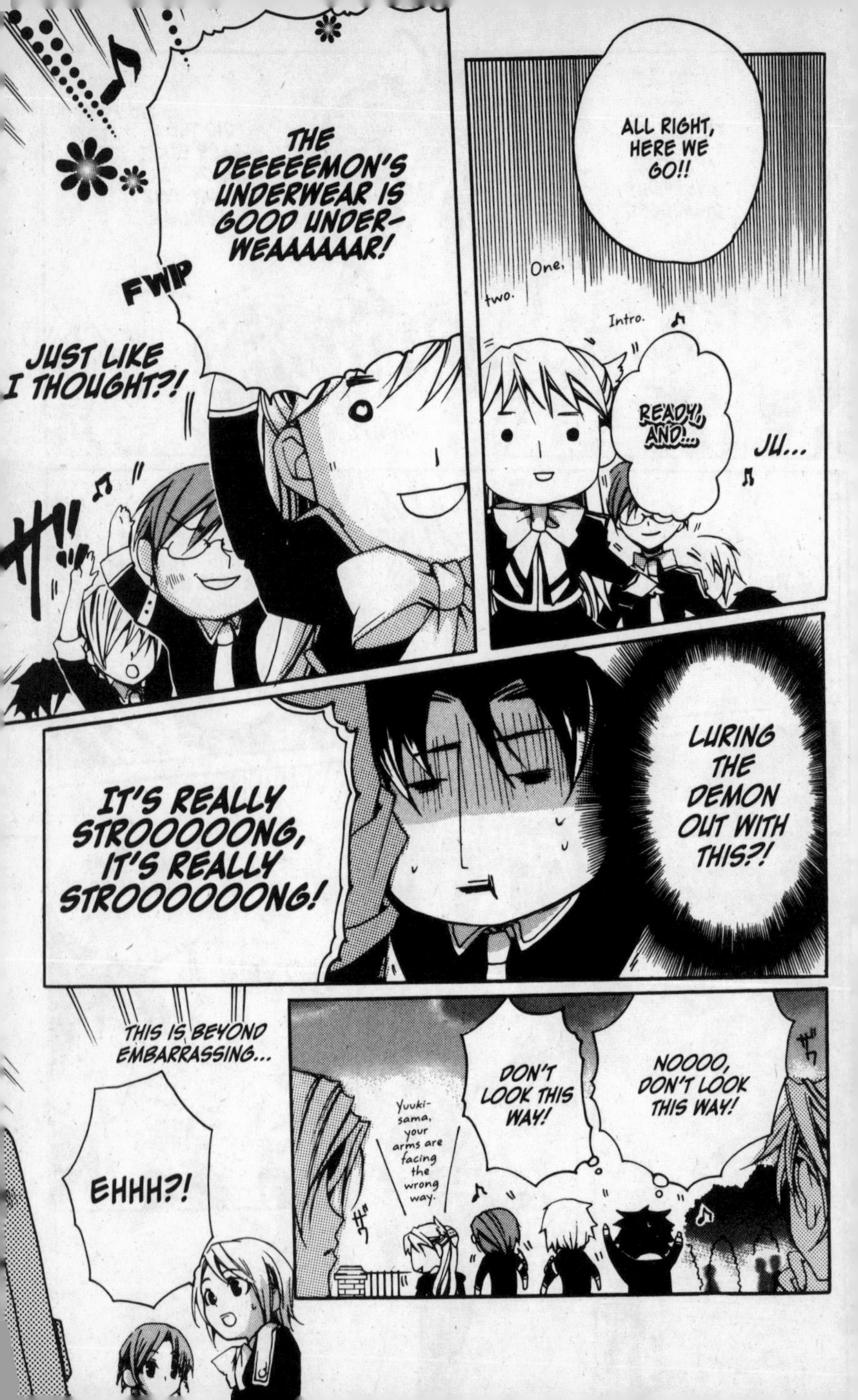
ALL RIGHT, HERE WE GO!!
One.
two.
Intro.
READY, AND...
JU...
THE DEEEEEEMON'S UNDERWEAR IS GOOD UNDER-WEAAAAAAR!
FWP
JUST LIKE I THOUGHT?!
LURING THE DEMON OUT WITH THIS?!
IT'S REALLY STROOOOOONG, IT'S REALLY STROOOOOOONG!
NOOOO, DON'T LOOK THIS WAY!
DON'T LOOK THIS WAY!
Yuuki-sama, your arms are facing the wrong way.
THIS IS BEYOND EMBARRASSING...
EHHH?!

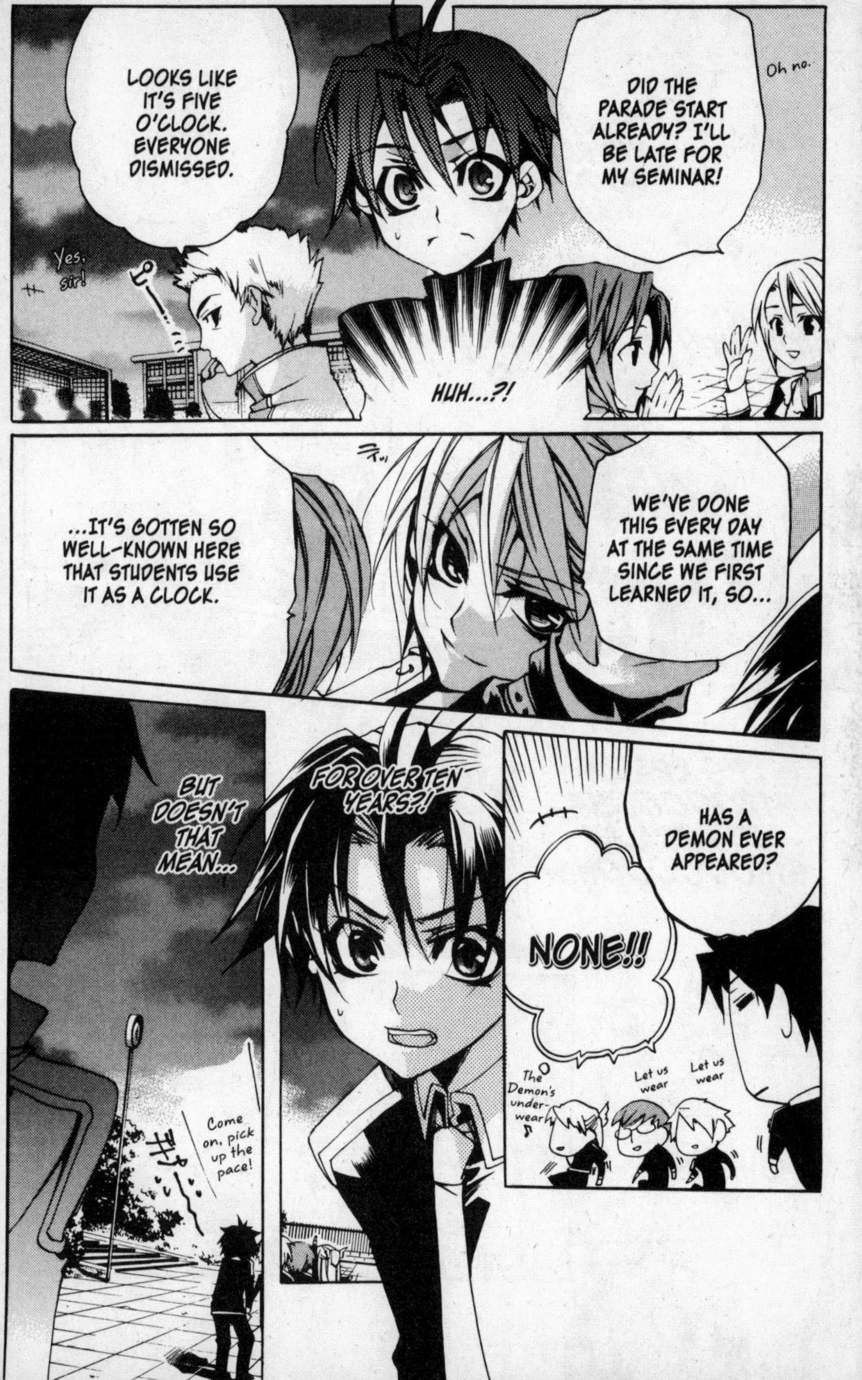
Oh no.
DID THE PARADE START ALREADY? I'LL BE LATE FOR MY SEMINAR!
HUH...?!
LOOKS LIKE IT'S FIVE O'CLOCK. EVERYONE DISMISSED.
Yes, sir!
WE'VE DONE THIS EVERY DAY AT THE SAME TIME SINCE WE FIRST LEARNED IT, SO...
...IT'S GOTTEN SO WELL-KNOWN HERE THAT STUDENTS USE IT AS A CLOCK.
HAS A DEMON EVER APPEARED?
NONE!!
Let us wear
Let us wear
The Demon's under-wear
FOR OVER TEN YEARS?!
BUT DOESN'T THAT MEAN...
Come on, pick up the pace!

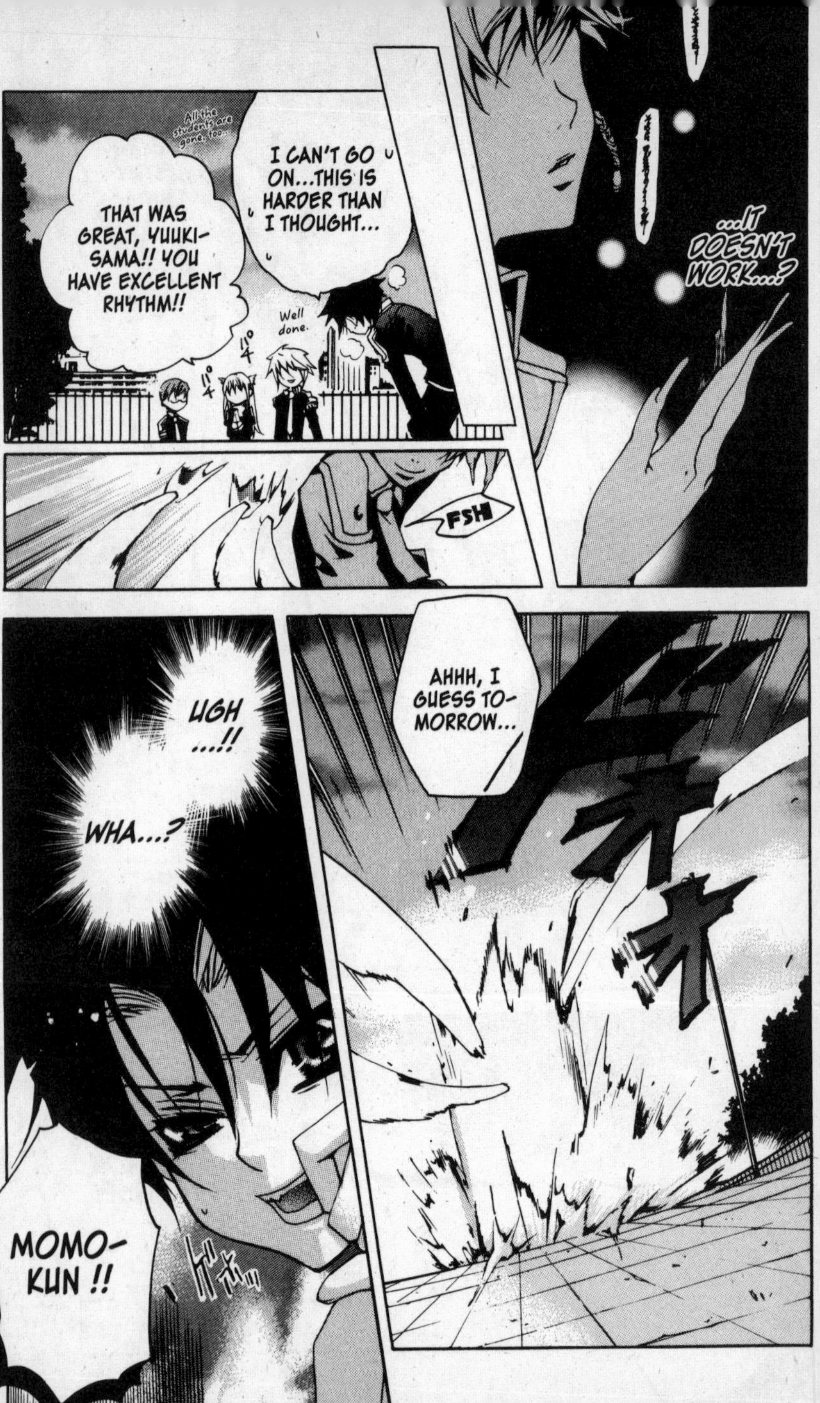
...IT DOESN'T WORK...?
All the students are gone, too...
I CAN'T GO ON...THIS IS HARDER THAN I THOUGHT...
THAT WAS GREAT, YUUKI-SAMA!! YOU HAVE EXCELLENT RHYTHM!!
Well done.
FSH
AHHH, I GUESS TO-MORROW...
UGH...!!
WHA...?
MOMO-KUN !!

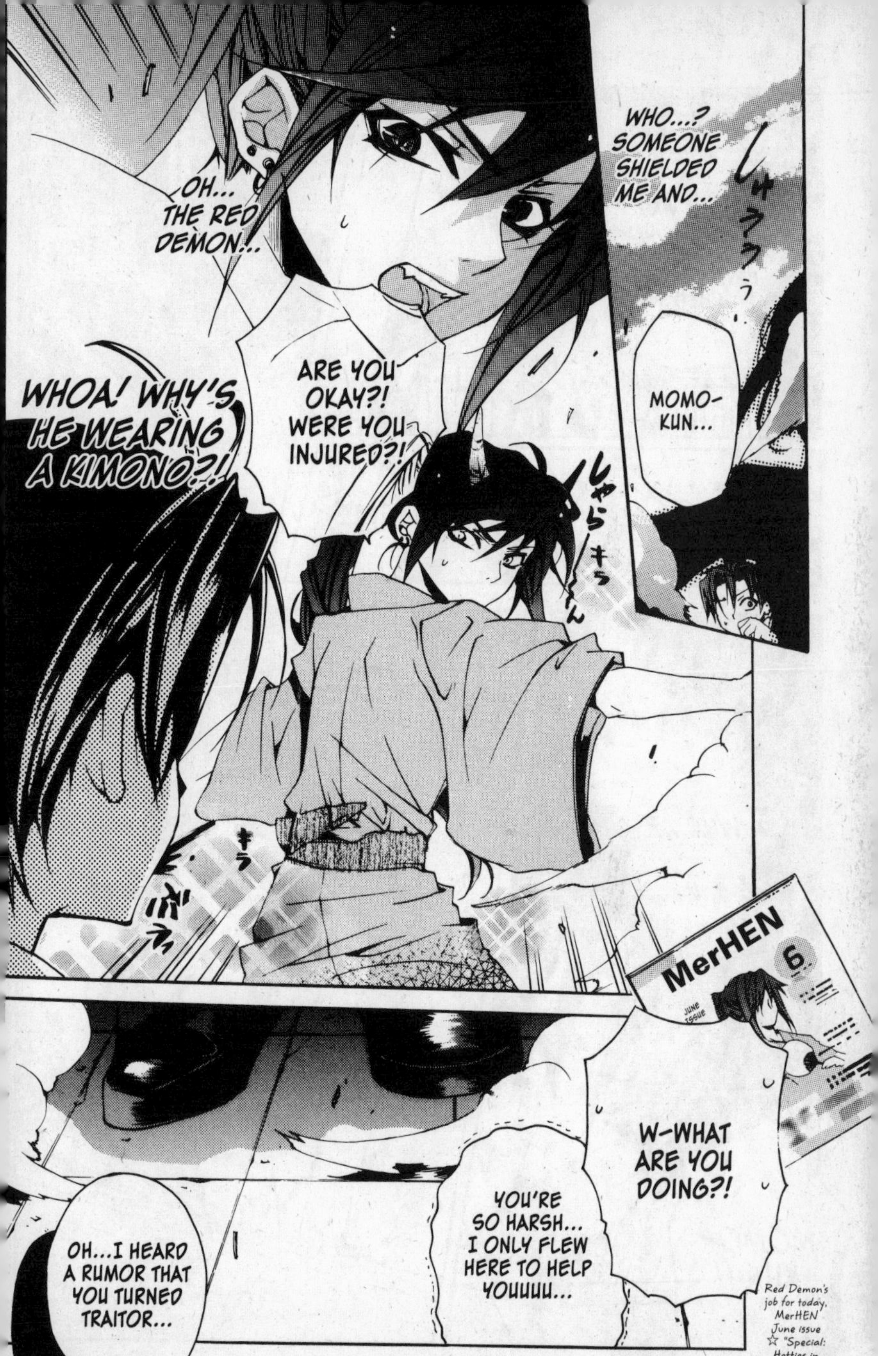
WHO...? SOMEONE SHIELDED ME AND...
MOMO-KUN...
OH... THE RED DEMON...
ARE YOU OKAY?! WERE YOU INJURED?!
WHOA! WHY'S HE WEARING A KIMONO?!
MerHEN
6
JUNE ISSUE
W-WHAT ARE YOU DOING?!
YOU'RE SO HARSH... I ONLY FLEW HERE TO HELP YOUUUU...
OH...I HEARD A RUMOR THAT YOU TURNED TRAITOR...

Red Demon's job for today, MerHEN June issue ☆ "Special: Hotties in Yukata"

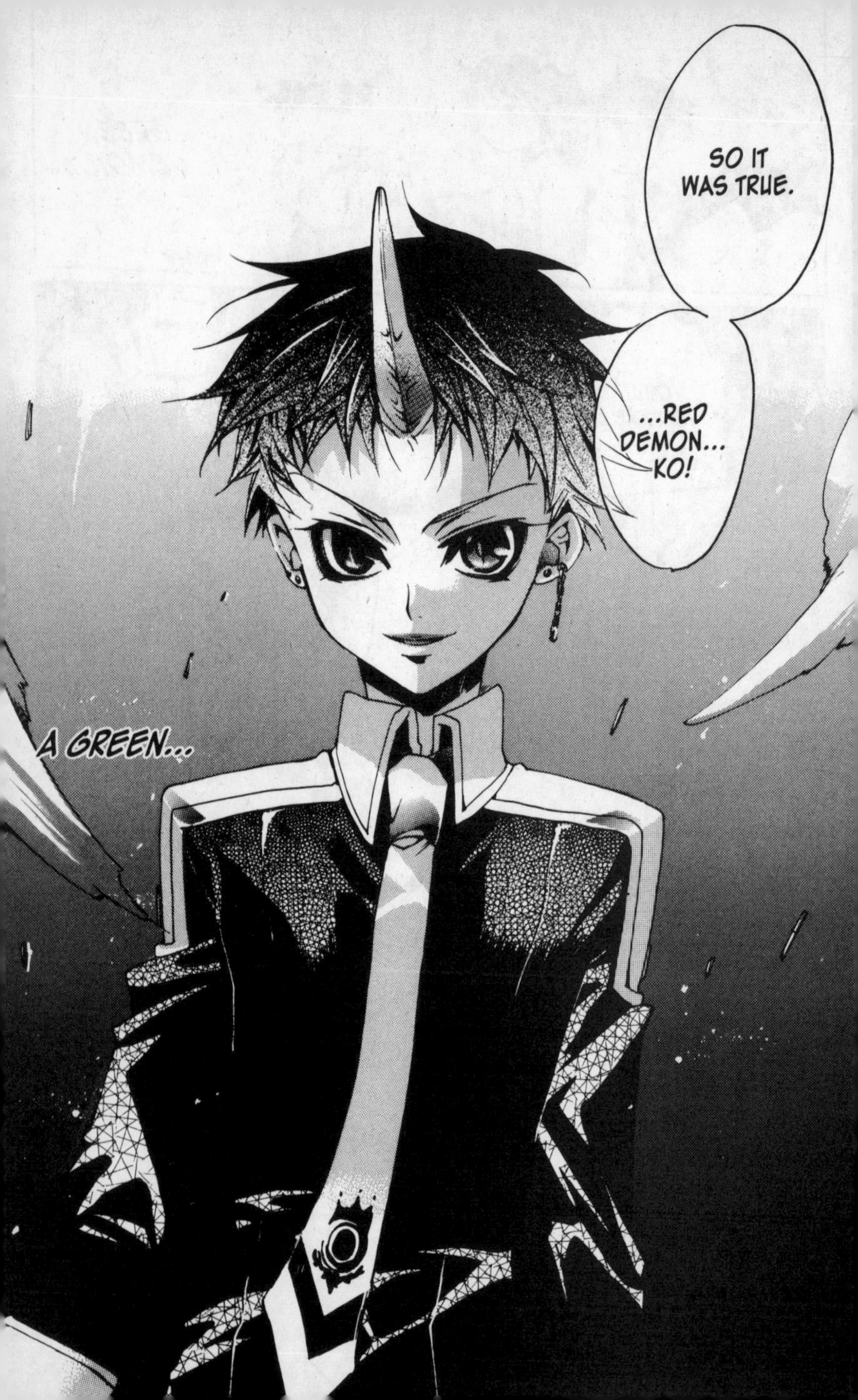
SO IT WAS TRUE.
...RED DEMON... KO!
A GREEN...

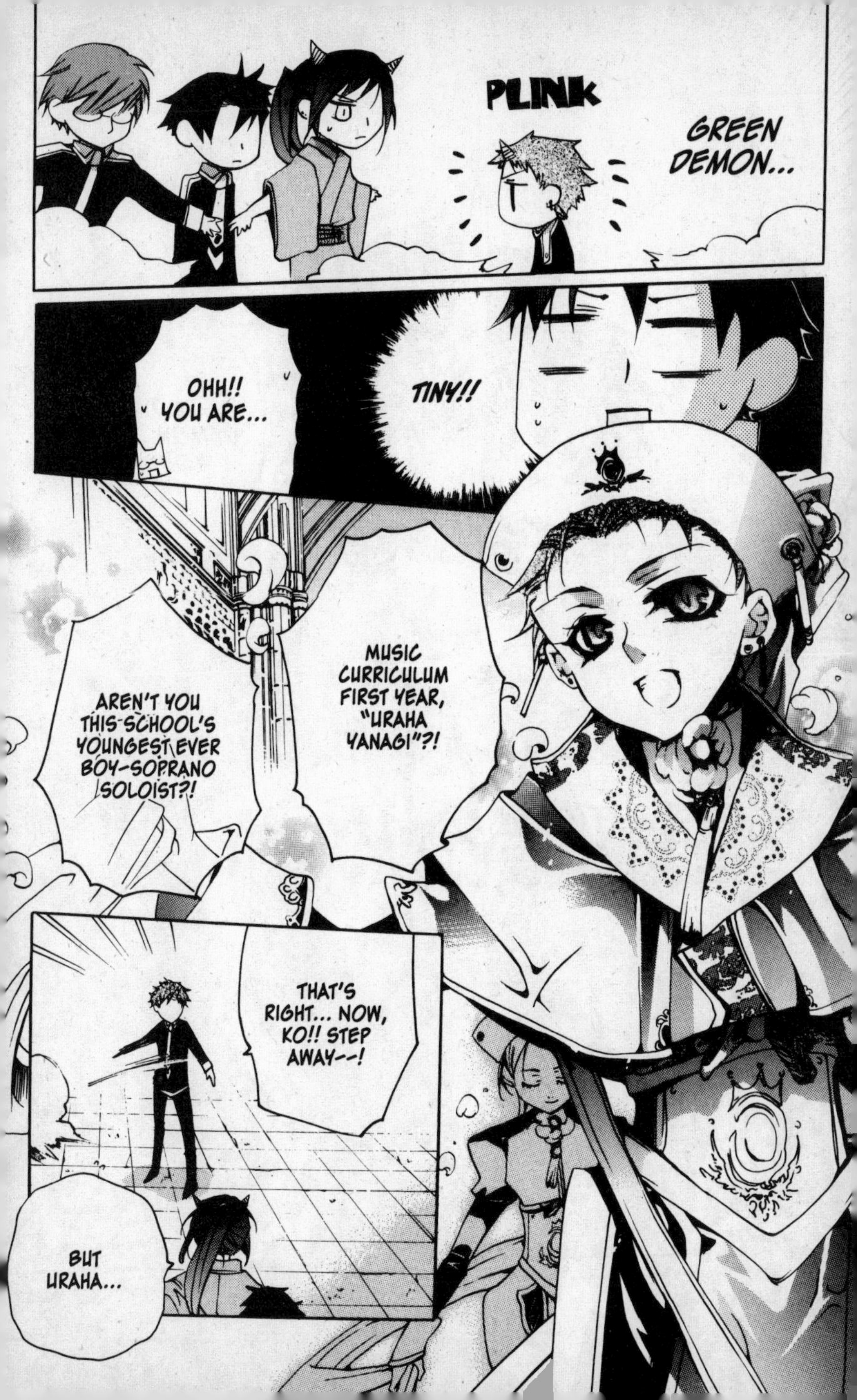
PLINK
GREEN DEMON...
TINY!!
OHH!! YOU ARE...
MUSIC CURRICULUM FIRST YEAR, "URAHA YANAGI"?!
AREN'T YOU THIS SCHOOL'S YOUNGEST EVER BOY-SOPRANO SOLOIST?!
THAT'S RIGHT... NOW, KO!! STEP AWAY--!
BUT URAHA...

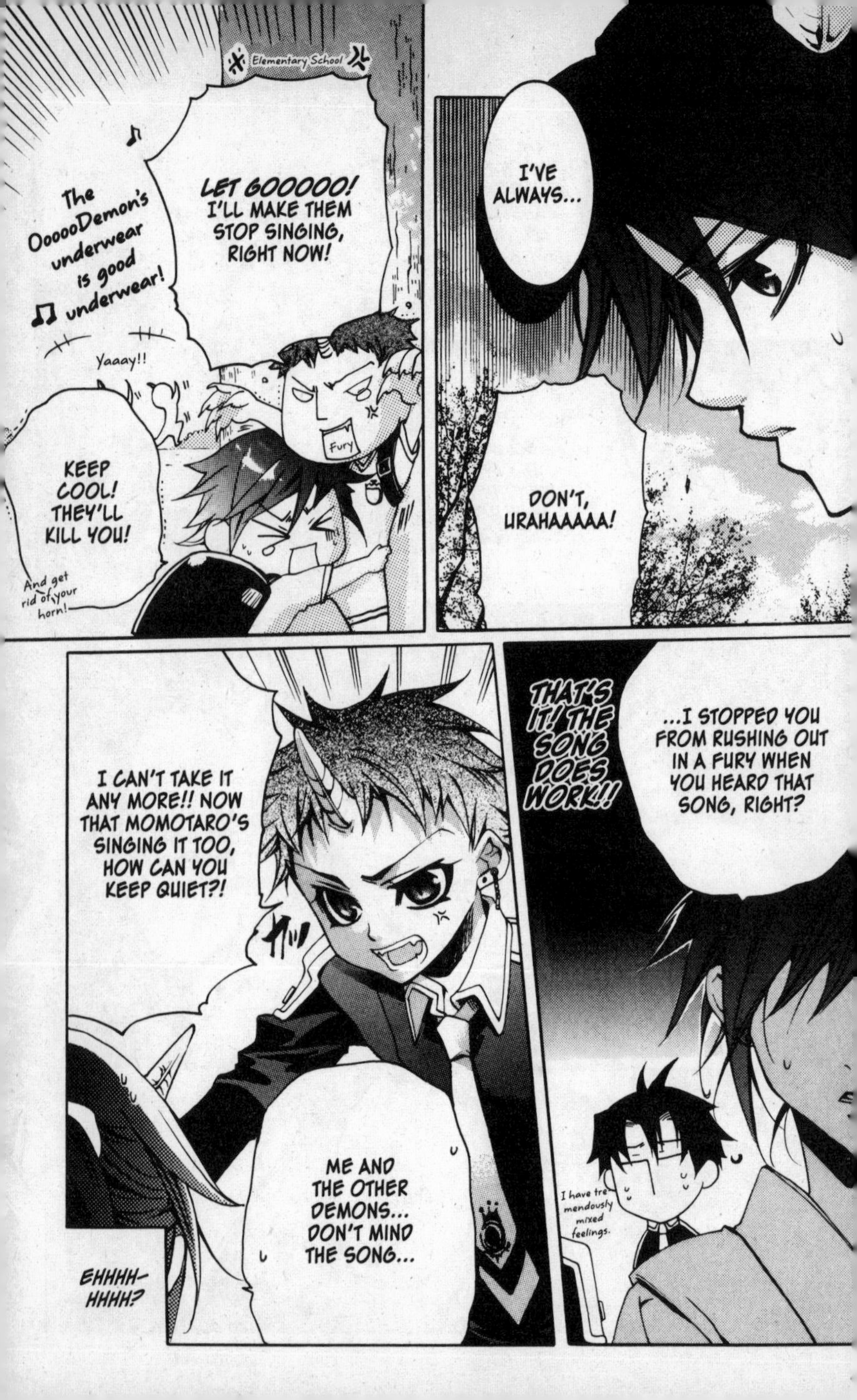
I'VE ALWAYS...
DON'T, URAHAAAAA!
Elementary School
The OooooDemon's underwear is good underwear! ♫
LET GOOOOO! I'LL MAKE THEM STOP SINGING, RIGHT NOW!
Fury
Yaaay!!
KEEP COOL! THEY'LL KILL YOU!
And get rid of your horn!
...I STOPPED YOU FROM RUSHING OUT IN A FURY WHEN YOU HEARD THAT SONG, RIGHT?
THAT'S IT! THE SONG DOES WORK!!
I have tremendously mixed feelings.
I CAN'T TAKE IT ANY MORE!! NOW THAT MOMOTARO'S SINGING IT TOO, HOW CAN YOU KEEP QUIET?!
ME AND THE OTHER DEMONS... DON'T MIND THE SONG...
EHHHH-HHHH?

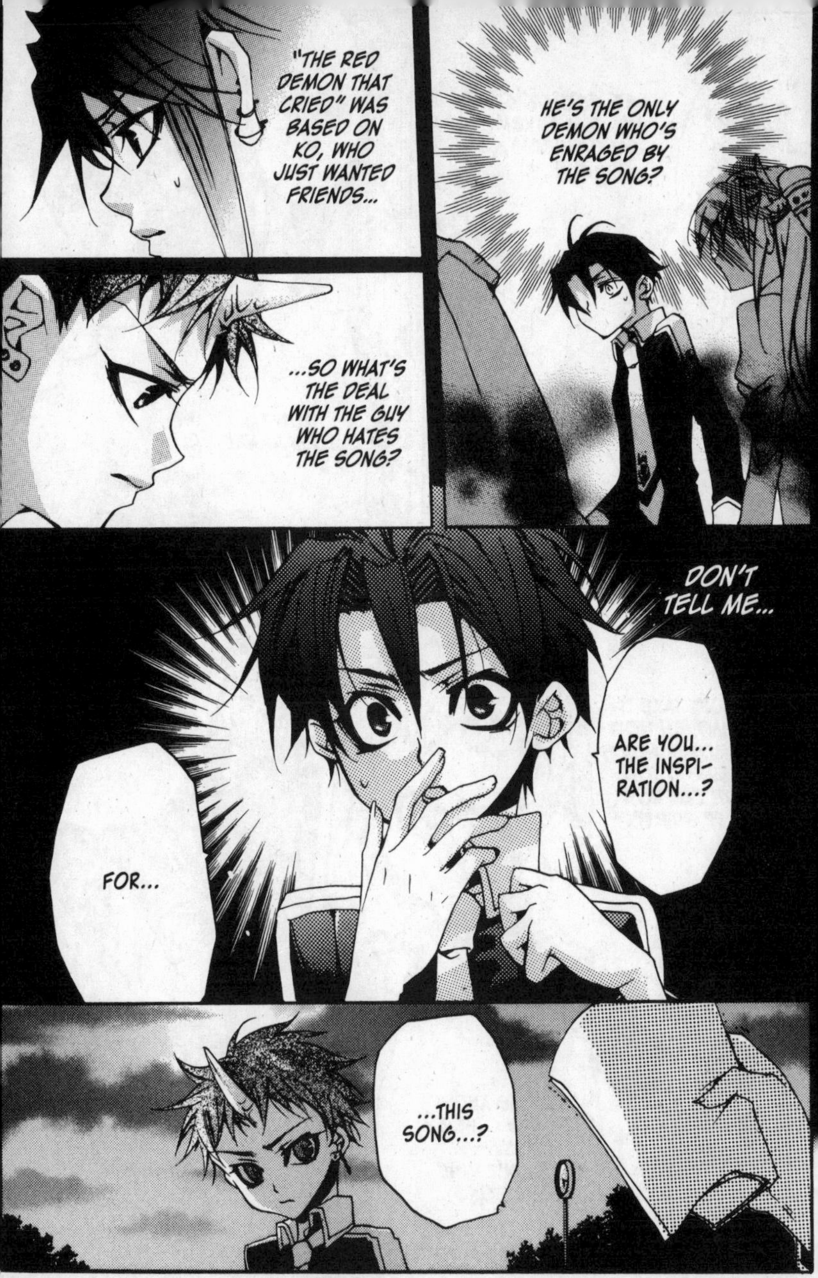
HE'S THE ONLY DEMON WHO'S ENRAGED BY THE SONG?
"THE RED DEMON THAT CRIED" WAS BASED ON KO, WHO JUST WANTED FRIENDS...
...SO WHAT'S THE DEAL WITH THE GUY WHO HATES THE SONG?
DON'T TELL ME...
ARE YOU... THE INSPIRATION...?
FOR...
...THIS SONG...?

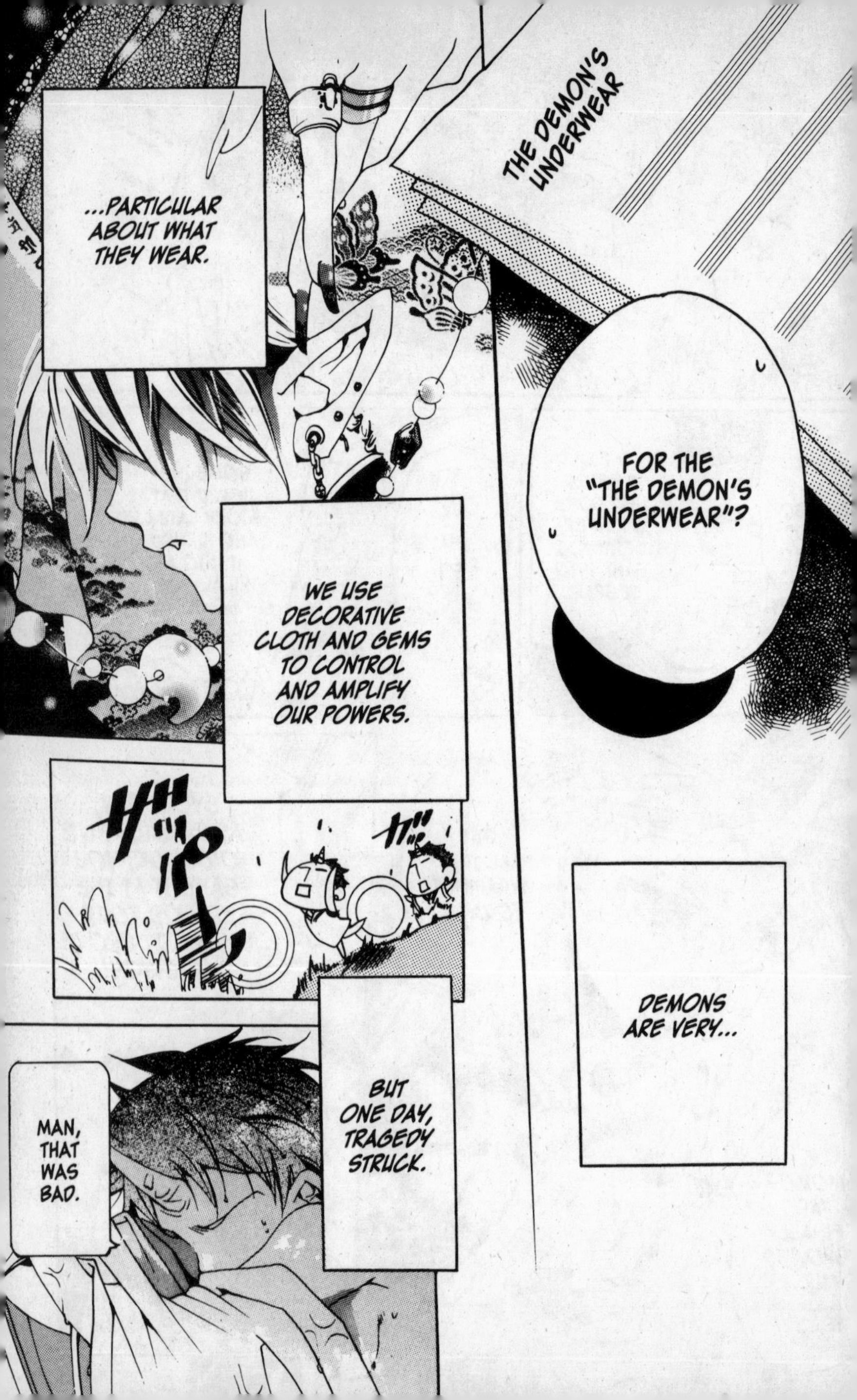
THE DEMON'S UNDERWEAR
FOR THE "THE DEMON'S UNDERWEAR"?
DEMONS ARE VERY...
...PARTICULAR ABOUT WHAT THEY WEAR.
WE USE DECORATIVE CLOTH AND GEMS TO CONTROL AND AMPLIFY OUR POWERS.
BUT ONE DAY, TRAGEDY STRUCK.
MAN, THAT WAS BAD.

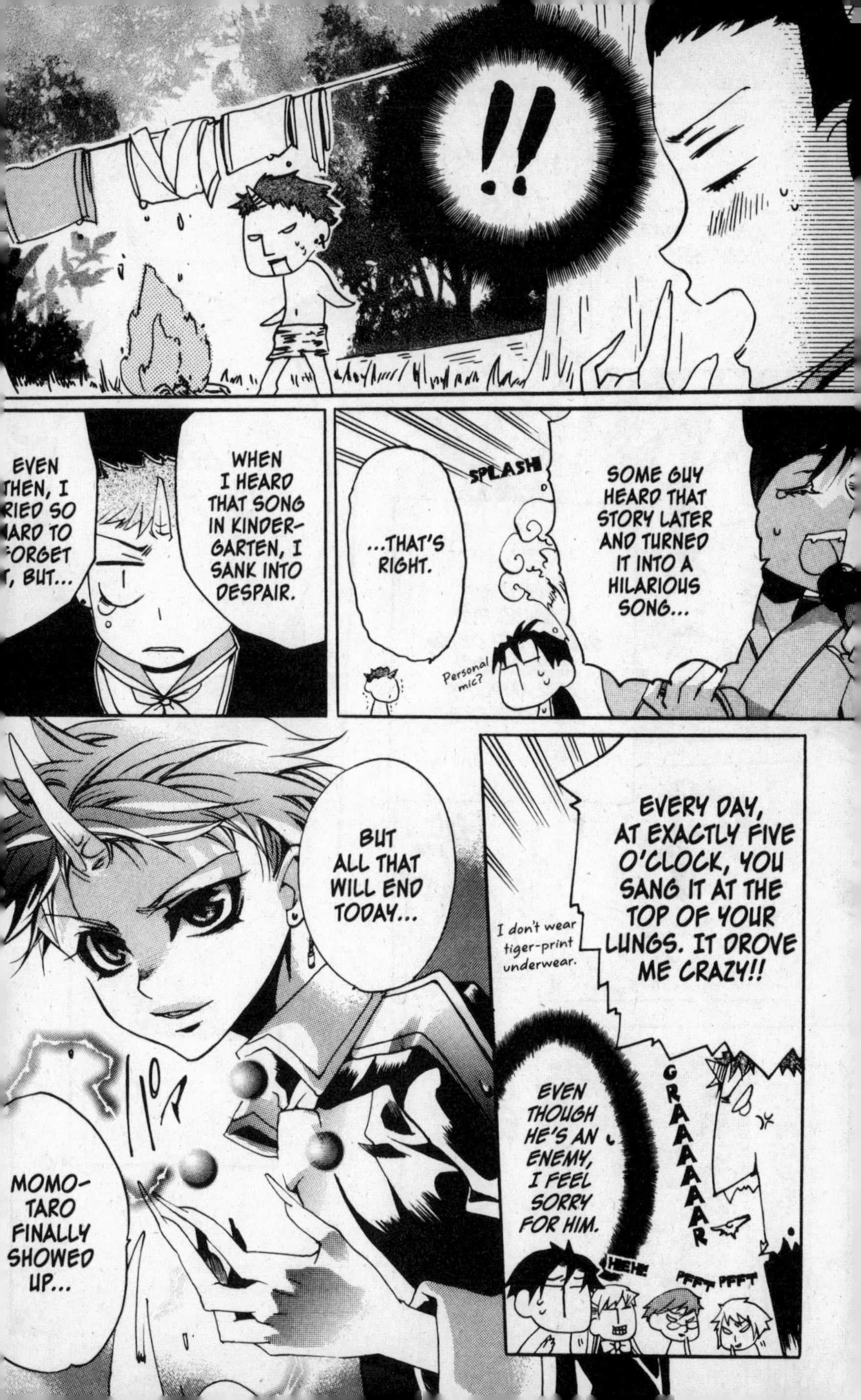
!!
SOME GUY HEARD THAT STORY LATER AND TURNED IT INTO A HILARIOUS SONG...
SPLASH
...THAT'S RIGHT.
Personal mic?
WHEN I HEARD THAT SONG IN KINDERGARTEN, I SANK INTO DESPAIR.
EVEN THEN, I RIED SO ARD TO FORGET , BUT...
EVERY DAY, AT EXACTLY FIVE O'CLOCK, YOU SANG IT AT THE TOP OF YOUR LUNGS. IT DROVE ME CRAZY!!
I don't wear tiger-print underwear.
GRAAAAAAR
EVEN THOUGH HE'S AN ENEMY, I FEEL SORRY FOR HIM.
HEH!
PFFT PFFT
BUT ALL THAT WILL END TODAY...
MOMOTARO FINALLY SHOWED UP...

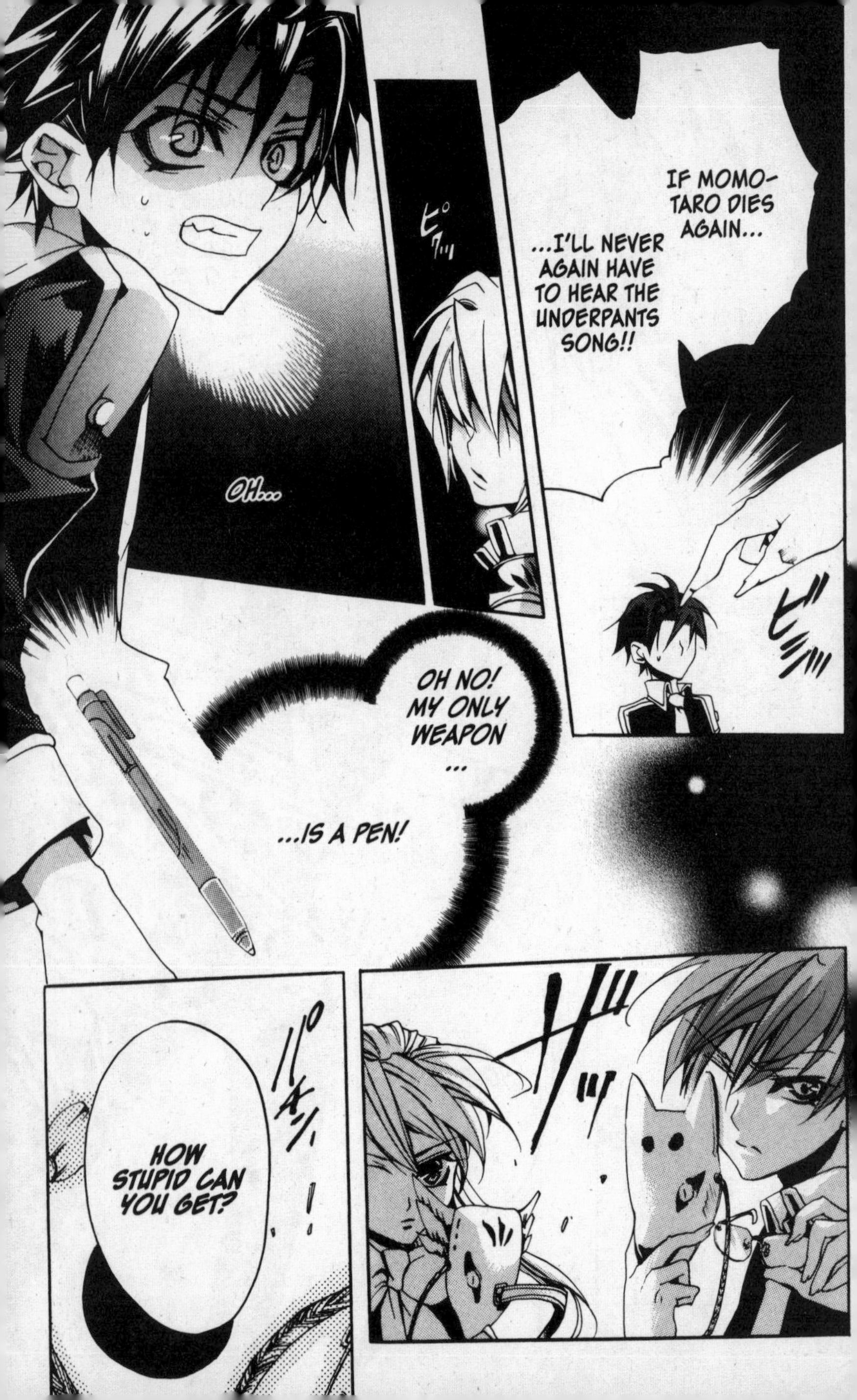
IF MOMO-TARO DIES AGAIN...
...I'LL NEVER AGAIN HAVE TO HEAR THE UNDERPANTS SONG!!
ピクッ
OH...
OH NO! MY ONLY WEAPON ...
...IS A PEN!
HOW STUPID CAN YOU GET?

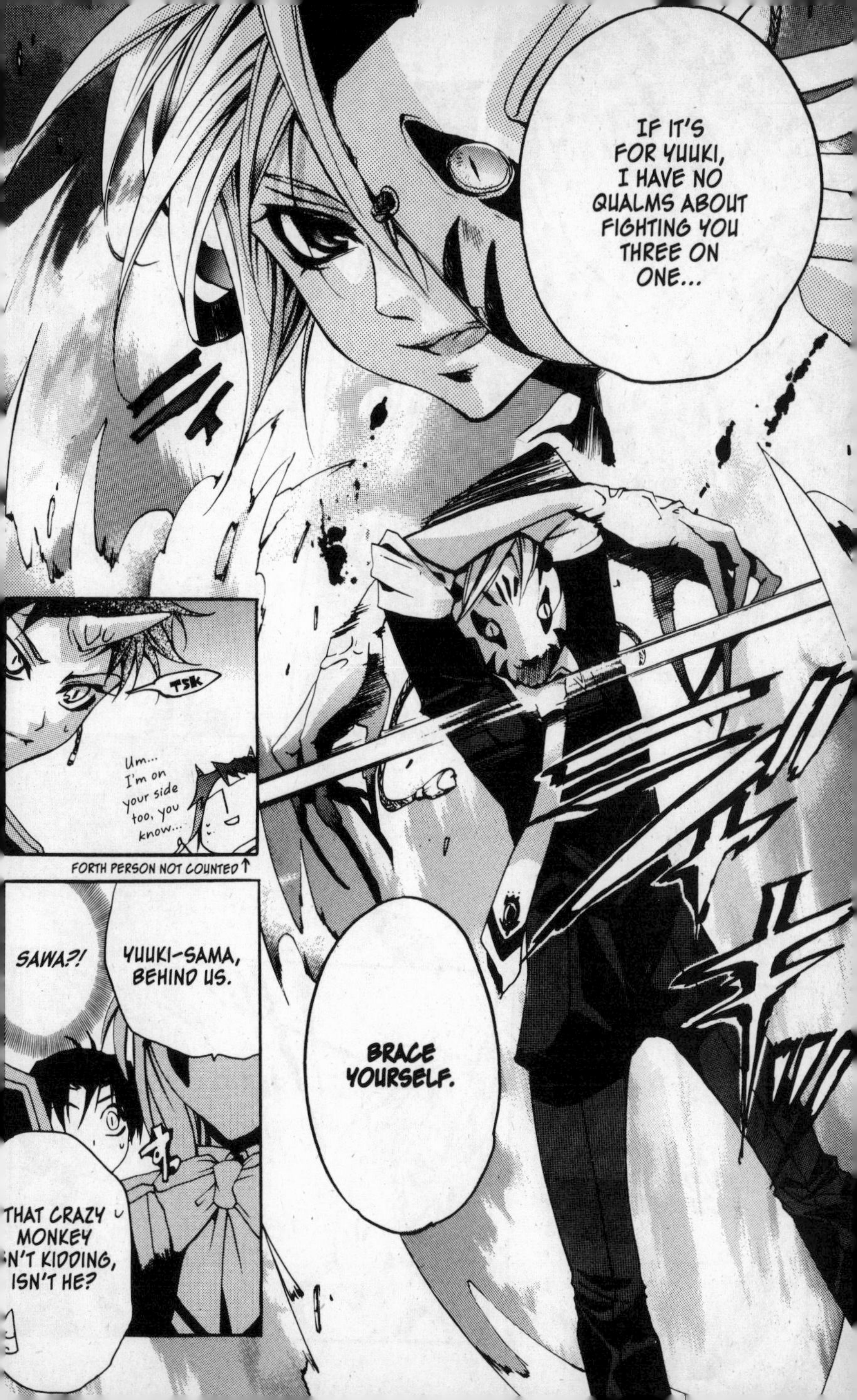
IF IT'S FOR YUUKI, I HAVE NO QUALMS ABOUT FIGHTING YOU THREE ON ONE...
TSK
Um... I'm on your side too, you know...
FORTH PERSON NOT COUNTED ↑
BRACE YOURSELF.
YUUKI-SAMA, BEHIND US.
SAWA?!
THAT CRAZY MONKEY N'T KIDDING, ISN'T HE?

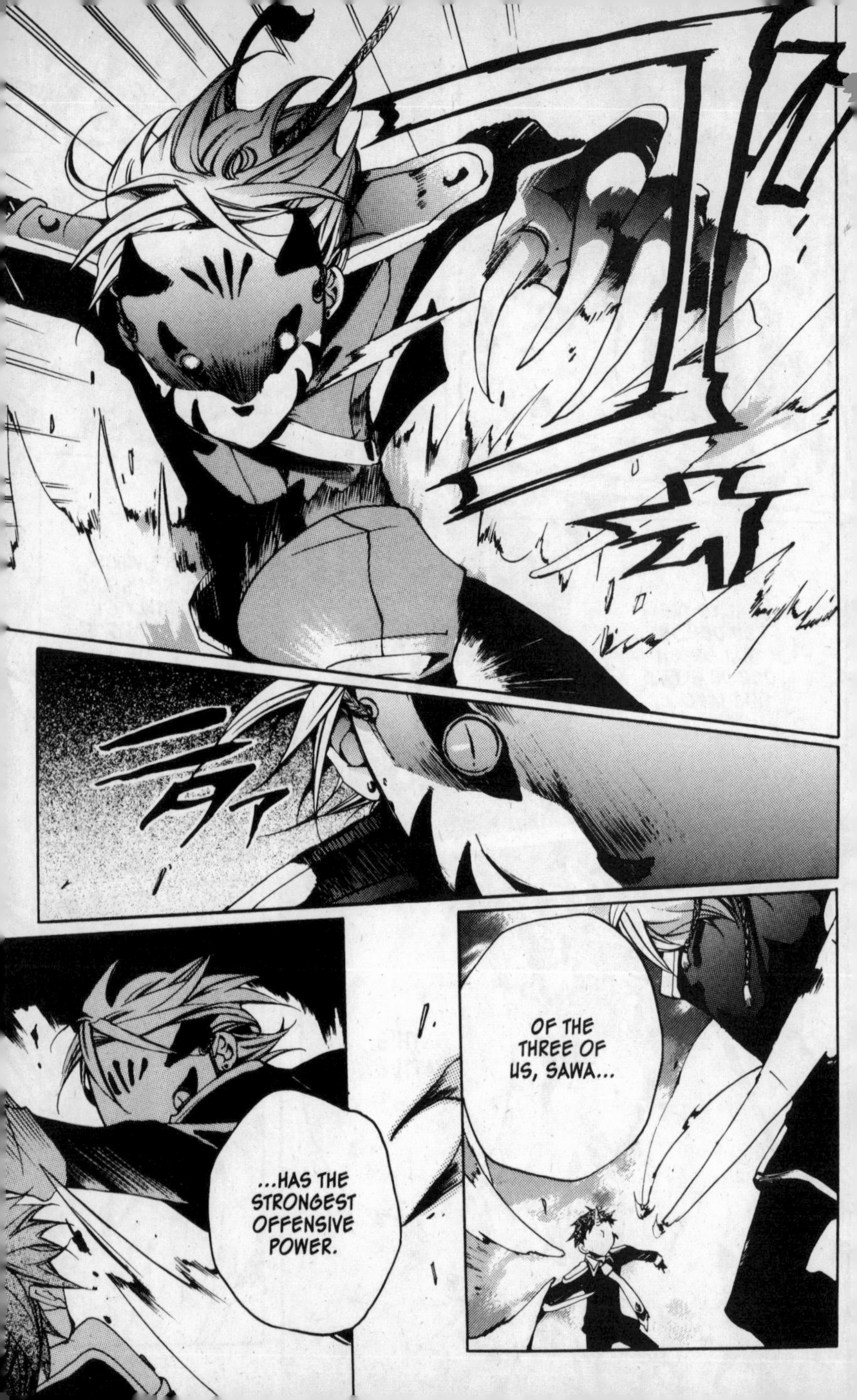
OF THE THREE OF US, SAWA...
...HAS THE STRONGEST OFFENSIVE POWER.

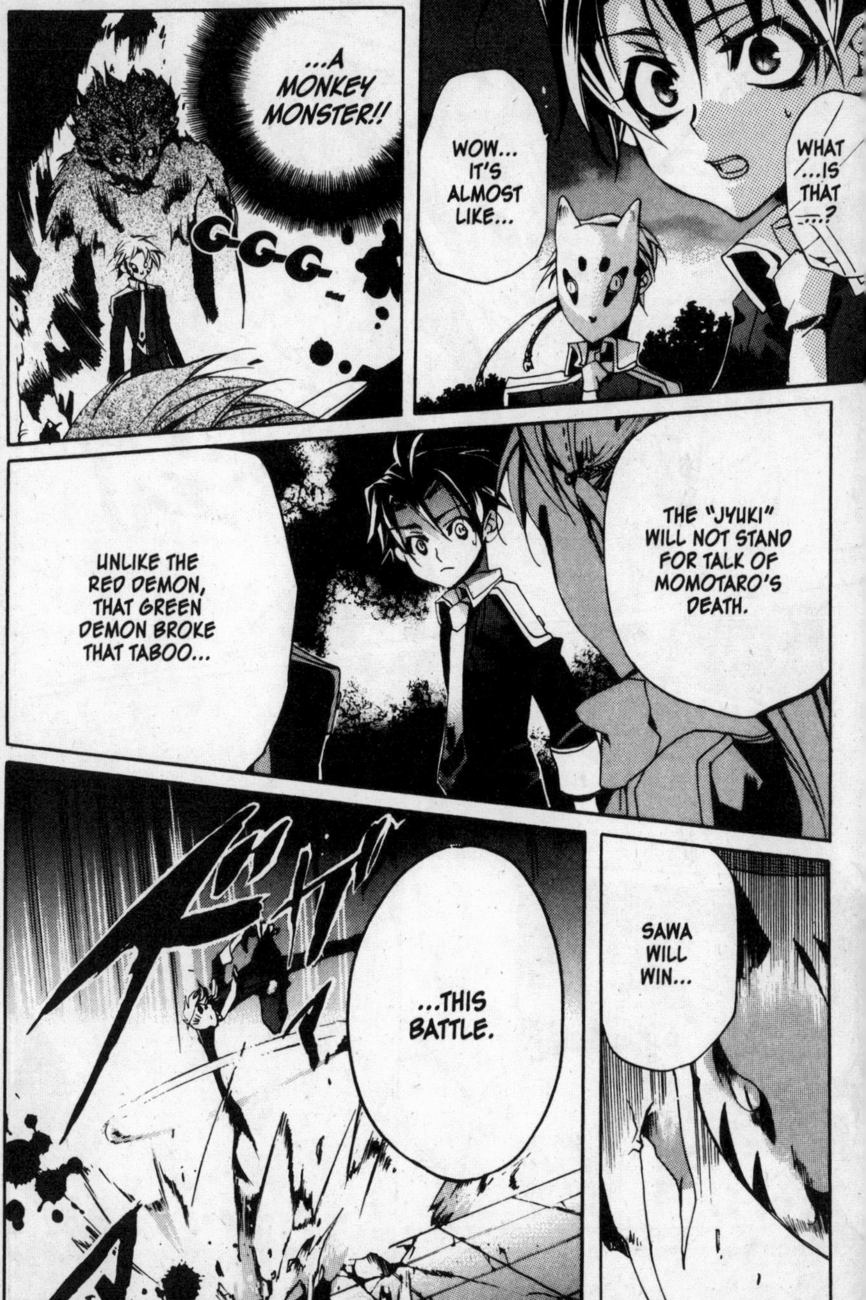
WHAT ...IS THAT ...?
WOW... IT'S ALMOST LIKE...
...A MONKEY MONSTER!!
G-G-G-
THE "JYUKI" WILL NOT STAND FOR TALK OF MOMOTARO'S DEATH.
UNLIKE THE RED DEMON, THAT GREEN DEMON BROKE THAT TABOO...
SAWA WILL WIN...
...THIS BATTLE.

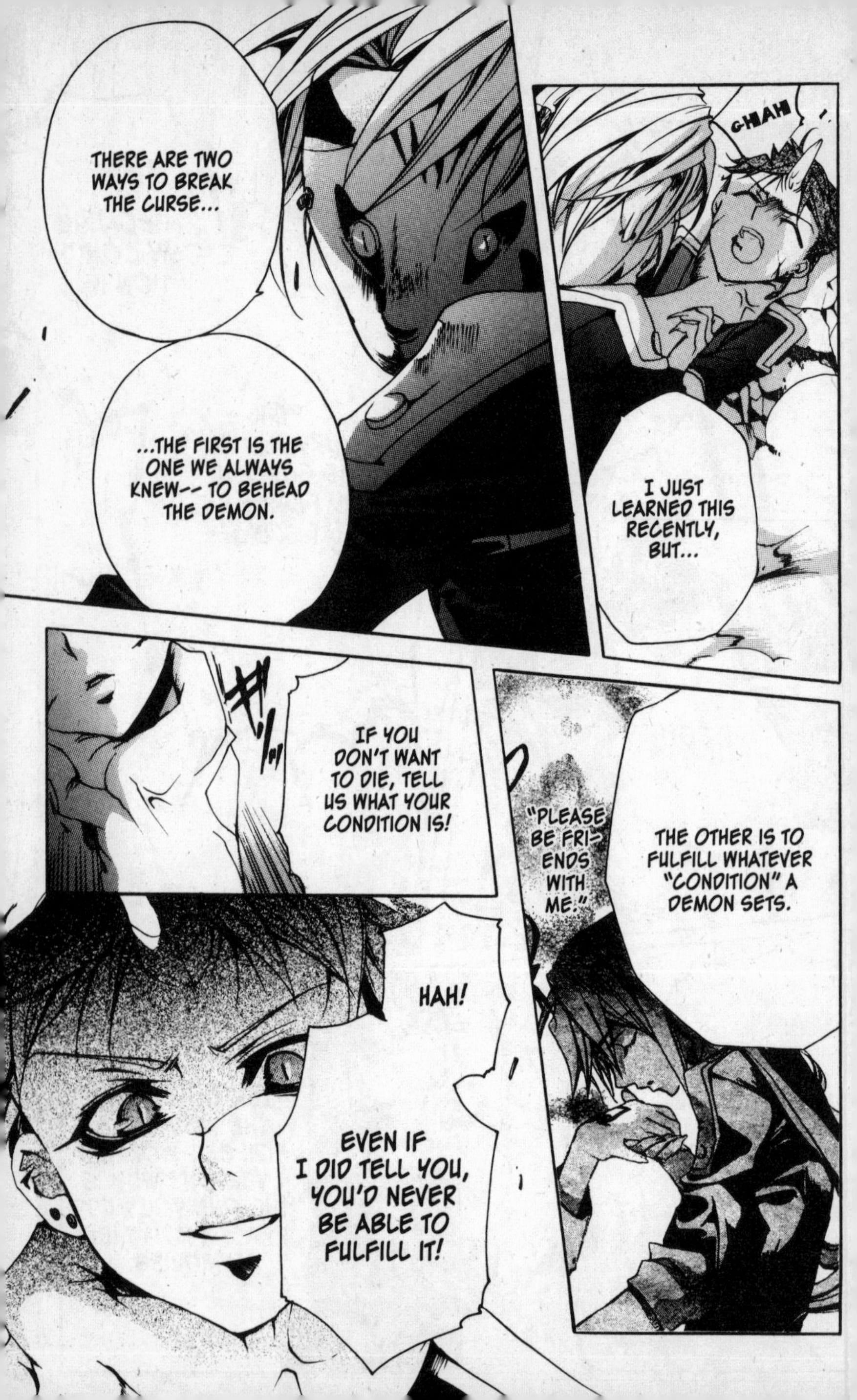
GHAH!
I JUST LEARNED THIS RECENTLY, BUT...
THERE ARE TWO WAYS TO BREAK THE CURSE...
...THE FIRST IS THE ONE WE ALWAYS KNEW-- TO BEHEAD THE DEMON.
THE OTHER IS TO FULFILL WHATEVER "CONDITION" A DEMON SETS.
"PLEASE BE FRI-ENDS WITH ME."
IF YOU DON'T WANT TO DIE, TELL US WHAT YOUR CONDITION IS!
HAH!
EVEN IF I DID TELL YOU, YOU'D NEVER BE ABLE TO FULFILL IT!

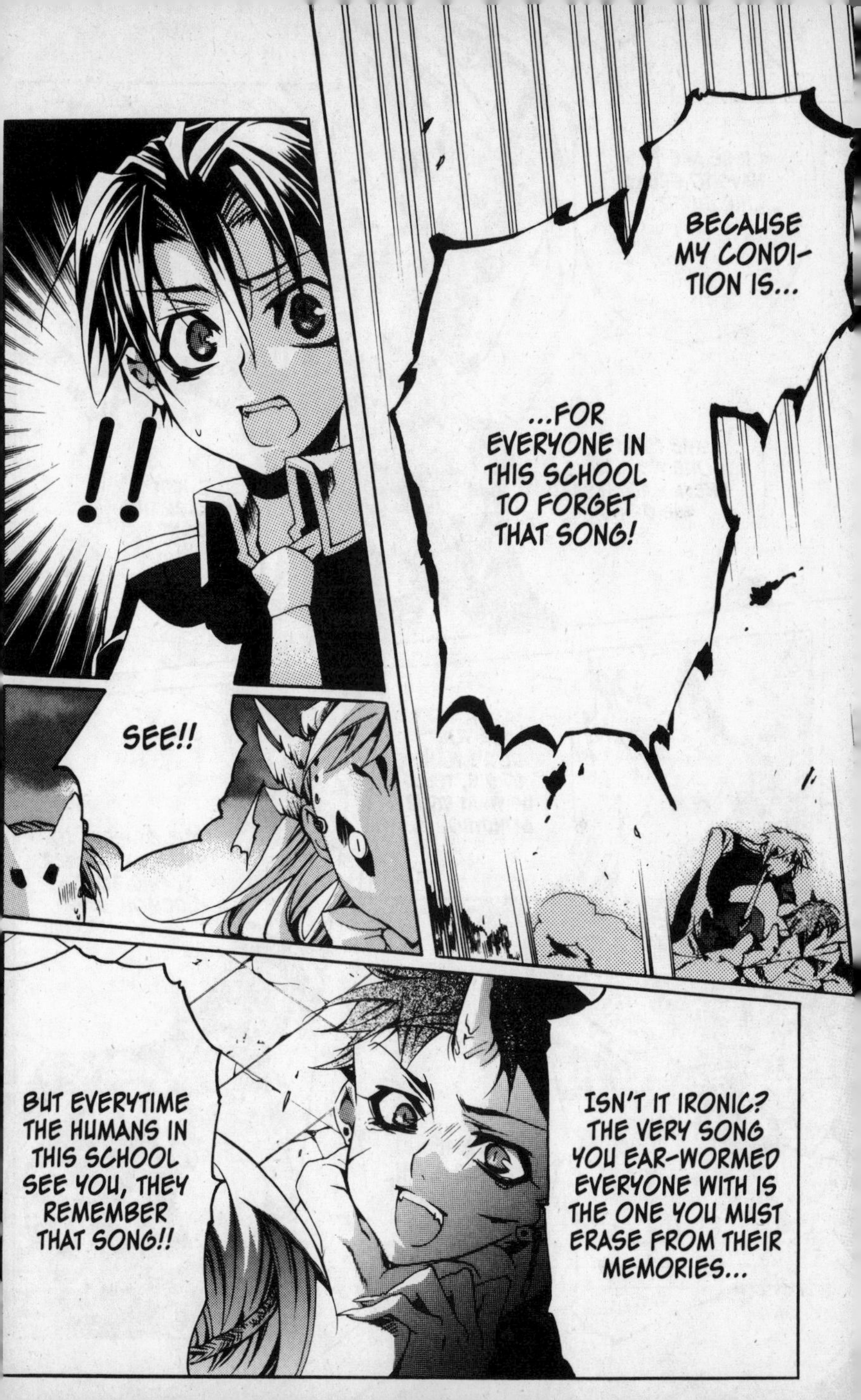
BECAUSE MY CONDI-TION IS...
...FOR EVERYONE IN THIS SCHOOL TO FORGET THAT SONG!
!!
SEE!!
ISN'T IT IRONIC? THE VERY SONG YOU EAR-WORMED EVERYONE WITH IS THE ONE YOU MUST ERASE FROM THEIR MEMORIES...
BUT EVERYTIME THE HUMANS IN THIS SCHOOL SEE YOU, THEY REMEMBER THAT SONG!!

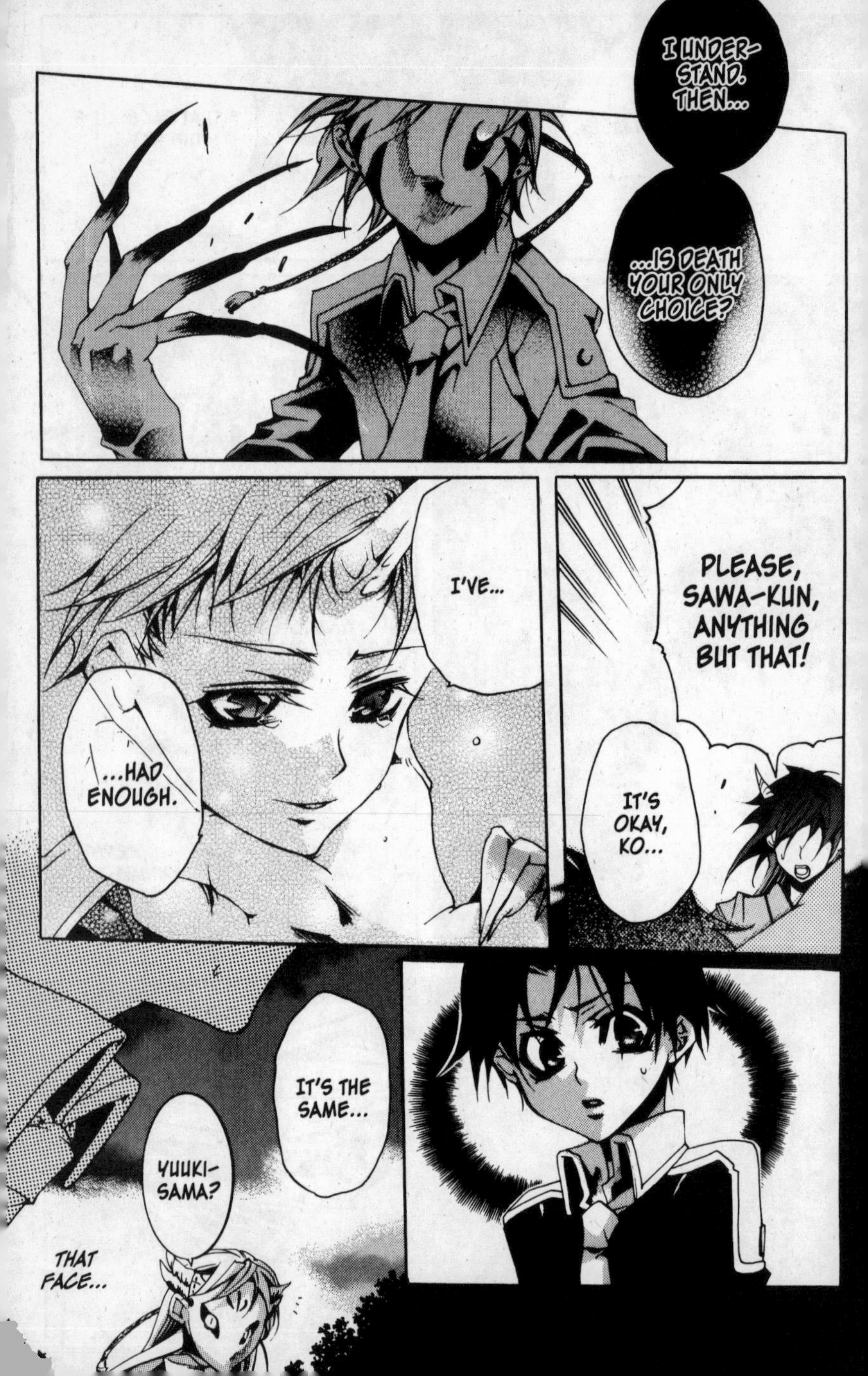
I UNDER-STAND. THEN...
...IS DEATH YOUR ONLY CHOICE?
PLEASE, SAWA-KUN, ANYTHING BUT THAT!
IT'S OKAY, KO...
I'VE...
...HAD ENOUGH.
IT'S THE SAME...
YUUKI-SAMA?
THAT FACE...

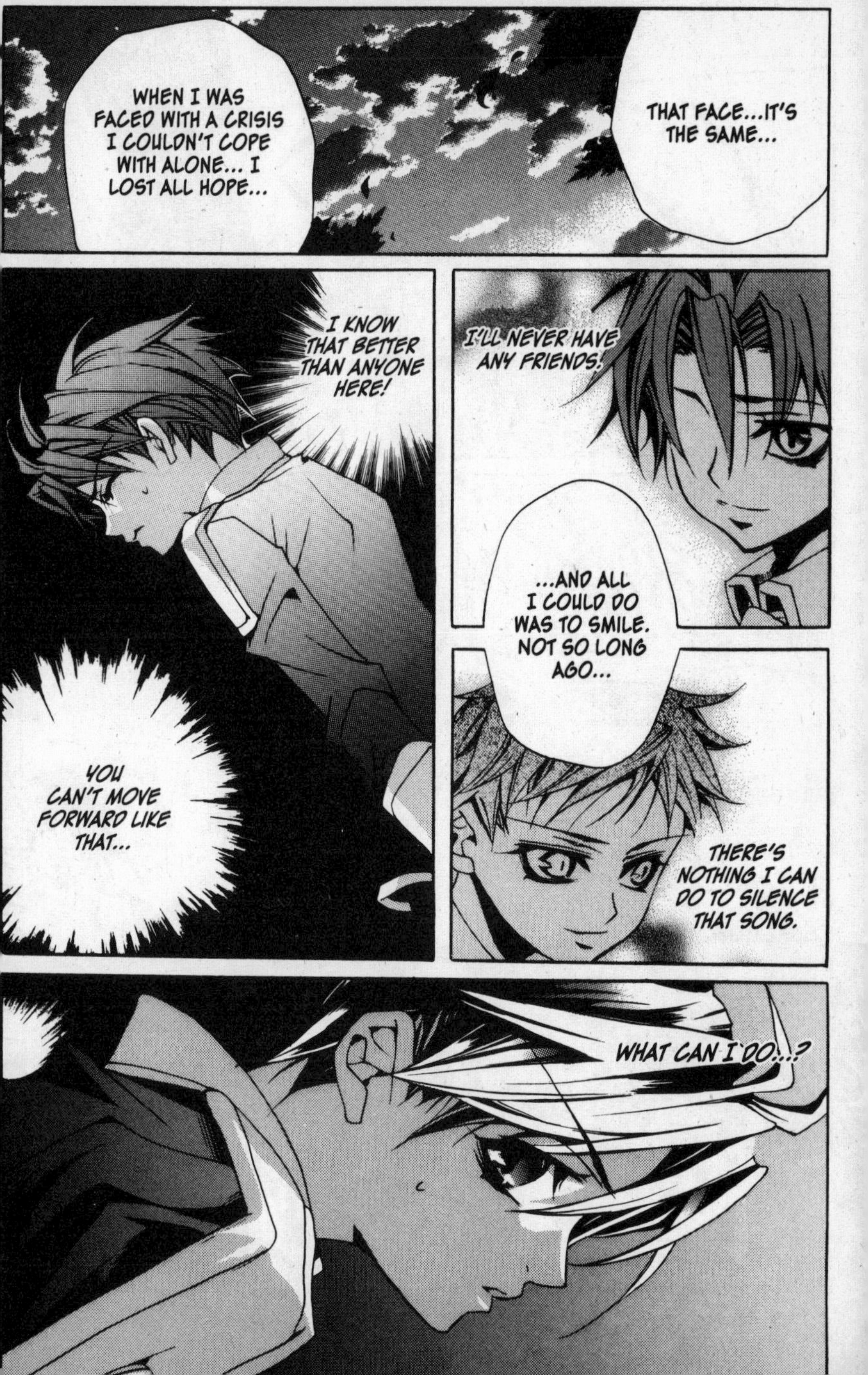
THAT FACE...IT'S THE SAME...
WHEN I WAS FACED WITH A CRISIS I COULDN'T COPE WITH ALONE... I LOST ALL HOPE...
I'LL NEVER HAVE ANY FRIENDS!
...AND ALL I COULD DO WAS TO SMILE. NOT SO LONG AGO...
THERE'S NOTHING I CAN DO TO SILENCE THAT SONG.
I KNOW THAT BETTER THAN ANYONE HERE!
YOU CAN'T MOVE FORWARD LIKE THAT...
WHAT CAN I DO...?

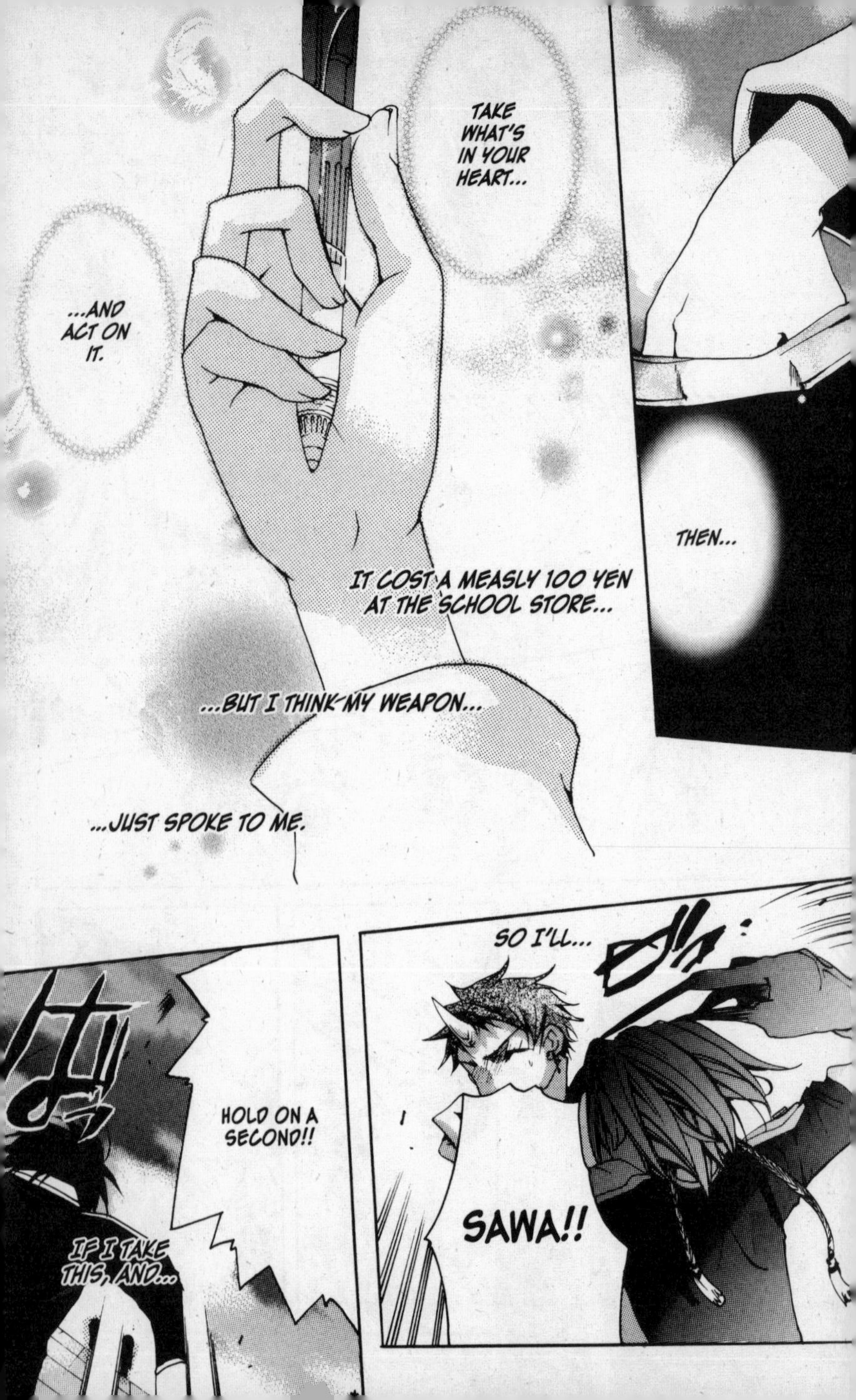
THEN...
TAKE WHAT'S IN YOUR HEART...
...AND ACT ON IT.
IT COST A MEASLY 100 YEN AT THE SCHOOL STORE...
...BUT I THINK MY WEAPON...
...JUST SPOKE TO ME.
SO I'LL...
SAWA!!
HOLD ON A SECOND!!
IF I TAKE THIS, AND...

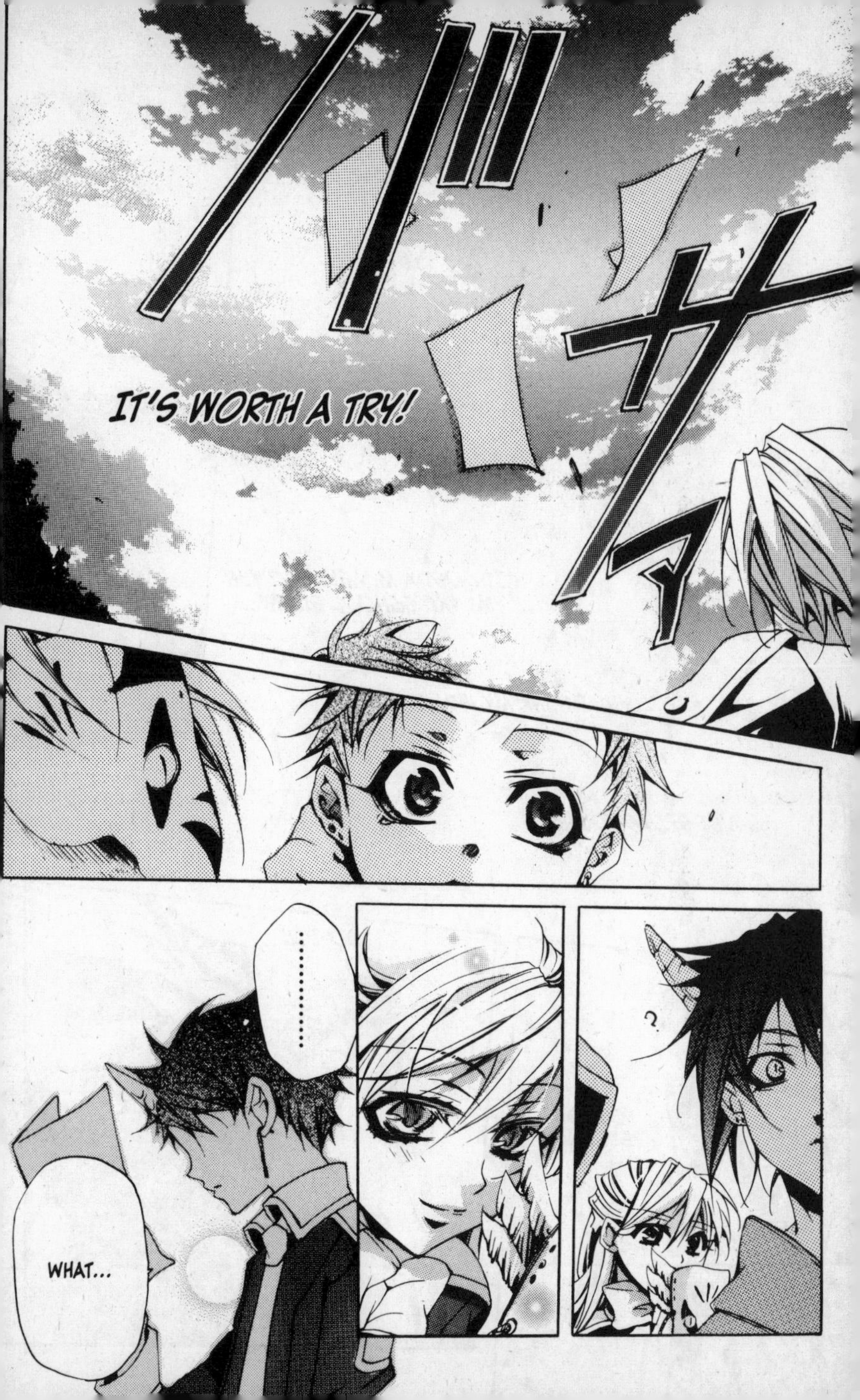
IT'S WORTH A TRY!
?
....
WHAT...

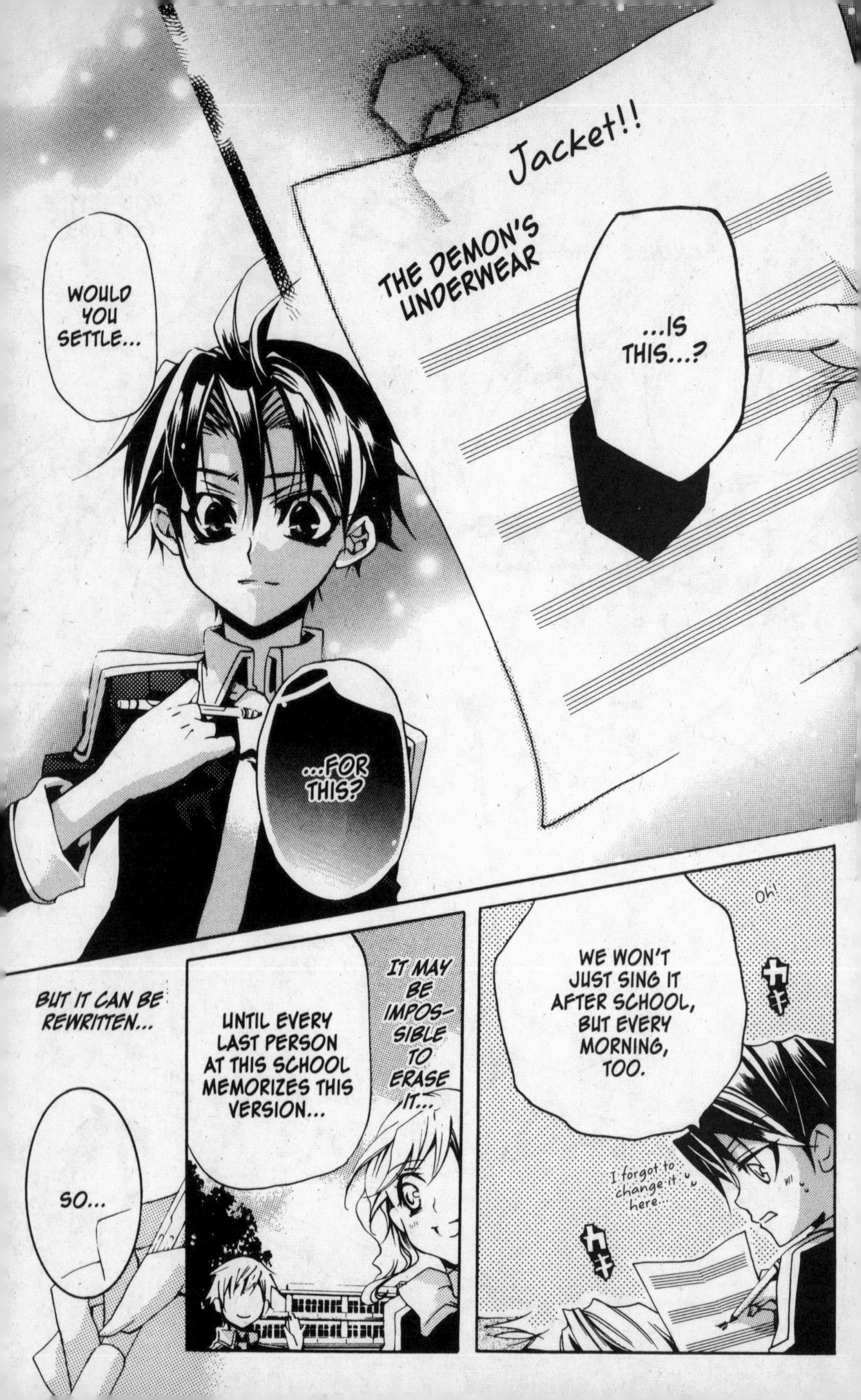
Jacket!!
THE DEMON'S UNDERWEAR
...IS THIS...?
WOULD YOU SETTLE...
...FOR THIS?
Oh!
WE WON'T JUST SING IT AFTER SCHOOL, BUT EVERY MORNING, TOO.
カキ
I forgot to change it here...
カキ
IT MAY BE IMPOS-SIBLE TO ERASE IT...
UNTIL EVERY LAST PERSON AT THIS SCHOOL MEMORIZES THIS VERSION...
BUT IT CAN BE REWRITTEN...
SO...

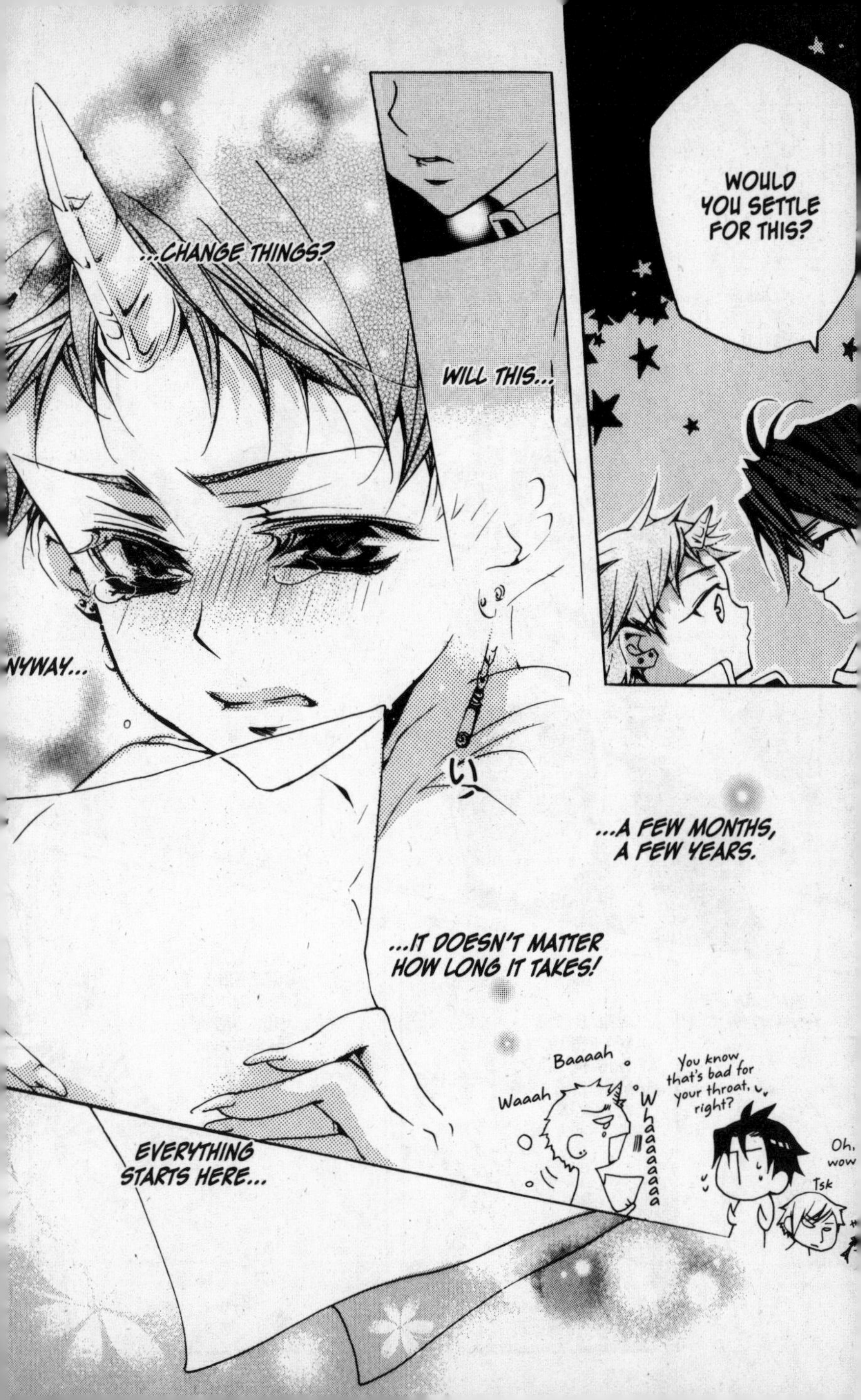
WOULD YOU SETTLE FOR THIS?
WILL THIS...
...CHANGE THINGS?
じ
NYWAY...
...A FEW MONTHS, A FEW YEARS.
...IT DOESN'T MATTER HOW LONG IT TAKES!
EVERYTHING STARTS HERE...
You know that's bad for your throat, right?
Oh, wow
Tsk
Baaaah
Waaah
Whaaaaaaaaa

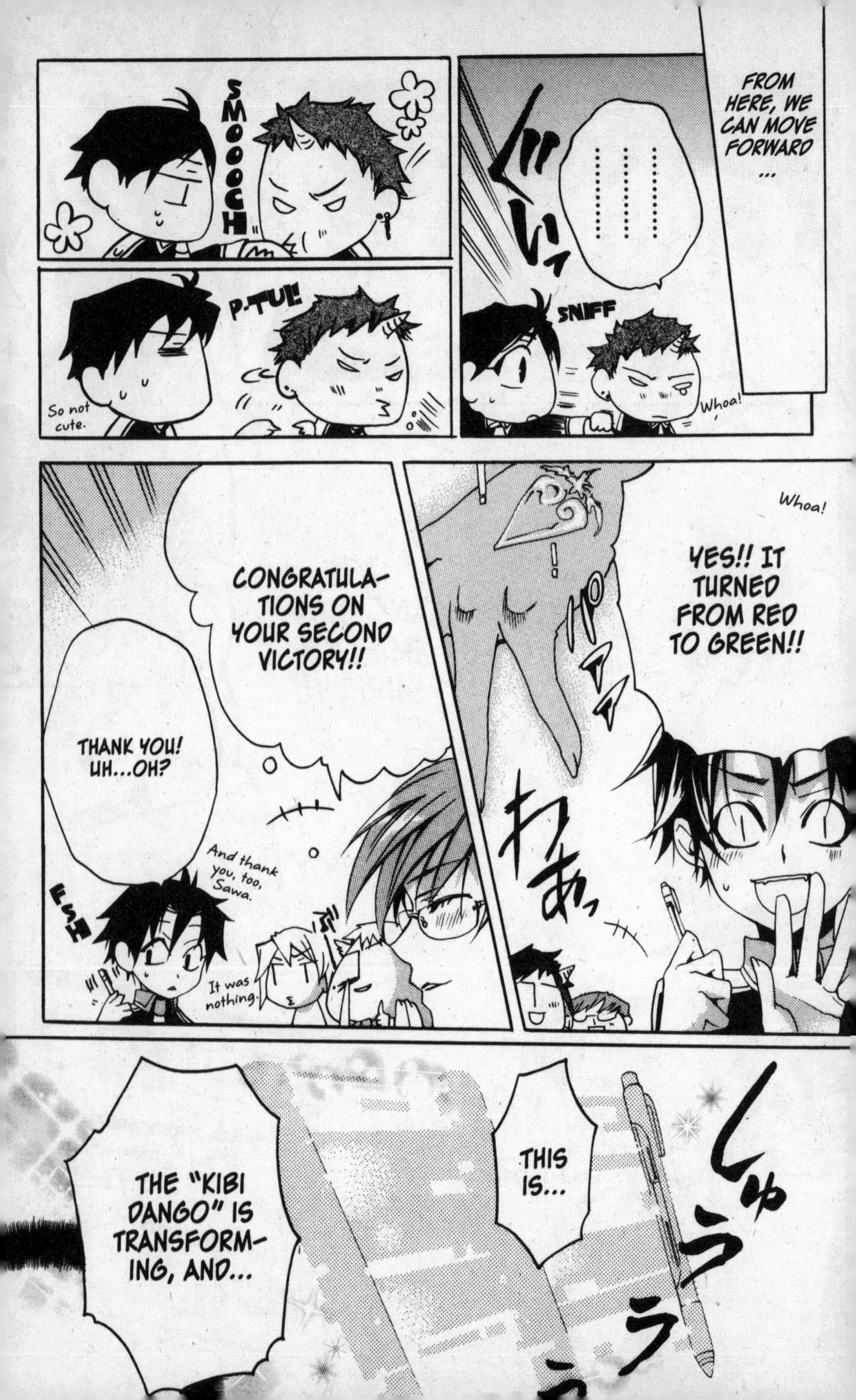
FROM HERE, WE CAN MOVE FORWARD ...
......
SNIFF
Whoa!
SMOOOCH
P-TUI!
So not cute.
Whoa!
YES!! IT TURNED FROM RED TO GREEN!!
わあっ
CONGRATULATIONS ON YOUR SECOND VICTORY!!
THANK YOU! UH...OH?
And thank you, too, Sawa.
It was nothing.
FSH
しゅうう
THIS IS...
THE "KIBI DANGO" IS TRANSFORMING, AND...

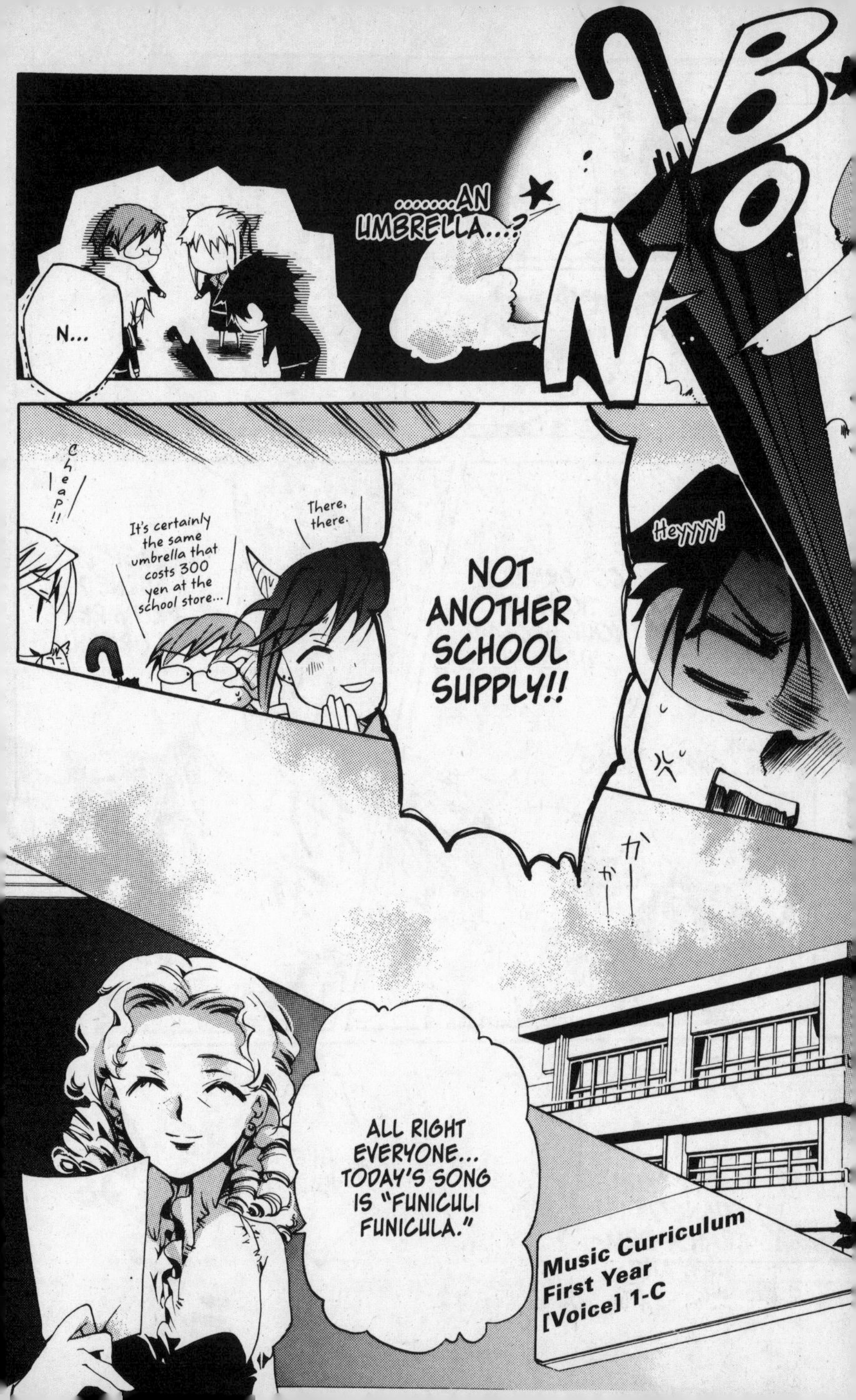
BON
........AN UMBRELLA...?
N...
Heyyyy!
NOT ANOTHER SCHOOL SUPPLY!!
There, there.
It's certainly the same umbrella that costs 300 yen at the school store...
Cheap!!
ガー
ガー
Music Curriculum
First Year
[Voice] 1-C
ALL RIGHT EVERYONE... TODAY'S SONG IS "FUNICULI FUNICULA."

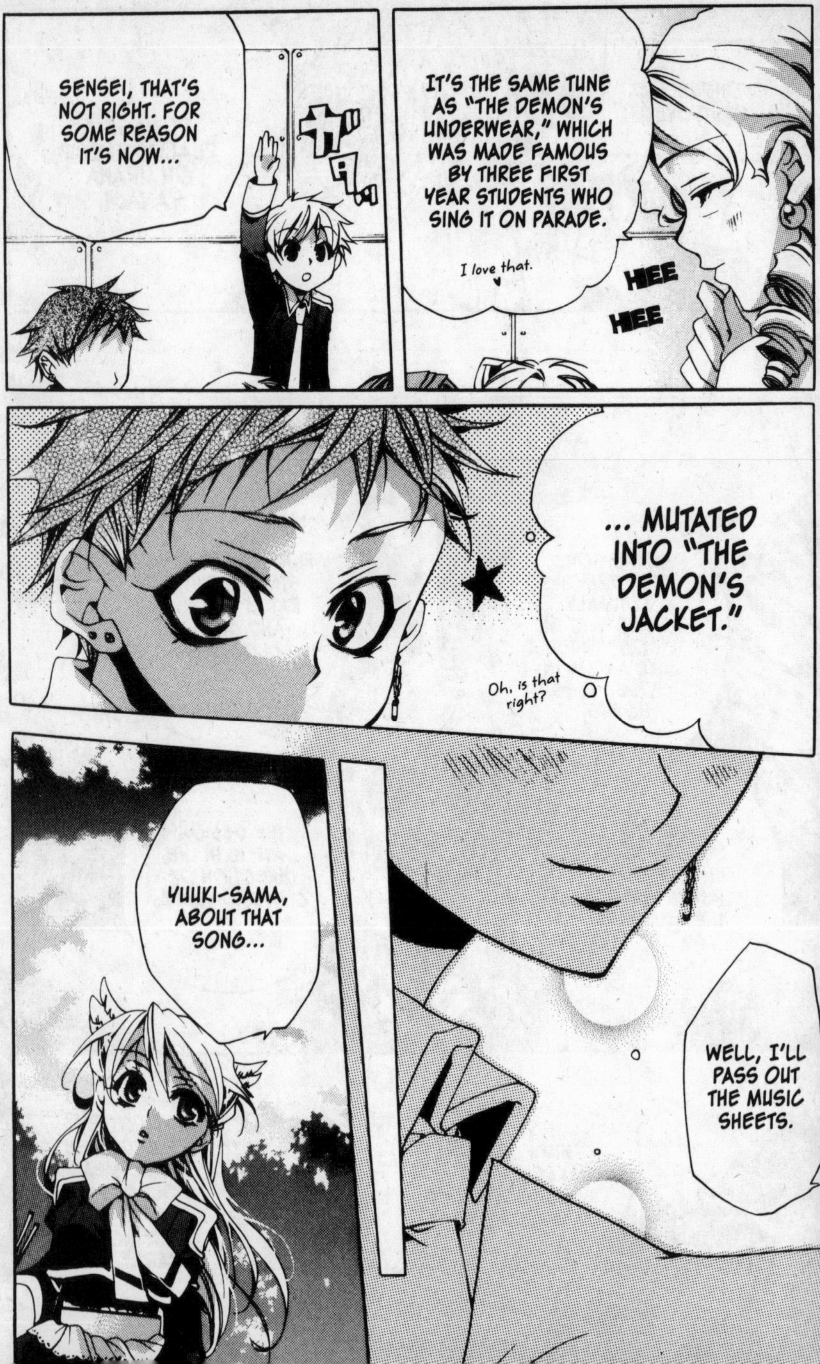
IT'S THE SAME TUNE AS "THE DEMON'S UNDERWEAR," WHICH WAS MADE FAMOUS BY THREE FIRST YEAR STUDENTS WHO SING IT ON PARADE.
I love that. ♥
HIEE
HIEE
SENSEI, THAT'S NOT RIGHT. FOR SOME REASON IT'S NOW...
... MUTATED INTO "THE DEMON'S JACKET."
Oh, is that right?
WELL, I'LL PASS OUT THE MUSIC SHEETS.
YUUKI-SAMA, ABOUT THAT SONG...

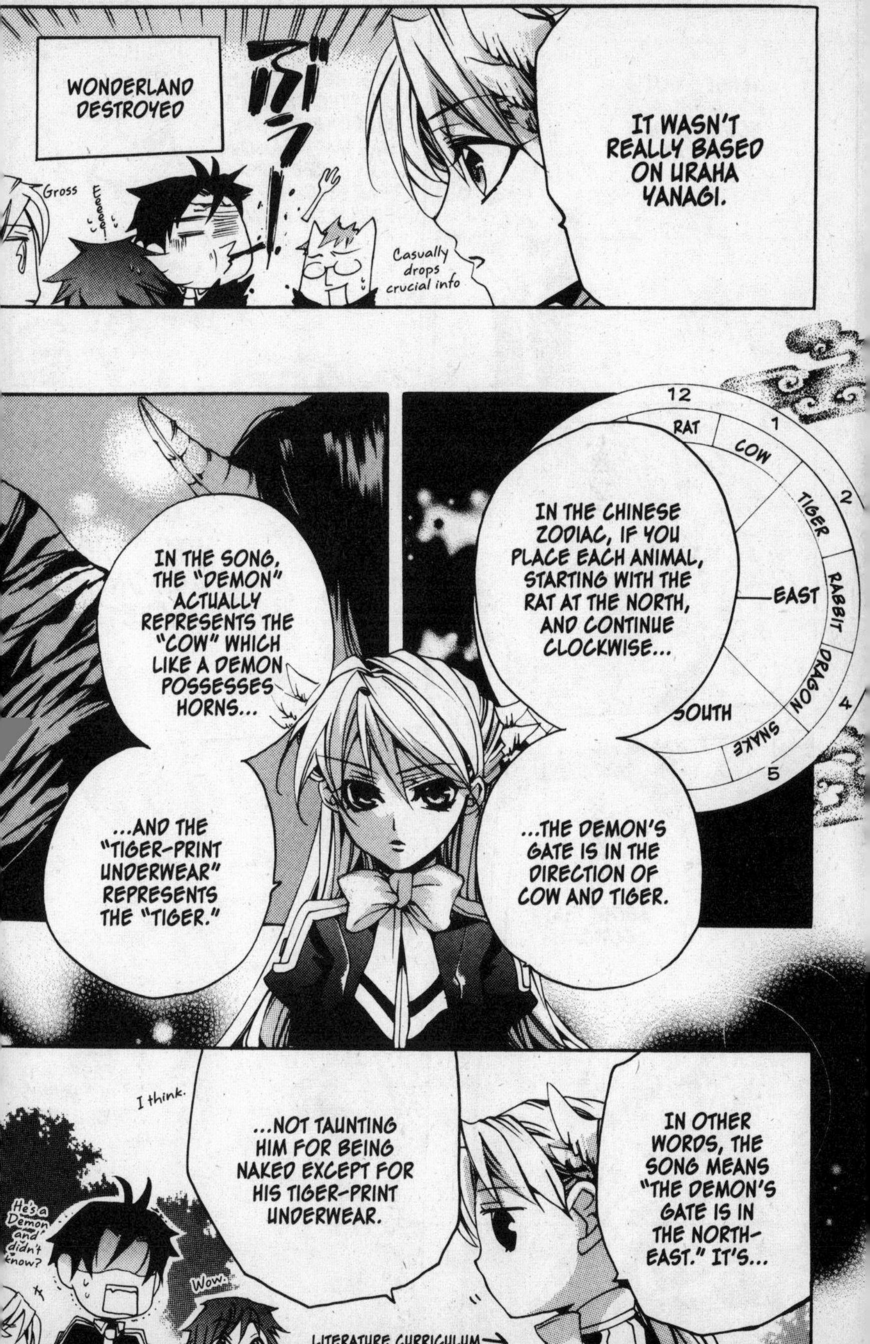
IT WASN'T REALLY BASED ON URAHA YANAGI.
Casually drops crucial info
WONDERLAND DESTROYED
Gross
IN THE CHINESE ZODIAC, IF YOU PLACE EACH ANIMAL, STARTING WITH THE RAT AT THE NORTH, AND CONTINUE CLOCKWISE...
12
RAT
1
COW
2
TIGER
EAST
RABBIT
DRAGON
4
SNAKE
5
SOUTH
...THE DEMON'S GATE IS IN THE DIRECTION OF COW AND TIGER.
IN THE SONG, THE "DEMON" ACTUALLY REPRESENTS THE "COW" WHICH LIKE A DEMON POSSESSES HORNS...
...AND THE "TIGER-PRINT UNDERWEAR" REPRESENTS THE "TIGER."
IN OTHER WORDS, THE SONG MEANS "THE DEMON'S GATE IS IN THE NORTH-EAST." IT'S...
...NOT TAUNTING HIM FOR BEING NAKED EXCEPT FOR HIS TIGER-PRINT UNDERWEAR.
I think.
Wow.
He's a Demon and didn't know?
LITERATURE CURRICULUM→

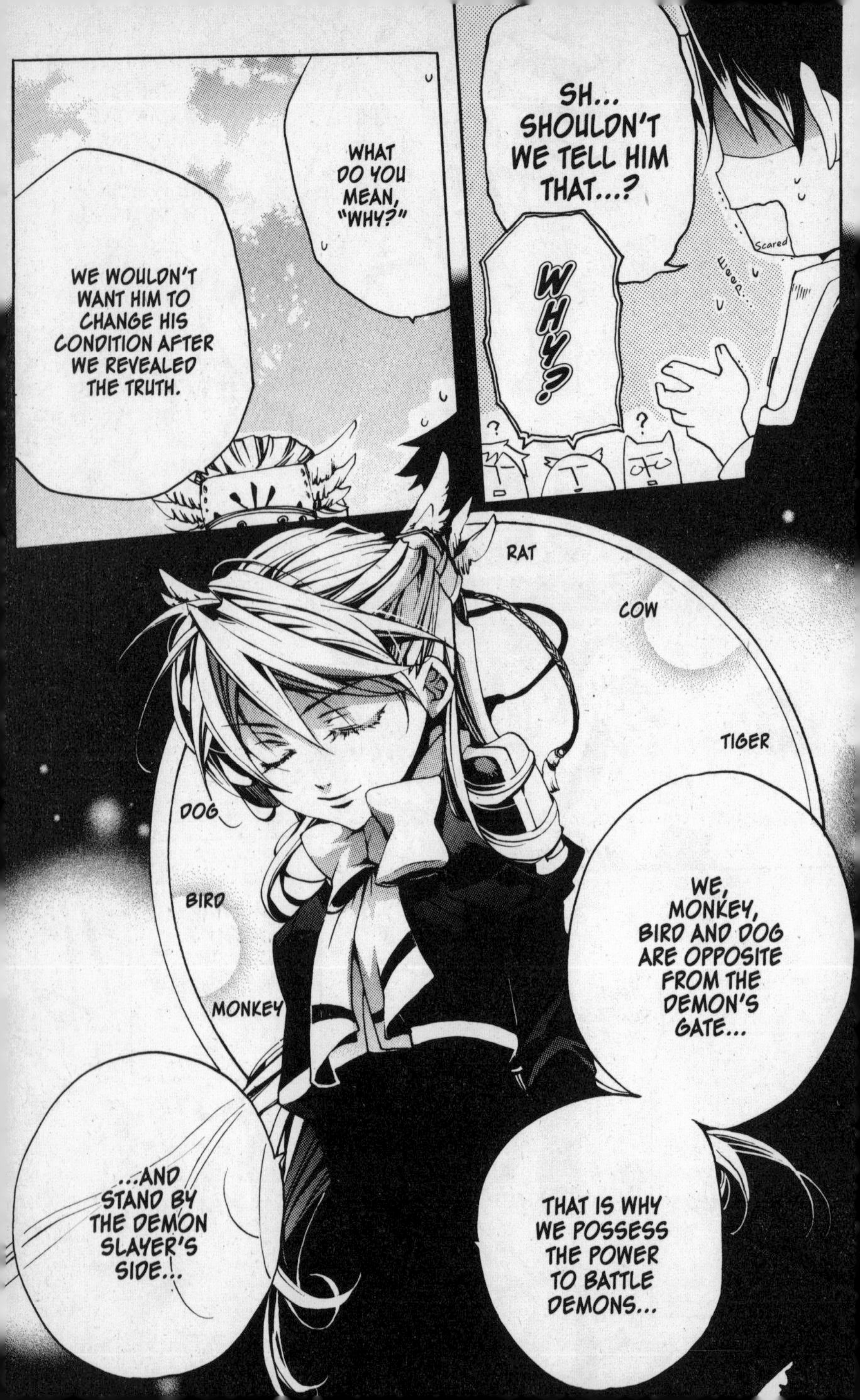
SH... SHOULDN'T WE TELL HIM THAT...?
WHY?
Scared
Weep...
WHAT DO YOU MEAN, "WHY?"
WE WOULDN'T WANT HIM TO CHANGE HIS CONDITION AFTER WE REVEALED THE TRUTH.
RAT
COW
TIGER
DOG
BIRD
MONKEY
WE, MONKEY, BIRD AND DOG ARE OPPOSITE FROM THE DEMON'S GATE...
...AND STAND BY THE DEMON SLAYER'S SIDE...
THAT IS WHY WE POSSESS THE POWER TO BATTLE DEMONS...

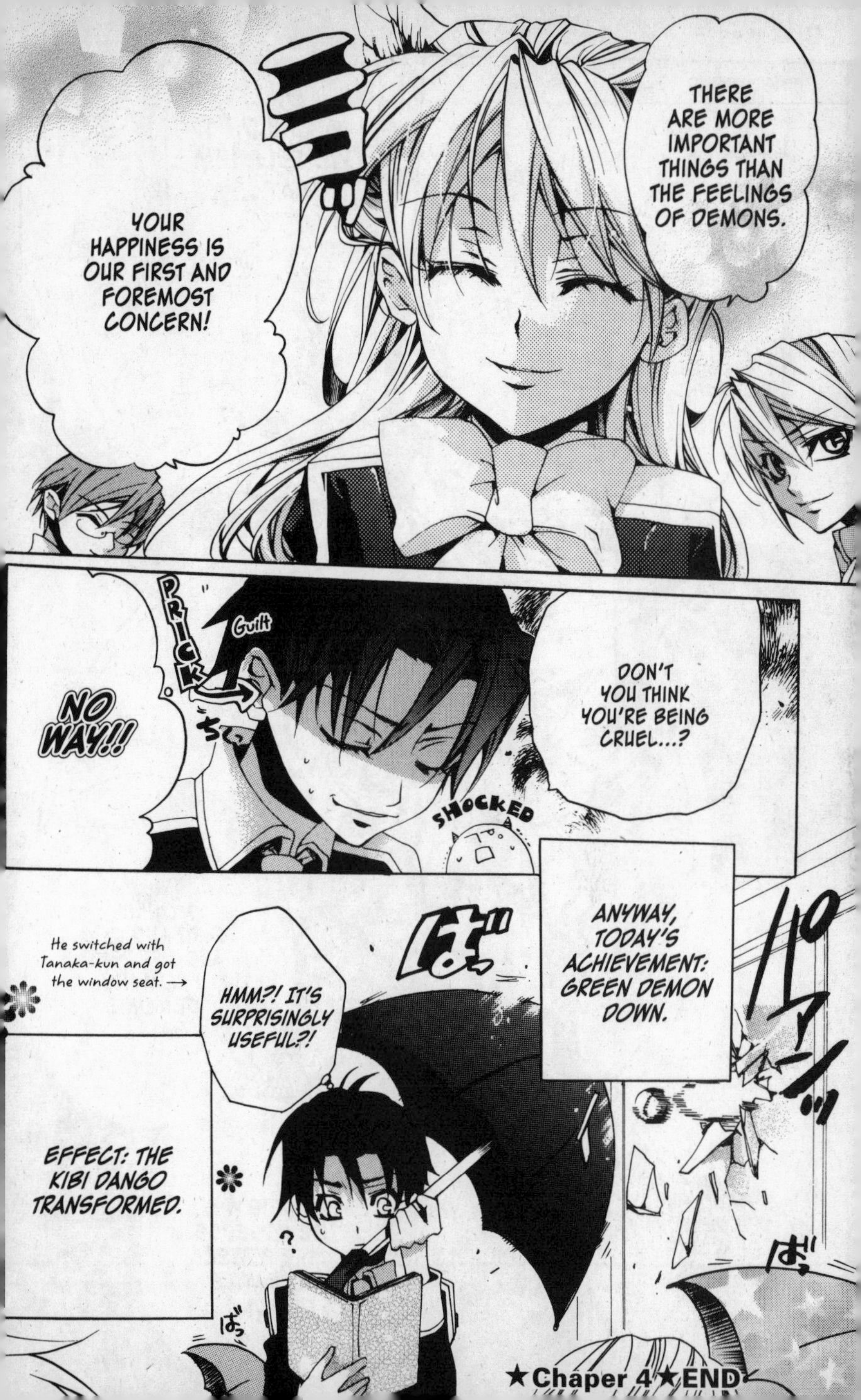
THERE ARE MORE IMPORTANT THINGS THAN THE FEELINGS OF DEMONS.
YOUR HAPPINESS IS OUR FIRST AND FOREMOST CONCERN!
DON'T YOU THINK YOU'RE BEING CRUEL...?
SHOCKED
Guilt
PRICK
ちく
NO WAY!!
ANYWAY, TODAY'S ACHIEVEMENT: GREEN DEMON DOWN.
HMM?! IT'S SURPRISINGLY USEFUL?!
He switched with Tanaka-kun and got the window seat. →
EFFECT: THE KIBI DANGO TRANSFORMED.
ぱっ
★Chaper 4★END

Chapter 5

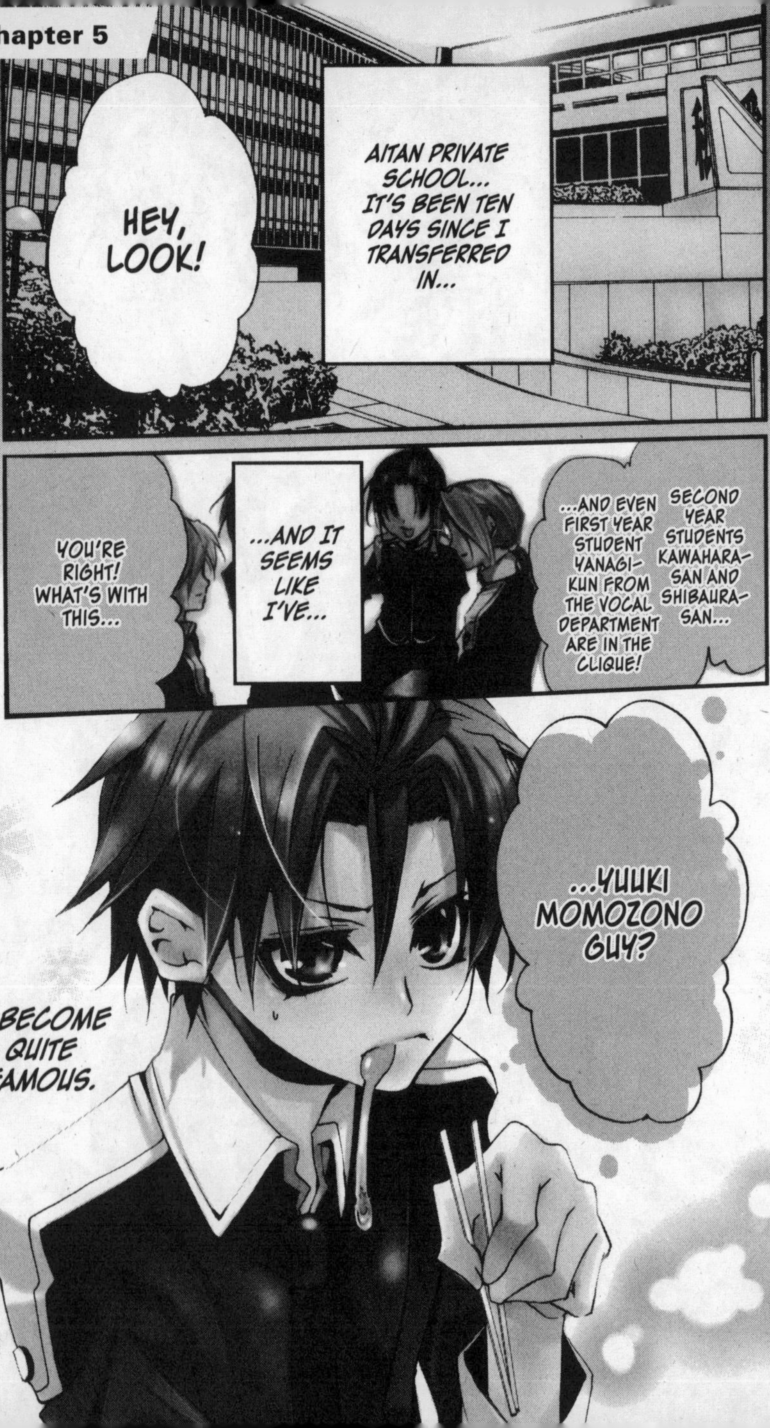
AITAN PRIVATE SCHOOL... IT'S BEEN TEN DAYS SINCE I TRANSFERRED IN...
HEY, LOOK!
SECOND YEAR STUDENTS KAWAHARA-SAN AND SHIBAURA-SAN...
...AND EVEN FIRST YEAR STUDENT YANAGI-KUN FROM THE VOCAL DEPARTMENT ARE IN THE CLIQUE!
...AND IT SEEMS LIKE I'VE...
YOU'RE RIGHT! WHAT'S WITH THIS...
...YUUKI MOMOZONO GUY?
...BECOME QUITE FAMOUS.

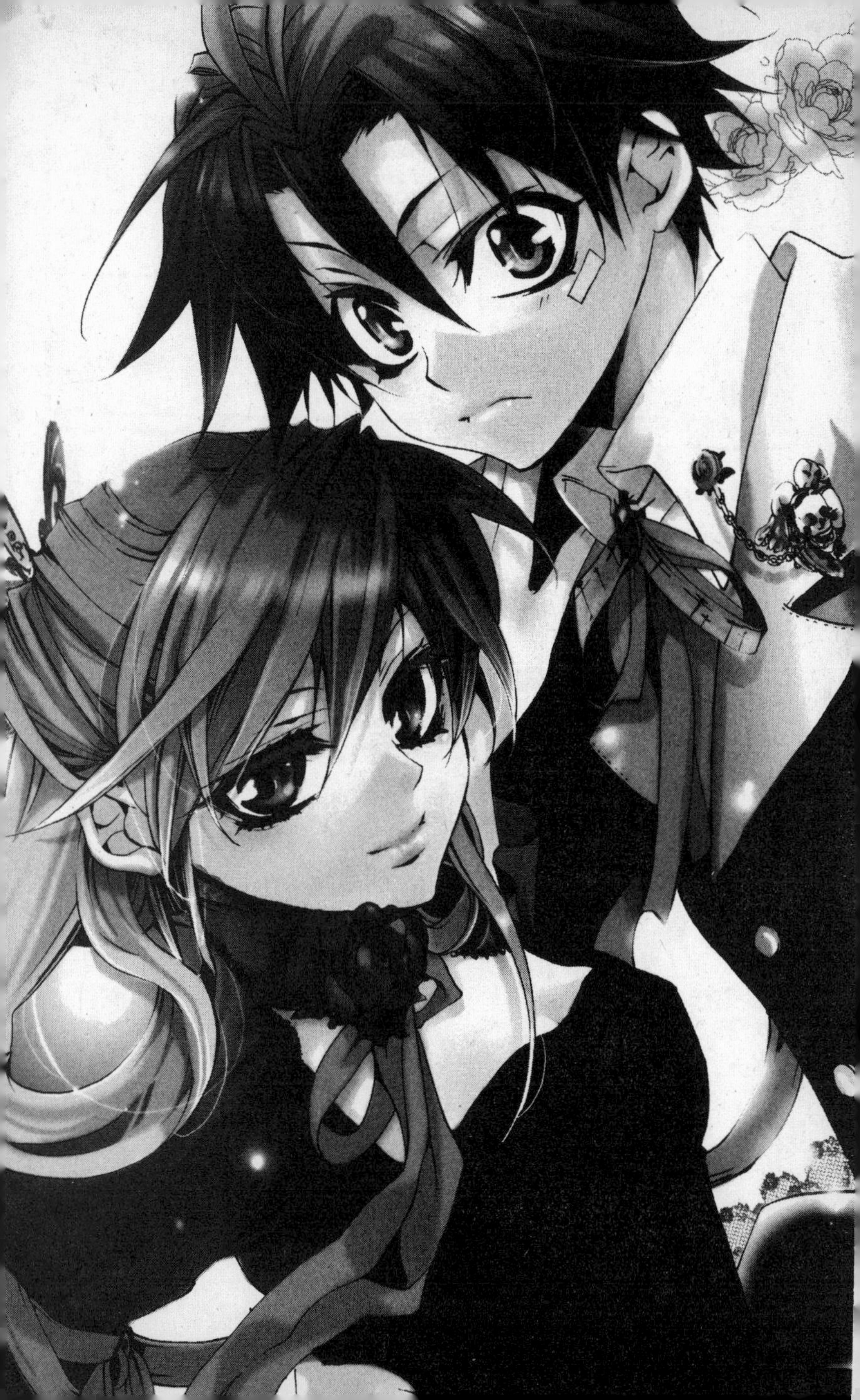

Chapter 5: Students and Quarrels

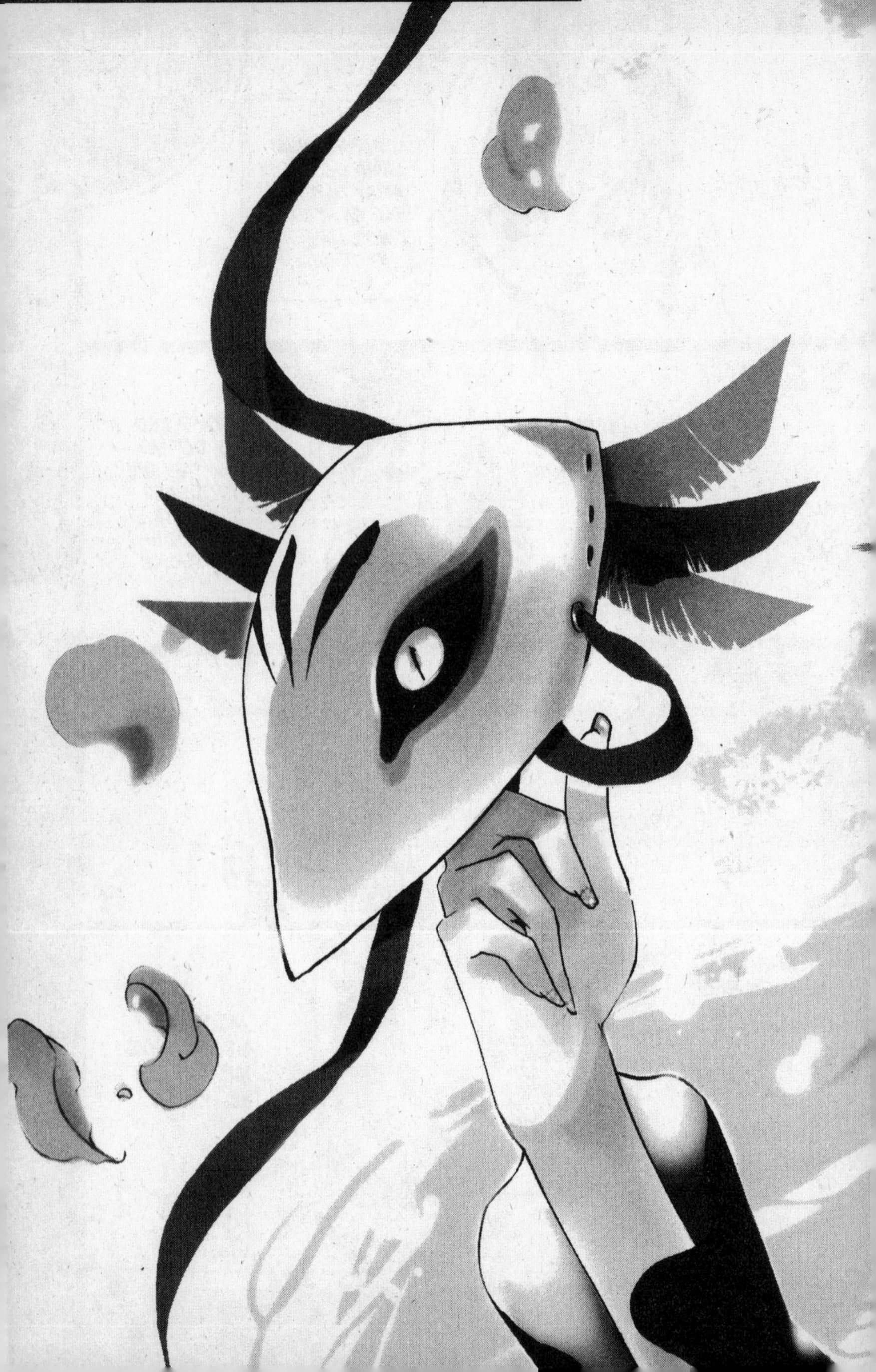

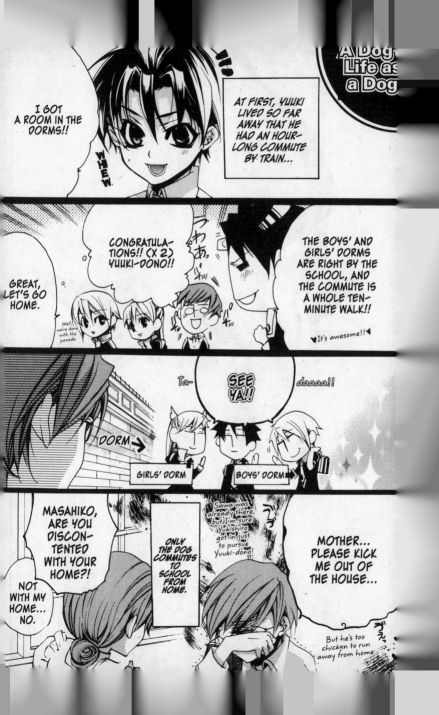

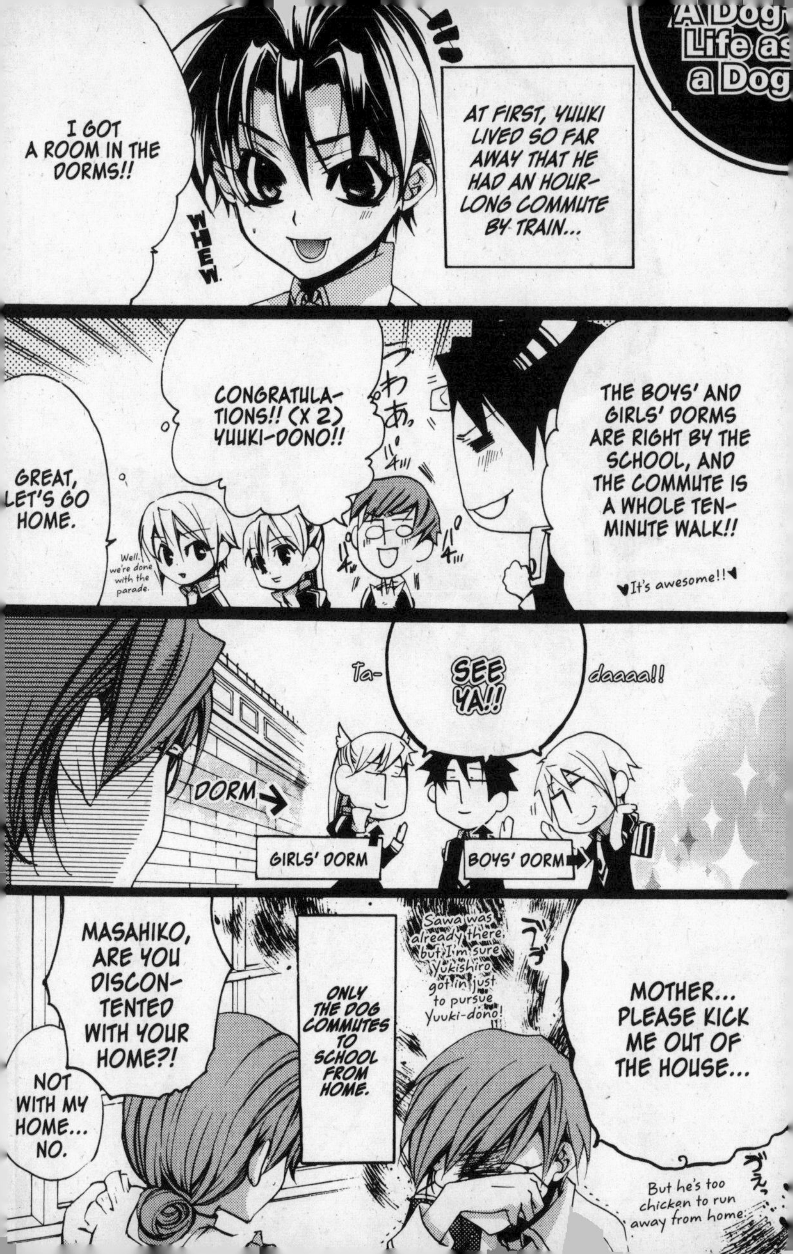
A Dog
Life as
a Dog
AT FIRST, YUUKI LIVED SO FAR AWAY THAT HE HAD AN HOUR-LONG COMMUTE BY TRAIN...
WHEW.
I GOT A ROOM IN THE DORMS!!
THE BOYS' AND GIRLS' DORMS ARE RIGHT BY THE SCHOOL, AND THE COMMUTE IS A WHOLE TEN-MINUTE WALK!!
It's awesome!!
CONGRATULATIONS!! (X 2) YUUKI-DONO!!
GREAT, LET'S GO HOME.
Well, we're done with the parade.
Ta-
SEE YA!!
daaaa!!
DORM
BOYS' DORM
GIRLS' DORM
MOTHER... PLEASE KICK ME OUT OF THE HOUSE...
But he's too chicken to run away from home.
Sawa was already there, but I'm sure Yukishiro got in just to pursue Yuuki-dono!
ONLY THE DOG COMMUTES TO SCHOOL FROM HOME.
MASAHIKO, ARE YOU DISCONTENTED WITH YOUR HOME?!
NOT WITH MY HOME... NO.

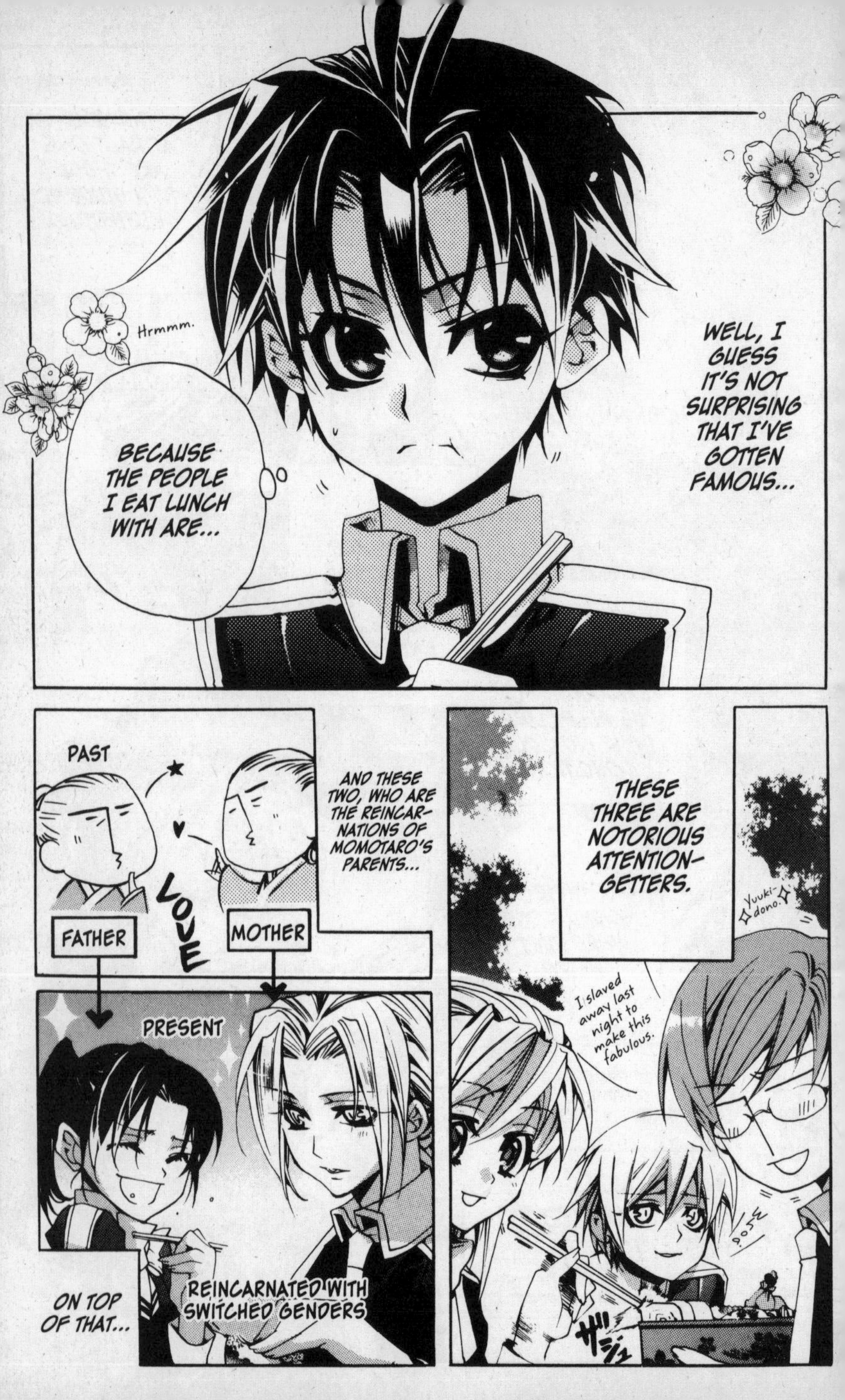
WELL, I GUESS IT'S NOT SURPRISING THAT I'VE GOTTEN FAMOUS...
Hrmmm.
BECAUSE THE PEOPLE I EAT LUNCH WITH ARE...
THESE THREE ARE NOTORIOUS ATTENTION-GETTERS.
Yuuki-dono.
I slaved away last night to make this fabulous.
AND THESE TWO, WHO ARE THE REINCARNATIONS OF MOMOTARO'S PARENTS...
PAST
LOVE
FATHER
MOTHER
PRESENT
REINCARNATED WITH SWITCHED GENDERS
ON TOP OF THAT...

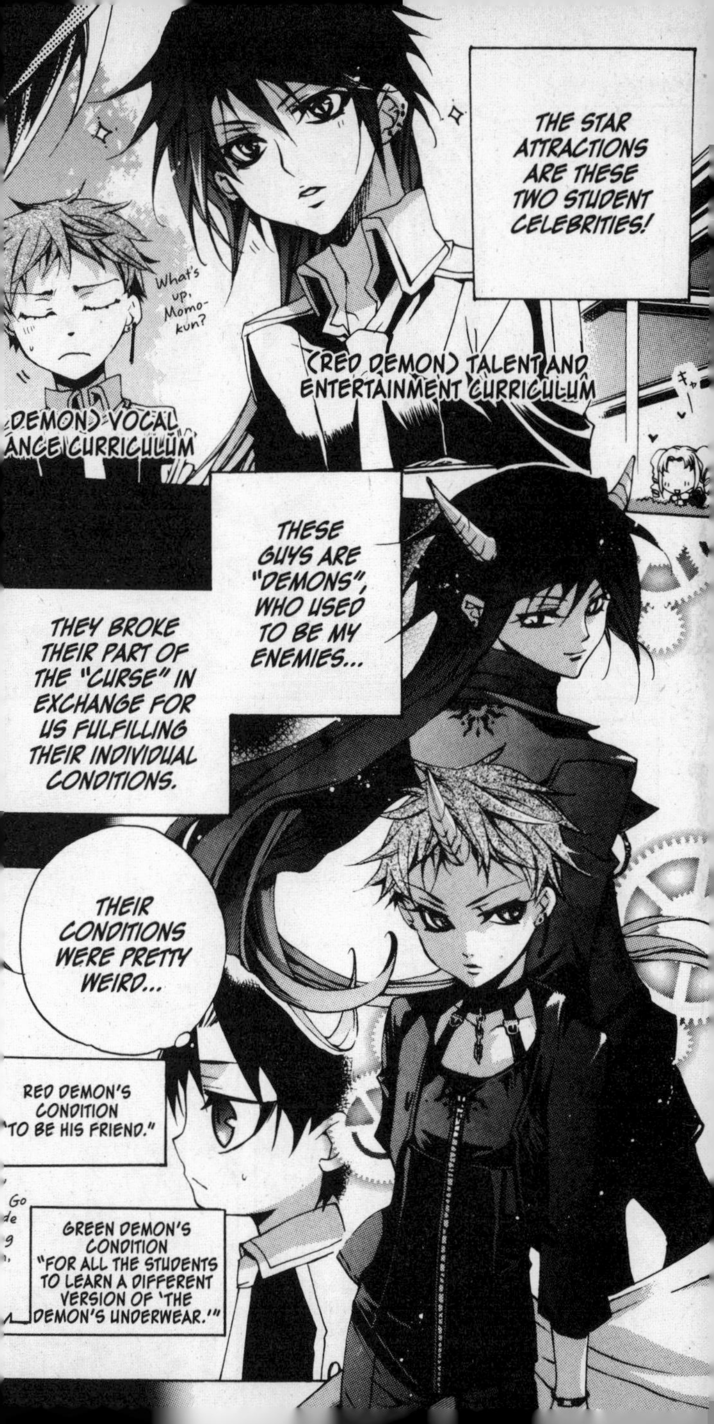
THE STAR ATTRACTIONS ARE THESE TWO STUDENT CELEBRITIES!
(RED DEMON) TALENT AND ENTERTAINMENT CURRICULUM
What's up, Momo-kun?
DEMON) VOCAL
ANCE CURRICULUM
THESE GUYS ARE "DEMONS", WHO USED TO BE MY ENEMIES...
THEY BROKE THEIR PART OF THE "CURSE" IN EXCHANGE FOR US FULFILLING THEIR INDIVIDUAL CONDITIONS.
THEIR CONDITIONS WERE PRETTY WEIRD...
RED DEMON'S CONDITION "TO BE HIS FRIEND."
GREEN DEMON'S CONDITION "FOR ALL THE STUDENTS TO LEARN A DIFFERENT VERSION OF 'THE DEMON'S UNDERWEAR.'"

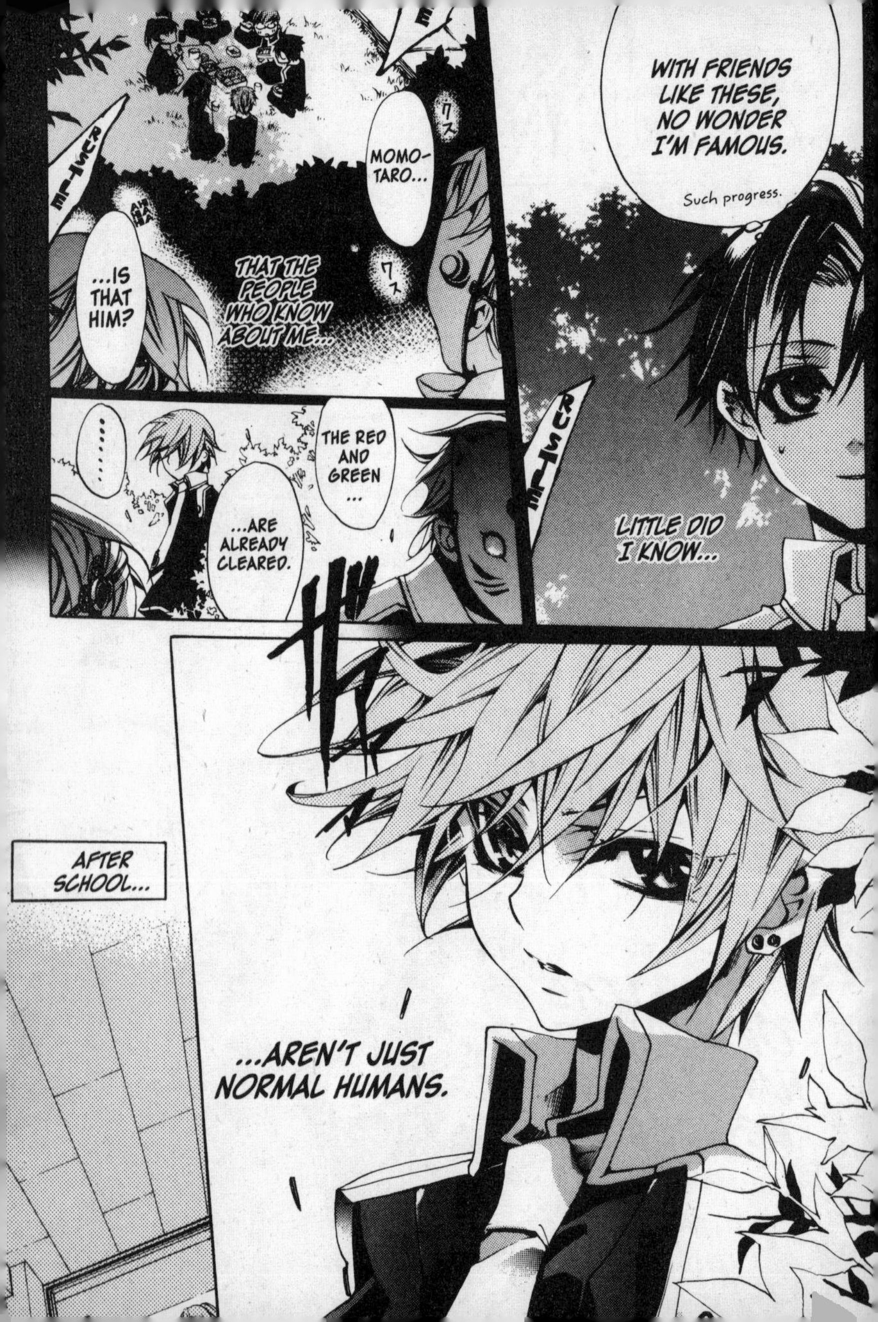
WITH FRIENDS LIKE THESE, NO WONDER I'M FAMOUS.
Such progress.
RUSTLE
LITTLE DID I KNOW...
MOMO-TARO...
クス
クス
RUSTLE
AHAHA
...IS THAT HIM?
THAT THE PEOPLE WHO KNOW ABOUT ME...
THE RED AND GREEN...
...ARE ALREADY CLEARED.
......
...AREN'T JUST NORMAL HUMANS.
AFTER SCHOOL...

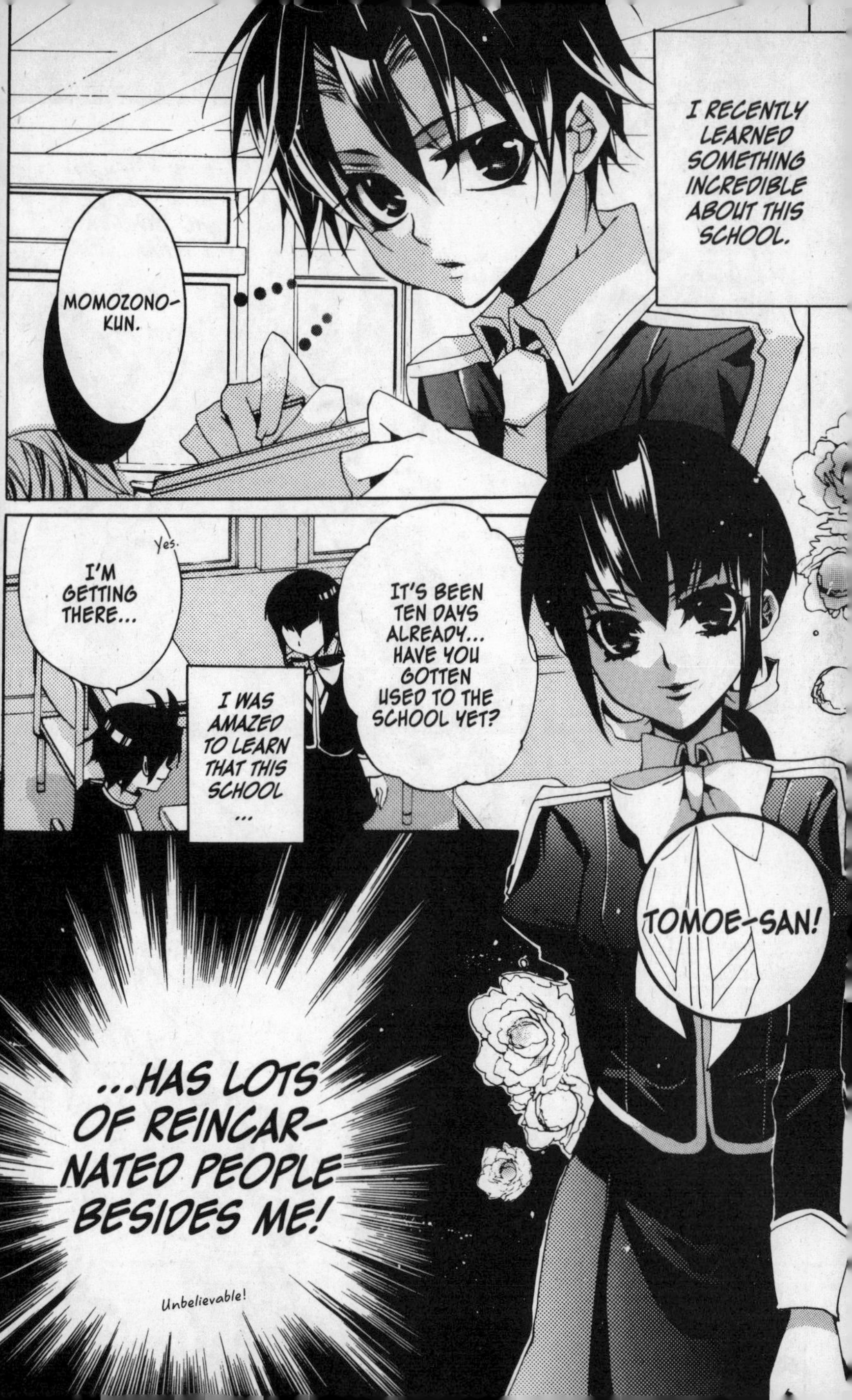
I RECENTLY LEARNED SOMETHING INCREDIBLE ABOUT THIS SCHOOL.
MOMOZONO-KUN.
IT'S BEEN TEN DAYS ALREADY... HAVE YOU GOTTEN USED TO THE SCHOOL YET?
I'M GETTING THERE...
Yes.
I WAS AMAZED TO LEARN THAT THIS SCHOOL ...
TOMOE-SAN!
...HAS LOTS OF REINCAR-NATED PEOPLE BESIDES ME!
Unbelievable!

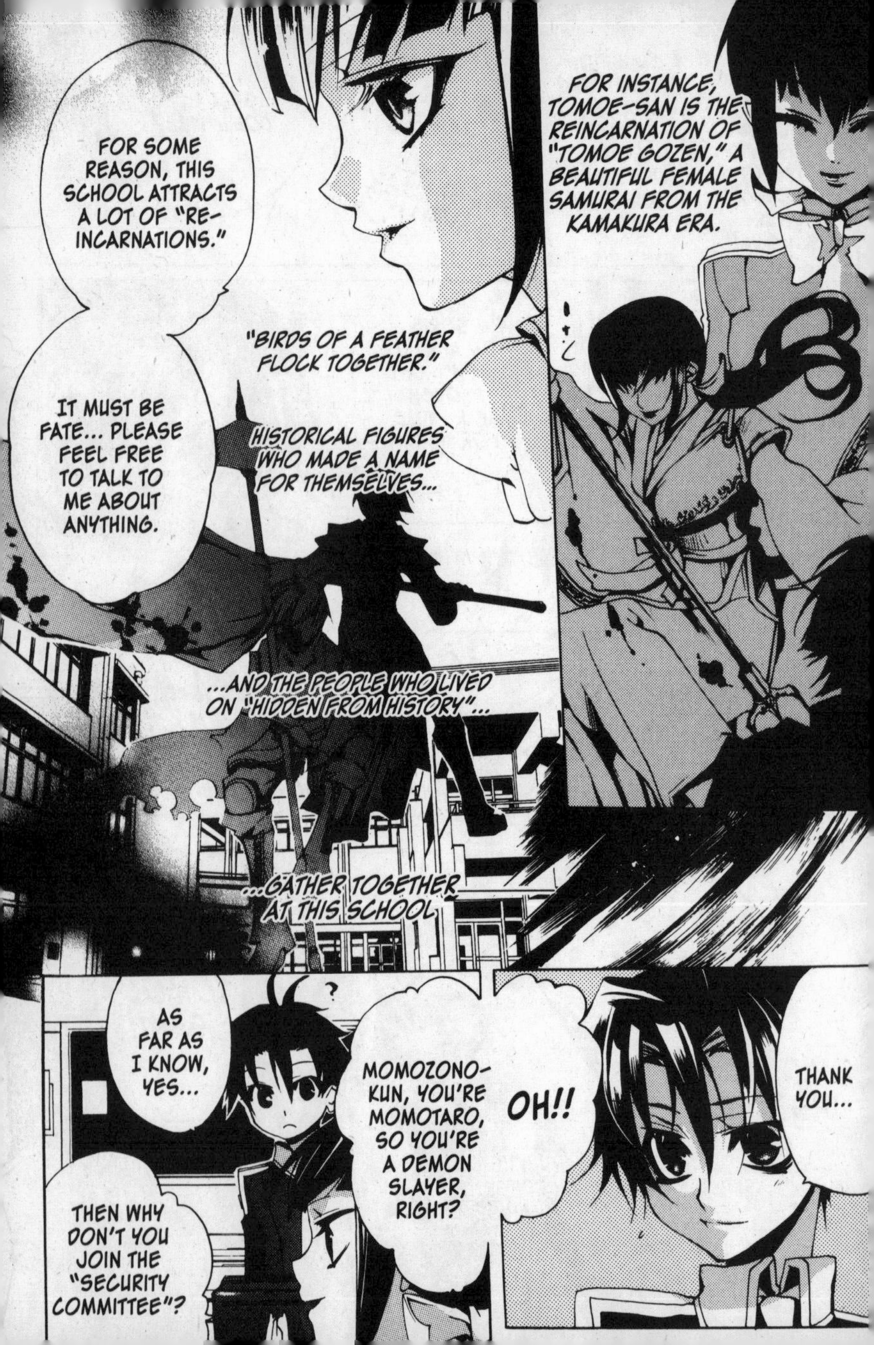
FOR INSTANCE, TOMOE-SAN IS THE REINCARNATION OF "TOMOE GOZEN," A BEAUTIFUL FEMALE SAMURAI FROM THE KAMAKURA ERA.
FOR SOME REASON, THIS SCHOOL ATTRACTS A LOT OF "RE-INCARNATIONS."
"BIRDS OF A FEATHER FLOCK TOGETHER."
IT MUST BE FATE... PLEASE FEEL FREE TO TALK TO ME ABOUT ANYTHING.
HISTORICAL FIGURES WHO MADE A NAME FOR THEMSELVES...
...AND THE PEOPLE WHO LIVED ON "HIDDEN FROM HISTORY"...
...GATHER TOGETHER AT THIS SCHOOL.
THANK YOU...
OH!!
MOMOZONO-KUN, YOU'RE MOMOTARO, SO YOU'RE A DEMON SLAYER, RIGHT?
?
AS FAR AS I KNOW, YES...
THEN WHY DON'T YOU JOIN THE "SECURITY COMMITTEE"?

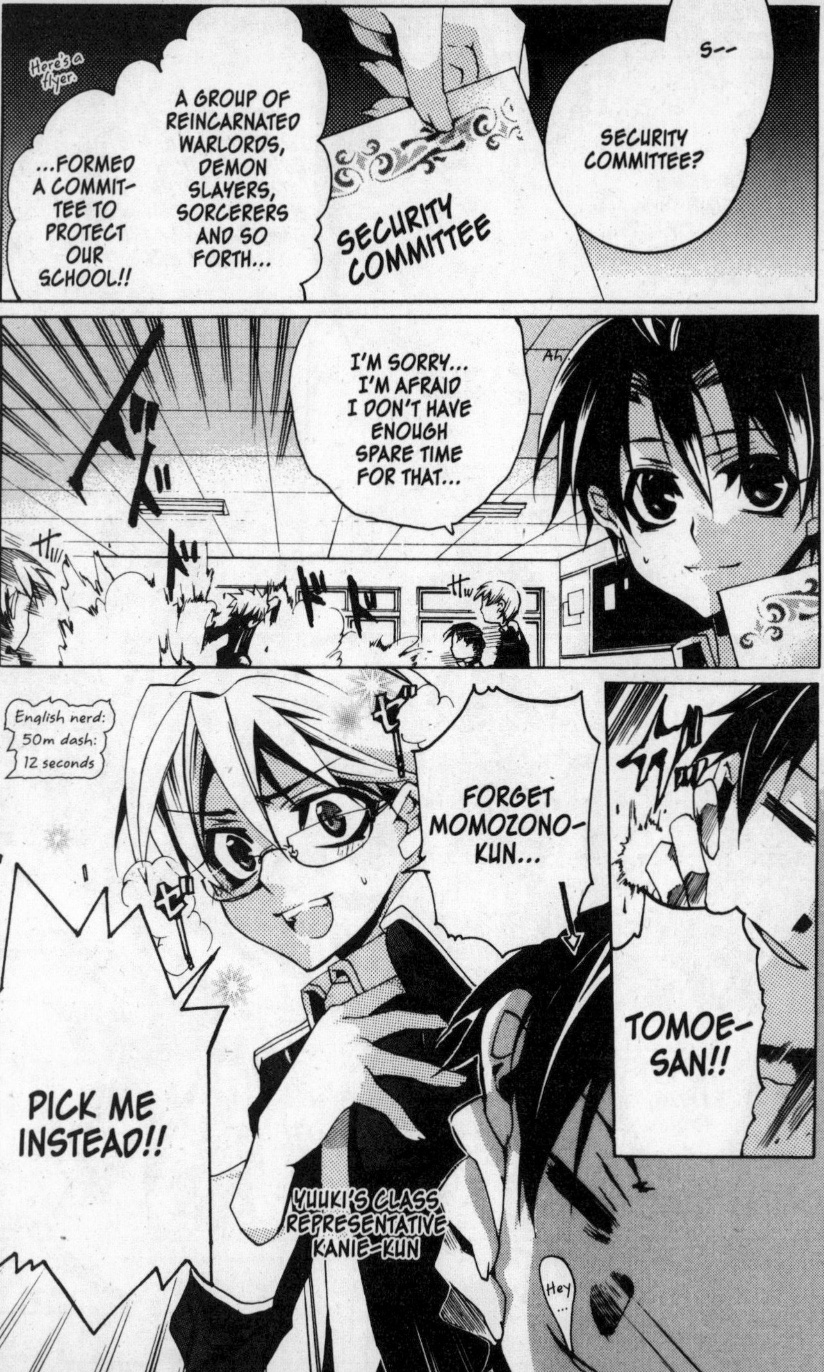
S--
SECURITY COMMITTEE?
SECURITY COMMITTEE
A GROUP OF REINCARNATED WARLORDS, DEMON SLAYERS, SORCERERS AND SO FORTH...
...FORMED A COMMIT-TEE TO PROTECT OUR SCHOOL!!
Here's a flyer.
Ah.
I'M SORRY... I'M AFRAID I DON'T HAVE ENOUGH SPARE TIME FOR THAT...
TOMOE-SAN!!
FORGET MOMOZONO-KUN...
English nerd: 50m dash: 12 seconds
PICK ME INSTEAD!!
YUUKI'S CLASS REPRESENTATIVE KANIE-KUN
Hey ...

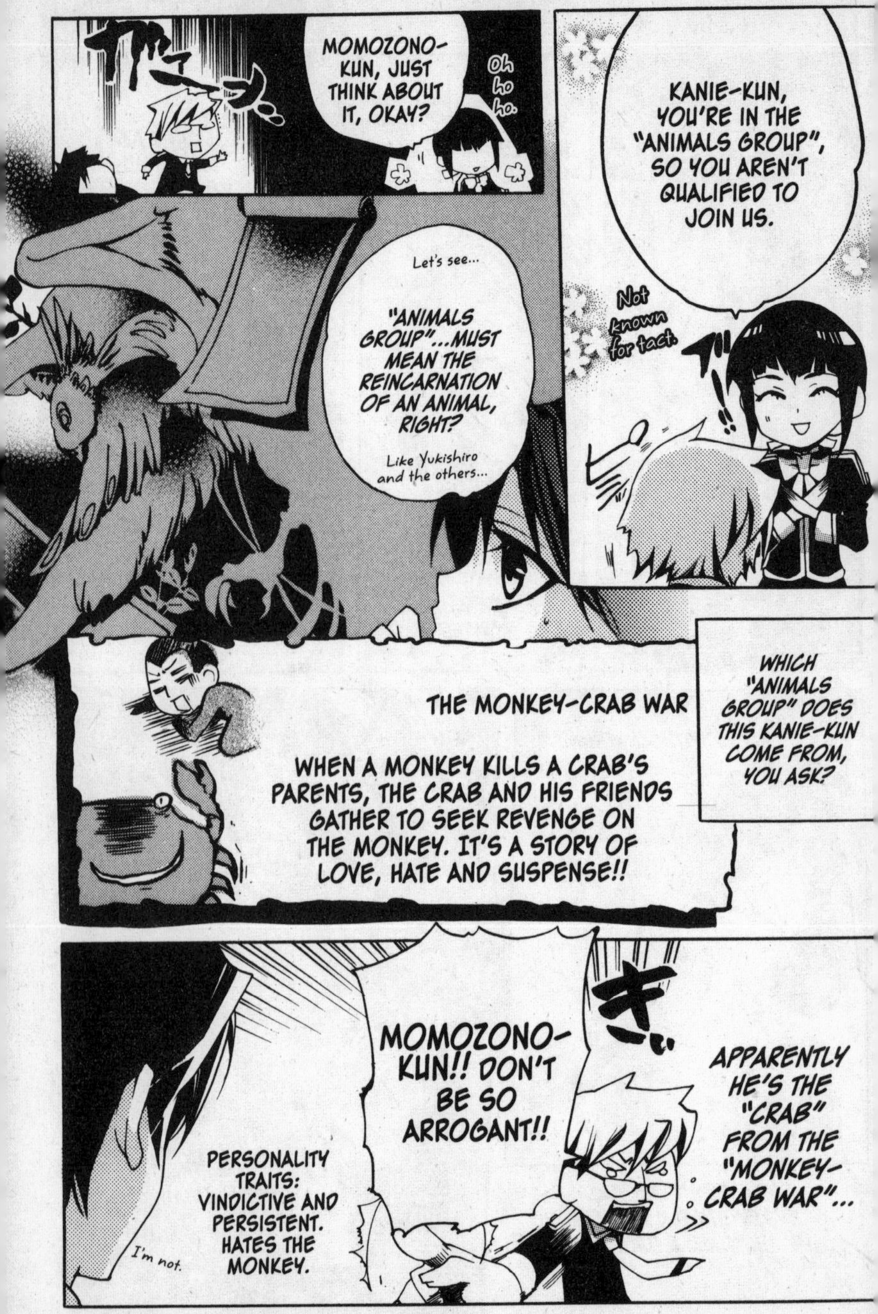
KANIE-KUN, YOU'RE IN THE "ANIMALS GROUP", SO YOU AREN'T QUALIFIED TO JOIN US.
Not known for tact.
MOMOZONO-KUN, JUST THINK ABOUT IT, OKAY?
Oh ho ho.
Let's see...
"ANIMALS GROUP"...MUST MEAN THE REINCARNATION OF AN ANIMAL, RIGHT?
Like Yukishiro and the others...
WHICH "ANIMALS GROUP" DOES THIS KANIE-KUN COME FROM, YOU ASK?
THE MONKEY-CRAB WAR
WHEN A MONKEY KILLS A CRAB'S PARENTS, THE CRAB AND HIS FRIENDS GATHER TO SEEK REVENGE ON THE MONKEY. IT'S A STORY OF LOVE, HATE AND SUSPENSE!!
APPARENTLY HE'S THE "CRAB" FROM THE "MONKEY-CRAB WAR"...
MOMOZONO-KUN!! DON'T BE SO ARROGANT!!
PERSONALITY TRAITS: VINDICTIVE AND PERSISTENT. HATES THE MONKEY.
I'm not.

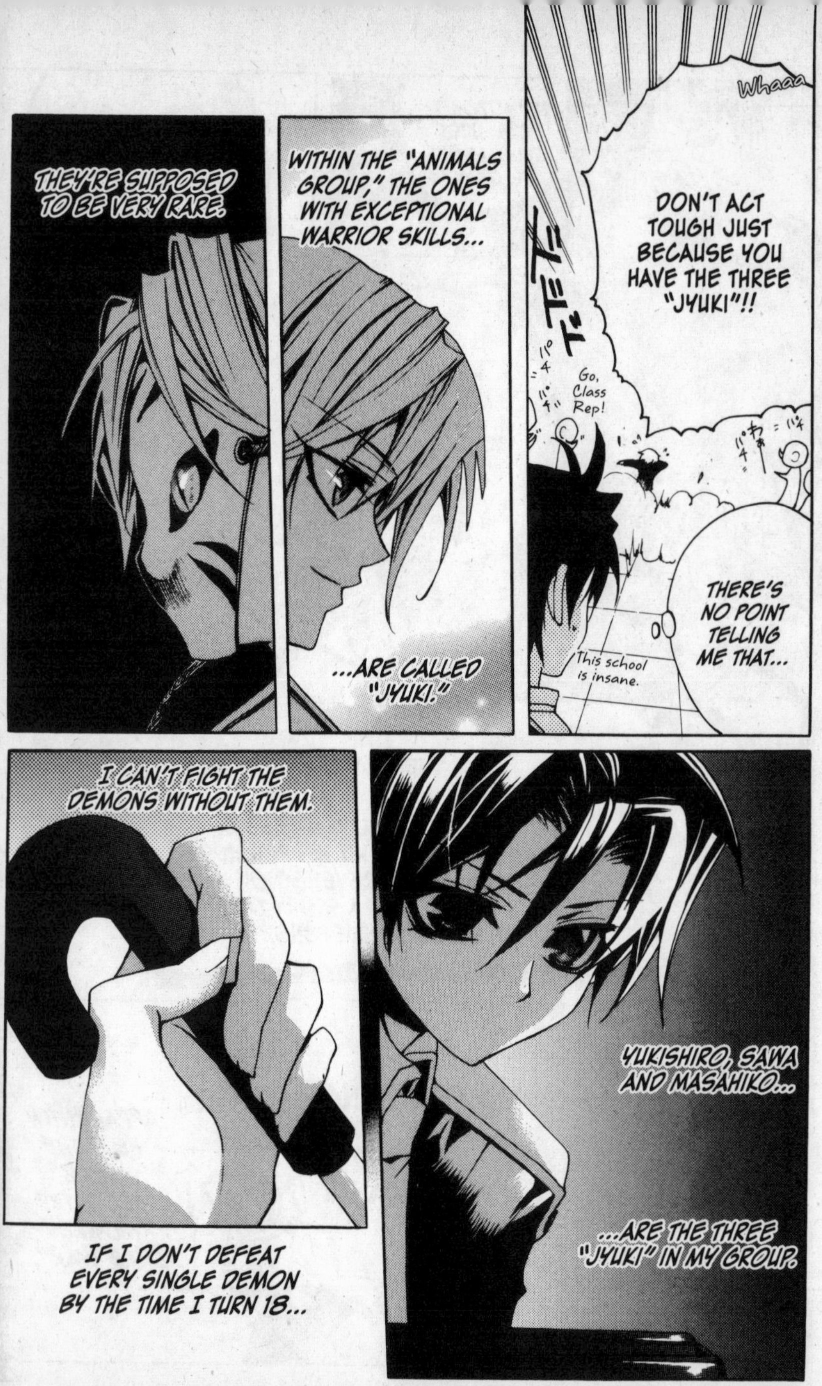
Whaaa
DON'T ACT TOUGH JUST BECAUSE YOU HAVE THE THREE "JYUKI"!!
Go, Class Rep!
This school is insane.
THERE'S NO POINT TELLING ME THAT...
WITHIN THE "ANIMALS GROUP," THE ONES WITH EXCEPTIONAL WARRIOR SKILLS...
...ARE CALLED "JYUKI."
THEY'RE SUPPOSED TO BE VERY RARE.
YUKISHIRO, SAWA AND MASAHIKO...
...ARE THE THREE "JYUKI" IN MY GROUP.
I CAN'T FIGHT THE DEMONS WITHOUT THEM.
IF I DON'T DEFEAT EVERY SINGLE DEMON BY THE TIME I TURN 18...

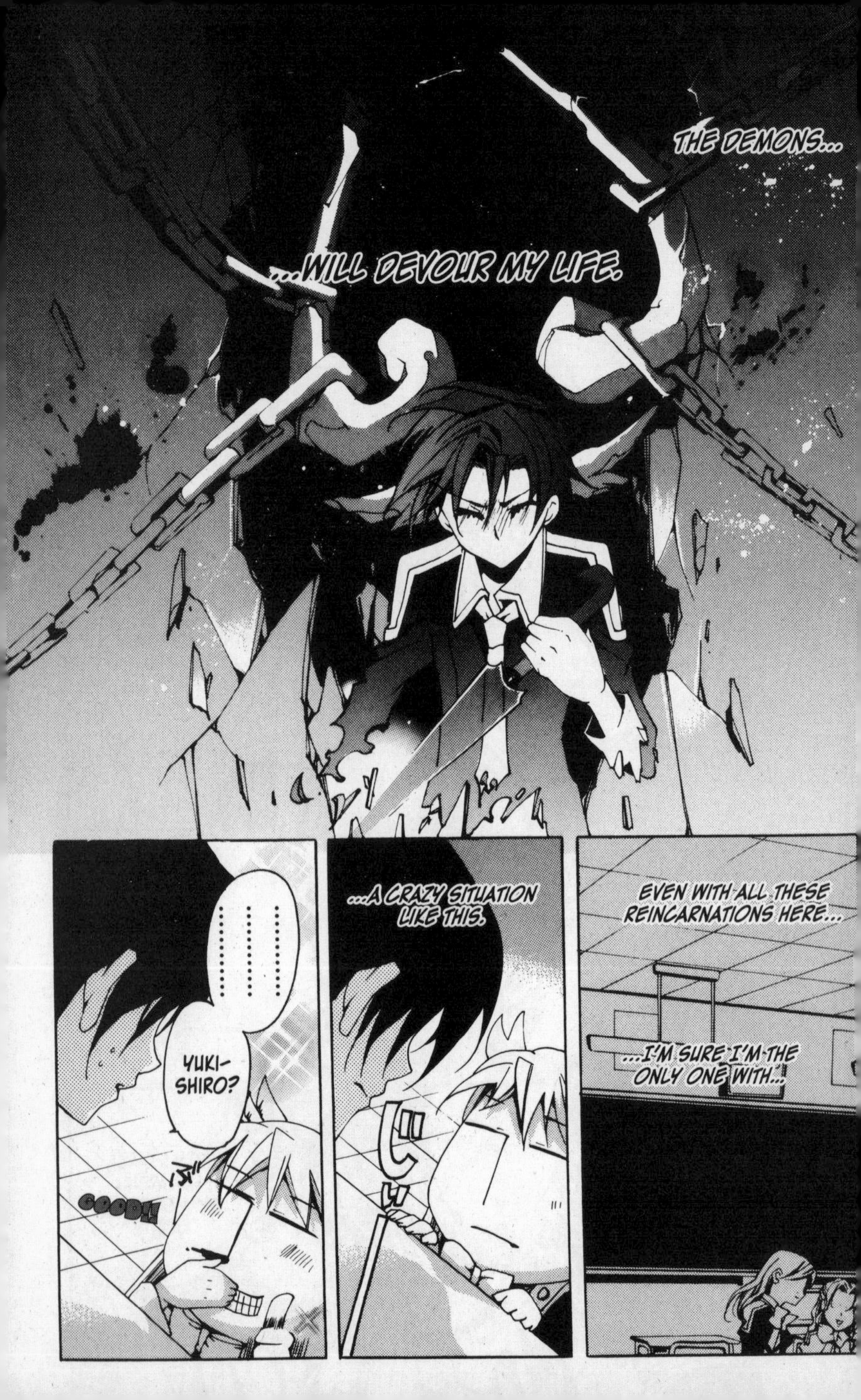
THE DEMONS...
...WILL DEVOUR MY LIFE.
EVEN WITH ALL THESE REINCARNATIONS HERE...
...I'M SURE I'M THE ONLY ONE WITH...
...A CRAZY SITUATION LIKE THIS.
......
YUKI-SHIRO?
GOOD!!

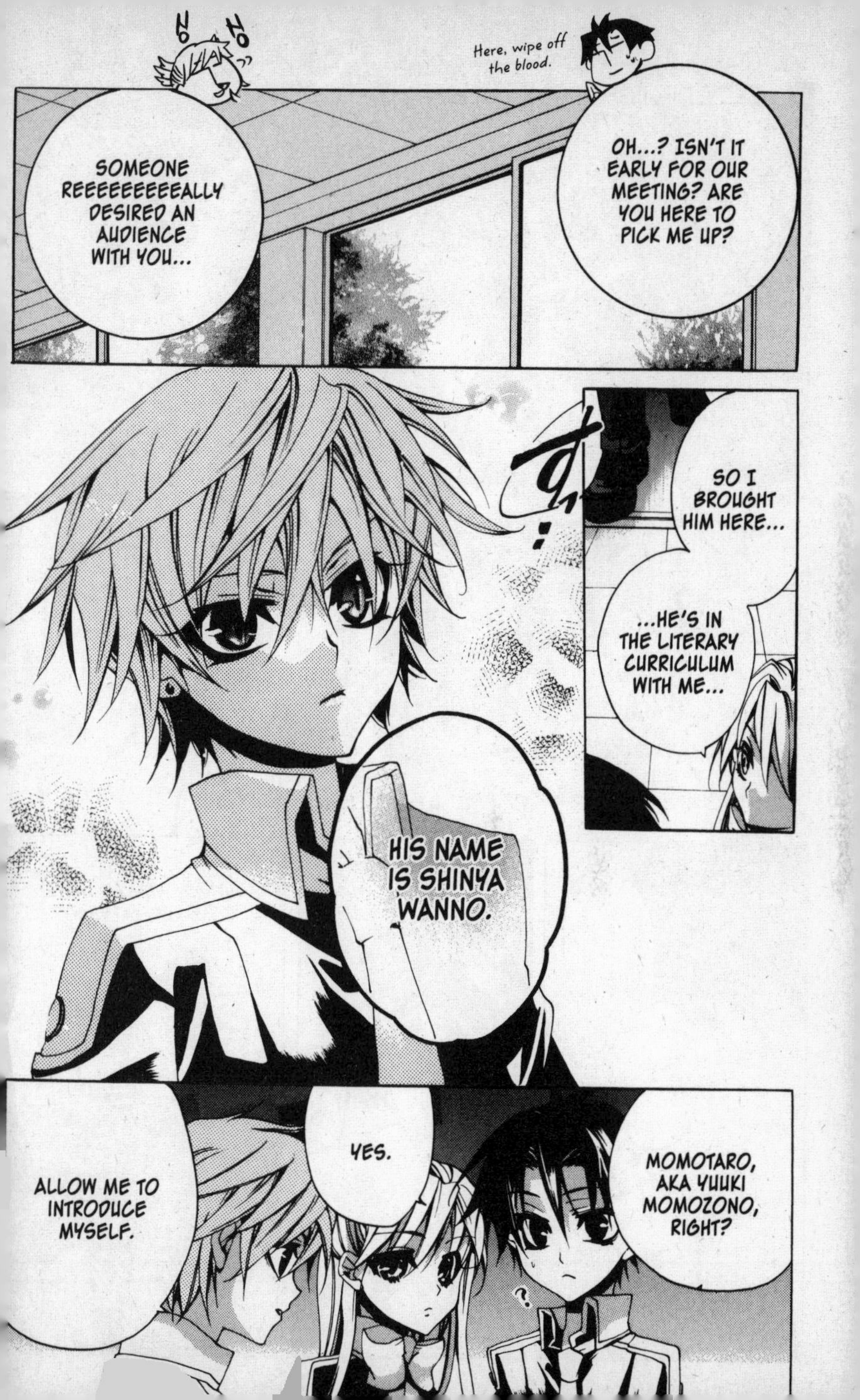
Here, wipe off the blood.
NO NO
OH...? ISN'T IT EARLY FOR OUR MEETING? ARE YOU HERE TO PICK ME UP?
SOMEONE REEEEEEEEEALLY DESIRED AN AUDIENCE WITH YOU...
SO I BROUGHT HIM HERE...
...HE'S IN THE LITERARY CURRICULUM WITH ME...
す
HIS NAME IS SHINYA WANNO.
MOMOTARO, AKA YUUKI MOMOZONO, RIGHT?
?
YES.
ALLOW ME TO INTRODUCE MYSELF.

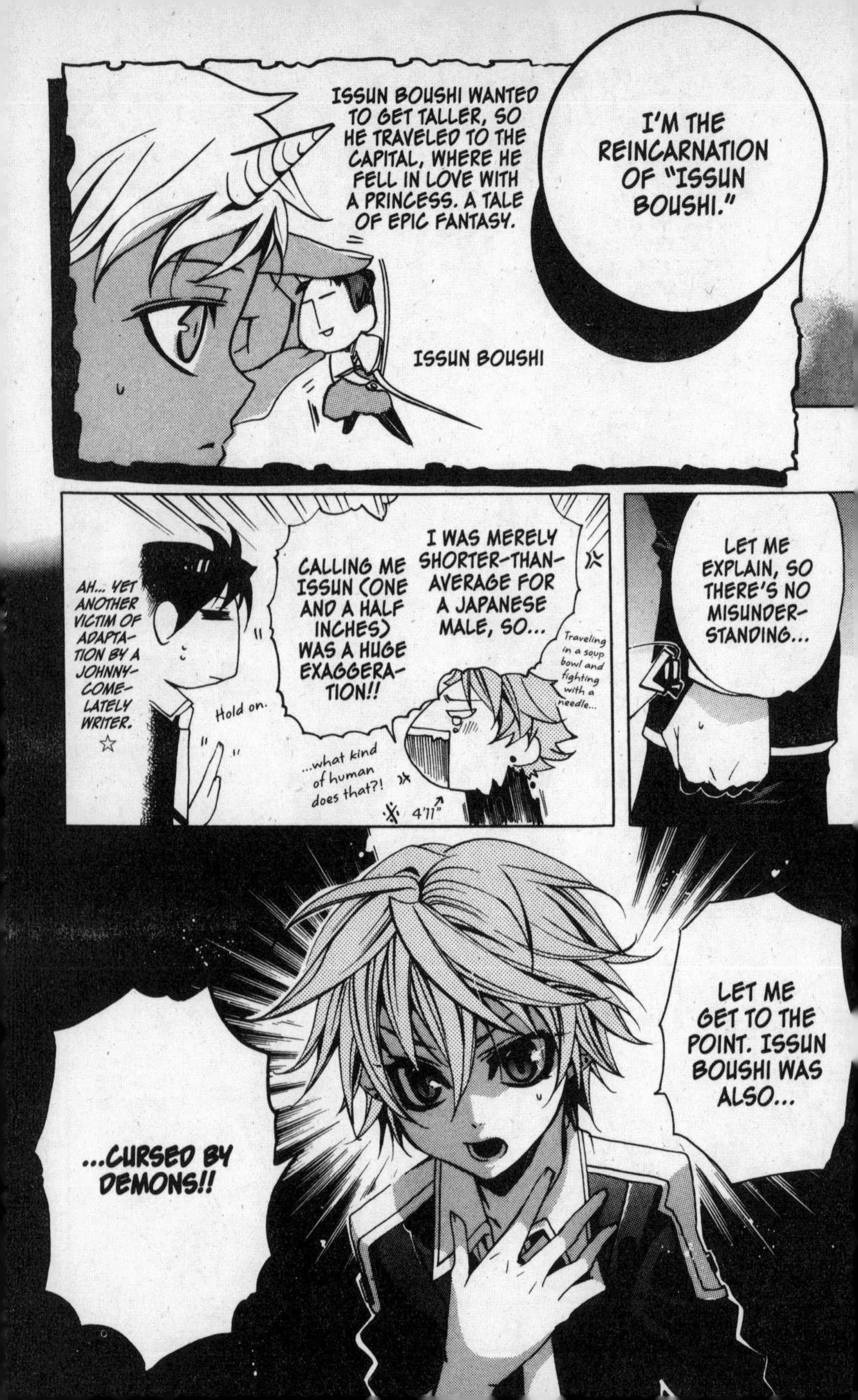
I'M THE REINCARNATION OF "ISSUN BOUSHI."
ISSUN BOUSHI WANTED TO GET TALLER, SO HE TRAVELED TO THE CAPITAL, WHERE HE FELL IN LOVE WITH A PRINCESS. A TALE OF EPIC FANTASY.
ISSUN BOUSHI
LET ME EXPLAIN, SO THERE'S NO MISUNDERSTANDING...
I WAS MERELY SHORTER-THAN-AVERAGE FOR A JAPANESE MALE, SO...
CALLING ME ISSUN (ONE AND A HALF INCHES) WAS A HUGE EXAGGERATION!!
Traveling in a soup bowl and fighting with a needle...
...what kind of human does that?!
4'11"
Hold on.
AH... YET ANOTHER VICTIM OF ADAPTATION BY A JOHNNY-COME-LATELY WRITER. ☆
LET ME GET TO THE POINT. ISSUN BOUSHI WAS ALSO...
...CURSED BY DEMONS!!

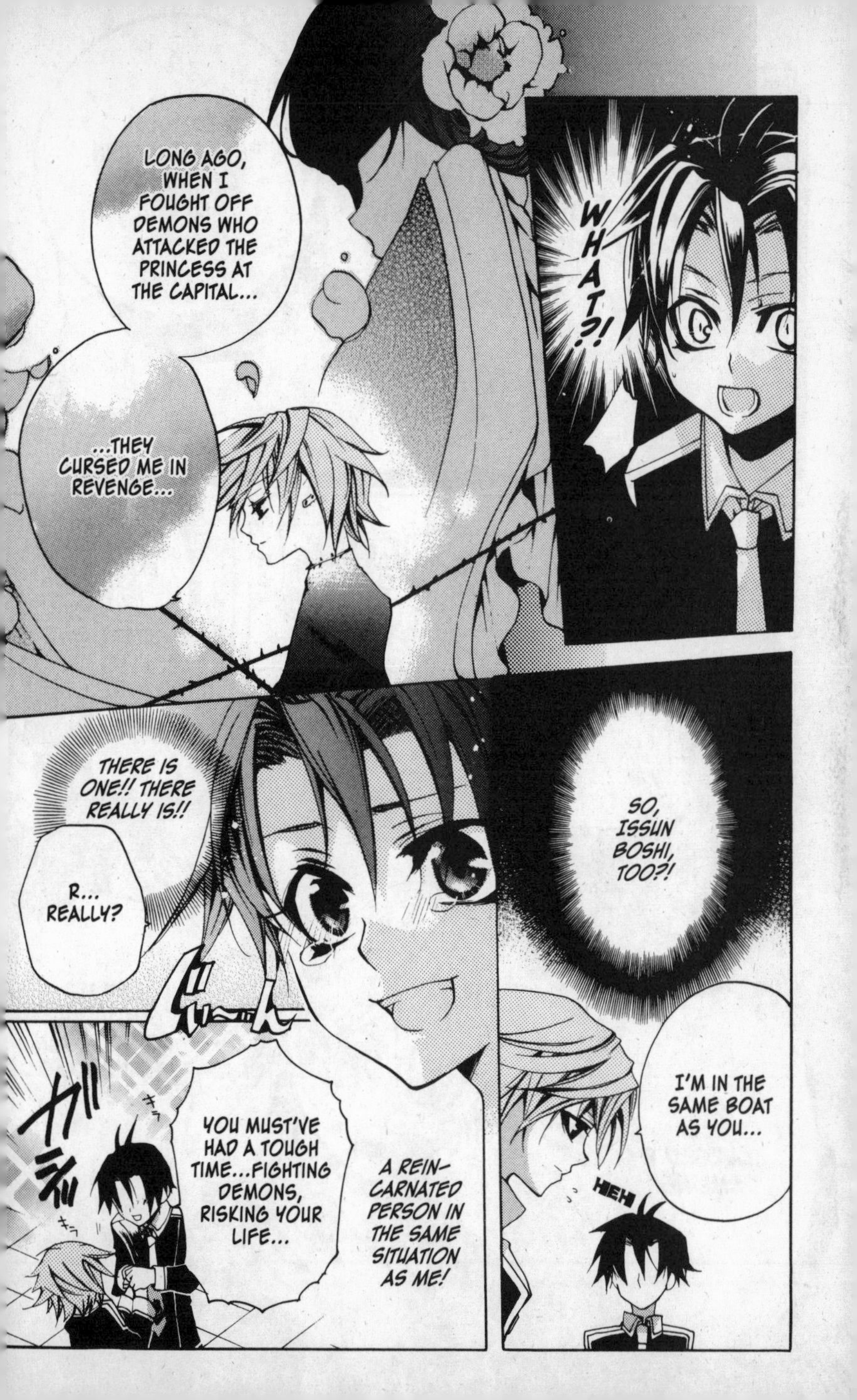
WHAT?!
LONG AGO, WHEN I FOUGHT OFF DEMONS WHO ATTACKED THE PRINCESS AT THE CAPITAL...
...THEY CURSED ME IN REVENGE...
SO, ISSUN BOSHI, TOO?!
THERE IS ONE!! THERE REALLY IS!!
R... REALLY?
I'M IN THE SAME BOAT AS YOU...
HEH
A REIN-CARNATED PERSON IN THE SAME SITUATION AS ME!
YOU MUST'VE HAD A TOUGH TIME...FIGHTING DEMONS, RISKING YOUR LIFE...

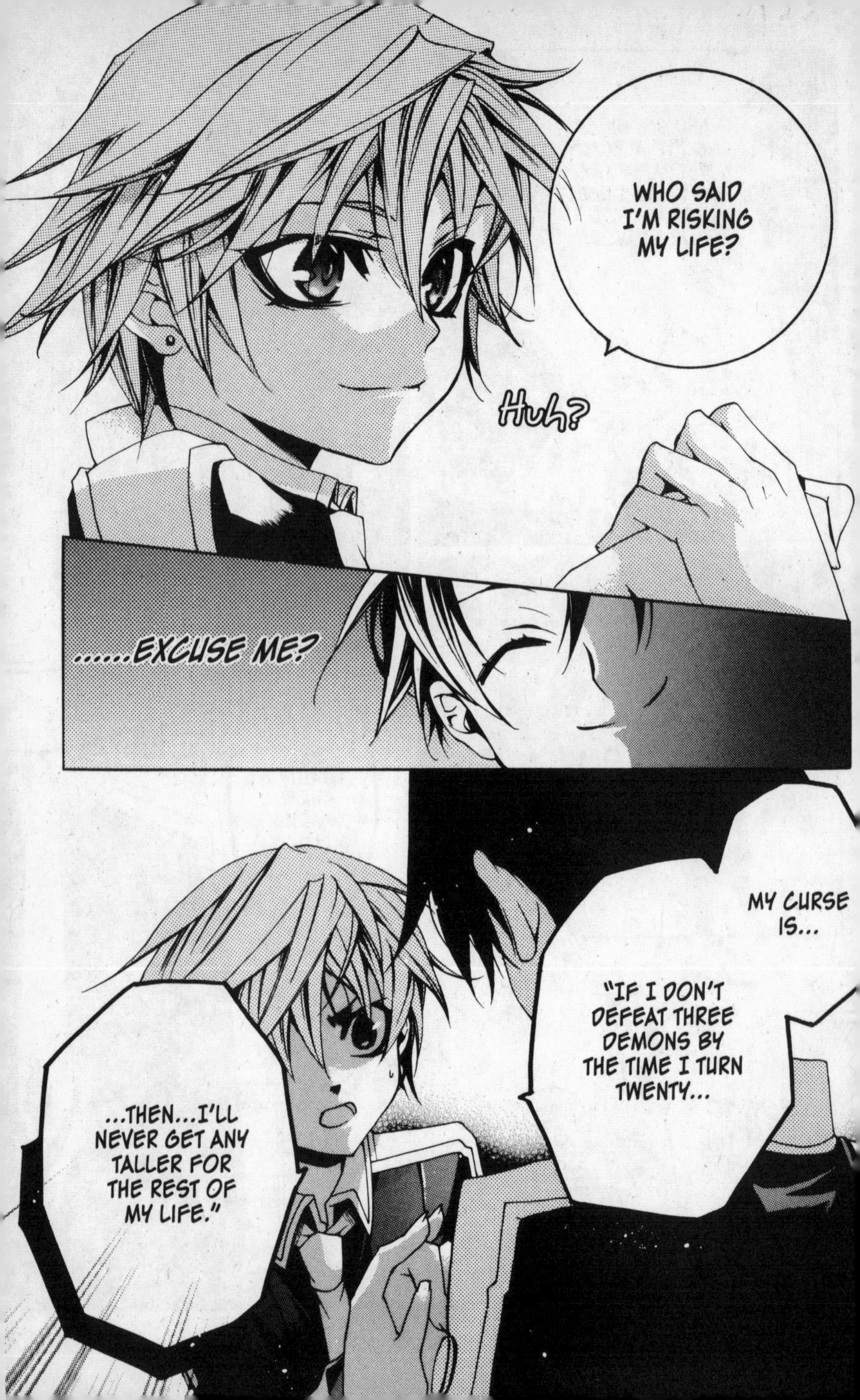
WHO SAID I'M RISKING MY LIFE?
Huh?
......EXCUSE ME?
MY CURSE IS...
"IF I DON'T DEFEAT THREE DEMONS BY THE TIME I TURN TWENTY...
...THEN...I'LL NEVER GET ANY TALLER FOR THE REST OF MY LIFE."

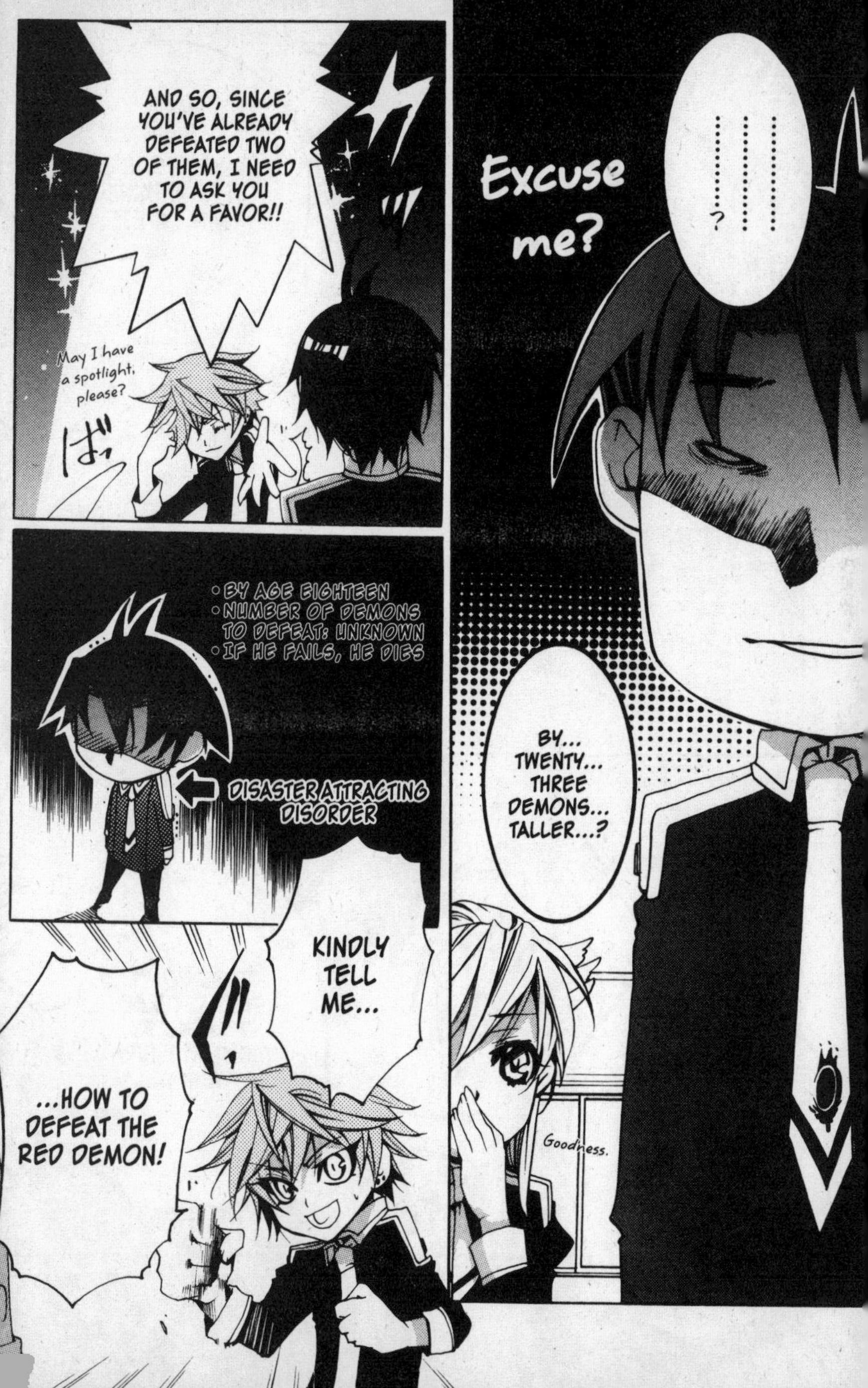
......?
Excuse me?
BY... TWENTY... THREE DEMONS... TALLER...?
Goodness.
AND SO, SINCE YOU'VE ALREADY DEFEATED TWO OF THEM, I NEED TO ASK YOU FOR A FAVOR!!
May I have a spotlight, please?
ばっ
• BY AGE EIGHTEEN
• NUMBER OF DEMONS TO DEFEAT: UNKNOWN
• IF HE FAILS, HE DIES
DISASTER ATTRACTING DISORDER
KINDLY TELL ME...
...HOW TO DEFEAT THE RED DEMON!

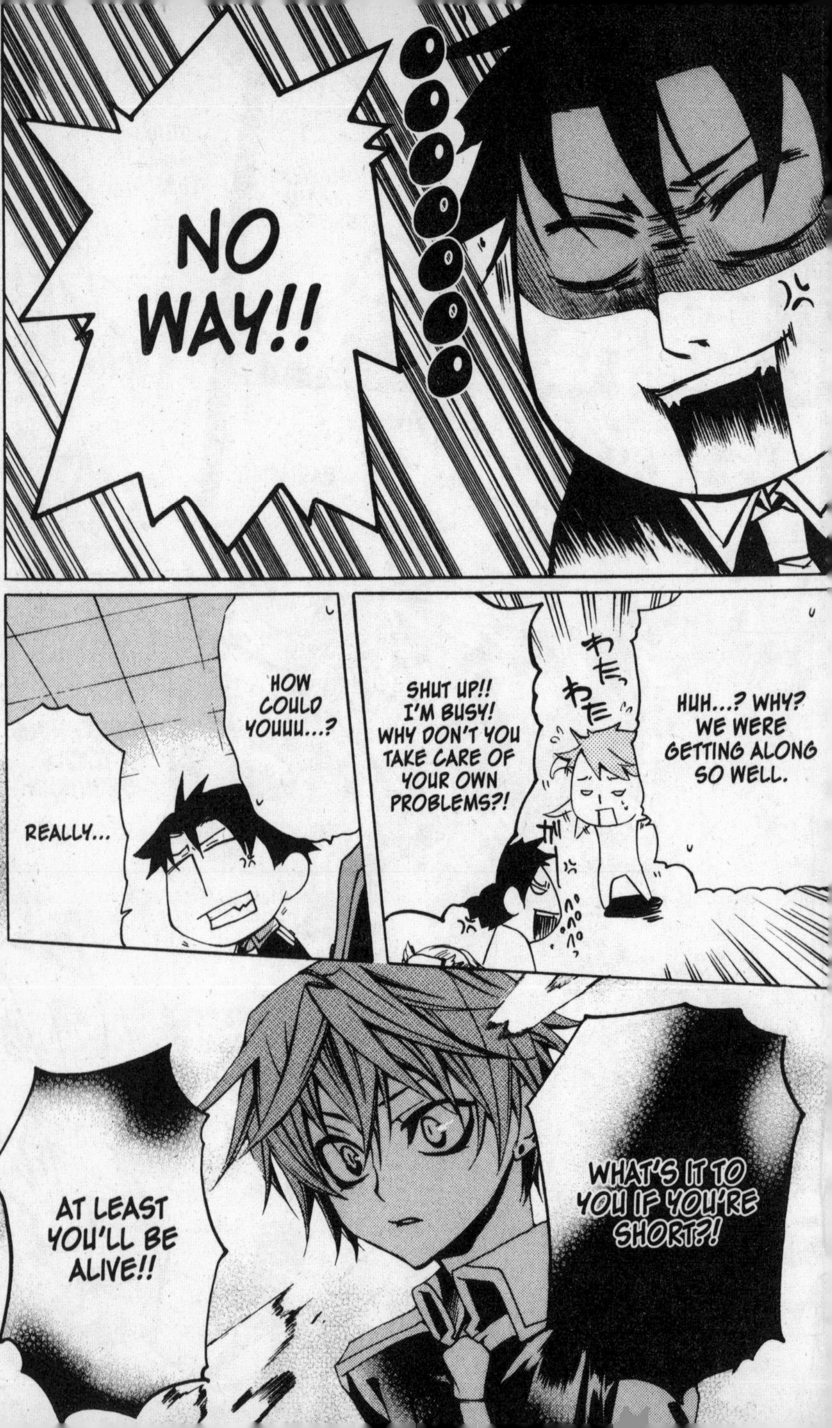
NO WAY!!
HUH...? WHY? WE WERE GETTING ALONG SO WELL.
わたっ わた
SHUT UP!! I'M BUSY! WHY DON'T YOU TAKE CARE OF YOUR OWN PROBLEMS?!
HOW COULD YOUUU...?
REALLY...
WHAT'S IT TO YOU IF YOU'RE SHORT?!
AT LEAST YOU'LL BE ALIVE!!

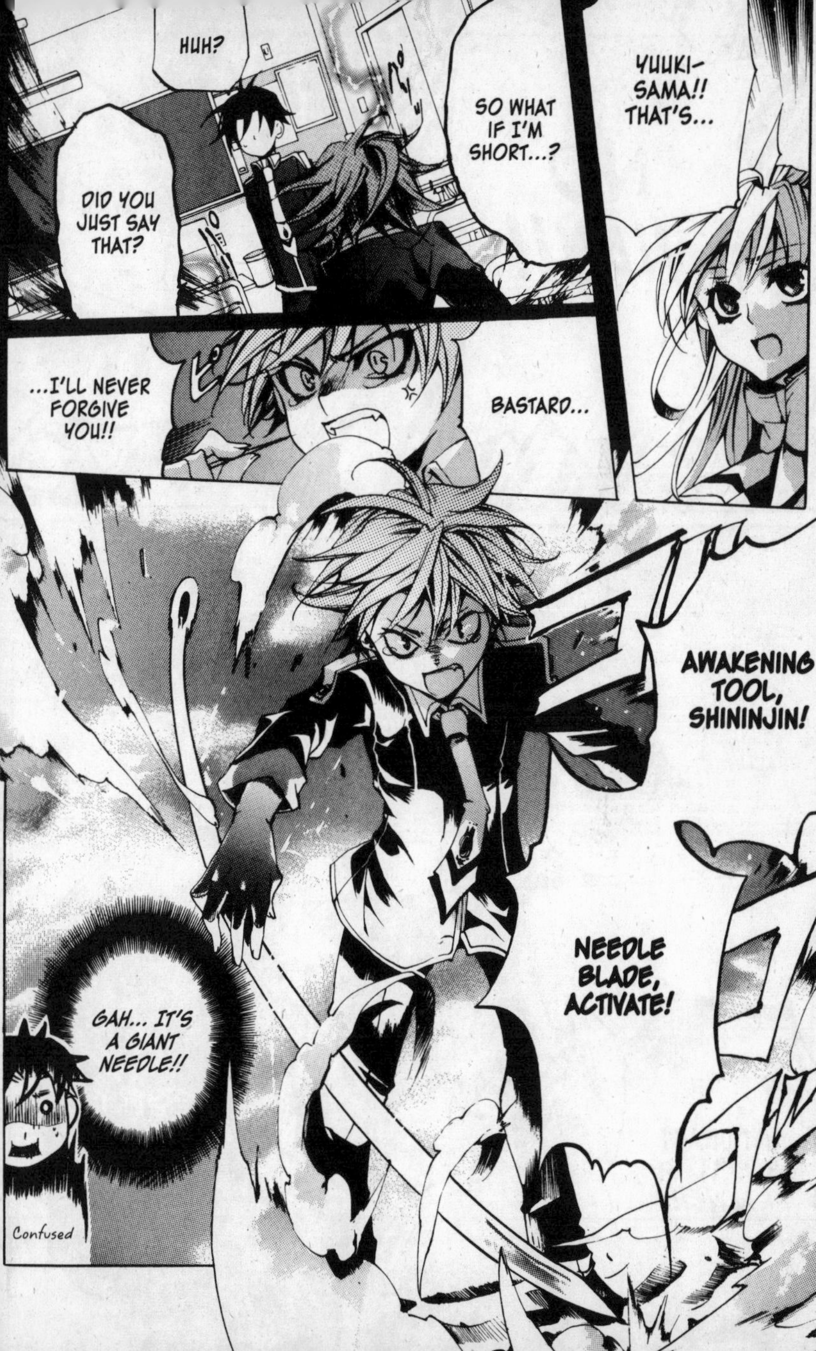
YUUKI-SAMA!! THAT'S...
SO WHAT IF I'M SHORT...?
HUH?
DID YOU JUST SAY THAT?
BASTARD...
...I'LL NEVER FORGIVE YOU!!
AWAKENING TOOL, SHININJIN!
NEEDLE BLADE, ACTIVATE!
GAH... IT'S A GIANT NEEDLE!!
Confused

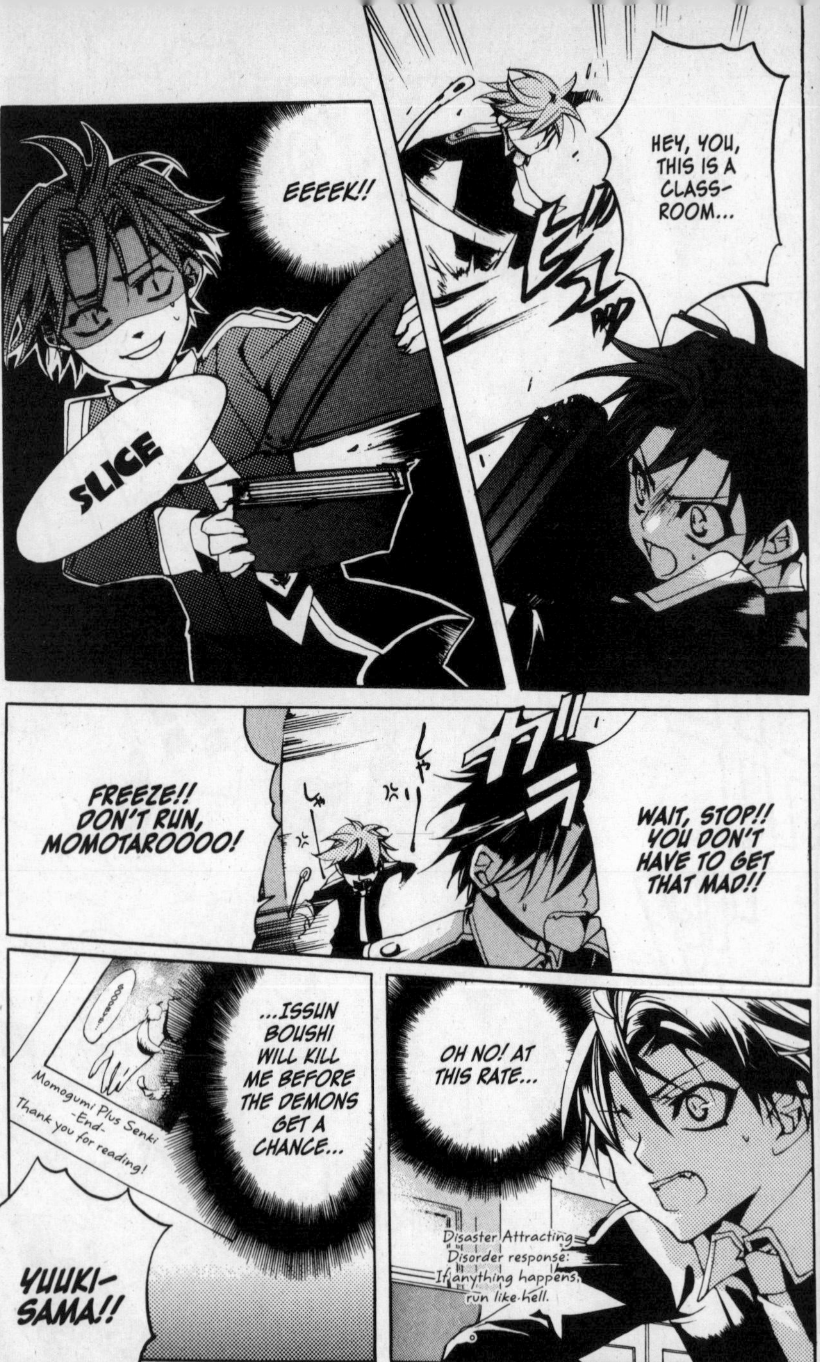
HEY, YOU, THIS IS A CLASSROOM...
EEEEK!!
SLICE
WAIT, STOP!! YOU DON'T HAVE TO GET THAT MAD!!
FREEZE!! DON'T RUN, MOMOTAROOOO!
OH NO! AT THIS RATE...
Disaster Attracting Disorder response: If anything happens, run like hell.
...ISSUN BOUSHI WILL KILL ME BEFORE THE DEMONS GET A CHANCE...
Momogumi Plus Senki -End- Thank you for reading!
YUUKI-SAMA!!

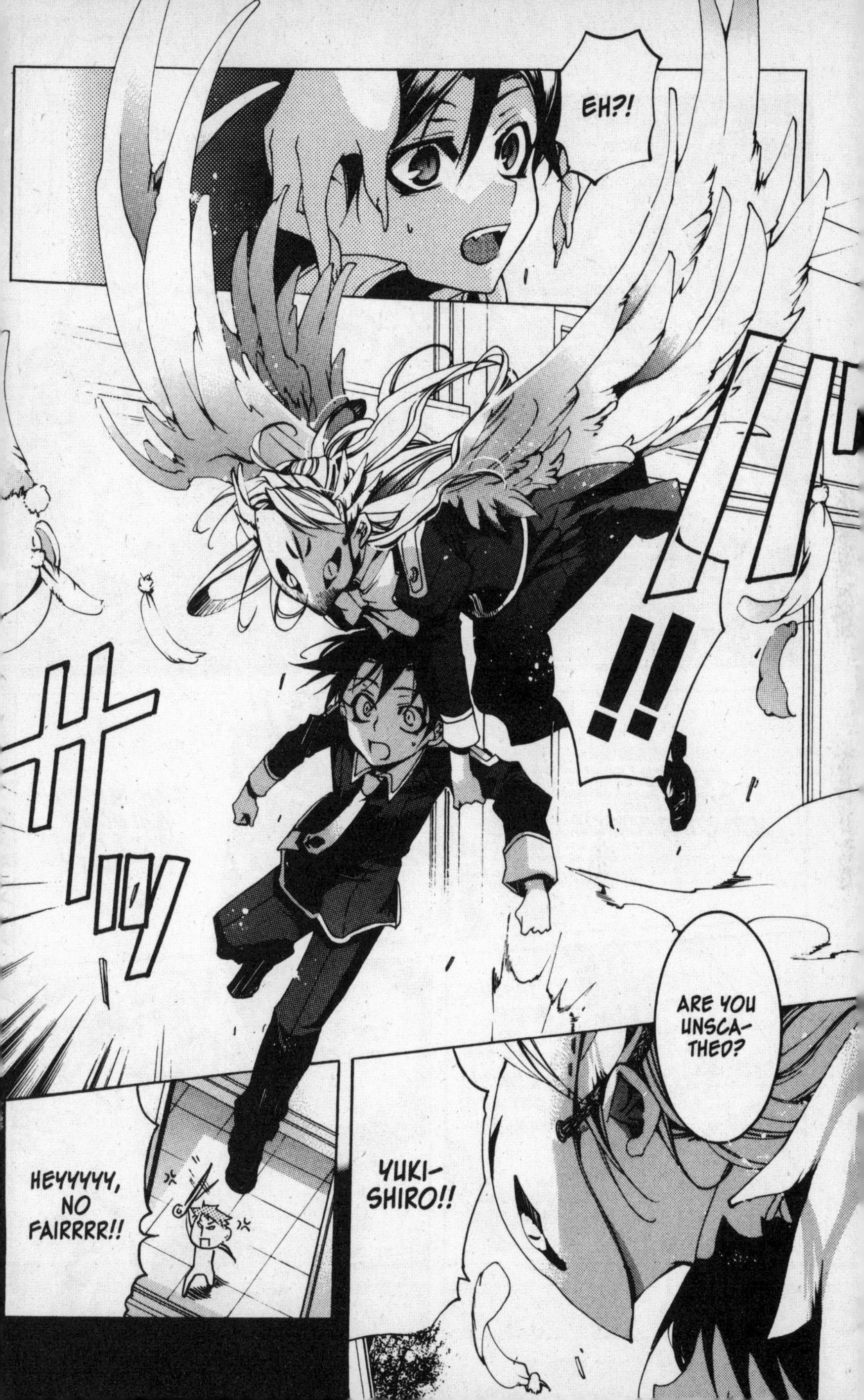
EH?!
ザッ
!!
ARE YOU UNSCA-THED?
YUKI-SHIRO!!
HEYYYYY, NO FAIRRRR!!

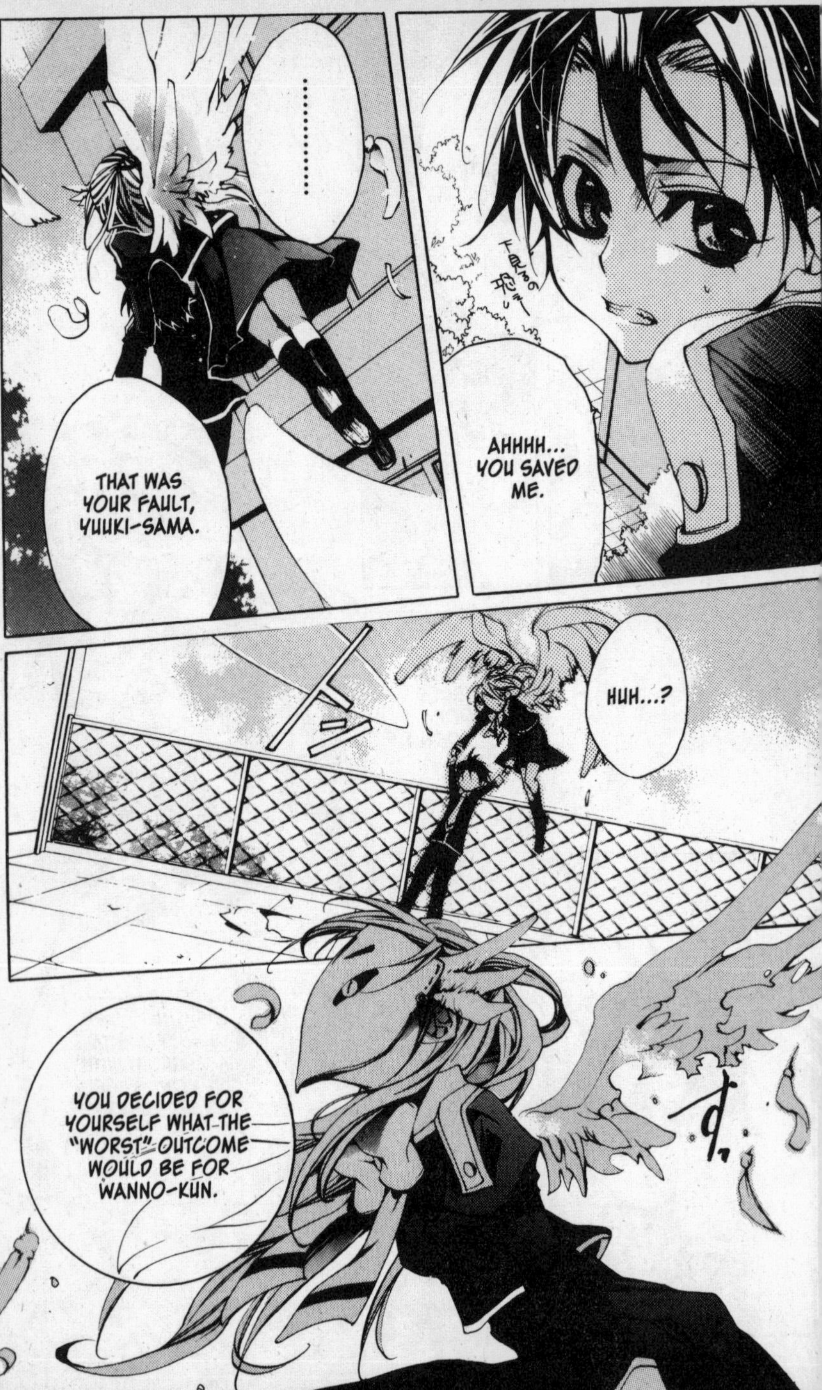
AHHHH... YOU SAVED ME.
……
THAT WAS YOUR FAULT, YUUKI-SAMA.
HUH...?
YOU DECIDED FOR YOURSELF WHAT THE "WORST" OUTCOME WOULD BE FOR WANNO-KUN.

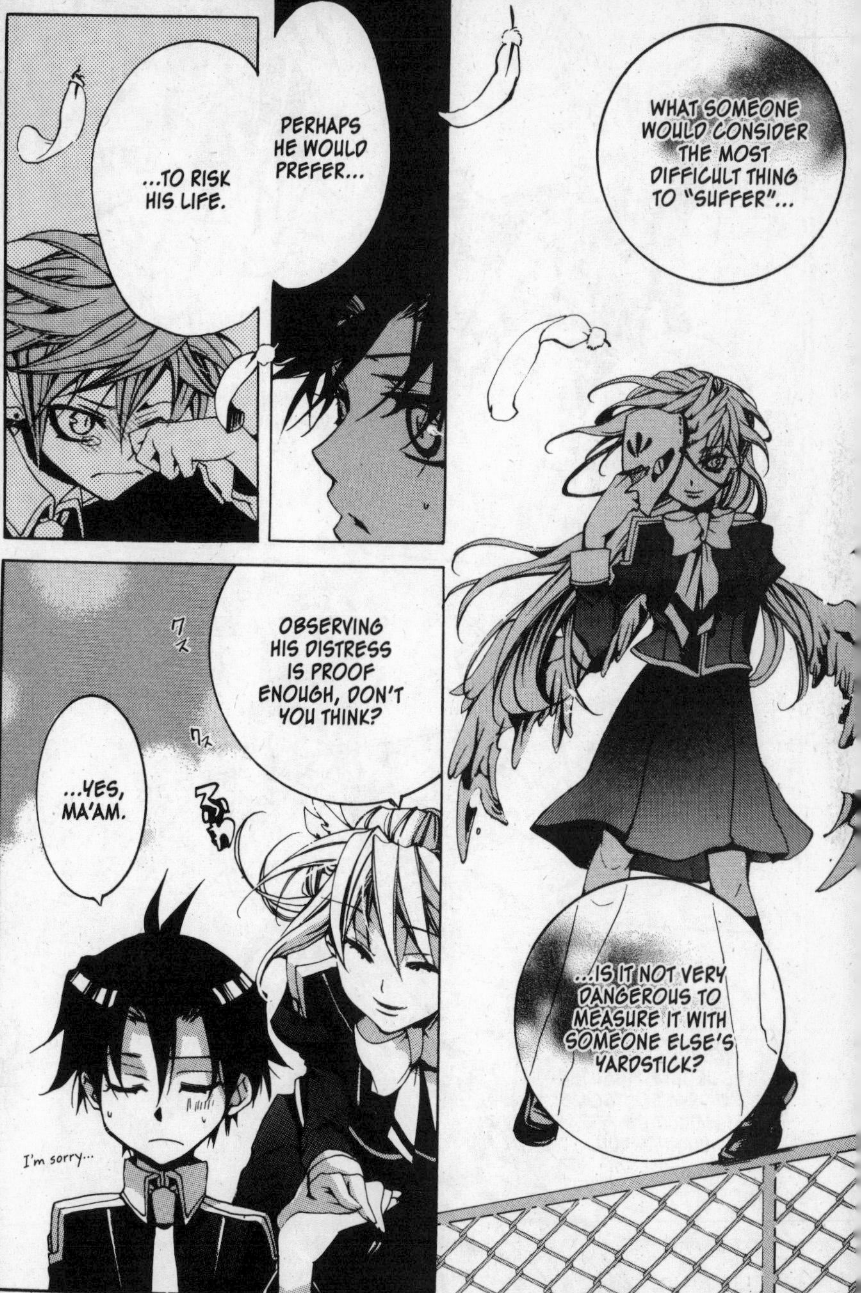
WHAT SOMEONE WOULD CONSIDER THE MOST DIFFICULT THING TO "SUFFER"...
...IS IT NOT VERY DANGEROUS TO MEASURE IT WITH SOMEONE ELSE'S YARDSTICK?
PERHAPS HE WOULD PREFER...
...TO RISK HIS LIFE.
OBSERVING HIS DISTRESS IS PROOF ENOUGH, DON'T YOU THINK?
クス
クス
...YES, MA'AM.
I'm sorry...

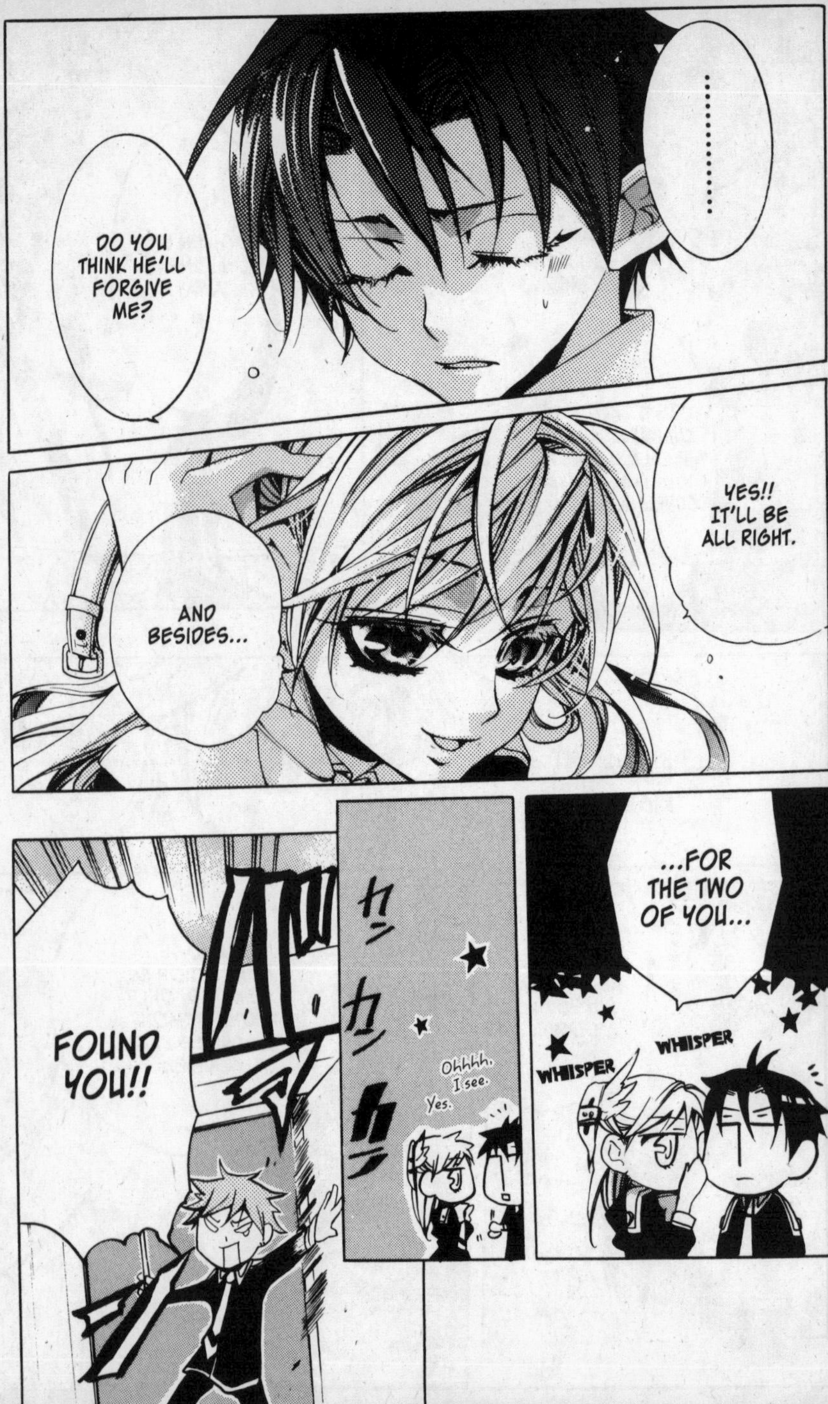
......
DO YOU THINK HE'LL FORGIVE ME?
YES!! IT'LL BE ALL RIGHT.
AND BESIDES...
...FOR THE TWO OF YOU...
WHISPER
WHISPER
カン
カン
カン
Ohhhh. I see.
Yes.
FOUND YOU!!

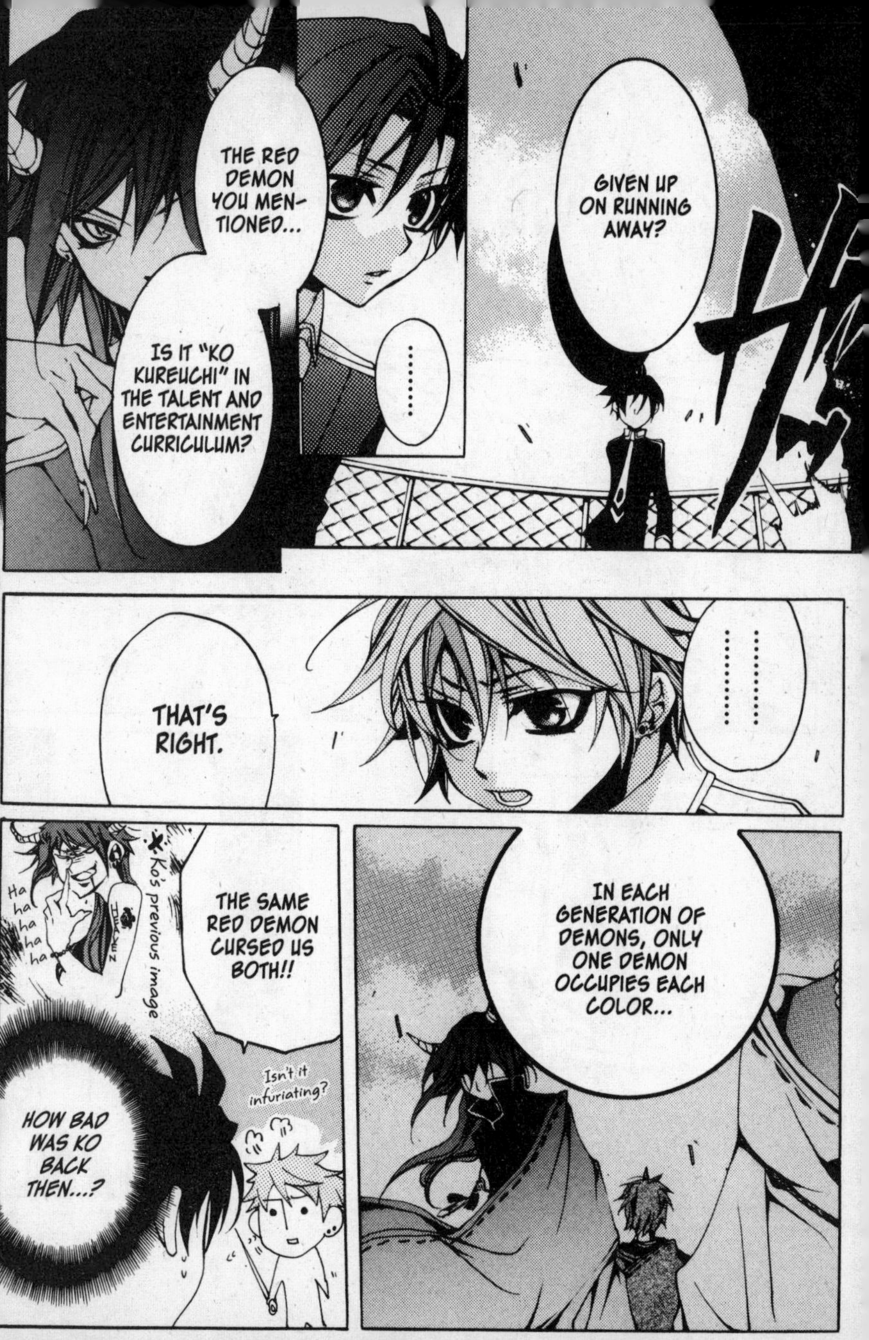
GIVEN UP ON RUNNING AWAY?
THE RED DEMON YOU MENTIONED...
IS IT "KO KUREUCHI" IN THE TALENT AND ENTERTAINMENT CURRICULUM?
......
......
THAT'S RIGHT.
IN EACH GENERATION OF DEMONS, ONLY ONE DEMON OCCUPIES EACH COLOR...
THE SAME RED DEMON CURSED US BOTH!!
Ko's previous image
Ha ha ha ha ha
HEAVEN
Isn't it infuriating?
HOW BAD WAS KO BACK THEN...?

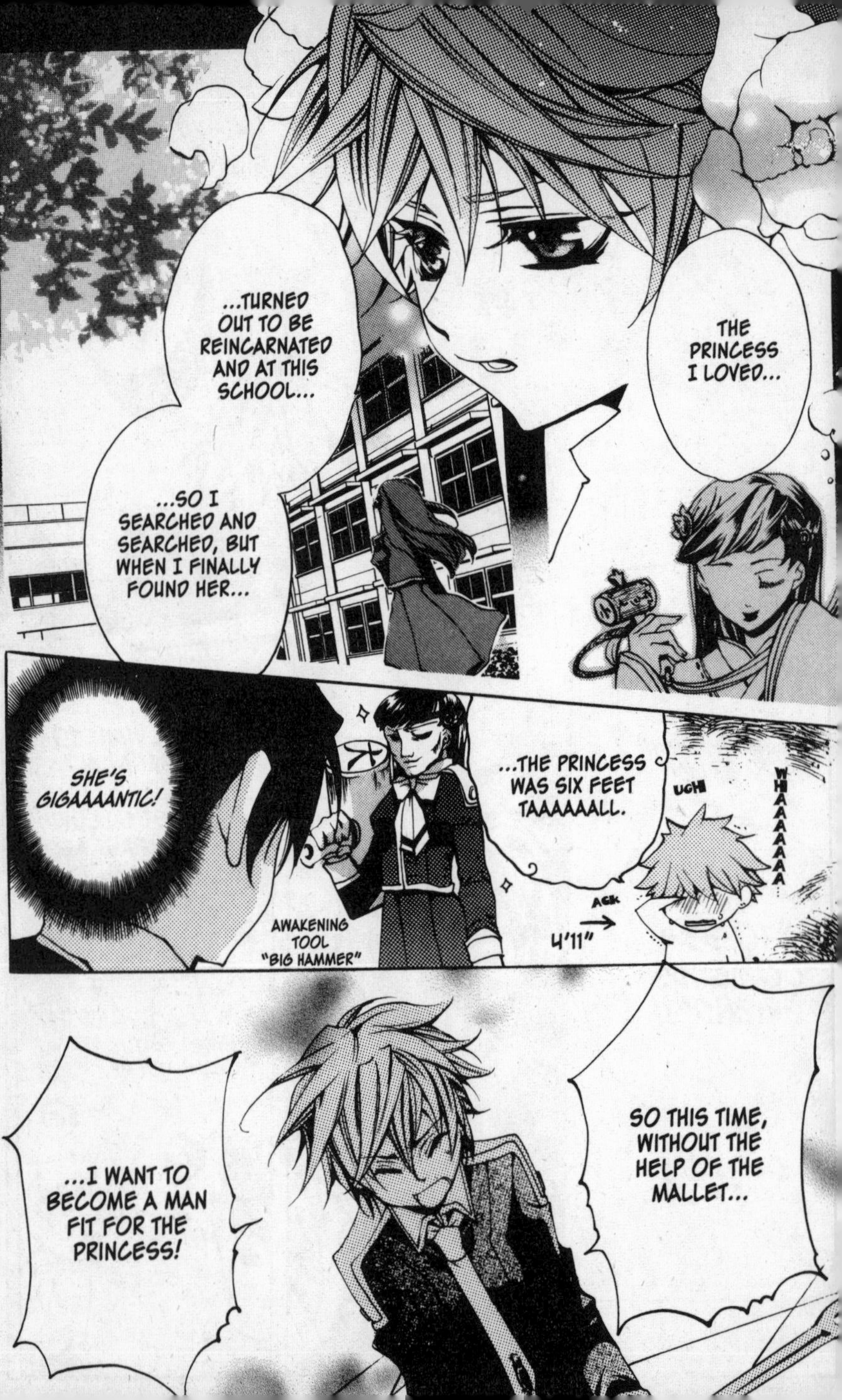
THE PRINCESS I LOVED...
...TURNED OUT TO BE REINCARNATED AND AT THIS SCHOOL...
...SO I SEARCHED AND SEARCHED, BUT WHEN I FINALLY FOUND HER...
WHAAAAAAAA...
UGH
...THE PRINCESS WAS SIX FEET TAAAAAALL.
ACK
4'11"
AWAKENING TOOL "BIG HAMMER"
SHE'S GIGAAAANTIC!
SO THIS TIME, WITHOUT THE HELP OF THE MALLET...
...I WANT TO BECOME A MAN FIT FOR THE PRINCESS!

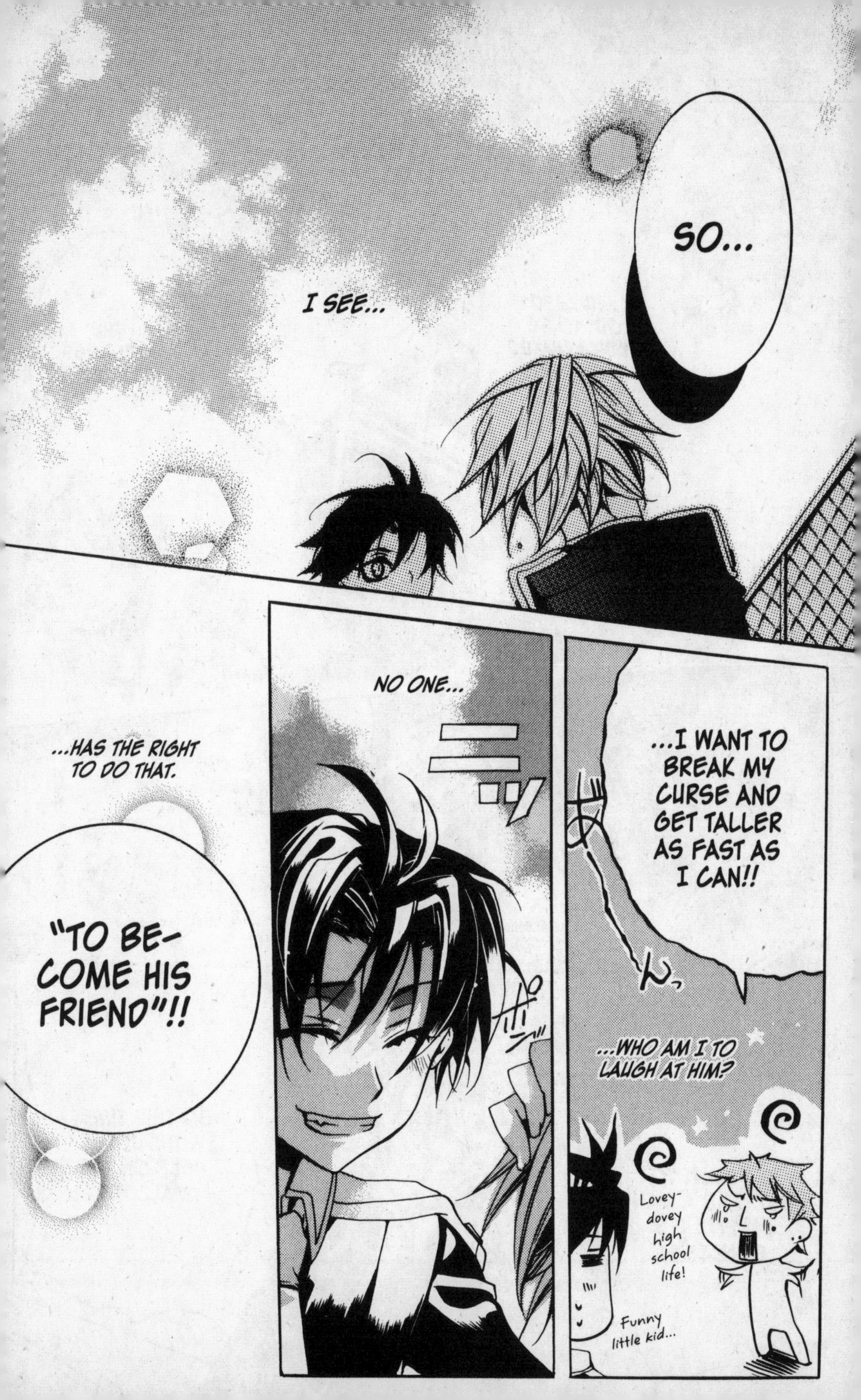
SO...
I SEE...
...I WANT TO BREAK MY CURSE AND GET TALLER AS FAST AS I CAN!!
...WHO AM I TO LAUGH AT HIM?
Lovey-dovey high school life!
Funny little kid...
NO ONE...
...HAS THE RIGHT TO DO THAT.
"TO BE-COME HIS FRIEND"!!

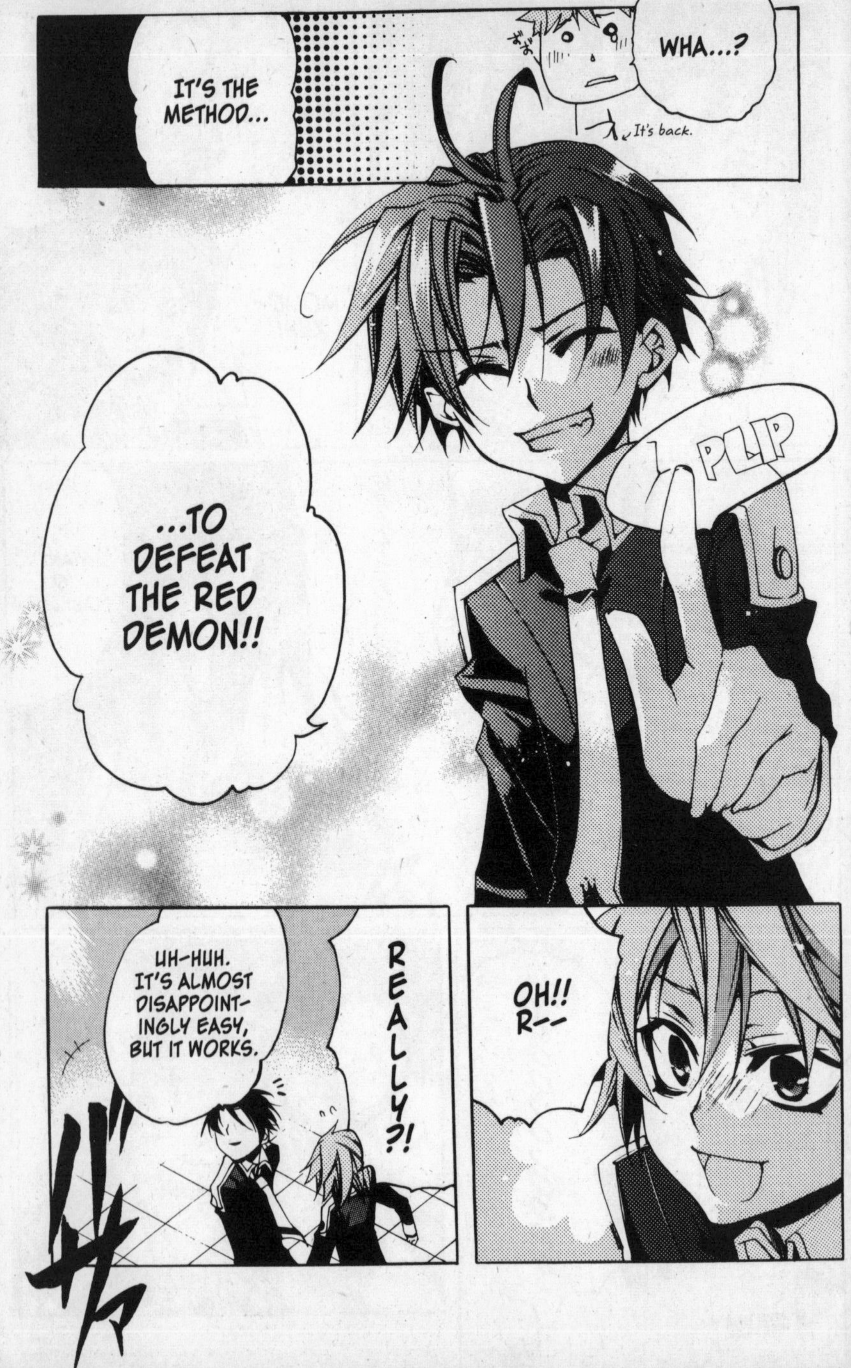
WHA...?
It's back.
IT'S THE METHOD...
PLIP
...TO DEFEAT THE RED DEMON!!
OH!! R--
REALLY?!
UH-HUH. IT'S ALMOST DISAPPOINT-INGLY EASY, BUT IT WORKS.

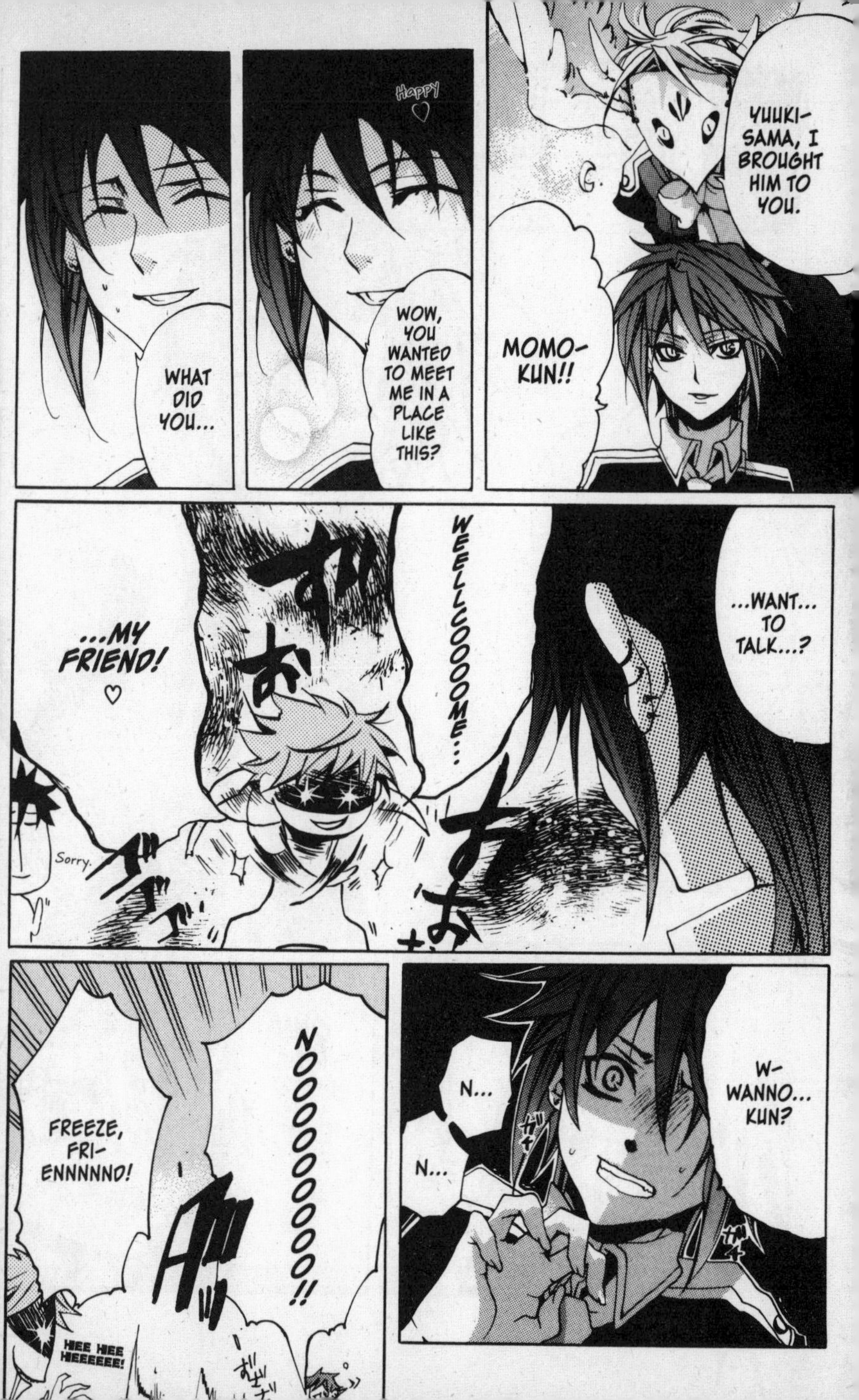
YUUKI-SAMA, I BROUGHT HIM TO YOU.
MOMO-KUN!!
Happy ♡
WOW, YOU WANTED TO MEET ME IN A PLACE LIKE THIS?
WHAT DID YOU...
...WANT... TO TALK...?
WEELLCOOOOOME...
...MY FRIEND! ♡
Sorry.
W-WANNO... KUN?
N...
N...
NOOOOOOOOOOOO!!
FREEZE, FRI-ENNNNND!
HEE HEE HEEEEEEE!

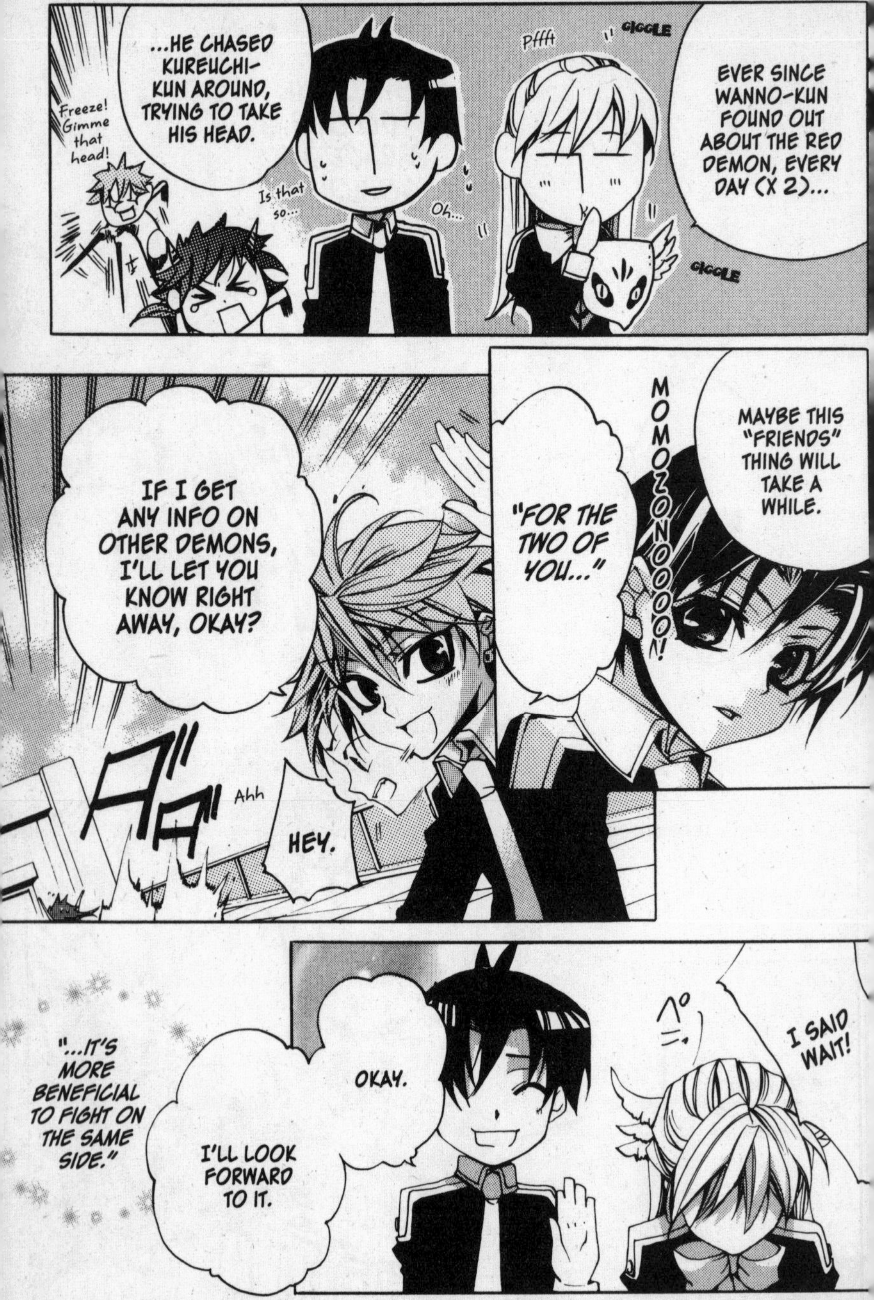
EVER SINCE WANNO-KUN FOUND OUT ABOUT THE RED DEMON, EVERY DAY (X 2)...
GIGGLE
Pffft
Oh...
GIGGLE
...HE CHASED KUREUCHI-KUN AROUND, TRYING TO TAKE HIS HEAD.
Is that so...
Freeze! Gimme that head!
MAYBE THIS "FRIENDS" THING WILL TAKE A WHILE.
MOMOZONOOOOOON!
"FOR THE TWO OF YOU..."
IF I GET ANY INFO ON OTHER DEMONS, I'LL LET YOU KNOW RIGHT AWAY, OKAY?
Ahh
HEY.
I SAID WAIT!
OKAY.
I'LL LOOK FORWARD TO IT.
"...IT'S MORE BENEFICIAL TO FIGHT ON THE SAME SIDE."

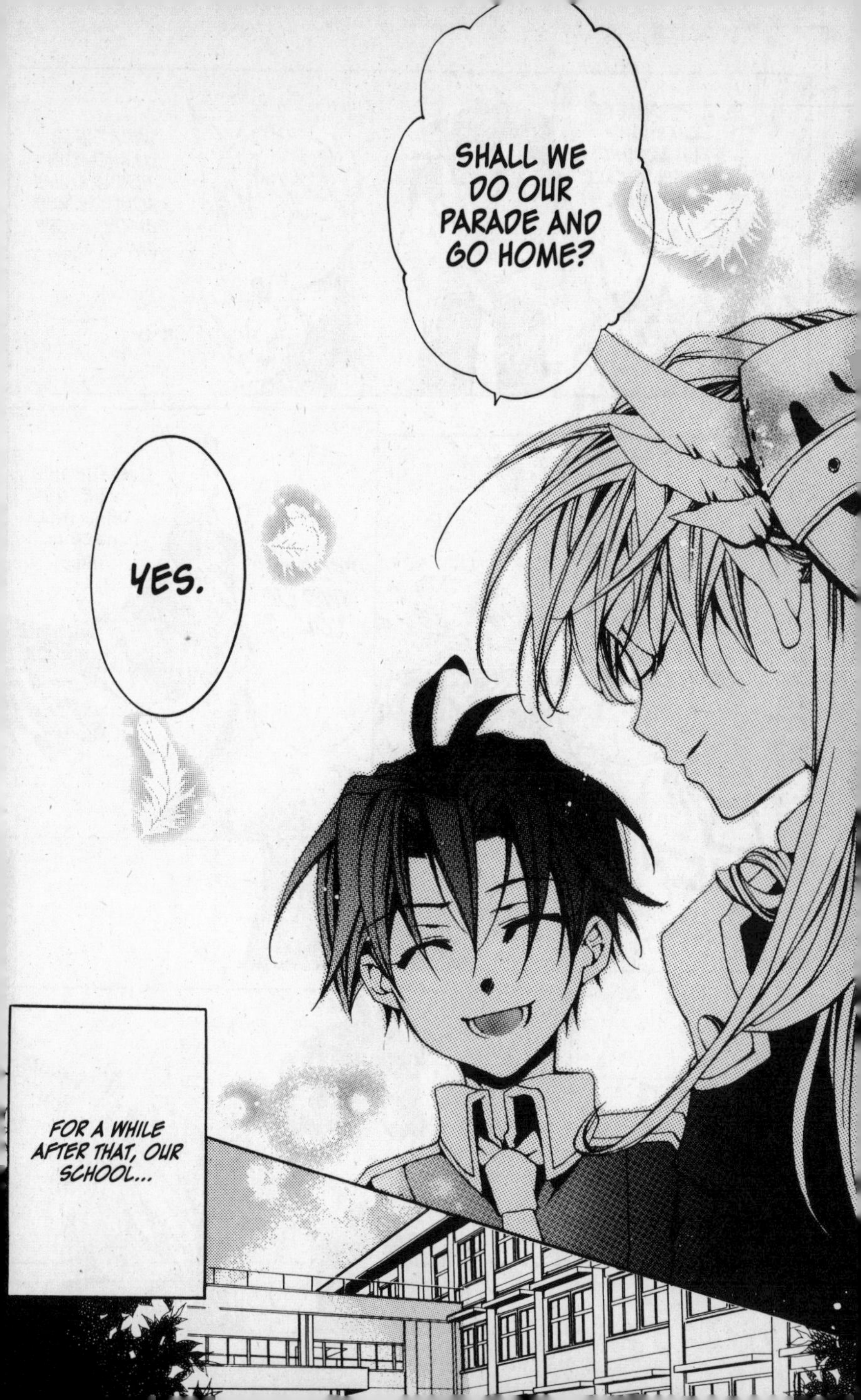
SHALL WE DO OUR PARADE AND GO HOME?
YES.
FOR A WHILE AFTER THAT, OUR SCHOOL...

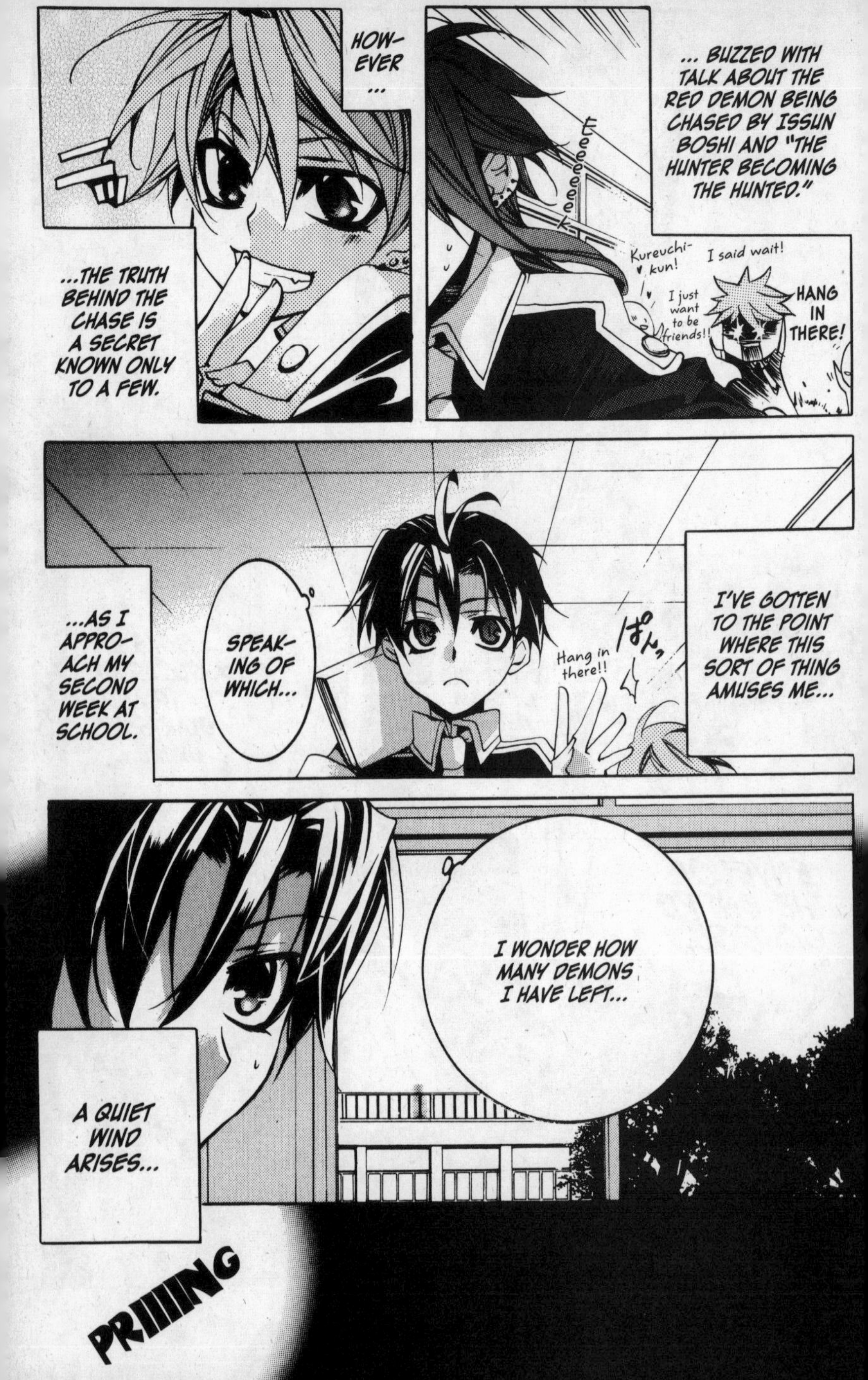
... BUZZED WITH TALK ABOUT THE RED DEMON BEING CHASED BY ISSUN BOSHI AND "THE HUNTER BECOMING THE HUNTED."
Eeeeeeek
Kureuchi-kun!
I said wait!
I just want to be friends!!
HANG IN THERE!
HOW-EVER ...
...THE TRUTH BEHIND THE CHASE IS A SECRET KNOWN ONLY TO A FEW.
I'VE GOTTEN TO THE POINT WHERE THIS SORT OF THING AMUSES ME...
Hang in there!!
SPEAK-ING OF WHICH...
...AS I APPRO-ACH MY SECOND WEEK AT SCHOOL.
I WONDER HOW MANY DEMONS I HAVE LEFT...
A QUIET WIND ARISES...
PRIIIING

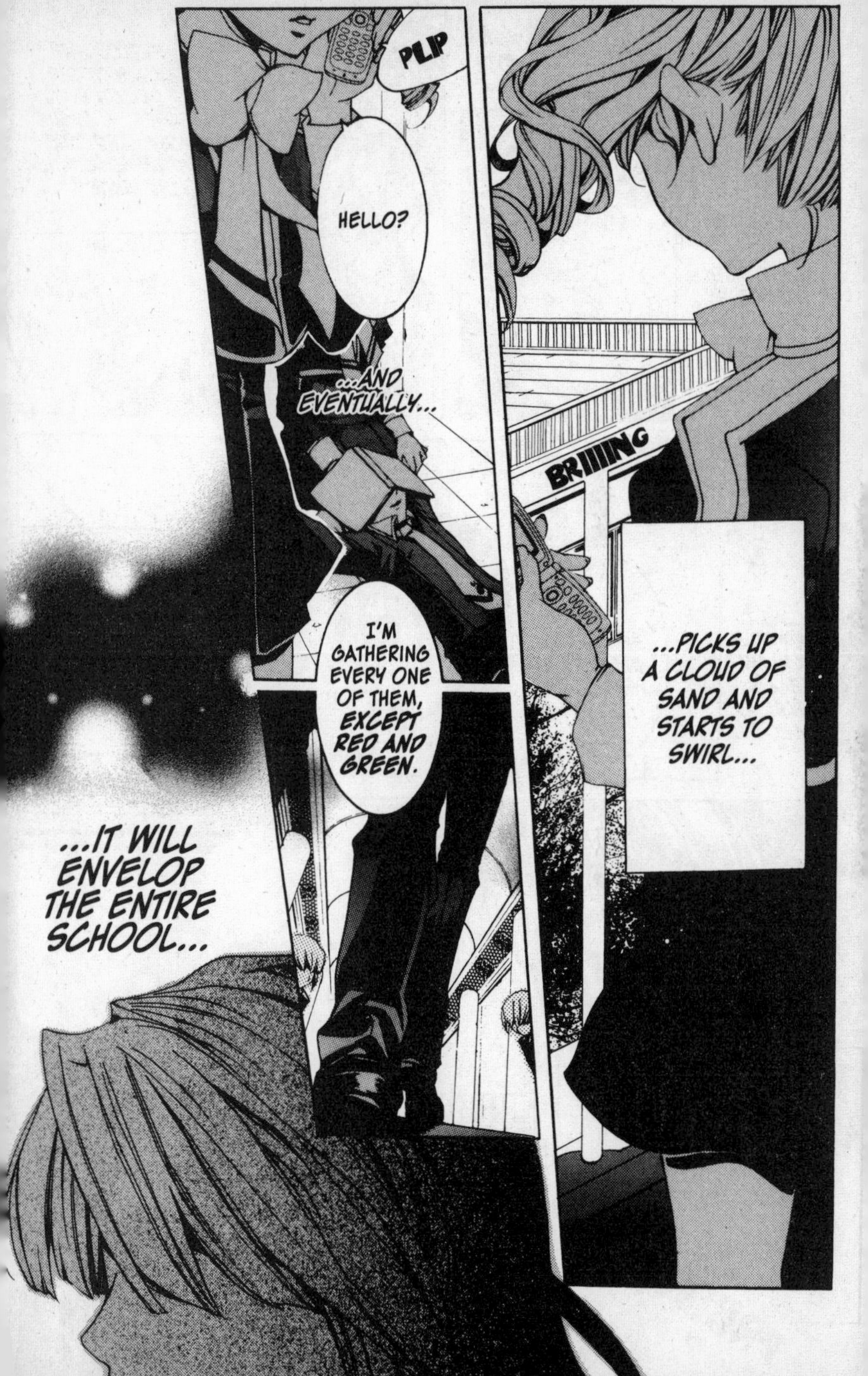
BRIIIING
...PICKS UP A CLOUD OF SAND AND STARTS TO SWIRL...
PLIP
HELLO?
...AND EVENTUALLY...
I'M GATHERING EVERY ONE OF THEM, EXCEPT RED AND GREEN.
...IT WILL ENVELOP THE ENTIRE SCHOOL...

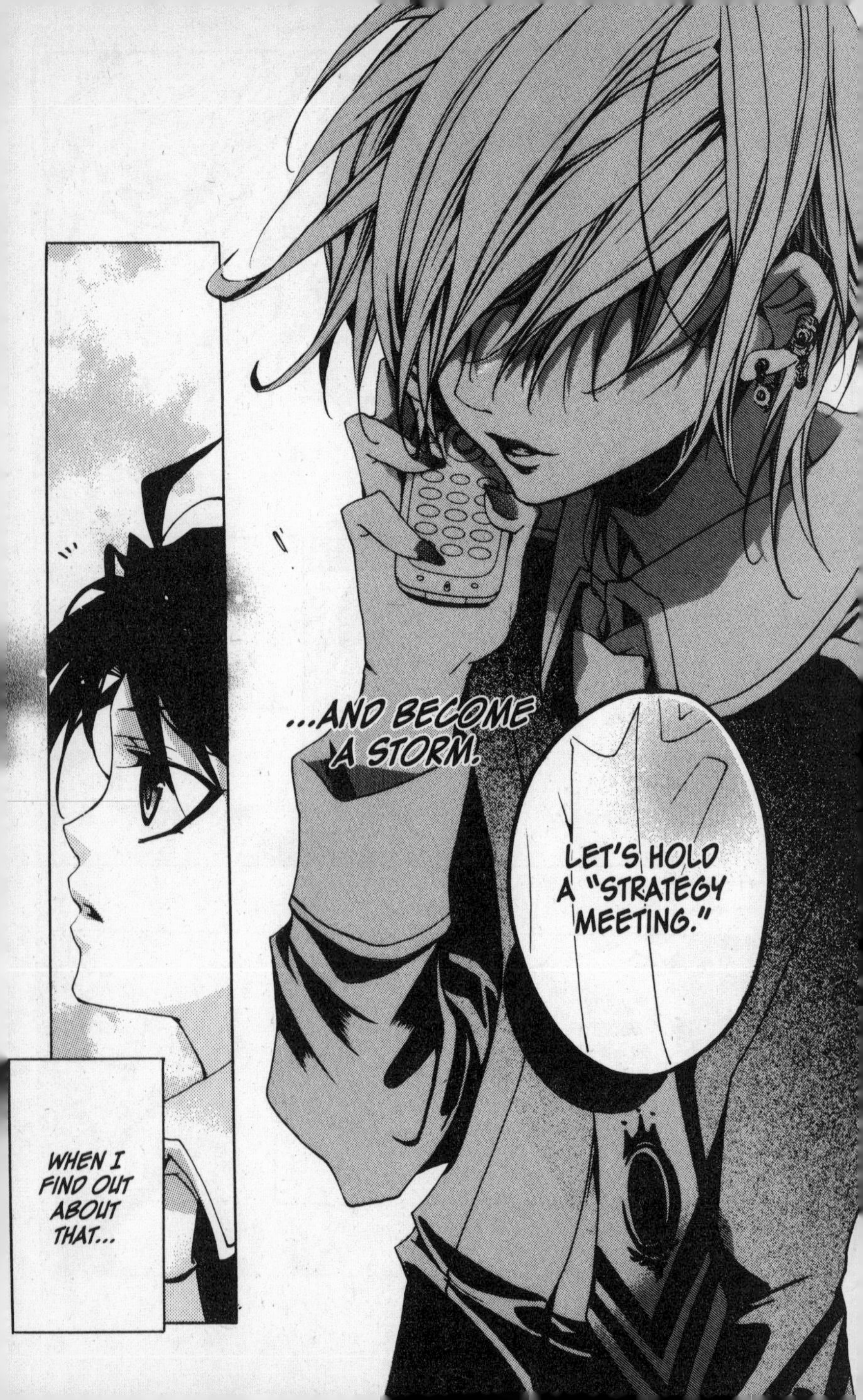
...AND BECOME A STORM.
LET'S HOLD A "STRATEGY MEETING."
WHEN I FIND OUT ABOUT THAT...

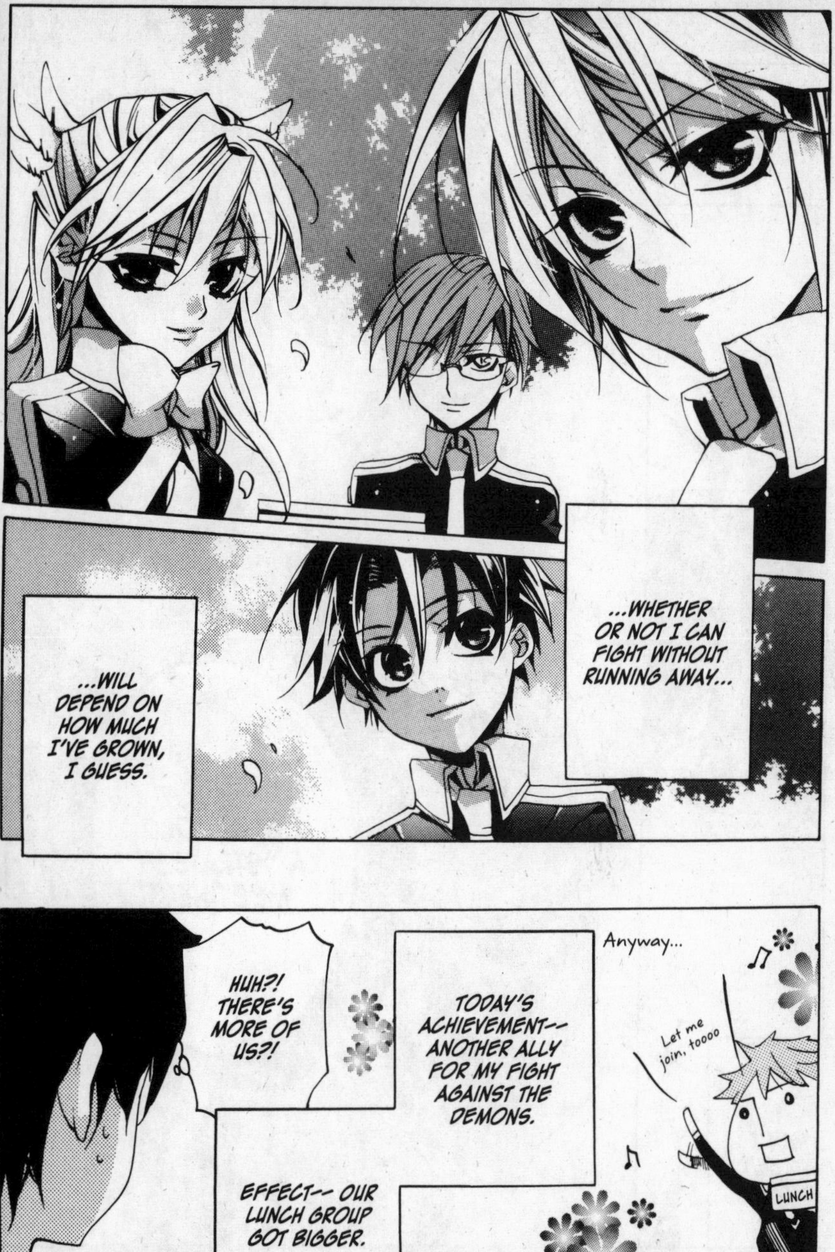
...WHETHER OR NOT I CAN FIGHT WITHOUT RUNNING AWAY...
...WILL DEPEND ON HOW MUCH I'VE GROWN, I GUESS.
Anyway...
Let me join, toooo
LUNCH
TODAY'S ACHIEVEMENT-- ANOTHER ALLY FOR MY FIGHT AGAINST THE DEMONS.
EFFECT-- OUR LUNCH GROUP GOT BIGGER.
HUH?! THERE'S MORE OF US?!

Bonus Chapter

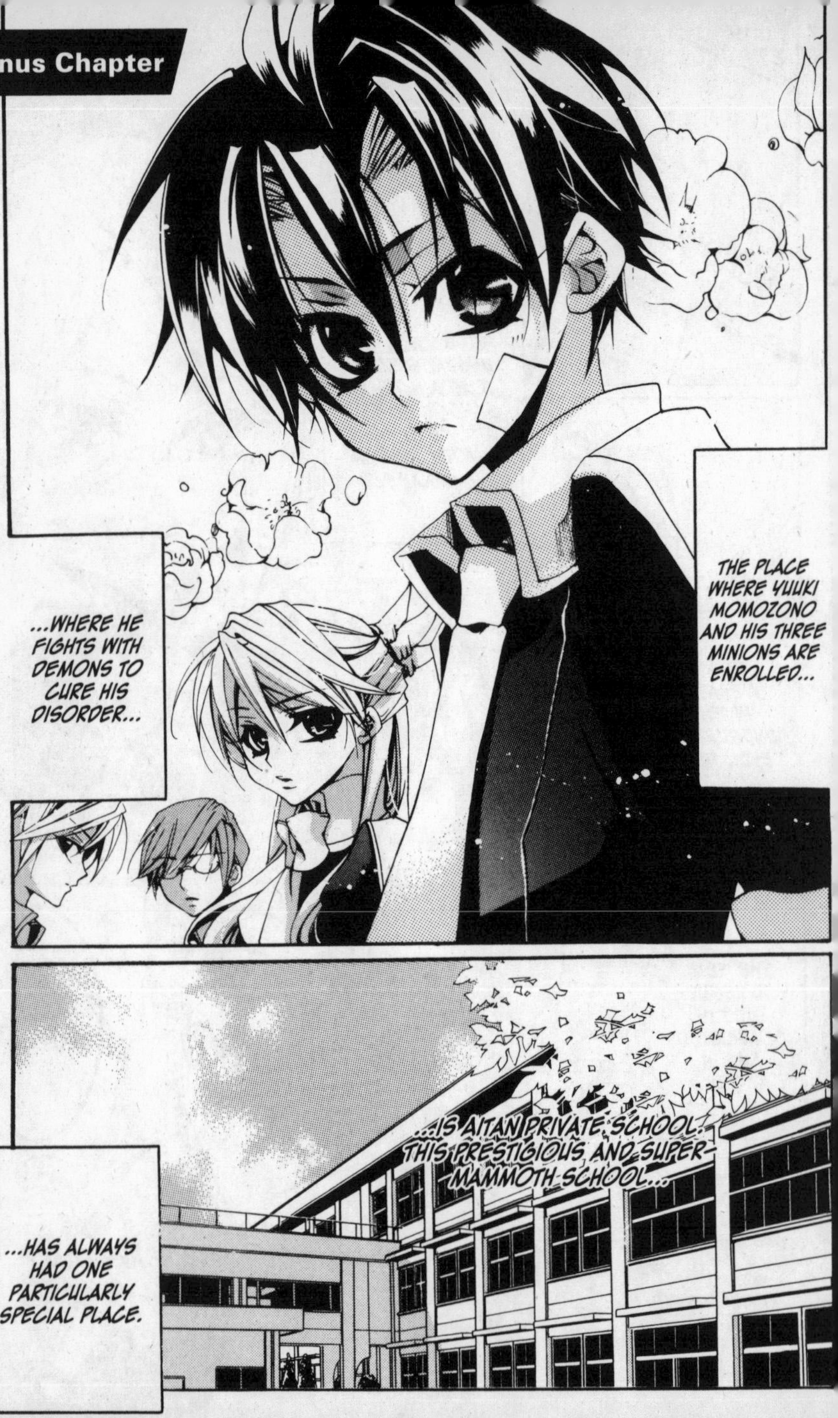
THE PLACE WHERE YUUKI MOMOZONO AND HIS THREE MINIONS ARE ENROLLED...
...WHERE HE FIGHTS WITH DEMONS TO CURE HIS DISORDER...
...IS AITAN PRIVATE SCHOOL. THIS PRESTIGIOUS AND SUPER-MAMMOTH SCHOOL...
...HAS ALWAYS HAD ONE PARTICULARLY SPECIAL PLACE.

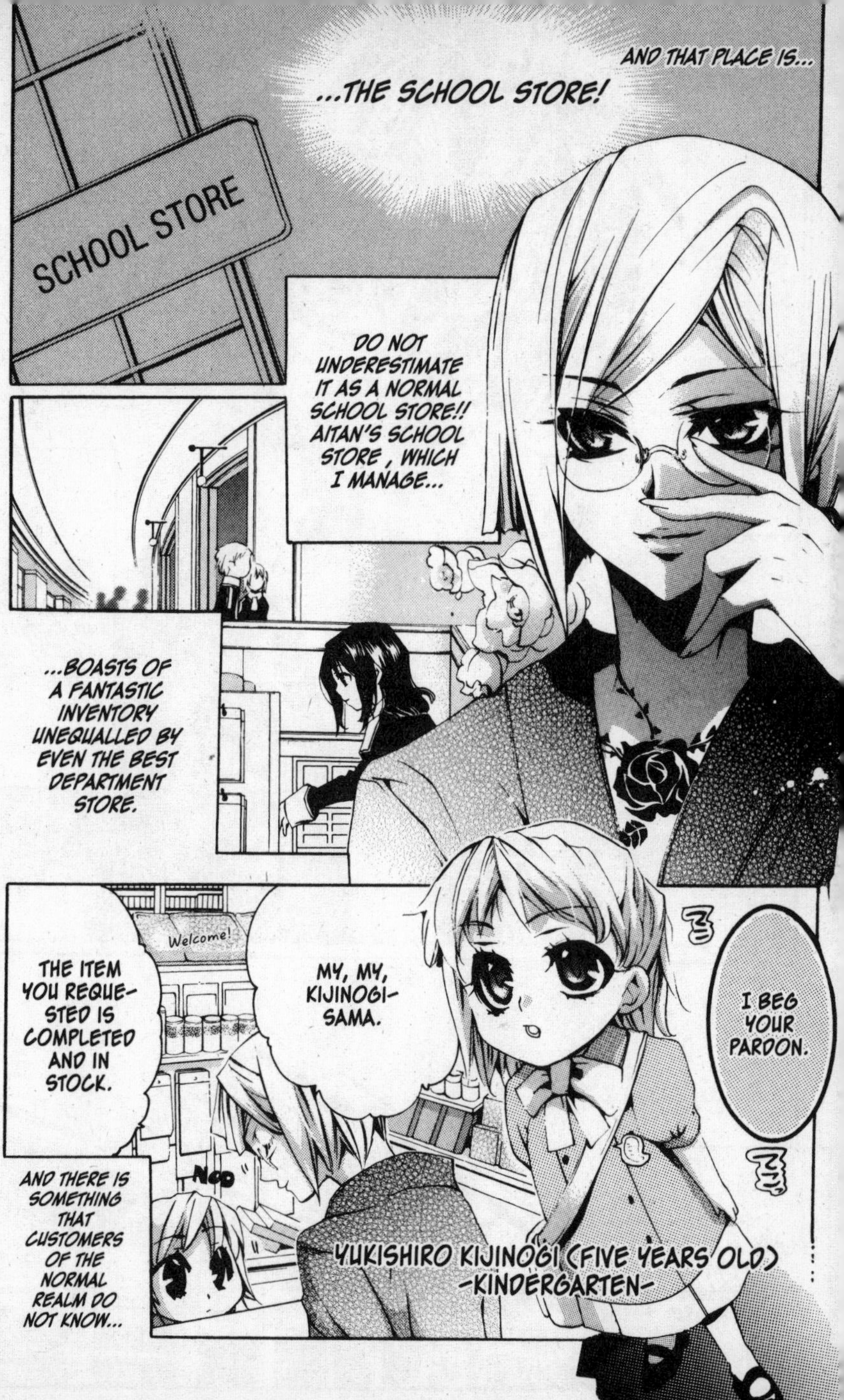
AND THAT PLACE IS...
...THE SCHOOL STORE!
SCHOOL STORE
DO NOT UNDERESTIMATE IT AS A NORMAL SCHOOL STORE!! AITAN'S SCHOOL STORE, WHICH I MANAGE...
...BOASTS OF A FANTASTIC INVENTORY UNEQUALLED BY EVEN THE BEST DEPARTMENT STORE.
I BEG YOUR PARDON.
YUKISHIRO KIJINOGI (FIVE YEARS OLD) -KINDERGARTEN-
MY, MY, KIJINOGI-SAMA.
Welcome!
THE ITEM YOU REQUESTED IS COMPLETED AND IN STOCK.
NOD
AND THERE IS SOMETHING THAT CUSTOMERS OF THE NORMAL REALM DO NOT KNOW...

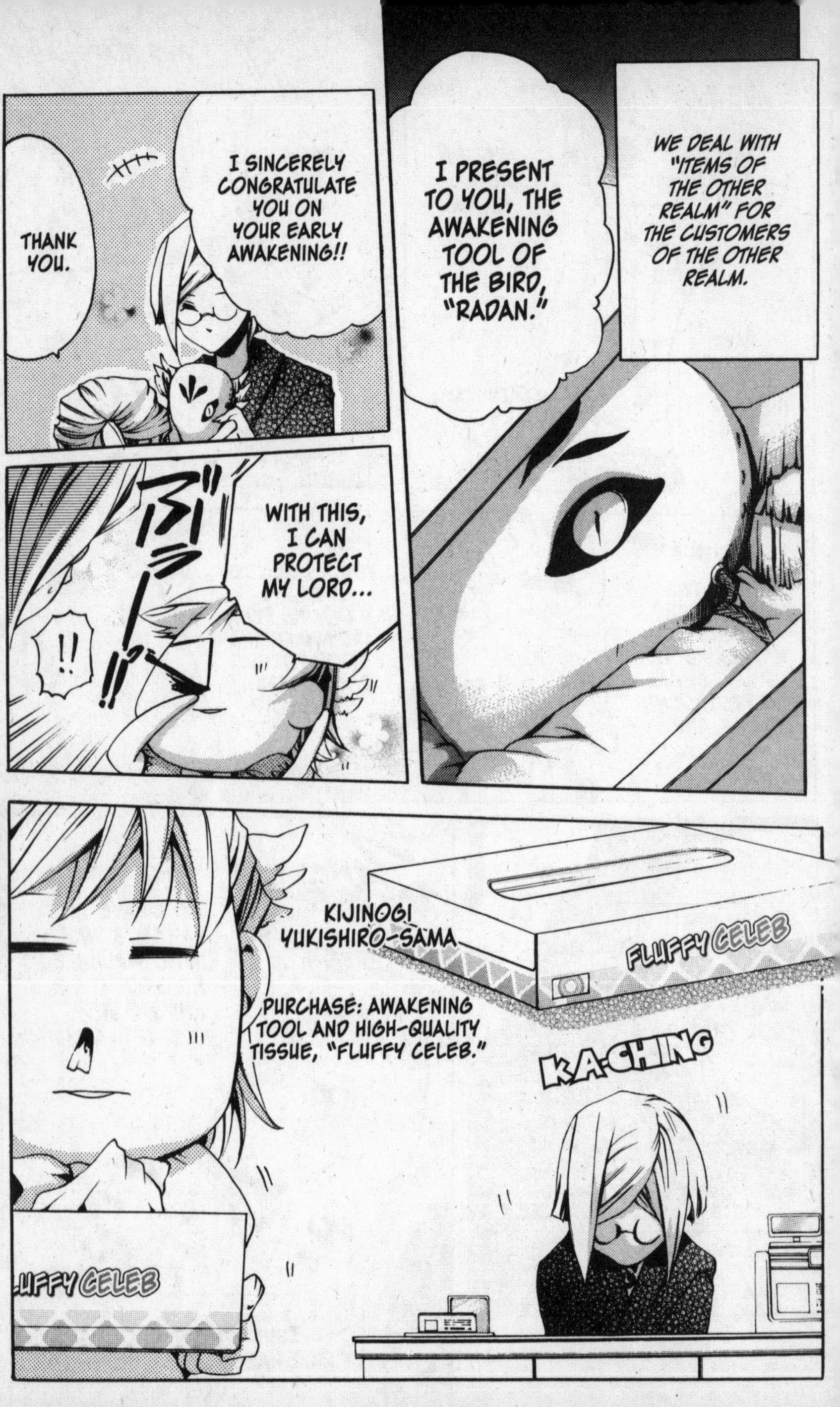
WE DEAL WITH "ITEMS OF THE OTHER REALM" FOR THE CUSTOMERS OF THE OTHER REALM.
I PRESENT TO YOU, THE AWAKENING TOOL OF THE BIRD, "RADAN."
I SINCERELY CONGRATULATE YOU ON YOUR EARLY AWAKENING!!
THANK YOU.
WITH THIS, I CAN PROTECT MY LORD...
!!
KIJINOGI YUKISHIRO-SAMA
FLUFFY CELEB
PURCHASE: AWAKENING TOOL AND HIGH-QUALITY TISSUE, "FLUFFY CELEB."
KA-CHING
LUFFY CELEB

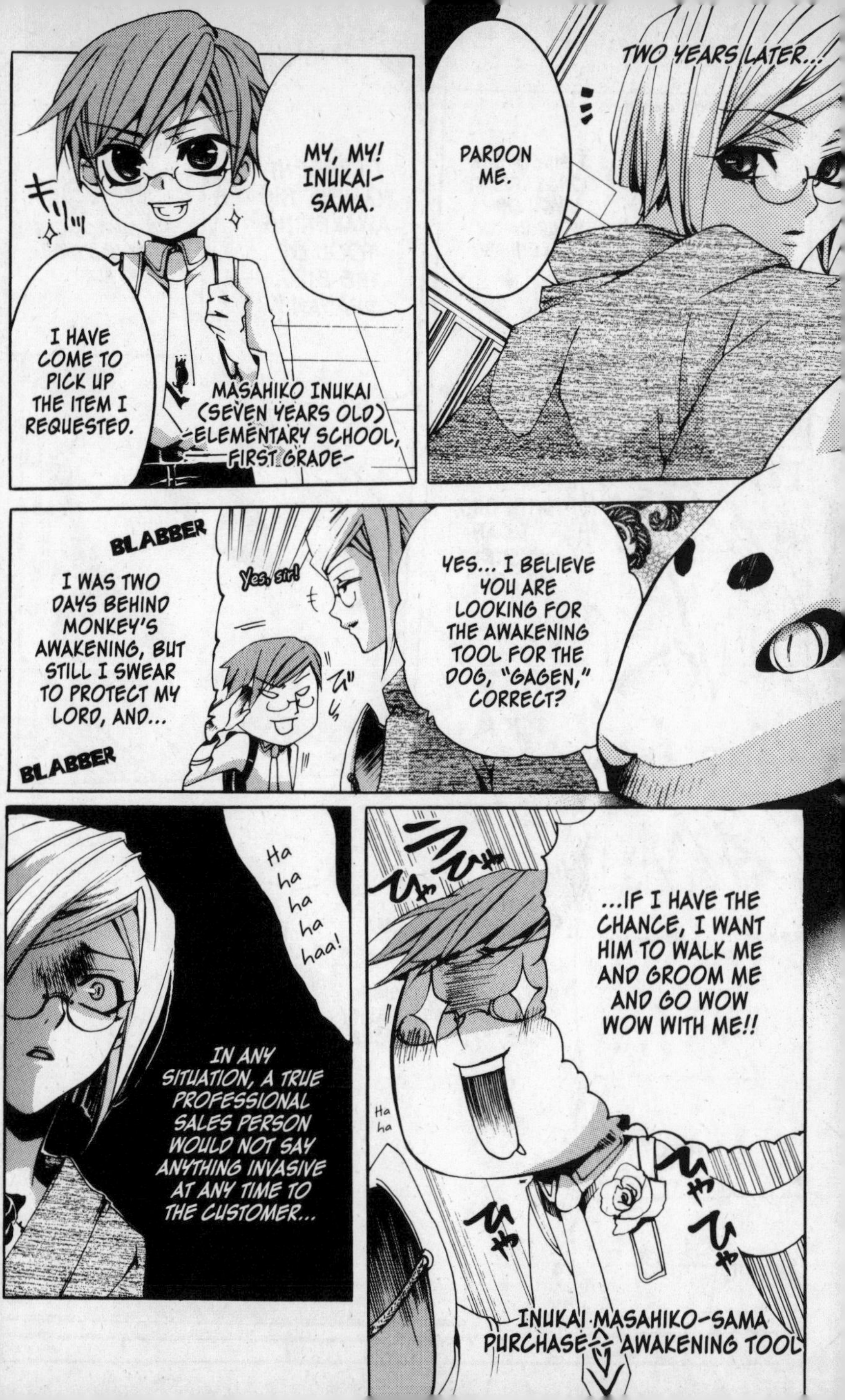
TWO YEARS LATER...
PARDON ME.
MY, MY! INUKAI-SAMA.
I HAVE COME TO PICK UP THE ITEM I REQUESTED.
MASAHIKO INUKAI (SEVEN YEARS OLD) -ELEMENTARY SCHOOL, FIRST GRADE-
YES... I BELIEVE YOU ARE LOOKING FOR THE AWAKENING TOOL FOR THE DOG, "GAGEN," CORRECT?
Yes, sir!
BLABBER
I WAS TWO DAYS BEHIND MONKEY'S AWAKENING, BUT STILL I SWEAR TO PROTECT MY LORD, AND...
BLABBER
...IF I HAVE THE CHANCE, I WANT HIM TO WALK ME AND GROOM ME AND GO WOW WOW WITH ME!!
Ha ha
INUKAI MASAHIKO-SAMA PURCHASE AWAKENING TOOL
Ha ha ha ha haa!
IN ANY SITUATION, A TRUE PROFESSIONAL SALES PERSON WOULD NOT SAY ANYTHING INVASIVE AT ANY TIME TO THE CUSTOMER...

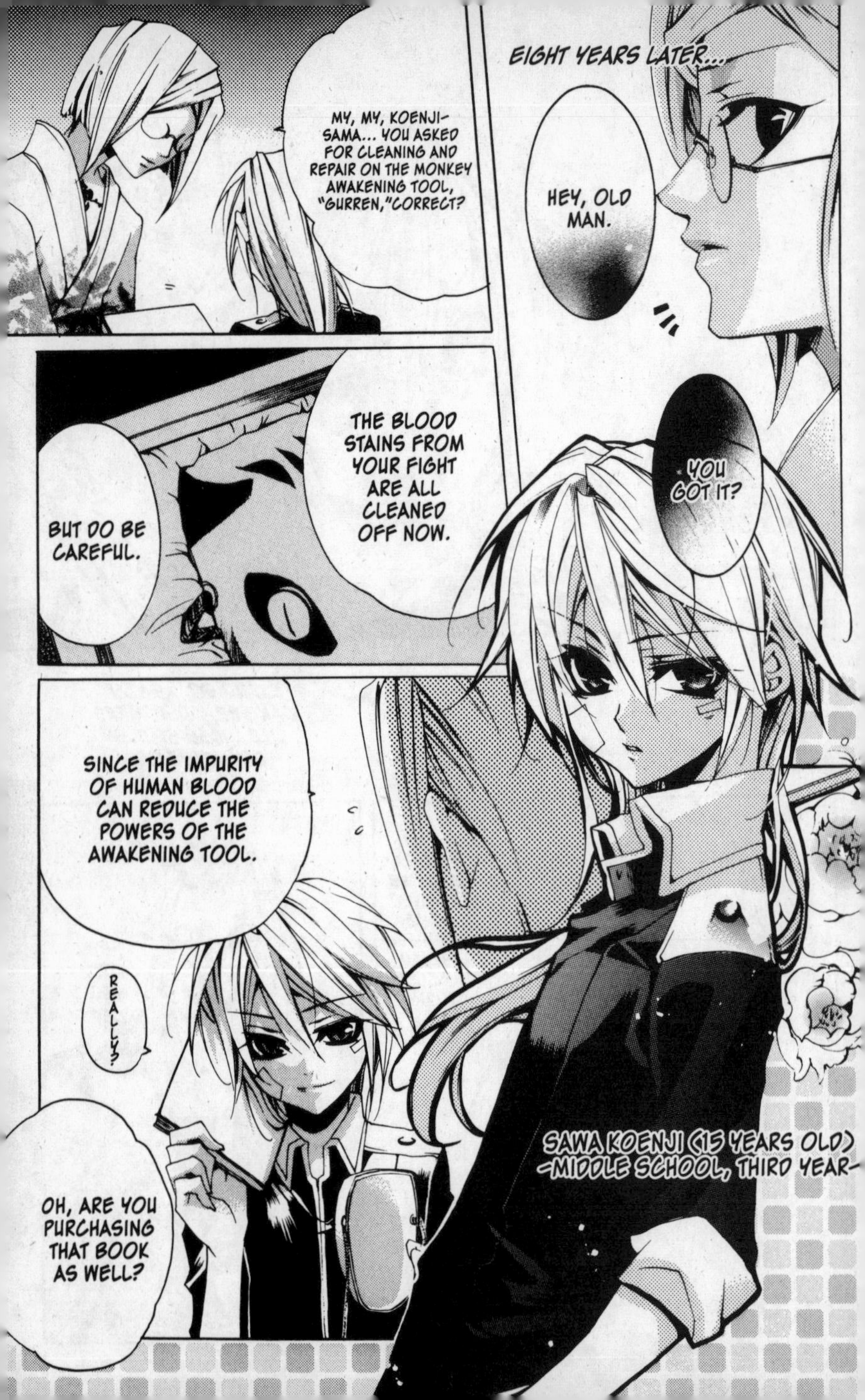
EIGHT YEARS LATER...
HEY, OLD MAN.
YOU GOT IT?
SAWA KOENJI (15 YEARS OLD) -MIDDLE SCHOOL, THIRD YEAR-
MY, MY, KOENJI-SAMA... YOU ASKED FOR CLEANING AND REPAIR ON THE MONKEY AWAKENING TOOL, "GURREN," CORRECT?
THE BLOOD STAINS FROM YOUR FIGHT ARE ALL CLEANED OFF NOW.
BUT DO BE CAREFUL.
SINCE THE IMPURITY OF HUMAN BLOOD CAN REDUCE THE POWERS OF THE AWAKENING TOOL.
REALLY?
OH, ARE YOU PURCHASING THAT BOOK AS WELL?

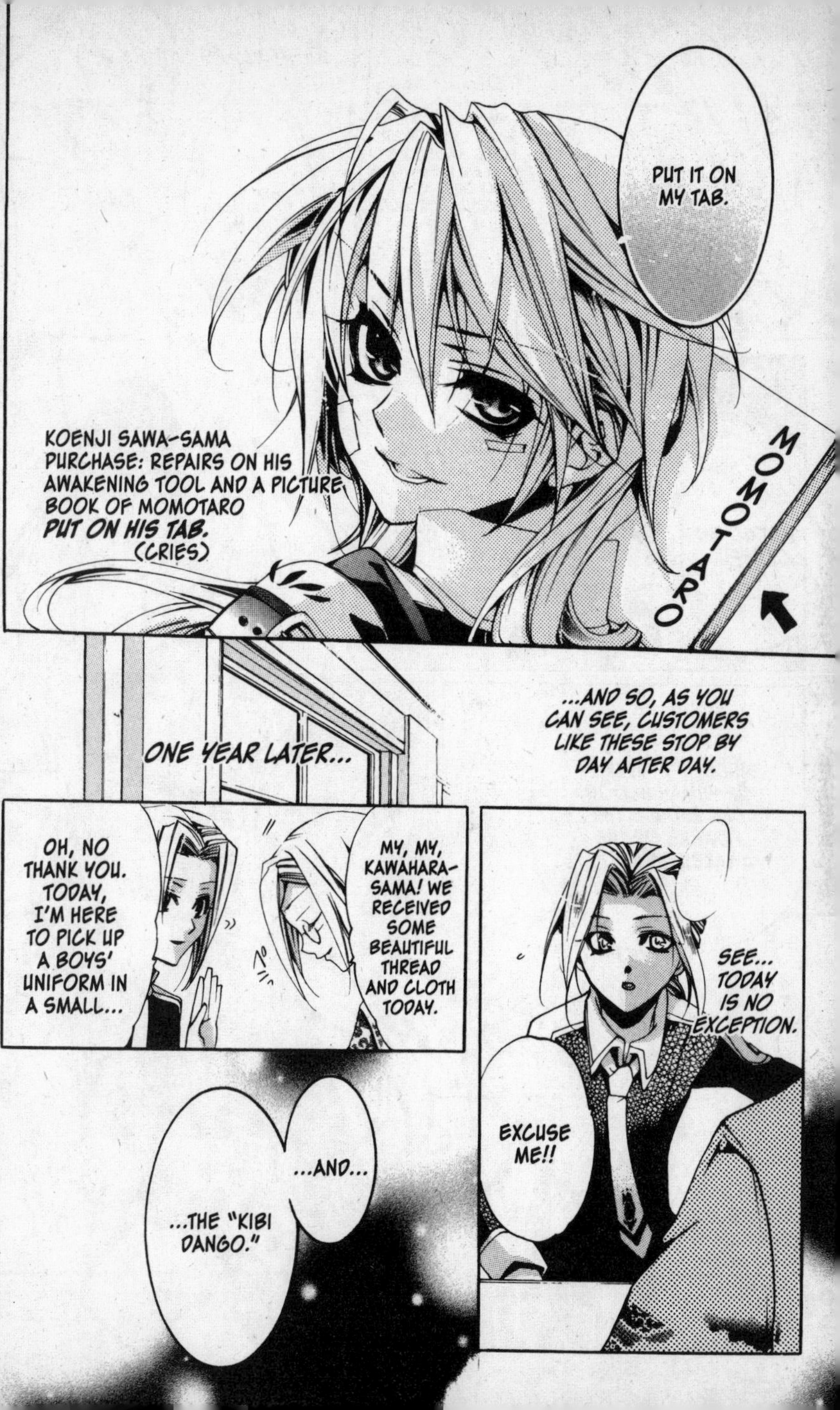
PUT IT ON MY TAB.
MOMOTARO
KOENJI SAWA-SAMA PURCHASE: REPAIRS ON HIS AWAKENING TOOL AND A PICTURE BOOK OF MOMOTARO *PUT ON HIS TAB.* (CRIES)
...AND SO, AS YOU CAN SEE, CUSTOMERS LIKE THESE STOP BY DAY AFTER DAY.
ONE YEAR LATER...
SEE... TODAY IS NO EXCEPTION.
EXCUSE ME!!
MY, MY, KAWAHARA-SAMA! WE RECEIVED SOME BEAUTIFUL THREAD AND CLOTH TODAY.
OH, NO THANK YOU. TODAY, I'M HERE TO PICK UP A BOYS' UNIFORM IN A SMALL...
...AND...
...THE "KIBI DANGO."

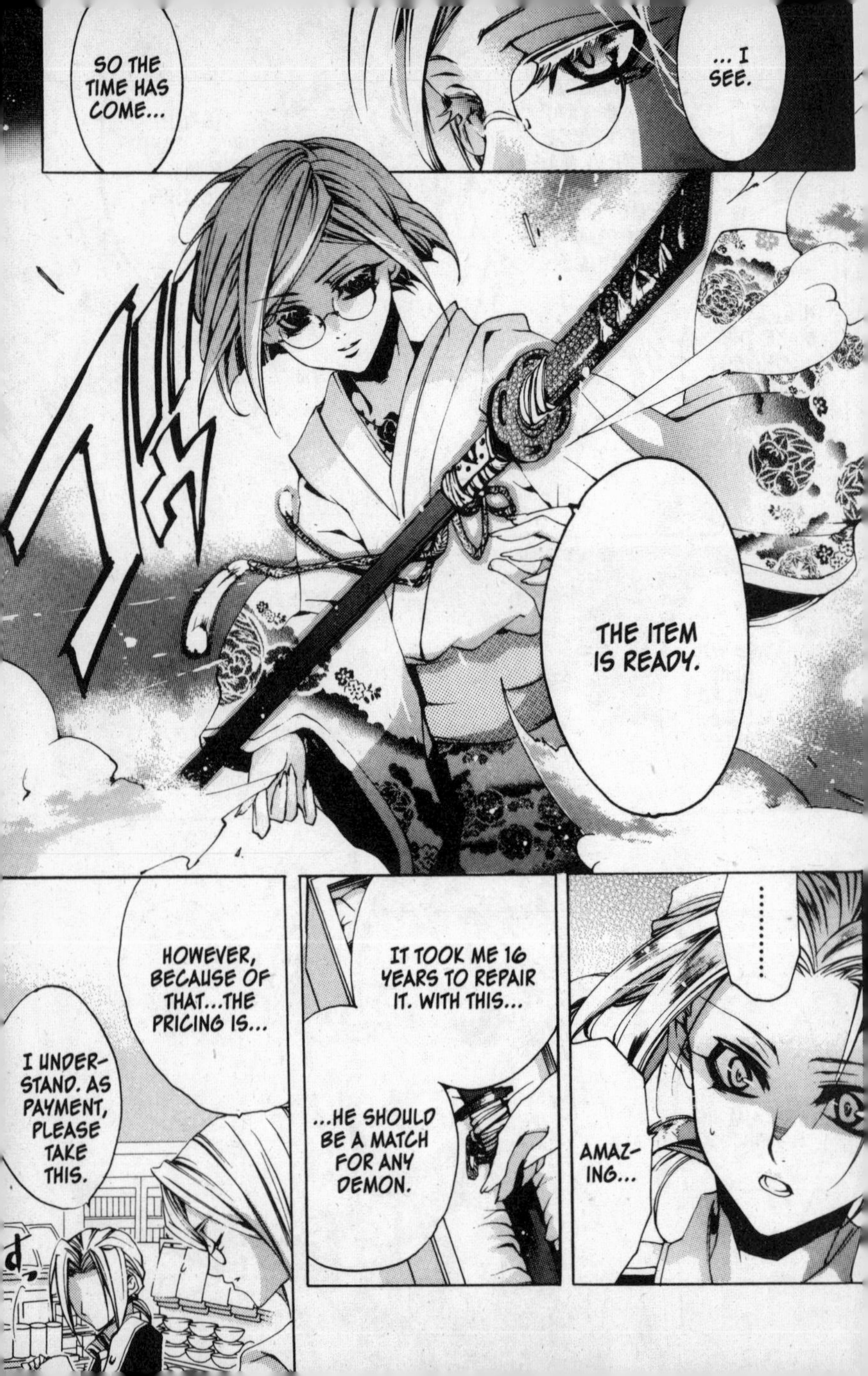
... I SEE.
SO THE TIME HAS COME...
THE ITEM IS READY.
......
AMAZ-ING...
IT TOOK ME 16 YEARS TO REPAIR IT. WITH THIS...
...HE SHOULD BE A MATCH FOR ANY DEMON.
HOWEVER, BECAUSE OF THAT...THE PRICING IS...
I UNDER-STAND. AS PAYMENT, PLEASE TAKE THIS.

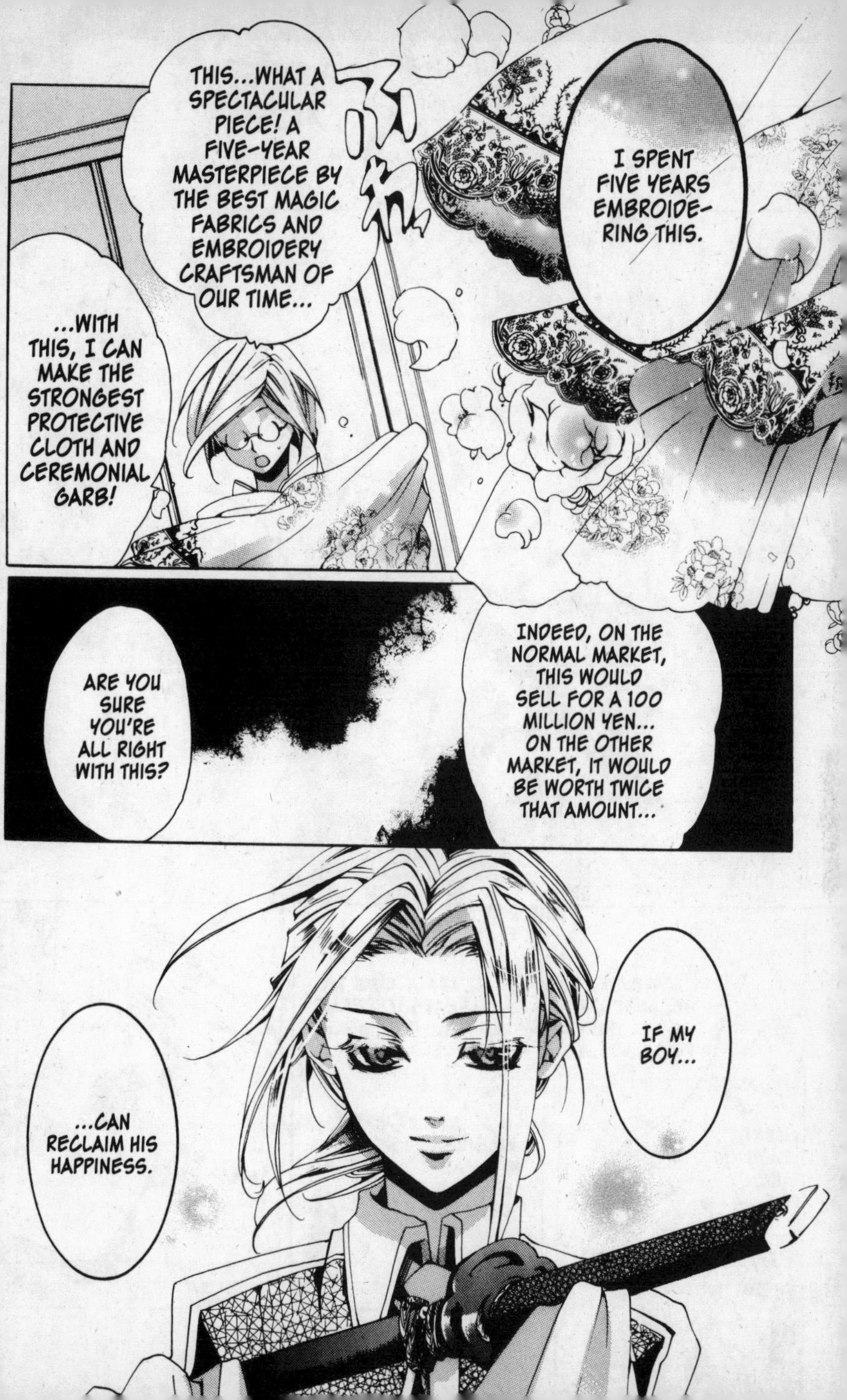
I SPENT FIVE YEARS EMBROIDERING THIS.
THIS...WHAT A SPECTACULAR PIECE! A FIVE-YEAR MASTERPIECE BY THE BEST MAGIC FABRICS AND EMBROIDERY CRAFTSMAN OF OUR TIME...
...WITH THIS, I CAN MAKE THE STRONGEST PROTECTIVE CLOTH AND CEREMONIAL GARB!
INDEED, ON THE NORMAL MARKET, THIS WOULD SELL FOR A 100 MILLION YEN... ON THE OTHER MARKET, IT WOULD BE WORTH TWICE THAT AMOUNT...
ARE YOU SURE YOU'RE ALL RIGHT WITH THIS?
IF MY BOY...
...CAN RECLAIM HIS HAPPINESS.

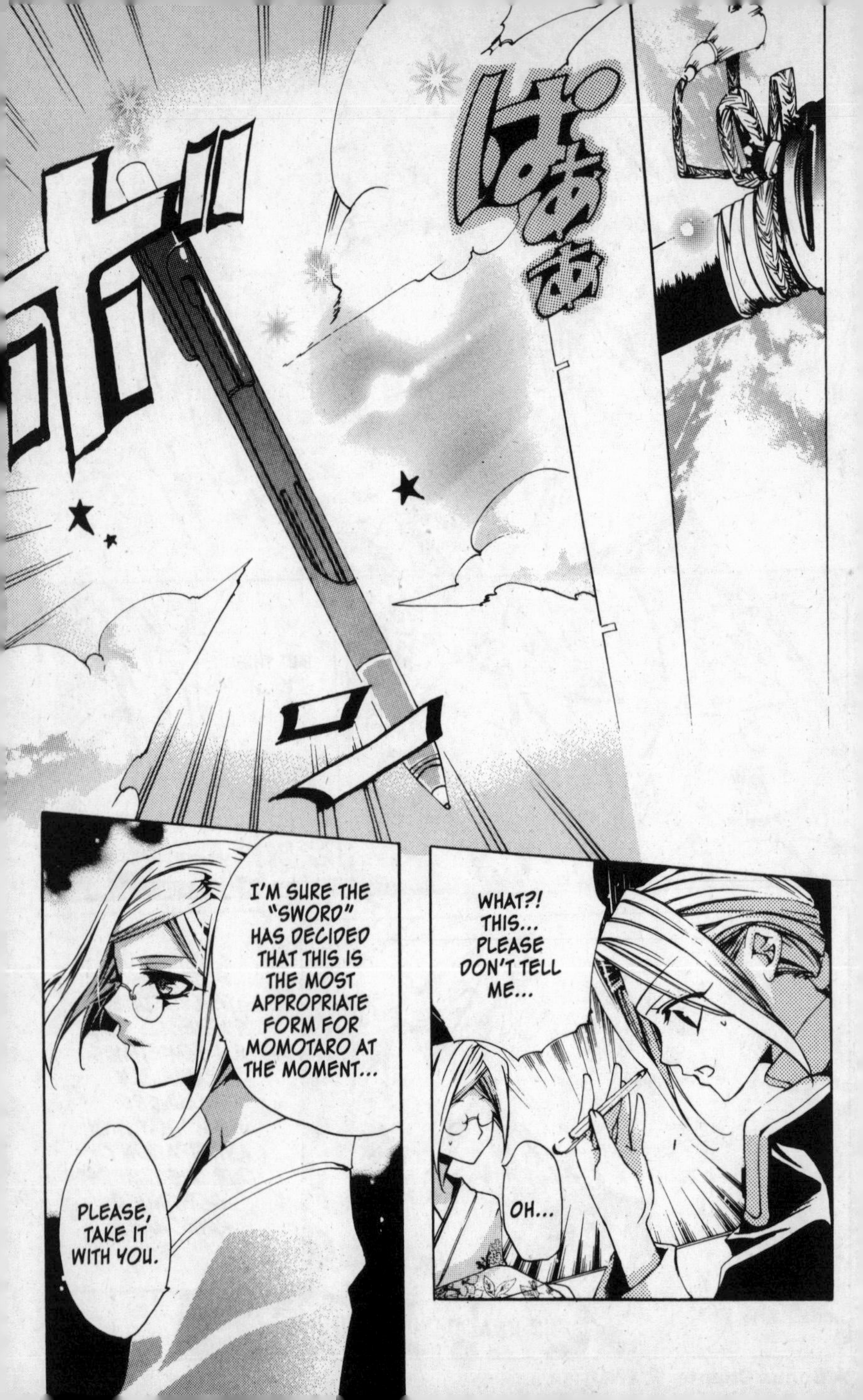
WHAT?! THIS... PLEASE DON'T TELL ME...
OH...
I'M SURE THE "SWORD" HAS DECIDED THAT THIS IS THE MOST APPROPRIATE FORM FOR MOMOTARO AT THE MOMENT...
PLEASE, TAKE IT WITH YOU.

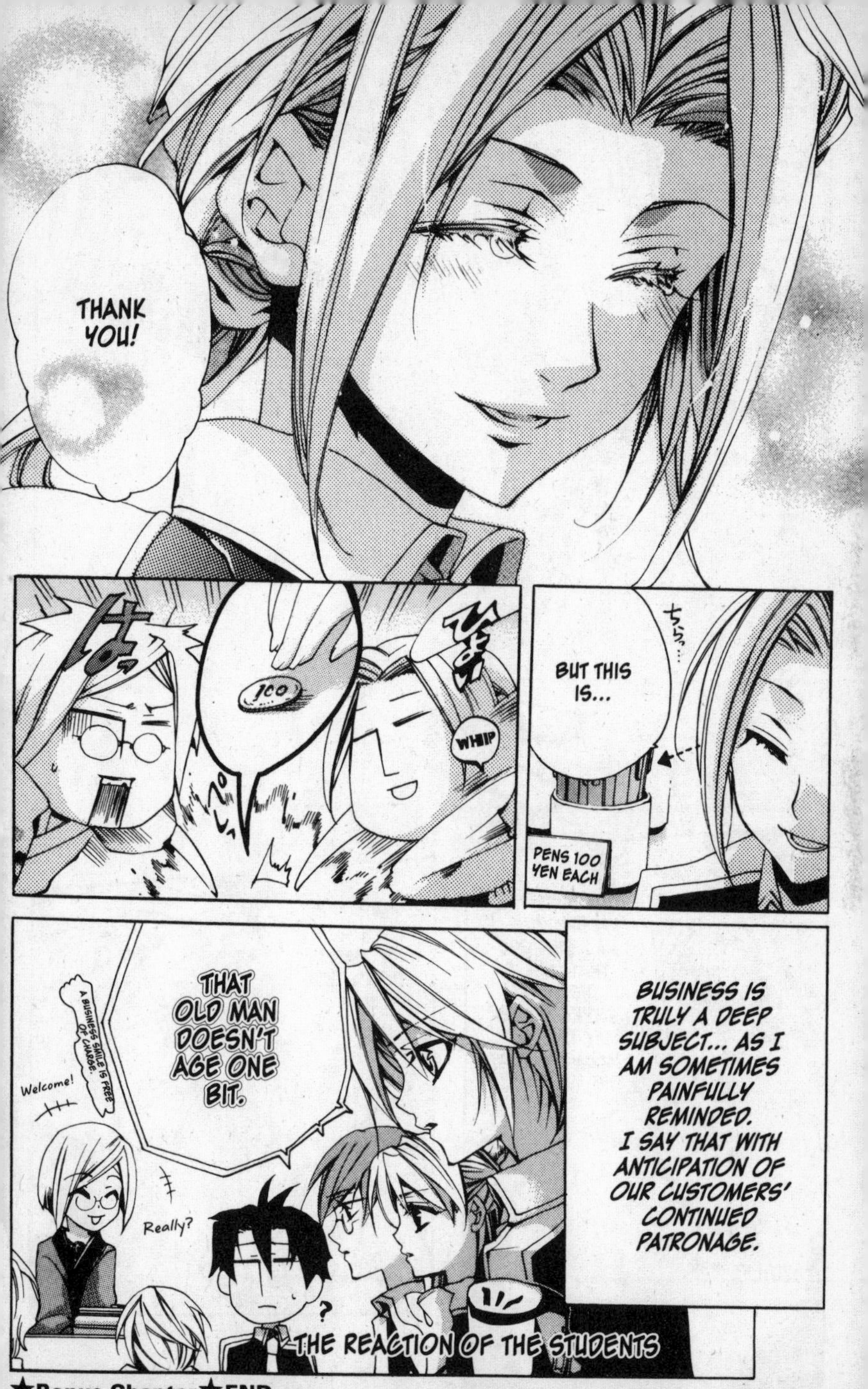
THANK YOU!
BUT THIS IS...
PENS 100 YEN EACH
WHIP
BUSINESS IS TRULY A DEEP SUBJECT... AS I AM SOMETIMES PAINFULLY REMINDED. I SAY THAT WITH ANTICIPATION OF OUR CUSTOMERS' CONTINUED PATRONAGE.
THAT OLD MAN DOESN'T AGE ONE BIT.
A BUSINESS SMILE IS FREE OF CHARGE.
Welcome!
Really?
?
THE REACTION OF THE STUDENTS

★Bonus Chapter★END

Postscript

- Hello and nice to meet you. This is Eri Sakondo. We've successfully published the first volume of Momogumi Plus Senki.

It's my first school-life story (it's out of this world, though) and I'm enjoying creating every chapter. Moreover, it's my first story with a major character who's a girl (Yukishiro), so... I'm happy. Oh, and nose bleeds are a first for me, too.

- Things will continue along, and so I'll be feeding off of your enthusiasm as I continue to do my best.

Until the next volume! Thank you very much!

Sawa is the most fun to move around. Yukishiro is most fun to draw. And the hardest are the Demon kids... I worry that I'll forget what kind of piercings they have.

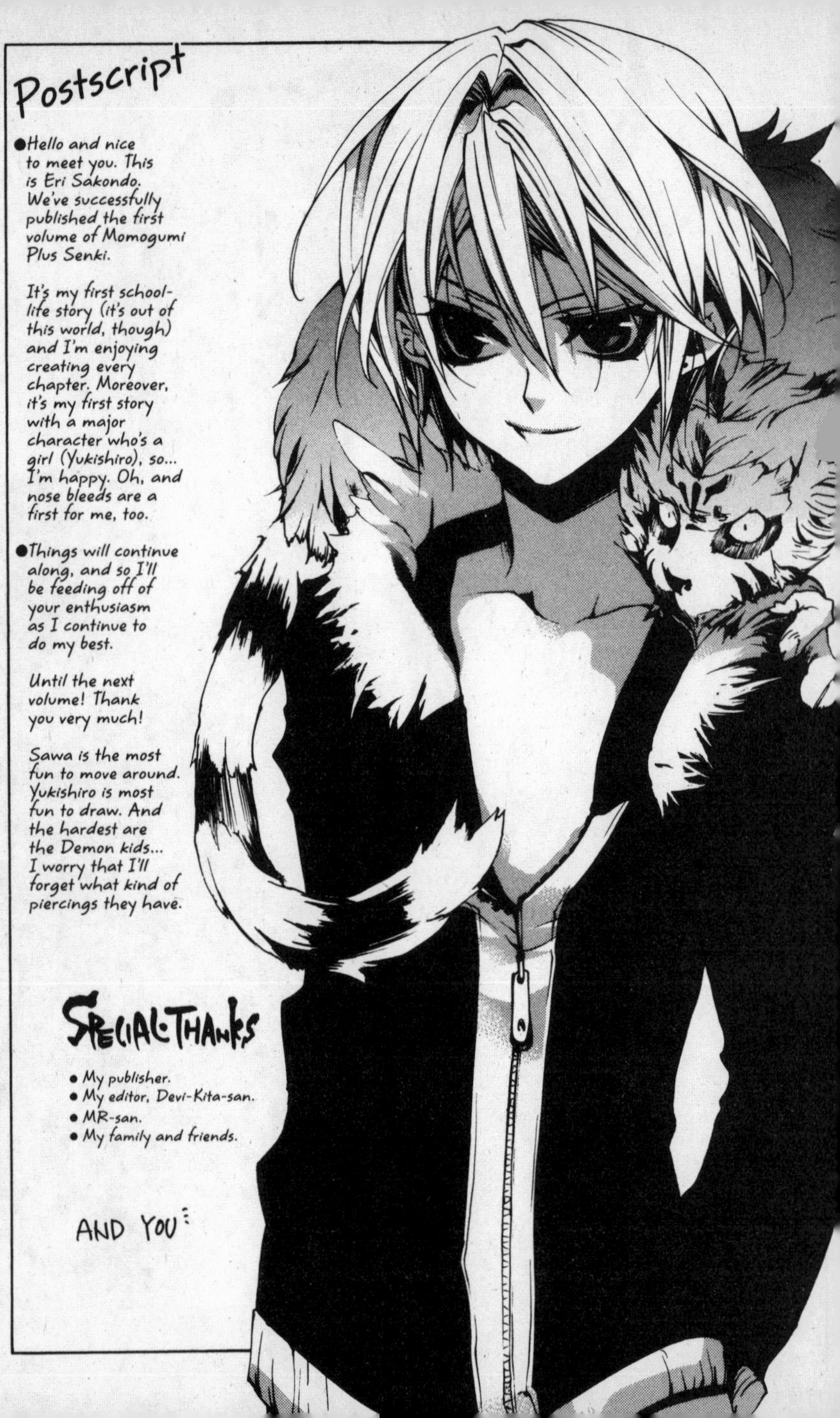

SPECIAL THANKS

- My publisher.
- My editor, Devi-Kita-san.
- MR-san.
- My family and friends.

AND YOU

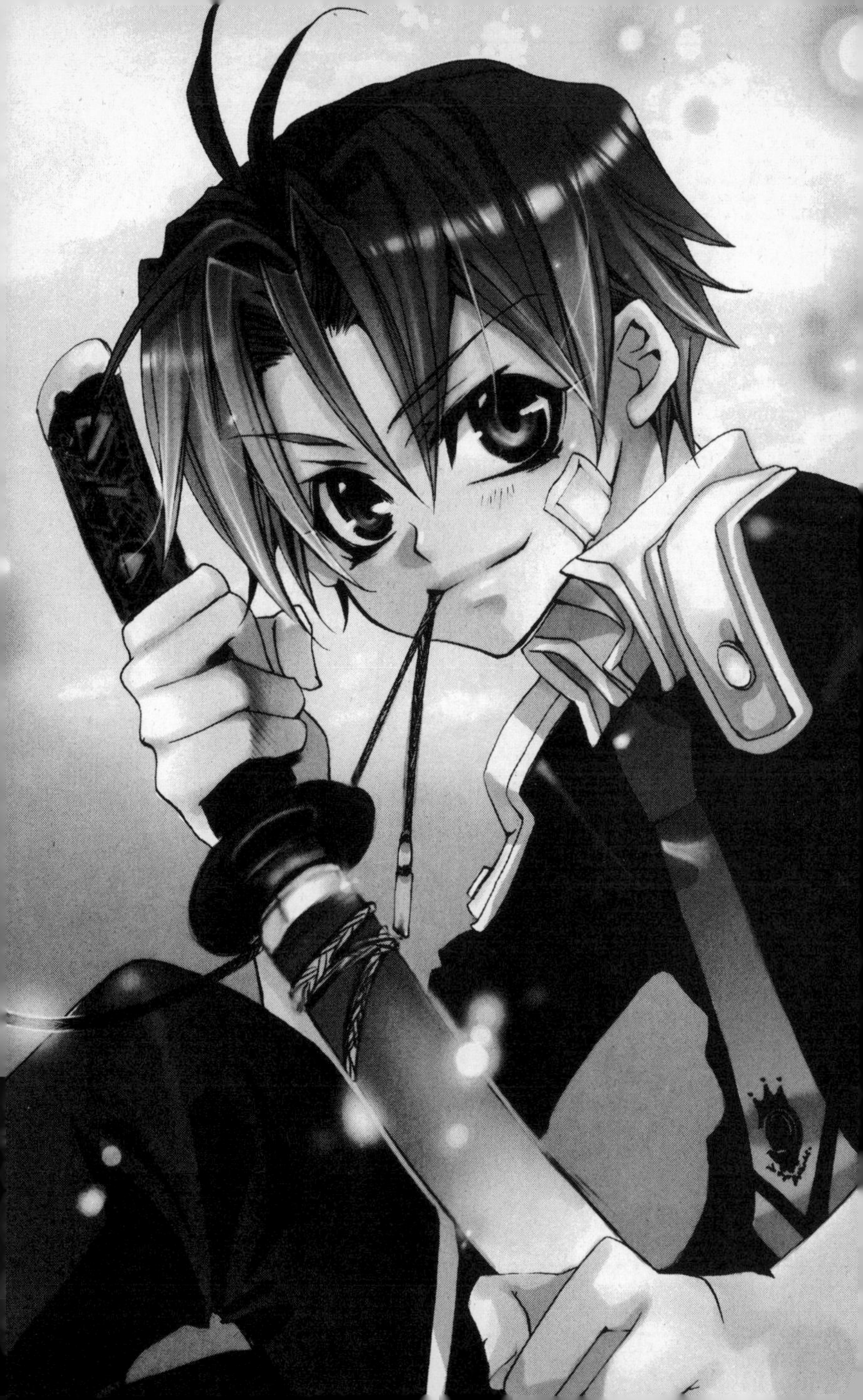

In the next volume of

MOMOGUMI PLUS SENKI

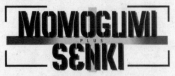

It's Spring Break for the students of Aitan Gakuen, and Sawa invites Yuki to go to the beach! But it turns out to be more of a "working vacation" when Yuki discovers he's actually there to continue his training as Momotaro, the Ogre Slayer. Eventually, the added training pays off, as one of Yuki's "senses" is reawakened, which leads to another power being rediscovered – Yuki's core weapon, the Kibi Dango!

The adventure continues in

MOMOGUMI PLUS SENKI

Volume 2!

Maid Sama!™

The class president has a little secret she's keeping from the sexy bad boy in school...

It's love at first fight in this shojo romantic comedy—with a hilarious spin on geek culture and... student government?!

As President of the Student Council, the overachieving feminist Misaki really socks it to the boys in an attempt to make the former all-boys' school attract a more female student body. But what will she do when the hottest boy in class finds out Misaki's after-school gig is in a maid café?!

Maid Sama!
Hiro Fujiwara
TOKYOPOP
1

ROMANCE

T TEEN AGE 13+

BE SURE TO VISIT WWW.TOKYOPOP.COM/SHOP FOR EVERYTHING YOU COULD EVER WANT!

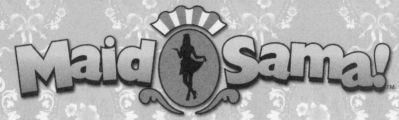

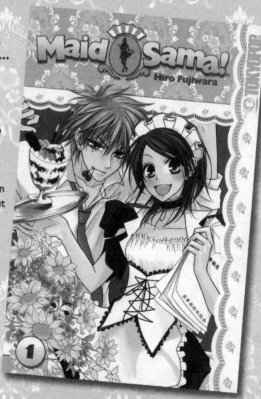

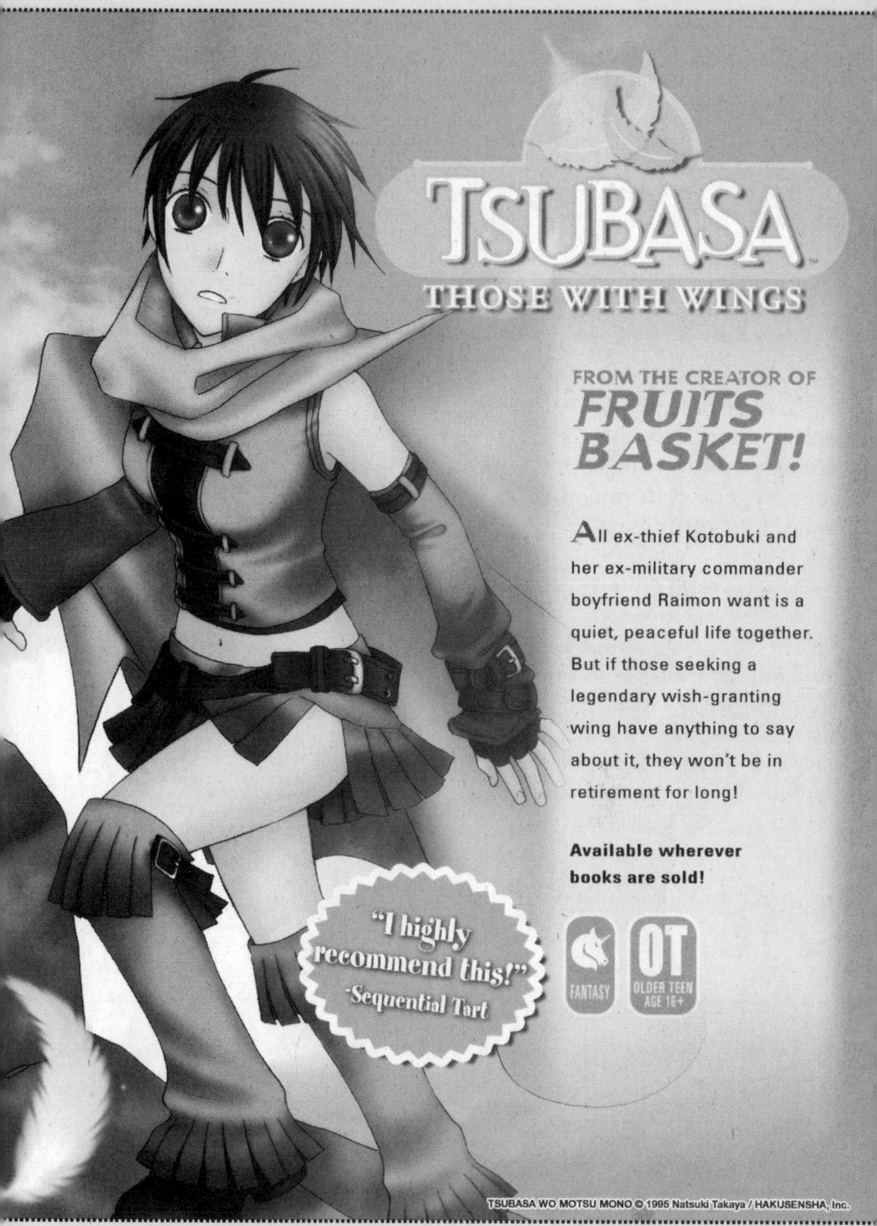
TSUBASA™
THOSE WITH WINGS
FROM THE CREATOR OF
FRUITS BASKET!
All ex-thief Kotobuki and her ex-military commander boyfriend Raimon want is a quiet, peaceful life together. But if those seeking a legendary wish-granting wing have anything to say about it, they won't be in retirement for long!
Available wherever books are sold!
"I highly recommend this!"
-Sequential Tart
FANTASY
OT
OLDER TEEN AGE 16+
TSUBASA WO MOTSU MONO © 1995 Natsuki Takaya / HAKUSENSHA, Inc.

Is the World's #1 Shojo Manga

**Fruits Basket Ultimate Editions
Volumes 1-3**

**Fruits Basket
Fan Book -Cat-**

**Fruits Basket
Sticker Collection**

**Fruits Basket
Journal**

**Fruits Basket 18-month
Planner**

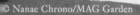

STOP!

This is the back of the book. You wouldn't want to spoil a great ending!

This book is printed "manga-style," in the authentic Japanese right-to-left format. Since none of the artwork has been flipped or altered, readers get to experience the story just as the creator intended. You've been asking for it, so TOKYOPOP® delivered: authentic, hot-off-the-press, and far more fun!

1
2
3
4
5
6
7
8
9
10

DIRECTIONS

If this is your first time reading manga-style, here's a quick guide to help you understand how it works.

It's easy... just start in the top right panel and follow the numbers. Have fun, and look for more 100% authentic manga from TOKYOPOP®!

THE MANGA REVOLUTION • LEADING THE MANGA REVOLUTION • LEADING
漫画革命